HerStory
Revelations

LCCN 2010920854
ISBN 9780984423309

 Your Time Publishing, LLC P.O. Box 872365 New Orleans Louisiana, 70187

Paulette Jones

HerStory
Revelations

A special thanks to:

Paula Tromp
Nicole Plain
Robert Warmsley
Kiana Ebony
Shannon Smith

For their support

 Your Time Publishing, LLC P.O. Box 872365 New Orleans Louisiana, 70187

Paulette Jones was first recognized when three of her stage plays were performed at the Black Repertory Theater in Berkeley, California in the early nineties. *HerStory: Revelations* is her first full length novel.

Your Time Publishing, LLC P.O. Box 872365 New Orleans Louisiana, 70187

HerStory
Revelations

ONE

These days, I find myself indulging in the simple joys of life while spending long, relaxed afternoons on my charming old porch, which sits under the broad, protective shade of my beloved magnolia tree. Its large, waxy leaves rustle gently in the breeze while the air is permeated with the sweet, intoxicating fragrance of its magnificent, creamy white blooms that seem to whisper stories of seasons gone by. I'm comfortably settled in a classic rocking chair, its timeless design a testament to the craftsmanship of old man Joel, who meticulously crafted it over a century ago. This porch, with its worn wooden boards that creak softly beneath me, is perfectly oriented to capture the refreshing coolness of the morning on one side while allowing the warm rays of the afternoon sun to bathe me in their golden embrace on the other. This contrast creates an idyllic atmosphere that evokes fond memories of yesteryears, imbuing my heart with deep love.

As summer unfolds, the dance of temperatures becomes an intriguing spectacle, showcasing nature's diverse moods. Just yesterday, I awoke to a delightfully cool morning that felt like a gentle caress, wrapping around me like a soft blanket. However, the heat intensified dramatically as the sun climbed higher in the crystalline blue sky, casting a warm glow over everything it touched. By midday, the temperature reached 90 degrees, enveloped by a steamy humidity that felt almost like a heavy, damp cloak clinging to my skin. Yet, when night descended, that familiar morning breeze returned like an old friend, wrapping me in its comforting embrace and providing a welcome reprieve from the day's oppressive heat. I relish the way the climate shifts throughout the seasons; there are days when the warmth resembles a heavy quilt draped over me, while on others, the cool breezes and fierce sun seem to engage in a playful competition. During those transitional periods, fierce weather battles unfold, often beginning with distant flashes of lightning that slice through the sky like silver blades and the rumbling growl of thunder that sound like World War three was going on outside. The atmosphere crackles with anticipation as the sky ultimately splits open, releasing brilliant flashes, and the thunder rumbles with a titanic resonance, sending shivers of exhilaration coursing through my body. And then comes the rain, sometimes warm and soothing, other times calm and invigorating, but it never feels truly cold in this part of the world, especially during this enchanting time of year.

These dramatic weather changes often transport me back to the more turbulent moments of my life, when uncertainty loomed large and it felt like the ground beneath my feet might give way. Yet here I stand today, a proud grandmother, looking back with gratitude and pride at how far I've journeyed. It's fascinating to witness the resilience of the human spirit, constantly evolving and adapting. I frequently reflect on my childhood, recalling those long, lonely, humid days spent confined in a dim, shadowy room, anxiously awaiting Mema's return. Back then, I was unaware that she was merely off at work as our mornings unfurled with the first light of dawn. Before embarking on her day, she would wake me for breakfast, a bowl of oatmeal and a glass of milk. Occasionally, she would step outside to gather luscious, sun-ripened berries or slice up a sweet, juicy pear that hung low on the trees. If I was fortunate, she would sprinkle a touch of brown sugar atop my oatmeal, infusing it with a hint of sweetness that turned each bite into a comforting hug.

Mema always urged me to stay inside, and away from the window. Our tiny room consisted of a modest brown sofa with faded upholstery sagging against a weary wall, a weathered wooden crate serving as our makeshift table, and two rickety chairs with wobbly legs, each seemingly steeped in history and tales of their own. In the corner, under the window, lay a simple mattress on the floor; it was my haven, cozily wrapped in Mema's familiar scent, which enveloped me in a sense of belonging and security.

In those quiet moments of solitude, I would often slip into imaginative play, pretending to be Mema herself as I meticulously set the stage for our cheerful breakfast. I would shuffle around the tiny kitchen, imitating her gentle movements as I placed pots on the stove, filling the air with the comforting aromas of our morning fare and mimicking the rhythm of our cherished routine. Those role-playing moments brought immeasurable joy and comfort, but my sense of security would waver when the rains came, as each raindrop fell. When Mema was at my side, the rain was merely a soothing backdrop, lulling me into tranquility; in her absence, it transformed into something formidable. There were occasions when the downpour lashed against the tin roof with such intensity that it felt like tiny metal pellets were raining down from the heavens. Peeking outside, I would see the trees swaying wildly, their branches thrashing in the intense wind, filling me with dread as I worried, they might snap and collapse, burying me beneath their weight. The loudness of the storm would quicken my breath, thumping heavily in my chest, and sharply bring the pain of loneliness to the forefront of my mind.

Yet, as I revisit those bittersweet memories, though they carry a hint of sadness, they also remind me of the considerable distance I've traveled and the strength I have cultivated. Each cherished recollection brings warmth to my heart and a deep-seated sense of gratitude for all the experiences, joyful and challenging, that have indelibly shaped who I am today. I embrace every moment and every lesson learned with an open heart and an optimistic spirit, ready to savor all that life still has to offer.

One morning after Mema left, I couldn't sit still; I started out sitting on the sofa, then to one of the chairs, where I rocked back and forth for a while; when I got tired of that, I went over to the window and stared into the woods. This nervousness had been building up in me for a while; between the rain, thunder, and loneliness, I was experiencing new feelings. It was no particular thing that day; I usually felt lonely, but this was different. At that time, I was about four years old and didn't know what to do, so I balled myself up in the bed and placed the covers over my head. As I lay on the mattress, in the corner, under the window, combating sleep, I found myself praying to God because Mema always talked about God. She said God loved everyone, no matter what color you were or how much money you had. As long as you are a decent human, God will pay attention to your prayers. She always told me I was a good girl, so I prayed because it felt like the right thing to do.

I had never been anywhere but in the house, so when I lifted my head from under the cover, I knew I wasn't home. The temperature was perfect, not too hot or cold, and everything was vivid, like when the sun would wake me mid-afternoon after my nap. As I looked around, I saw people everywhere, some above the clouds, some below, some far away, and some singing. Some were flying through the cumulus clouds, but all had smiles, similar to Mema's when she brought something delicious home for me, like pralines, fried fruit pie, or a piece of caramel fudge. Everything was so beautiful, and it reminded me of a picture Mema once showed me; she said they were flying angels in heaven. My mind felt liberated from the loneliness as if I were part of something significant. To this day, I can still feel the tranquility that flowed through my body.

While standing there enjoying the landscape, someone yelled my name, Lillian, stop staring, and come on. I had no idea what she was talking about, so I asked her what I should do; she stopped in the middle of a cloud and yelled, fly, you can fly. I thought to myself, fly, how could I fly? I'm not a bird. I had never seen anyone fly before, but maybe it was something Mema hadn't gotten around to showing me yet, so I yelled at her to tell me what I should do.

Start running, stretch out your arms as far as you can, and concentrate on your feet. Before you know it, you will be airborne.

As I ran, she kept saying faster, faster, and just as I was about to abandon my attempt, it happened, I was flying, and the cool breeze was blowing in my face. I extended my body as far as possible to increase speed because I wanted to pull alongside the old woman who knew my name. When I pulled beside her, she said, hi, Lillian, are you enjoying yourself, and with a gigantic smile on my face and my arms whaling, I yelled I'm flying, I'm flying, look at me, I'm flying. She smiled, saying yes you are, baby, flying. When I asked her how she knew my name, she told me it wasn't important now, that we would meet again someday. I was so excited and overwhelmed that I couldn't think fast enough to ask another question.

Before I could gather my racing thoughts, a booming voice reverberated through the air, calling my name with such intensity that it echoed in my ears like a thunderclap. I spun around, my heart pounding in my chest, eager to uncover the source of this unexpected shout, but the voice felt like a riddle cloaked in mystery, just waiting for me to solve it. As the sound surged and swelled ominously, it became increasingly challenging to maintain my flight's stability. My body, caught in a battle to keep balanced, began a rapid descent, and in a heart-stopping instant, panic washed over me like a tidal wave. When I finally collided with the earth, the impact sent a jolt through my entire being, and it struck me that I wasn't the only one spiraling down. All around me, I could hear the chaotic thuds of others landing; each impact resonated like cannon fire, creating a thunderous symphony that filled the air with a chaotic yet oddly exhilarating melody.

With newfound determination and adrenaline rushing through my veins, I sprang to my feet as if the ground itself were a hotbed of energy, invigorating my every movement. I dashed away, desperate to escape the lingering weight of that mysterious call echoing in my mind. But as I pivoted on my heel, my foot caught on an unseen obstacle, sending me tumbling forward near a massive, dark hole. Curiosity sparked in my chest, compelling me to crawl to the edge and peer into the abyss. The shadows slowly dissipated as I leaned over the edge, revealing an astonishing sight that took my breath away: Mema.

But she was not the woman I remembered. Gone were her characteristic work clothes, those sensible blouses and sturdy shoes that spoke of her no-nonsense approach to life. Instead, she stood before me adorned in a striking purple dress that shimmered and glinted as if woven from fragments of the night sky. Her outfit was perfectly complemented by an eye-catching, quirky green bonnet and oversized yellow shoes that curled like crescents at the tips, and seemed to dance with her every move giving her an air of whimsical enchantment. What seized my attention the most, however, were her eyes, they glowed with a vibrant, intense orange light, flickering like embers in a fireplace, hinting at an adventurous spirit just waiting to ignite.

Lillian, come down here. You don't belong up there. Don't you know anything, little girl? The voice rang out with a sharpness that cut through the air, filled with a blend of authority and concern. My heart pounded, but an unwavering confidence rose like a shield. I was confident of my place up there; after all, God loved everyone without exception, which included me. I took a deep breath, willing my legs to move, to spring up and escape the stifling atmosphere of judgment, but it felt as though I were ensnared by a heavy shroud that kept me rooted to the spot. A tremor rippled through my body, a shiver that started deep within and spread outward, and then, amidst the chaos, I heard a soft and gentle voice calling my name. This sound was a soothing balm, starkly contrasting to the harsh reprimand that had pierced my earlier haze, Mema was beckoning me to awaken.

As I slowly opened my eyes, the scene around me flickered back into focus, revealing the familiar contours of the house. Mema was perched at my side, her warm hands gently shaking me like a delicate flower awakening after a long winter. Panic bubbled within me, and I instinctively cried out, begging her to let me go, desperate to remain in a realm devoid of shadows and loneliness. Yet, when I met her gaze, that initial fear began to diminish, replaced by an overwhelming wave of love and assurance. Her eyes, large and expressive, radiated a deep concern that seemed to reach out and envelop me, banishing the remnants of my distress.

Drawing me close, Mema wrapped her arms around me, the enveloping warmth of her embrace reminiscent of a cozy blanket on a frost-laden morning. She rocked me gently back and forth, instilling a sense of calm that seeped into my bones. The soft murmur of her voice floated around me, soothing and rhythmic. Though the words eluded my understanding, they carried an emotional weight that resonated deeply within.

As she pulled back just enough to create a small distance, she gazed into my eyes with such intensity that it felt like she was peering into the depths of my soul. Time seemed to suspend itself; we were locked in a connection that transcended spoken language, a communion of heart and spirit. I noticed a single tear glimmer as it traced a path down her cheek, and the sight provoked a wave of understanding within me. Her empathy was intense, echoing my feelings of vulnerability and fear, yet as I looked at her, I recognized that I was not alone in this emotional storm.

Together, we navigated this sacred moment, both shaken yet anchored by our bond. Every heartbeat that passed brought with it a reminder of the love that encircled us, a protective cocoon woven from shared experiences and mutual understanding. Mema and I existed in that space, the weight of our emotions crystallizing into something beautiful, a testament to the enduring strength of love that connects us, no matter the distance or darkness that may surround us.

After the day of that unforgettable dream, Mema donned her work clothes, her favorite floral-patterned dress and sturdy shoes, before heading out the door, her footsteps echoing softly against the wooden floor. Before leaving, she placed a simple candle on the stove, its wax a delicate ivory hue. As the wick caught fire, the flame flickered to life, casting warm, dancing shadows across the kitchen walls. She turned to me with a reassuring smile, her eyes crinkling at the corners, and said, as long as you don't touch the candle, God will always be with you, watching over you. I felt a wave of determination wash over me; I resolved to keep my hands firmly away from the flame. It was a promise I made, not just to her but to myself.

Whenever loneliness crept into the corners of my heart, I would find myself drawn to that flickering light. Its gentle glow felt like a friend in the solitude, an assurance that I was never truly alone. I would sit for hours, mesmerized by how the light danced and swayed, swirling with a life of its own, wrapping me in a cocoon of warmth and hope. I often reflected on the magical persistence of that tiny candle, how it defied the dark with its steadfast glow, burning brightly through the long hours of the day until the night draped its inky cloak over everything.

Mema embodied warmth, filling my days with her vibrant spirit and infectious laughter. Her conversations sparkled with life, and her hugs enveloped me like a favorite old sweater, soft and reassuring. But it was her singing that genuinely captivated my soul. Her voice flowed like a gentle river, smooth and rich, evoking the soulful resonance of a finely tuned piano or the heartfelt notes sung by the legendary Aretha Franklin. On those magical evenings, Mema would sing sweet lullabies that wrapped around me like a beloved blanket, each note weaving a spell of comfort that lulled me to sleep. The melodies lingered in the air, encasing me in a cocoon of safety where dreams could flourish, transforming ordinary moments into cherished memories.

Though the specifics of our conversations during those times have blurred with age, one day stands out vividly in my memory. In her usual contemplative manner, Mema began to peel back the layers of her past, sharing a significant story that resonated deeply with me. She explained, her voice tinged with nostalgia and sorrow, that she had never known the presence of her mother or father. When she said father, a flood of curiosity sparked inside me. What is a father? I asked, my young mind grappling with the concept.

Mema's gaze drifted, momentarily lost in the abyss of her thoughts, moving from the flickering flame to the door that led outside and then back to my eager eyes. Her expression shifted to one of solemnity as if the weight of her words demanded respect. She continued softly, it's a rough world out there, and being a young girl in a house full of strangers can be quite challenging. At that moment, I recognized the depth of her wisdom, her eyes glistening and reflecting light like raindrops clinging to vibrant green leaves after a storm.

She unfurled more of her story with delicate precision. Many years ago, I belonged to someone, and that meant I had to be obedient to survive. That man, he is your father. As she spoke those words, I could see the clouds of emotion gathered in her gaze. Her eyes squinted slightly, her lips pursing together as though she struggled to recount a chapter of her life fraught with complexity. The idea of belonging puzzled me, sending a flurry of questions racing through my mind. However, I sensed that what she needed most from me at that moment was not inquiries but rather the comfort of my presence and the willingness to listen.

As she held me close, her gentle, rocking motion began to comfort me like the soothing tide of the ocean, making it challenging to keep my eyes open. The rhythm was mesmerizing, steady like a heartbeat, and I could feel her love enveloping me in warmth, a feeling I didn't fully understand back then but would later realize was the essence of unconditional motherly love. Over the years, that cherished sensation became a rare treasure, and many seasons before we dared to discuss that dream or that profound evening again.

Looking back, I am deeply grateful for those intimate moments with Mema. They shaped my understanding of love, a love that transcended words, rich with resilience and beauty. Life undoubtedly presents its share of challenges, but as I reminisce about the light of that candle and Mema's sweet voice, I am reminded that love can illuminate even the darkest paths, guiding us with hope and clarity as we journey through life.

TWO

As time passed, I became restless because being inside the house alone began to drive me crazy. Sometimes, I would imagine heads coming through the walls and legs and arms dropping from the ceiling, and the whole house would be full of chaos, but when I looked outside, there would be calmness. I wondered how it felt to be out there, and at the peak of my curiosity, I thought about flying away and never coming back, but reality set in, and I thought about Mema being all alone like I am. I frequently sat at the window speculating whether I could fly, thinking that maybe it was why Mema didn't want me outside because she didn't want me to fly away. I'd walk to the door, position my hand on the knob, and turn it, but I couldn't open it because, in my mind, I could hear her say, stay in the house. One day, I reckon I couldn't resist; I must have walked from the door to the window twenty times before it happened; the next thing I knew, I was standing outside the house. I felt enchanted by the way the sun shone on my face, and the cool breeze of the blowing wind reminded me of my vision of flying. I stood there with my head pointing straight up to the sky, but I could still not see the tree tops. My eyes slowly strolled down the barks of the trees, where I noticed gray silky moss that looked like a spider web hanging to the ground. It surrounded the house like a canopy of fog, and when I first saw it, I thought I was in heaven because of its beauty. I began galloping like a horse through the trees, but I wanted to know if I could fly. As I ran, I started flapping my arms like a bird and leaping like a deer, but nothing happened; even though I couldn't fly, I was still having fun. I lay on the ground and watched the birds and the butterflies fly around the trees in and out of the blue and white lilies.

All the while I lay there, I was intoxicated by the flowers' aroma. While lying there, I heard the leaves rustle; it frightened me because I thought it was Mema. I jumped to my feet and ran behind a tree, and when I peeped to see who was there, to my surprise, two people looked similar to me. They seemed to be playing some kind of game; they were giggling and shoving each other, and I thought I heard one of them say tic tag, you're it. When I stepped from behind the magnolia tree and said my name is Lillian, I must have frightened them because they grabbed at each other. They began pointing and laughing at me once they realized I wasn't a threat. I didn't know what was funny, but I started laughing too, and when I started, they stopped. One of them asked me what I was doing out there, and when I didn't answer, the other one said, *what, cat got your tongue.* All of a sudden, I became short of breath and couldn't say anything, I tried to run, but my feet refused to budge. They started walking toward me, I was so afraid my body started quivering, and as they got closer, I felt water running down my legs. When they walked past me, one of them lowered their shoulder and rammed their body into mine, and I went flying to the ground. They both turned and said, *Crazy nigger.* They walked away laughing, giggling, and shoving each other. This was an unfamiliar word, so I tried to figure it out but came up with nothing. I picked myself up, returned to the house, and changed my clothes.

When Mema finally stepped through the front door, I felt a flutter of excitement, but a part of me hesitated to divulge the whirlwind of events that had colored my day. As we gathered around the old wooden table, I could see Mema's warm smile, yet her inquisitive eyes were scanning my face intently.

Throughout dinner, she filled the air with curious questions about my daily adventures. Her tone was light and playful, but there was an undercurrent of concern that I couldn't entirely ignore. Somehow, it felt like she already knew I had been outside, her intuition finely tuned like a well-crafted instrument. Perhaps a little birdy had flown in with snippets of gossip about my escapades, or was it simply a mother's knack for sensing when her child had strayed from the expected?

As her questions continued, I found it increasingly difficult to hold my composure. Each passing moment seemed to amplify the tension between us, and I could sense an anxious energy building in her. The nervous flutter in my stomach grew more vigorous. At just four or five years old, navigating Mema's feelings felt like trying to solve a puzzle with missing pieces.

With a gentle hand reaching out to touch my arm, she leaned slightly closer and asked again, how was your day, baby? Her voice, though soft, held a weight that made my heart race. I feared that if I answered truthfully, I might summon disappointment or worry from her, and the thought of causing her distress sent a fresh wave of tears threatening to spill from my eyes.

Gathering my courage, I took a deep breath and admitted that I had played outside, my words tumbling out with the hesitance of a timid breeze. Just as I began to weave the details of my day into a colorful tapestry of adventure, Mema's voice sliced through the moment with urgency, If I've told you once, I've said it a thousand times: please stay in the house when I'm not here. I worry about you, and I can't help but think of all the things that could happen.

Her voice, although raised, was laced with concern and love, each word a testament to her protective nature. The tension in the room thickened, but amidst that palpable anxiety, I could feel the unwavering warmth of her love. Mema's fierce concern was a vivid reminder of her devotion, and I recognized then that her heart was simply echoing her desire for my safety, and beneath her worried gaze lay a steadfast commitment, a testament to how a mother would shield her child from harm.

I told her that I saw two little people who looked like me when I was outside. When they saw me, they began laughing, and one of them pushed me down and called me a name. When she asked what they called me, I started to cry even harder, and for the life of me, I couldn't remember what they said. Then she asked, did they call you a nigger? I thought about it briefly and said it could have been that word, but I wasn't sure. I wanted to ask her what it meant, but I was scared because, from the look in her eyes, I knew it was a bad word, and she detested it.

She looked at me for a moment, her eyes softening with empathy, and then her tone shifted to a nurturing timbre as if she were trying to wrap my heart in a protective layer. You are not that word; you are my precious child, and I love you dearly, she reassured me, her voice warm like a sunbeam breaking through a cloudy sky. Those kids who called you that were absolutely wrong. It's important to realize that some people, in their ignorance, mistakenly believe they are superior to others based solely on appearances. Do you understand what I'm saying?

Detecting the uncertainty that clouded my thoughts, she decided to illustrate her message in a way that might resonate with me. The kids you encountered, they looked different from you, didn't they? While they may think their differences elevate them above others, such beliefs are rooted in ignorance and fear. Tragically, some individuals allow these misguided notions to justify mistreating others and even inflicting harm simply because they believe they are better. But let me tell you, my dear, your worth is not and never will be defined by their hurtful words or narrow-minded views. It is shaped by the love, kindness, and resilience that you carry within your heart.

I could sense a palpable shift in the atmosphere when she began speaking to me; her gaze drifted beyond my presence as if she were peering through the enclosed walls. Each word she uttered tumbled in a hurried cascade, a flurry of thoughts that slipped through my fingers like water. I strained to follow her train of thought, but her rapid-fire delivery left me grasping at elusive fragments of meaning. As she finally paused, a wave of relief washed over me, soothing my frazzled nerves momentarily. But then she stood up abruptly, her silhouette tense and alert, as the realization flickered across her face that there was still more to convey. She turned around, her voice cutting through the air with an unsettling urgency: Did they ask you where you live? Did they see you come into the house? I told you not to go out when I'm at work.

Her frustration puzzled me, knotting my insides into tight little spirals. When our eyes met, I must have worn an expression painted with terror because she quickly crossed the room, her footsteps swift and purposeful, gathering me into her arms. Her warm embrace wrapped around me like a protective shield, offering a fleeting sense of sanctuary amidst the storm of her worries.

That evening, as the day faded into twilight, the serenity of night was punctured by her restlessness. I could feel her constant movement, and the occasional sigh escaping her lips; she tossed and turned beneath an apparent whirlwind of unease that stirred my anxieties. The first hints of dawn crept into the room, revealing a different facet of her, eyes puffy and tinged with pink, lips drawn tight like a wrestling line of tension. This was a familiar sight, one that appeared during her unpredictable moments, a sign of the looming chaos often lurking just beneath the surface.

With a heavy yet tender sigh, she gently set me down, her hands lingering on my shoulders as she shared words that hung in the air like a thick fog: if she didn't come home, she wanted me to go to bed without her. Her voice, though soothing, carried an intense weight as she urged me to venture outside if she hadn't returned by morning. She pointed toward the narrow, winding road that stretched behind our home, her eyes searching mine for understanding as she reassured me, keep walking until you find people who look like me.

Confusion twisted in my gut, but I nodded obediently when she asked if I understood, even as fear simmered beneath the surface. A thousand unarticulated fears bubbled within me, a rising tide of dread at the thought of being left alone. Yet, she knelt down to my level, her presence grounding and calming as she pressed her lips gently against my forehead, whispering, I love you, before stepping out into the uncertain world beyond our door. Her last words echoed in my mind as she left, sparking a whirlwind of unanswered questions. I spent the day lost in thought, consuming me with uncertainty: where would I go, why did her eyes betray such an unsettling glimmer, and what might transpire if she didn't come back?

As the hours dragged on and the sun dipped lower in the sky, casting long shadows that crept across the room, the suffocating wave of worry again crashed over me. Tears pooled in my eyes as I wondered if I would ever see her smile again. With a heavy heart, I found solace in the corner of the room, curled up beneath the window, watching the world outside fade into twilight while time stretched into an endless void. When darkness enveloped the space, and Mema had still not returned, I laid down, yearning for sleep to grant me peace and the sweet oblivion of dreams.

The following day arrived with a heavy blanket of silence, and an unsettling worry clutched at my chest as I realized she still hadn't returned. The fading memories of her last comforting words echoed in my mind, yet a gnawing apprehension rooted me in place despite the reassurance they once provided. I sank deeply into the softness of the mattress, surrounded by the covers that held the lingering warmth of her presence. My thoughts swirled around her absence like autumn leaves caught in a whirlpool, each one heavier than the last, pulling me deeper into my anxious trance.

Just as I felt myself drifting into a fretful slumber, a warm, enticing aroma wafted through the air, stirring me from my thoughts. It was a scent that tugged at my heart, rich and comforting, like freshly baked biscuits with a hint of cinnamon. As my senses sharpened, I heard the familiar, gentle strains of Amazing Grace floating softly through the house, pulling me toward the source.

Excitedly, I leaped up from the bed, my bare feet meeting the cool wooden floor as I dashed across the room. I flung myself into her arms, an impulsive wave of joy washing over me, wrapping us in a cocoon of warmth. You're back, I exclaimed, my voice thick with relief, the weight of my fears melting away in her embrace. I was scared I wouldn't see you again. Please, Mema, don't leave me alone.

She settled me onto her lap, her arms enveloping me in a protective embrace, the familiar scent of her body mingling with the kitchen smells around us. Do you remember when I told you I belonged to someone? She murmured; her voice soft yet filled with a poignant intensity. I was just about your age when this began for me. It fills me with concern that what happened to me could happen to you. I made a promise to myself that I would protect my child at all costs, even if it meant sacrificing everything.

For a moment, her gaze drifted out of the window, and I could see how her thoughts seemed to unfurl painful memories. The silence stretched between us, heavy with unspoken fears and unyielding love. Eventually, she gently reminded me that it was getting late and that I should change into my pajamas and prepare for bed.

As I lay curled up in the darkness, the weight of her words settled around me like a thick fog. I didn't notice when she finally slipped under the covers beside me, but I could feel her restlessness radiating as the night wore on. Her movements broke the stillness and pulled me from sleep's gentle grasp.

The following morning, I awoke with a sense that something had shifted within her, an undercurrent of unease lingered in her eyes, the tension intense as if she was bracing for an unseen storm. She began to stay up later, her silhouette outlined against the dim light streaming through the window as she peered into the night, her brow crumpled with worry. Her demeanor oscillated between quiet determination and a gnawing apprehension, making it clear that something lay out of reach, waiting to reveal itself.

Despite the tumult of emotions swirling around us, her steadfast presence offered a comforting balm. I found solace in the belief that no matter what challenges were ahead, we would face them together, our bond unshakeable and resilient against whatever the world might throw our way.

THREE

I often found myself spending long, languid days nestled by the window like an eager bird, gazing out at the enchanting woods that sprawled beyond the confines of the house. Each afternoon, I would spot the two children I had met during my excursion into the vibrant outside world. Their laughter floated in the air like music, weaving through the branches of the trees, a melody I could almost reach out and touch. Although I remained confined within the four walls of my little sanctuary, I envisioned a world where we were inseparable friends.

In my vivid daydreams, those lively children would come bursting through the door to visit Mema, their faces aglow with excitement as they asked if I could join them for play. With her warm smile and twinkling eyes, Mema would always say yes, and we'd dash out into the inviting woods together, our laughter mingling with the rustling leaves as we played for hours, spinning tales of fantasy and adventure floating on the wind. Sometimes, I even pictured the warmth of cozy slumber parties at their house, where their parents would prepare fluffy, sugary popcorn that melted in our mouths. At the same time, we huddled under blankets, sharing thrilling ghost stories that sent shivers down our spines. Those moments of imagination painted vibrant colors on my otherwise gray days, wrapping me in a soft cocoon of happiness that helped me cope with the solitude that enveloped me.

One day, as I drifted deeper into these whimsical daydreams, I suddenly noticed one of the children pointing in my direction, their little fingers outstretched as if they had discovered treasure. A jolt of surprise shot through me; this was no ordinary afternoon. They had passed my window many times before, but their gaze seemed focused, inquisitive, almost magical this time. A rush of unexpected excitement coursed through me, filling my chest with butterflies, yet instinctively, I found myself retreating from that window like a rabbit, seeking safety. I curled up on the mattress, in the corner under the window wrapping my arms tightly around my knees as if shielding myself from the world outside.

When I carefully peeked back through the gap in my makeshift fortress, I saw them gazing curiously into another window, their expressions a mix of wonder and intrigue. My heart raced, would they come closer? I was suddenly struck by the realization that I had extinguished the only flickering candle, plunging my small realm into an unfathomable darkness that felt alive and oppressive. Enveloped by fear, I remained frozen in my corner, trembling like a leaf caught in a sudden winter gale. Hours faded away in silence, and when Mema finally returned, I was still huddled there, feeling small and fragile.

As she stepped through the doorway, her presence radiated warmth, but the sharpness of her gaze caught me off guard. Her eyes quickly assessed the room, landing on the darkened stove, and I could see worry etching across her features as she realized the candle was extinguished and the room remained shrouded in gloom. She rushed to my side in an instant, her arms enveloping me in a warm, protective embrace. What happened? she asked, her voice tinged with urgency. I stumbled through my explanation about the children peeking in, but her only concern was whether they had seen me, whether I was safe.

The palpable panic in her voice sent chills down my spine as she darted her gaze back and forth between the window and me, urgently insisting that it was time for us to leave. I was utterly puzzled, a thousand questions swirling in my mind, unsure of what she was implying, and she offered no further explanation to ease my distress. The following morning, she moved about her familiar routine as if nothing had shifted, a facade of normalcy that deepened my confusion and dread. I had thought that when she said we would leave together, it meant that we would embark on our journey side by side, not that I would be left behind to face the unknown alone.

As I sat there, abandoned to my thoughts, the weight of solitude pressed down on my chest. My mind danced with the idea of walking down that road she often shared stories about, the one that led to new wonders. Yet, a flicker of uncertainty gnawed at me; a desperate hope lingered that she would never abandon me, though the shadow of something ominous lay heavy in the air. Lost in thought, I suddenly heard footsteps approaching the house, each crunch echoing like the beat of a wild drum in my heart. Panic surged through me, and in a frenzied rush, I darted back to my safe corner, a sanctuary amidst my fears. I could hear the footsteps drawing closer, the tension thick like fog, and in a burst of terror, I shouted, go away, please go away.

To my astonishment, the door swung open with a creak that filled the silence, revealing Mema standing there, her expression a tempest of fury and protectiveness. Her voice thundered through the air, filled with a primal instinct to shield me as she shouted, Leave my baby alone. Get out of here.

In that electrifying moment, a torrent of emotions crashed over me. Tears streamed down my face as I raced into her arms, a wave of relief washing away my fears. You're back, you're back. I cried, my voice thick with emotion, I thought I wouldn't see you again. When you said it was time to leave this place, I feared you didn't want me anymore.

In that raw, vulnerable moment, amidst the swirling storm of fear and the sweet surge of joy, we clung tightly, knowing that our bond was an unwavering force capable of overcoming any challenge life throws our way. Together, we could face the unknown, and in that realization, I felt a renewed sense of hope ignite within me, a spark that promised brighter days ahead.

As Mema wrapped her arms around me in a warm embrace, the world outside melted away, and all that mattered was her soothing presence. Her voice, soft yet confident, floated through the air, telling me how deeply she loved me and whispering that it was time for us to set forth on an adventure. The following morning, Mema, bustling about as she prepared for work, bestowed upon me a radiant smile that eased my worries. I'll be back soon, and there's nothing for you to worry about, she promised, her words wrapping around me like a warm blanket. I clung to those assurances, repeating them to quiet the nervous flutter in my chest, focusing on staying calm and convinced that Mema would return before I could even miss her. Somehow, amidst the day's endless clock ticking, I managed to keep hope alive, eagerly anticipating our journey.

Mema stepped inside when the door swung open later that evening, her excitement bursting forth like a spring flower. Pack your things. We're leaving tonight. she exclaimed, her eyes twinkling as brightly as the stars. My heart raced, pulsing with a blend of joy and anxious anticipation. As we ventured outside, a canopy of darkness wrapped around us, and the silhouettes of towering trees loomed like silent sentinels, their branches swaying in the cool night breeze. Shadows danced at the edges of our path, sending delightful shivers down my spine. Gripping my hand firmly yet gently, Mema asked, Are you ready? Together, we began walking along a path lined with majestic trees, their thick, sturdy trunks rising above us. The air was crisp and refreshing, filled with the earthy scent of damp soil and fallen leaves, as if the very essence of nature was beckoning us forward.

The journey felt like drifting through a dream, and as we walked, the midnight sky transformed before our eyes. Shades of indigo and violet melted into the horizon, revealing beautiful cypress trees rising gracefully from the glistening waters nearby, their reflections shimmering like jewels in the soft glow of the moonlight. Each step took us farther from the ordinary, and I was swept away by the magical atmosphere surrounding us.

After what felt like an eternity of wandering, fatigue began to seep into my little legs, and a soft whine escaped my lips. Mema, with her reassuring smile, the kind that could chase away doubt, bent down and said, hang in there, we're almost there. Sensing my weariness, she effortlessly scooped me up into her arms, cradling me like a precious bundle as warmth radiated from her body. It wasn't long before I succumbed to sleep, Mema's heartbeat lulling me into a peaceful slumber.

Suddenly, I was jolted awake by the loudest sound I had ever heard, a deafening roar that filled my ears and rattled my bones. My heart raced, pounding like a drum as I instinctively clung to Mema, my wide eyes darting around to find the source of the commotion. Mema remained a calming anchor, her serene demeanor unfazed by the chaos. Just beyond the trees, a colossal black shape barreled toward us, and my heart soared. It was my first encounter with a train. As it thundered past, the ground shook beneath us, each vibration sending excited tremors through my body, thrilling me to my core as I watched the massive engine roar into the night.

After the train finally faded into the distance, I nestled back into Mema's comforting embrace, slipping into a serene sleep once more. When I awoke again, a delightful surprise awaited me: the sweet, nutty aroma of pecans mingled with the vibrant scent of blueberries perfumed the air. Mema had brought my favorite treats. The blueberries were dark and velvety, bursting with sweetness that danced on my tongue like a sugary kiss. After savoring our delicious snack, we resumed our adventure, though a nagging twinge of doubt crept into my thoughts, where exactly where we headed? The sky began to deepen into shades of navy blue, yet the full moon ascended higher, illuminating our path with its ethereal glow.

Just when despair threatened to creep in, Mema's bright and full-of-wonder voice broke through the stillness of the night. Look, there they are, she exclaimed, and my heart leaped with anticipation. As I turned to follow her gaze, I was astonished to see an enchanting house glowing softly in the moonlight, its beauty stopping me in my tracks.

As we approached the front door, a sweet, intoxicating scent, wafted through the air, enveloping us like a comforting embrace. The house stood tall and proud, elongated and slender, painted in a brilliant shade of white that gleamed against the dark sky. Cheerful green window frames adorned the inviting windows, and a bright door beckoned us forward, exuding warmth and cheer. It rested gracefully upon a charming porch, a feature I had never encountered before, sending waves of excitement coursing through me. The roof, a stunning dark rainbow of colors, glimmered as if glistening with dewdrops, shimmering in the moonlight. I would later learn that this delightful home was known as a shotgun house; a unique design allowed a straight view from the front door to the back, a curious architectural wonder.

We climbed the steps with bated breath, knocked on the door, and awaited an answer, hearts pounding in eager anticipation. A woman opened the door, her eyes widening in surprise at our unexpected appearance, two weary travelers ready for rest and adventure. Come in here, child. What are you doing out there all alone this time of night? Get in here, she exclaimed invitingly, warmth washing over us and instantly making us feel at home.

As we stepped inside, a wave of delight washed over me at the sight that greeted my eyes. The interior was just as enchanting as the exterior. The living room unfolded before me, with pristine white walls adorned with cheerful pictures that seemed to capture moments of joy and laughter, punctuated by vibrant floral curtains that danced gently in the light breeze from the open window. We ventured deeper, discovering a cozy bedroom tucked away, though darkness made it a mystery I would explore later. Our gaze then drifted to the kitchen, where my eyes widened in awe at the sight of a lovely wooden table surrounded by six sturdy chairs resting on beautiful wooden floors that shimmered under the warm glow of overhead lights. It felt so inviting and cozier than our little house back home.

Every sight, sound, and scent filled me with a deep sense of wonder and excitement, and in that moment, I realized that this journey, was truly just beginning, an enchanting tale waiting to be told.

The woman's soft voice cut through the ambient sounds of the kitchen, asking if I was hungry. Mema's eyes twinkled with encouragement as I looked up, and a knowing smile graced her lips. With her gentle nod, a rush of excitement coursed through me, my heart racing at the prospect of a delicious meal. I settled into my seat at the table. While I waited, my gaze wandered to an intriguing door set into the wall, half-open and beckoning. Curiosity ignited me; I tiptoed across the cool floorboards, intrigued by what lay beyond.

Peeking through the door, I was greeted by several children nestled under soft, colorful blankets, their cherubic faces glowing in the dim light. The room was filled with a delicate stillness, the peacefulness of their slumber wrapping around me like a comforting embrace. My heart swelled with delight at seeing their innocent forms, and the playful spirit within me couldn't resist the urge to enter their little sanctuary. I slipped inside with laughter bubbling in my chest and gleefully shouted, wake up. The startled children stirred, their eyes blinking open in confusion, and although they weren't thrilled at being jolted awake in the middle of the night, I felt a profound joy at witnessing their sleepy, bemused faces.

Suddenly, a familiar voice called me back, and I turned to find Mema summoning me to join her for the meal prepared by the woman. I scampered back to the kitchen, my feet barely touching the ground as I raced enthusiastically. The emotions swirling within me were intoxicating, a beautiful dance of happiness, anticipation, and a deep sense of belonging.

When the woman placed a plate before me, I couldn't help but gawk at the vibrant presentation: a round, flat potato dish cradling golden-brown codfish balls that shimmered enticingly in the warm light. This was to be my first taste of codfish balls, and as I took my first bite, a burst of flavor exploded in my mouth, the combination of savory spices and tender fish creating a culinary experience I knew I would always cherish. Even now, whenever the scent of codfish wafts through the air, it sweeps me back to that moment of pure delight. After savoring each morsel, Mema unfurled a cozy, colorful blanket and spread it on the floor of the welcoming front room. I settled down, my heart racing from the day's enchanting experiences as dreams of playing with the children swirled in my mind. Sleep did not come quickly; the excitement of having new friends nearby buzzed in my thoughts while Mema's warm, melodic voice intertwined with the woman's gentle laughter, creating a soothing backdrop that finally lulled me into slumber.

The next morning, sunlight streamed through the windows, bathing everything in a golden hue as I leaped up, energized by the day's possibilities. I rushed to the room where I had glimpsed the children the night before, but to my dismay, it stood empty, the beds unoccupied. For a fleeting moment, doubt crept in, twisting my thoughts, had it all been a dream akin to the imaginary companions I often conjured in the woods? Determined to uncover the truth, I dashed to find Mema, my heart pounding with curiosity and hope. With a gentle, reassuring smile, she told me the children were outside playing, and my pulse quickened with excitement. But just as I was about to sprint out into the sunshine, Mema's voice stopped me. There was one critical thing I needed to do first: eat, my heart sank slightly at the thought of missing another round of the delicious codfish balls I had so eagerly anticipated, but instead, I was served fluffy flour bread paired with creamy scrambled eggs. The meal disappeared quickly as I devoured it with enthusiasm, and with my mouth full, I exclaimed, Can I go play now? Mema smiled warmly at me, her eyes sparkling with approval, and when she nodded, joy erupted within me like a bursting firework. I dashed over to envelop her in a grateful hug, the relief and happiness radiating from her filling my heart with warmth as I bolted outside.

Outdoors, I was greeted by a lively scene that ignited my heart with joy, children leaping and laughing, their voices ringing like music as they played an animated game of tag, running in circles and squealing with delight. This was the moment I had long envisioned, and my heart raced with anticipation and thrill. But as I stood there, ready to join in, the others suddenly paused, their playful laughter turning to hushed giggles, fingers pointing in my direction. Confusion washed over me like a cold wave, dragging me back to the lonely times I had felt isolated in the woods. Overwhelmed, I hurried back inside, seeking Mema, desperate to understand why they laughed when they saw me. She looked at me with a thoughtful gaze, a mix of understanding and empathy, as if contemplating how best to prepare me for the truth.

With gentle care, she broached the subject of my uniqueness, explaining that I appeared a bit different from the other children, a representation of my father's lineage. A tangle of emotions twisted inside me as I grasped her words; while confident kids shared my skin color, others sported darker hair, and some had lighter skin that contrasted with my own hair color. Mema listened intently as I expressed my confusion, then touched my cheek gently, explaining that my distinctive features made me stand out in this community, where such combinations were rare, skin as dark as mine with white blonde hair. Yet, she emphasized that these differences did not dictate my value and that her love for me transcended any physical appearance.

One afternoon, as I lounged lazily on the front porch, the sweet scent of blooming flowers drifting in the air, I overheard Mema conversing deeply with her friends, Mrs. Bernadette and Mrs. Florence. Their tones were serious, laced with concern, and I leaned in closer, curious about the matters they were discussing. Mema spoke of needing to leave our home in the woods, sharing that it had become unsafe and those shadows of unease lingered as people began intruding. Mrs. Bernadette expressed surprise, her voice tinged with concern, revealing she hadn't known Mema had a child, asking why she had kept it a secret. Mrs. Bernadette's inquiry about my father filled the room like a heavy fog, muffling Mema's response. Driven by the thought of clarity, I furtively peeked through the window, catching a glimpse of Mema with tears glistening in her eyes.

With a soft, nurturing smile, Mrs. Bernadette reached out to Mema, offering comfort in her words: You don't have to cry; you're safe with friends now. Mema's heartfelt tears, she explained, were tears of joy, for the first time, someone had shown a genuine interest in her life, treating her as an equal, a friend. Mrs. Florence and Mrs. Bernadette wrapped Mema in a beautifully warm embrace, their friendship enveloping her like a soft blanket, a reminder that she was cherished and loved.

HerStory

It was a stunning moment, an intertwining of connection and support, radiating a deep sense of belonging. In this poignant moment, I felt an overwhelming gratitude swell within my heart for the love surrounding us, wrapping us in a comforting cocoon of warmth and acceptance, a feeling that we were not alone in this big, sometimes intimidating world.

HerStory

FOUR

After two incredible years of living with Mrs. Bernadette, Mema finally opened up and shared the most personal chapters of her life story. I still wonder what made her wait, but her timing was destined to be perfect. I was about seven years old, happily enjoying a delicious shrimp po-boy for lunch in the kitchen, when I overheard Mema deep in conversation with Mrs. Bernadette and Mrs. Florence.

With courage, she recounted a heartbreaking part of her childhood, how, at just four years old, her father had dropped her off, and she never saw him or her mother again. She was given as a birthday gift to Mr. Tommy's son, Danny, who was thirteen then. Every evening, Danny would come into her room, and she would try to defend herself, swinging her tiny fists and kicking, but he was much stronger, and his laughter rang out as she fought back. Mema held onto this hope that her father would return for her, and she dreamed of telling him everything, envisioning him standing up for her. Unfortunately, that hope faded with time.

She remembered how, day after day, someone would tell her that she was living the way God intended. At first, it was hard for her to believe, as she could recall happier times from her past. However, those memories started to slip away, leaving only echoes of what she'd been told. Mema spent many years in that same room, occasionally seeing others, and when she spotted black people walking by, she thought they must have their own rooms, too.

Then came a day when Mr. Tommy ordered her to leave, threatening her if she ever spoke about her experiences. Just a week later, she took that brave step into the unknown, and after a few months, her body started changing in ways that bewildered her. One morning, she woke up feeling a lot of pain, and shortly after, I was born.

Reflecting on those times, Mema returned to work, knowing it was what she was meant to do. She was worried Mr. Tommy might be angry at her return, but to her surprise, he never uttered a word. I still remember the day Mrs. Bernadette yelled about it so passionately that I nearly bumped my head on the wall, you damn right he ain't say nothin', and I bet he was glad to see you. He probably thought the police were waiting outside to take his ass to jail. He can't get away with this; you should've called the police right after you left. We, as black folks, have come too far for this kind of shit; too many have cried, and too many have died to stop this type of mess from happening. Many years ago, that sort of thing was acceptable behavior for their folks, and people like us had no rights, and all because of the color of our skin. We are still not free because they think they're the only civilized ones. I find that so damn peculiar given the fact that they were the ones who hung, burned, raped, and sold other human beings, and they think we the savages, huh, that I will never understand.

Even at the tender age of seven, I intuitively understood the immense pain and horror that Mrs. Bernadette must have endured over the years. Her voice trembled, thick with disbelief, as she exclaimed, Florence, can you believe what's happening? In this day and age, something like this could occur right under our noses.

Her eyes, usually filled with a spark of warmth, were now wide with anguish and disbelief as she spoke. She recounted, I dedicated over twenty years of my life working for him, constantly aware that he had his issues, but this, this is simply incomprehensible. I had no idea of the dark shadows lurking behind those closed doors. I would have moved heaven and earth to end it if I'd known. It always struck me odd when that room suddenly became off-limits; the air around it felt tense and unwelcoming. The mere thought of your being confined in there for years on end fills me with a deep, consuming rage. I often saw little Danny, his slight figure darting toward that doorway, and curiosity would gnaw at me mercilessly, making me wonder what was happening behind those walls. One day, I could no longer hold back my worries and asked him directly what was happening there. With the innocent sincerity of a child, he replied that his father had bought him a pet and that it couldn't be allowed out. The idea struck me as woefully cruel, but I hesitated to intervene, feeling powerless against the adults around me. When I mustered the courage to raise my concerns with Mr. Tommy, he merely brushed me aside with a dismissive wave, insisting I stay out of matters that were not my concern.

Since Viola passed away, that once-vibrant house has felt like an empty shell, haunted by the ghost of what it once was. She was such a nurturing spirit, her laughter echoing in every corner; I know she would have never tolerated such behavior within her home. It's absolutely devastating to witness how Mr. Tommy has lost his way. I must ask, why in the world would you choose to work for that man again after everything he put you through?

A heavy silence enveloped the room, thick with unspoken fears and shared pain, and then Mema spoke up, her voice quivering with emotion as fragile as spun glass. I thought what I lived through was normal; that's all I had ever known. It wasn't until I began listening to your stories, each heartfelt confession, that I realized life could be vastly different. Your conversations about your children sparkled with hope and possibility, illuminating my darkness and filling me with the belief that my little one could have a brighter future. The fear that my child would be doomed to suffer the same torment I had endured, the same isolation and sadness, gripped my heart in a vise. But your words opened my eyes to the reality that something was wrong. I desperately yearned to share my experiences, but the shame felt like a heavy blanket, suffocating and binding. No one knew about my child because I wanted to shield her from Mr. Tommy's insidious reach. I couldn't bear the thought of him thinking he could inflict upon her the same pain he inflicted on me.

As her heart-wrenching confession poured forth, tears cascaded down her cheeks, each droplet telling its own story of suffering and resilience. Once she finished, her friends instinctively gathered around her, forming a protective circle filled with warmth and understanding. They embraced her as if their collective strength could lift the burdens from her shoulders, assuring her that the dark chapters she had endured was finally behind her while insisting that such unbearable circumstances would not rear their heads again. Yet, deep within their hearts, they all knew these harrowing memories hung like an ominous shadow, a constant reminder of pain's lingering presence.

Mrs. Florence, with the gentle grace and wisdom born from hardship, reached out to Mema, her voice encouraging. Sweetheart, you've been living with us for a while; it's time you shed your fears like an old coat and take those first shaky steps toward independence. She paused, her gaze lingering thoughtfully on Mema, adding with a sense of nurturing warmth, you genuinely have no idea that you can stand on your own two feet in this world, do you?

Mema, overwhelmed by their loving support, felt a tidal wave of anxiety swell within her, crashing over her like a turbulent sea. What should I do? How can I prevent this from happening again? she pleaded, her voice trembling with uncertainty and desperation. I don't have anywhere to go. Please don't make me leave. Her friends, understanding the depths of her fears, recognized the critical moment unfolding before them, one that signaled the urgency for Mema to embrace the next chapter of her life. They gently reassured her that they were not pushing her away;

instead, they were offering her an incredible opportunity to begin anew, reclaiming the life that was rightfully hers.

As Mema internalized their words, understanding their foundation of love and care, she felt the weight of their support, a hopeful lifeline guiding her toward a better future. Yet I could see the anxiety wash over her as she stumbled toward a nearby chair, one hand resting on its back for support and the other pressed against her forehead, lost in thought. It was almost as if you could hear her inner dialogue echoing in the silence, wondering, What's next for me? However, with her steadfast friends standing resolutely by her side, rays of hope began to pierce through the clouds of doubt, suggesting that perhaps the future held something profoundly brighter, an opportunity for renewal, growth, and joy.

FIVE

After Mema had her profoundly emotional conversation with her friends, we dove headfirst into an exciting new chapter: house hunting for a charming little place we could call our own. The entire process was an exhilarating adventure, and I took immense joy in the thrill of searching for a home. However, the real treasure was our time exploring the neighborhoods. Our busy routines often confined us within our home's walls, so this was a rare and precious opportunity for us to connect and enjoy the world outside.

Yet, I began to notice something troubling, Mema seemed to struggle with the search. Each house we visited seemed to dim her spirit, and despite my eagerness to explore, it became clear that she wasn't truly connecting with any of them. It was as if the house whispered secrets, she wasn't ready to hear.

One house stands out in my memory with vivid clarity. As we approached, we were greeted by the sight of two tall, slender Christmas trees, their greenery strikingly contrasting with the front yard's soft earth. The porch beckoned, inviting us to sit and relax, while a swing tucked away in the corner promised lazy afternoons filled with laughter. Hope ignited in my chest as we stepped inside, could this be the one? The entrance opened into a stunning interior where a wide, inviting archway led into a spacious living room with sunlight. The gleaming wooden floors added warmth, while the walls painted a bright, cheerful yellow uplifted my spirits. The kitchen sprawled out to my left, and my heart raced at the thought of future dinners and gatherings.

However, as I admired the beauty surrounding us, I glanced back and noticed Mema had paused at the entrance, her expression a mixture of contemplation and sorrow. It was clear our search was far from over. She stepped inside, took a slow, deliberate breath, and scanned the room as if trying to uncover something hidden. It was all too apparent when she turned to leave without a word. Intrigued, I later asked her what had held her back, and she revealed that the house evoked memories of a difficult chapter in her past,

With each subsequent house visit, it dawned on me that Mema's heart wasn't indeed in this house-hunting journey. Rather than examining each home closely, she would enter, breathe deeply as if testing the air, and make a quick decision based on that moment. Unfortunately, many homes simply didn't resonate with her, leaving a lingering feeling of disappointment.

In stark contrast, my experience house hunting with Mrs. Florence was filled with laughter and camaraderie. We found ourselves admiring the same homes, sharing our thoughts and dreams as we explored neighborhoods like Gentilly, Pontchartrain Park, and the Lower Ninth Ward. I was particularly drawn to Pontchartrain Park; it was near the beautiful, serene lake and boasted a charming park just across the street from a house we considered. The allure of lush greenery and the sound of children's laughter wafting through the air made my heart swell.

After six long months of searching, Mema finally settled on a house that, despite my initial reservations, unfolded into an unexpected adventure. Located on Deslonde Street, just a block away from the levee and a couple of blocks from the back bridge, it had its unique blend of charm and challenges. The Bayou-like surroundings were picturesque, but the relentless mosquitoes during the summer months could feel overwhelming, an endless swarm that turned sweltering afternoons into a test of endurance. Yet, amidst the challenges of our new home, a delightful silver lining emerged. Mema discovered a passion for making and selling treats: frozen cups bursting with flavor, decadent pralines, crunchy popcorn balls, and crisp candy apples that tantalized taste buds. Suddenly, our doorstep transformed into a lively hotspot, a hub resonating with laughter and excitement from eager neighborhood children flocking for her sugary creations. Initially, I thought her entrepreneurial venture would provide some much-needed relief, allowing me to retreat into the quiet of our home. Instead, the bustling atmosphere became a whirlwind of joy and energy. Thankfully, the unyielding mosquitoes kept many of the kids indoors during the hot summer days, and once school resumed, I found the perfect excuse to enjoy the comfort of our home.

We lived on Deslonde for two long, transformative years before finally moving to Reynes Street. This new location promised a friendlier neighborhood that was alive with children. At first, I hesitated to step outside, unsure how I would cope with the teasing that had taunted me in the past. But when I eventually mustered the courage to venture out, I was met with the familiar din of playful mockery, laughter, hair-pulling, and good-natured name-calling were all part of the daily routine in this spirited neighborhood.

In search of tranquility, I often escaped to the nearby park or the canal, where I would sit and watch children eagerly dipping their nets into the shimmering water, speculating on the treasures they might unearth. There were moments of solitude when I relished in catching crawfish all by myself. I would catch just a handful but always returned them to the water, acutely aware that Mema would be pretty upset if she knew I ventured near the canal without company.

One afternoon, as I sat on the porch, lost in thought about the possibilities ahead of me, a group of neighborhood kids approached. Their energy was infectious, and they invited me to join them at the canal. My heart raced with excitement, and I leaped to my feet without hesitation. When we arrived, the atmosphere turned electric: everyone settled into a rhythm, casting their nets into the water and engaging in animated chatter. For the first time, it finally felt as though I was a part of this vibrant group.

However, just as I began to believe they had truly accepted me, playful chaos erupted. One of the kids raced behind me and playfully seized me, tugging me backward with surprising strength. Amidst the wild laughter, I felt something slimy and messy rubbed into my hair. When I was finally set free, I rushed to touch my hair and face, only to discover mud smeared all over me. In a torrent of embarrassment, I sprinted home, heart pounding, wishing that no one else would see the disheveled state I found myself in.

In a moment of self-reflection, I paused in front of the mirror as I rushed through the house, finally confronting the differences that often made me uneasy. A wave of realization washed over me, and I quietly thought, *I sure am ugly.* Without wasting another moment, I sprinted to the backyard and rinsed my hair with the cool, refreshing spray of the hose, reminding myself that I would rise above these and not let them define me.

From that day forward, whenever I saw those kids, it was with a newfound understanding. I came to realize that their laughter didn't diminish my worth. Each experience, whether joyful or painful, was part of my evolving story, and with every passing day, I felt more prepared to embrace whatever adventures lay ahead, ready to carve my own unique place within this colorful tapestry of life.

Since leaving our little house in the woods, my life had been pure unadulterated hell, but I couldn't have anticipated the degree of brutality I would have to undergo. The teasing started with the kids pointing and laughing at my hair whenever I was in their presence, and when that got old, they started making fun of my complexion, then my height, my weight, the way I talked and the way I walked. They were relentless in keeping me in misery, I had overheard them many times say that Mema was stupid to live the way she lived, and to make things worst she had a deformed baby, by who knows what. I'm sure they didn't know I heard, but I bet they really didn't care if I did or didn't. It wasn't only the kids who were cruel, I remember a child asking her mother what was wrong with me, why was my hair different from everyone else's, and she told her child that Mema must have been an evil woman, and God wanted the whole world to know. That really disappointed me because I thought adults knew better, from the way she stared at me, I knew my life would be frustrating as long as I looked the way I did. I thought if I changed the color of my hair possibly it would make a difference, but Mema refused and told me when I got older, I could change it myself, but I shouldn't be surprised if other people's attitude didn't change.

As Mema began to share stories of her past, the trials she faced and the hurdles she overcame, I felt the threads of connection between us weaving a more substantial fabric of understanding. Yet, despite those shared moments, my feelings of being an outsider loomed large, pressing against me like a heavy cloud. One afternoon, as golden light streamed through the trees, casting dappled shadows on the floor, I found the courage to confide in Mema about my unique struggles because of my appearance. I poured out my heart, worries, and deep-seated fears of never fitting in. Mema listened attentively, her warm eyes reflecting her concern. She gently encouraged me to let others see and appreciate my individuality instead of retreating at the first hint of judgment.

It was a difficult lesson, but I gradually understood that her unwavering faith in humanity was deeply rooted in her life experiences of overcoming adversity. I often found myself wandering through memories of my childhood days spent on the mattress in the corner, under the window of the dimly lit room, yearning for playmates and the simple joys of companionship. A part of me wondered if solitude was a safer refuge than the pain of rejection, a bittersweet realization that sometimes wrapped around me like a heavy quilt. Certain days embodying a relentless struggle felt overwhelming at times, as though I were carrying the weight of the world on my young shoulders. There were moments when it felt like the air around me grew heavy, constricting my breath like the world collapsing.

One day, I found myself sitting on the back porch, overwhelmed by everything life had thrown my way. The weight of it all felt unbearable, and I was wrestling with thoughts I didn't truly want to entertain. But just as I was lost in those dark thoughts, a familiar voice called out my name. It stirred memories of a simpler time, bringing to mind the dreams and aspirations of my childhood. I looked around, hoping to see someone, but the porch was empty, until out of the blue, Mrs. Florence appeared. It was as if she had sensed my solitude. She took a seat beside me and, with a warm smile, remarked on the beauty of the day, noting that the lovely weather would be lingering for a while.

Though my silence lingered, I appreciated her presence. Just then, Mrs. Florence continued, sharing her insights on life's unexpected twists. You know, she said thoughtfully, life can be quite funny. It rarely goes as we expect. Take your journey, for instance. You and your mother lived in the woods, just the two of you. She wanted you to have more opportunities, to be around others and live a better life. Yet, even in a crowd, you can still feel profoundly lonely. This loneliness is different, it can make you feel as though happiness is beyond reach. She then quoted Eleanor Roosevelt, saying, nobody can make you feel inferior without your permission.

Mrs. Florence paused after her words, giving me a moment to reflect, anticipating my reaction. I remained silent, but her next words caught my attention: You know, I had a daughter.

Surprised, I asked where she was now. I recognized the grief in her eyes, the telltale signs of sorrow etched across her face. She shared the story of her daughter, Josephine, who would often sit on that same porch, mirroring my own expression of turmoil. Mrs. Florence had assumed Josephine was content in her solitude, believing that having friends wasn't everything. But Josephine faced her own challenges; she was born with a clubbed foot, which made her different. The teasing from other children deeply affected her, a pain that Mrs. Florence only began to comprehend too late.

Mrs. Florence said she could only imagine what Josephine was going through because it got to the point where she could no longer take the ridicule or the pain of rejection, so she took her life. Mrs. Florence realized she could've helped her if she would have paid more attention to what was going on, but sometimes parents just can't see what's happening to their children. Before she died, she begged for her life because in the end, she realized she didn't want to die, but it was too late she had taken a meat clever and just about chopped off her foot, by the time help arrived she had lost too much blood. Being different wasn't worth losing her life and she knew it. Josephine asked her mother for forgiveness, Mrs. Florence loved her daughter very much, and made a promise that if she ever saw anyone in a bad situation, she would make sure it didn't end the same way it ended for Josephine.

As she spoke, I could feel the depth of her sorrow. Do you understand? She pleaded; her voice filled with compassion. The grief I carry is not something I wish upon anyone. Think of Mema, how would she feel?

With tears streaming down my face, I nodded, feeling understood for the first time. I get it, I whispered. But some days, it feels like I can't carry this burden any longer. With Mema preoccupied, it feels like I have no one to talk to. I feel so lonely, as if there's no love for me.

Mrs. Florence listened intently, allowing my feelings to flow, then gently reassured me. Mema loves you, and so do I. When things feel too hard, promise me you'll reach out to me. I'm here for you. From that day forward, Mrs. Florence became my anchor and my closest friend.

Years later, I discovered that Mrs. Florence never actually had a daughter; she had shared that story to help me confront my struggles and recognize my need for support. I carry a deep appreciation for her to this day. If it weren't for her kindness and strength, I might have taken a very different path that day. She spoke with Mema about our conversation, leading to a heartfelt dialogue. Mema revealed that even when it seemed like she wasn't listening, she heard me. Her own battles often left her feeling overwhelmed, and at times it felt like she was barely holding herself together. I realized then that she too, relied on me, and our connection was mutual and vital.

As I grew older, I understood the magnitude of Mema's struggles. She fought battles that no one should have to face, and she needed me just as much as I needed her. That realization ignited a new sense of empathy within me; I saw her not just as a caregiver but as a fellow fighter wrestling with her own challenges.

SIX

The school had always felt like a challenging maze, filled with twists and turns that often left me feeling lost and isolated. As I grew more accustomed to the rhythm of high school life, I learned to navigate the tumultuous social landscape on my own, forging a path through the halls, keeping my head down and my thoughts to myself. One fateful afternoon, however, as I made my way home along the familiar route lined with towering trees that dappled the sidewalk with sunlight, a boy unexpectedly stepped into my path.

Hey, how are you doing? he called out, his voice breaking through my contemplation. I must have been around sixteen at the time, enveloped in my own world of worries and thoughts, when his sudden approach startled me.

Surprise washed over me like a cold splash of water. I instinctively shifted to the side, quickening my pace, my heart rate increasing at this unwanted interruption. I could still hear him call after me, Hey I'm talking to you. A flicker of curiosity sparked within me, but I squashed it down, forcing my legs to carry me forward. My instincts screamed caution; I wasn't ready to discover who he was or his intentions. Evading a confrontation with strangers had become second nature by then.

As the weeks rolled on, I noticed a shift in my surroundings. The once-vibrant chaos of high school life seemed to quiet down, like a once-boisterous crowd gradually thinning out, leaving only a few relentless figures who persisted in their berating. I was left unsure whether this boy was one of them. I told myself he was just another face, perhaps even a source of amusement for others, and I imagined the scenario where the kids of the school would leap from the hedges, laughing, as if unveiling an elaborate prank at my expense. But I was determined not to offer them any satisfaction.

Yet, amidst my steady rhythm of evasion, a longing began to bloom within me during those solitary walks home. I wished for the very thing I instinctively pulled away from, a genuine conversation. The boy resurfaced in my daily life, each time asking the same cheerful, light-hearted questions, and though I answered with the same brevity, I couldn't help but notice the peculiar way his eyes lit up, revealing a glint of interest. I tried convincing myself that I wasn't captivated by him, for he bore an endearing oddness, a slight awkwardness in his demeanor that initially made me wary. But deep down, I recognized my heart betraying my logic; he was strikingly handsome. Towering over most of his peers at six feet, he possessed an athletic build, with thick black hair and deep brown eyes brimming with warmth and undeniable charm.

My hesitation to engage in conversation was rooted in those frightening memories from my childhood, sitting like shadows in my mind. I recalled a boy named Jordan, who had once sparked a flicker of hope in me. I had thought he genuinely liked me, only to discover too late that he was merely a pawn in a cruel game orchestrated by others. He had once handed me a note, a single slip of paper that sent my heart racing with the possibility of affection. It invited me to the swings after school, and for a moment, I allowed myself to dream. As we chatted, he complimented me, saying, you look as pretty as Billie Holiday, my heart soared with joy.

But that blissful moment fractured like glass when he playfully yanked my hair, his laughter mingling with his friends hiding nearby. The brutal shock of betrayal suffocated any warmth in my heart, replacing it with a thick layer of mistrust that clung to me like a second skin. That day marked a turning point; my innocence shattered, and I learned to harden my heart against any feeling.

Days turned into weeks, and the boy continued to greet me with cheerful questions, each meeting lessening my resolve. But then came the day when I arrived at our usual meeting spot, an old tree with gnarled branches, my heart racing within my chest, only to find him absent. Disappointment washed over me like a wave crashing on the shore. I had resolved to finally engage him in a real conversation, but as I walked home feeling dejected, I remembered Mema's wisdom, she always said to give people a chance. As I settled into a muddled sadness, he suddenly materialized from behind a tree, startling me.

Rushing toward me, his face broke into a wide, crooked smile that melted away my lingering worries. How are you doing? he asked again, his voice light with curiosity. I could hardly respond as nerves tightened around my throat. Fine, I managed to mumble, my cheeks flushing crimson as I stammered. To my astonishment, he replied, that's obvious, a playful grin dancing across his face. Intrigued, he pressed on, asking why I was always in such a hurry and jokingly wondering if I was married.

He expected laughter from me, and I could sense the lightness of his spirit, but as he spoke, my mouth went dry, and my mind spiraled into a whirlwind of confusion. I had rehearsed what I would say a hundred times, yet when I came face to face with him, all my carefully chosen words vanished, leaving me feeling foolish and small.

His warm gaze started to shift as he sensed my struggle. What? Cat got your tongue? he teased lightly, though his tone had an undertone of discomfort. I attempted to gather my thoughts, hoping to articulate a coherent response, but the words felt trapped like butterflies in a jar, fluttering helplessly against the glass. Watching his expression morph from amiable curiosity to frustration was disheartening, and wondered was this how this charming connection was meant to unfold? Suddenly, in an outburst of frustrated eloquence, he exclaimed, oh, I see. I'm not good enough for you. People like you just walk around thinking you're superior to everyone else.

His words sliced through the air with the sharpness of a knife, igniting a wave of confusion and hurt. Before I could respond, caught off guard by the unexpected anger, my instincts kicked in. Fueled by panic, I felt an overwhelming urge to flee. In a heartbeat, I turned on my heels and bolted down the street, my legs carrying me faster than I could process, my heart pounding wildly in my chest as if trying to escape the assault of emotions.

Finally, when I reached the sanctuary of home, I collapsed into a whirlwind of thoughts, frantically replaying the exchange that had just transpired. His words echoed in my mind, a conundrum that deepened with every passing moment. How could he think that someone who felt like a perpetual outsider could see themselves above others?

Despite the years of sorrow and mistrust I had accumulated, a tiny ember of hope ignited within me. I could learn to extend my hand toward others and accept the fragile prospect of friendship. It was a sliver of optimism in a dark and isolating world. Faced with my fears, the world might reveal surprising joys I had long since stopped believing existed. If I dared to open myself up and take that leap, I could begin to uncover the beauty of connection that had evaded me for so long.

As the weeks meandered past, I found myself enveloped in an unexpected and comforting relief that came from not having crossed paths with him again. I was resolute in my determination to avoid that confusing whirlwind of emotions, especially after suffering through the pain of betrayal. One bright, sun-soaked afternoon, I settled into the embrace of our grand magnolia tree in the front yard, its fragrant white blooms framing a perfect escape from the world. With the gentle breeze rustling the leaves above me, I lost myself in the day's tranquility. Suddenly, a voice broke through the serene moment, calling, hi, how are you doing? The familiarity of the voice sent a jolt through me, and even before I turned to look, I instinctively knew it was him. With a friendly smile, I replied, I'm fine, and you?

There was a momentary pause as if he were gathering his thoughts before continuing, A friend of yours told me where I could find you. I couldn't suppress a chuckle that bubbled to the surface; having a go-between was amusing, since my social circle was practically nonexistent.

Robert elaborated earnestly, explaining that he wanted to extend a heartfelt apology for how he had spoken to me the last time we met, and he realized that his behavior was ultimately out of line. His sincerity resonated deeply, a refreshing change from the callousness I had often encountered. It was akin to hearing a sweet melody after a long silence, and I felt my heart soften as I responded with a smile, assuring him that he had nothing to apologize for. Yet, in reply, he offered up his enchanting smile, stepping a little closer to me, which set my soul alight. My name is Robert, and you're Lillian, right? he asked, his voice warm and inviting. I nodded, feeling a delightful flutter of shyness mixed with intrigue. Without waiting for an explicit invitation, he settled beside me, his presence a bright beacon in the afternoon light.

As we began to converse, a natural rhythm emerged. Robert spoke animatedly about various aspects of his life, how his family uprooted him and moved here just over a year ago. He had a passion for sports, especially the electrifying game of football. He vividly shared his dreams, telling me about his ambitions to play for LSU and how he aspired to go pro, all while making a name for himself with the New Orleans Saints. I listened intently, captivated by his enthusiasm and how his eyes sparkled with the thrill of possibility. He confessed that he had been admiring me from afar, marveling at my beauty and desiring a chance to truly get to know me. It took him considerable courage to finally approach me, especially when I was often wrapped up in my world. After his previous misstep, he understood an in-person apology was crucial. He had asked around, seeking guidance until a mutual acquaintance finally pointed him in my direction. While he had my address, he carefully conveyed that he completely understood if I wasn't interested in meeting him. Nevertheless, his genuine desire to connect shone through, and I sensed his hopefulness.

Curiosity streamed through him as he inquired if I was studying for the SAT or ACT, noting how I tended to keep to myself rather than socialize with the other kids. I replied that I enjoyed my own company, a subtle half-truth, as I wasn't ready to unveil my complex backstory. Our conversations gradually blossomed into a delightful routine, with Robert patiently explaining the intricacies of football, a sport I began to find remarkably fascinating. When he finally mustered the courage to ask me out, exhilaration surged through me, our first date was set for a Saints game. Although the match's outcome wasn't in our favor, the experience was exhilarating and electric with the crowd's energy. Being with him felt like living in a romantic narrative, and he treated me with such kindness that I felt indeed seen as if he appreciated me for who I was beyond my exterior.

Life shifted dramatically around me as if the universe conspired to bring light into my world. More and more people began to acknowledge my presence, using my name with a warmth I hadn't experienced before, stopping to greet me with genuine smiles, and engaging in lively conversations. I cherished each moment spent in Robert's company; he was a breeze of joy, and his warmth elevated my spirits in ways I hadn't believed possible. My mother, Mema, was thrilled at the prospect of meeting him. She made a concerted effort to ensure we both felt warmly welcomed, orchestrating delightful little picnics in the yard and making it her mission to learn about Robert's favorite foods. Her legendary red beans, simmered with double D spicy smoked sausage, paired exquisitely with her infamous fried chicken, which soon became our go-to meal. At least once a month, she would whip up that culinary masterpiece, a succulent chicken soaked in a fragrant blend of cayenne pepper and water, meticulously tossed in a well-seasoned flour mixture, and fried to a golden, crispy perfection. It was a dish that could rival the best-fried chicken anywhere in southern Louisiana.

Everything began to fall into place beautifully, a tapestry woven of attention and excitement that filled me with wonder. Every new day brought fresh joys, and being part of something special with Robert felt like a beautiful awakening.

SEVEN

Mema's journey took a challenging turn as she began to lose weight, and her skin became pale and thin, nearly translucent. Her hair started to turn grey, and it seemed she was struggling with signs of depression. I often found her wandering around in her slip, sometimes mumbling to herself. Although her behavior became unpredictable, I still held hope for brighter days ahead. One night, I awoke to a startling vision of her standing over me with a knife, blood dripping from it. I leaped to my feet and realized it was only a dream; things had gotten so bad that it caused my dreams to turn to nightmares. I thought it was because her past was colliding with the present.

On another day, I found myself feeling a mix of excitement and curiosity, so I decided to ask Mema if I could attend a Mardi Gras Parade. To my surprise, her reaction was intense and emotional; it felt as if a storm had erupted all around us. For a brief moment, I genuinely feared for my life. Her unpredictable outburst left me feeling uneasy, prompting me to seek support from Mrs. Florence, who had been a reliable ally for me in the past.

When I approached Mrs. Florence, she shared her insights about Mema. She explained that Mema was on a journey of self-discovery, trying to untangle the threads of her life story. It was intriguing to learn that the people who raised Mema had significantly influenced her sense of self, often to the extent of stifling her identity. Although Mema held a great deal of resentment towards them, they were also the only family she had ever known, and there was a complex web of love intertwined with her feelings. Mrs. Florence described it as a classic love/hate relationship, noting that grappling with such deep emotional connections can be one of life's greatest challenges. It became clear that Mema needed to delve into her past, her true past, the one that lay before her current memories.

As Mema wrestled with her unraveling world, my own life began to feel increasingly difficult. I noticed her slipping into a repetitive routine of gazing out of the window, reminiscent of her days in that quaint little house tucked away in the woods. Sometimes, when passersby caught her attention, her reaction was dramatic: she would shout, even spit from the window, jumping up with an urgent plea for them to leave her and her baby be. In the beginning, I knew just how to soothe her troubled mind, but over time, she began to lash out verbally at me. Any attempt I made to reach out was met with her accusations, as she insisted that I must have shared our address with the outside world.

Although Mema and I had experienced similar conditions, our perspectives could not have been more different. To me, those events seemed to be mere chapters in my life story, while for Mema, they encapsulated her entire existence. She seemed trapped in a past she couldn't rewrite, lost in a present she couldn't interpret, and anxious about a future she couldn't envision. While Mema navigated her challenges, I found comfort in spending time with Robert. I cherished our moments together. Even with Mema's apprehensions about the Mardi Gras Parade.

Being at the parade was nothing short of magical. It illuminated why Mema had reservations; with throngs of people and vibrant chaos, it certainly wasn't her cup of tea. Yet, despite the bustling atmosphere, I was completely captivated. The sights of individuals in flamboyant feathered costumes, beautiful horse-drawn carriages, and lively dancing girls, all paired with the uplifting music enveloping the streets, created an unforgettable experience. The energy was contagious, there was hardly room to move as trinkets flew through the air, adding an exhilarating touch to the occasion.

To this day, I look forward to the Zulu Parade every year, embracing the joy and wonder it brings. It's a celebration that, despite Mema's feelings, has become a cherished part of my own journey.

One wonderful afternoon, Robert and I decided to escape into the enchanting world of movies, eager to immerse ourselves in a story that would sweep us off our feet. While the details of that particular film have faded over time, the vibrant atmosphere of that day is etched in my memory like a cherished snapshot. What truly stands out is the breathtaking moment when Robert, a mix of excitement and vulnerability shining in his eyes, opened his heart to me. Nestled close in the soft glow of the theater, he turned towards me, a sparkle in his gaze that spoke volumes. With heartfelt sincerity, he shared his dreams and his deep affection, expressing his desire for us to build a life together. Each word he spoke wrapped around me like a warm embrace, lifting my spirit to new heights. In that magical moment, I truly understood the depth of my feelings for him. As the credits rolled and we stepped back into the sun-drenched world outside, I felt as if I were soaring, filled with a vibrant sense of joy and endless possibilities.

As if the universe had more in store for me that day, I found myself summoned into Mema's bedroom. She was nestled against her fluffy pillows, her brow furrowed, and a blend of concern and contemplation reigned on her expression. I settled onto the edge of her bed, the plush quilt beneath me offering comfort amidst the tension in the air, a palpable anticipation, reminiscent of the calm before the storm. Looking into her eyes, I sensed a whirlwind of unspoken thoughts, and I promised myself I would remain grounded, ready to face whatever was about to unfold.

Breaking the silence, Mema gently began to explore the topic of my feelings for Robert. There was an undercurrent of concern in her tone that hinted at disapproval, leaving me feeling a bit rattled. The urge to escape the discomfort of the conversation bubbled up inside me, but deep down, I knew that running away wouldn't resolve anything. Gathering all my strength, I took a deep breath and declared, I love Robert very much. The air in the room shifted dramatically, and it felt as if a dam had burst, releasing a flood of emotions. Mema's reaction was immediate and intense; frustration crossed her face, and her voice rose with urgency. It felt as though we were caught in a whirlwind of conflict, challenging yet charged with the potential for understanding. Despite the emotional storm swirling around us, I held onto the flicker of hope that we could find our way through this together.

In that tense moment, she exclaimed, Love? What the hell do you know about love? If you think that boy truly cares for you, you're being stupid. He's just a man, and men have a tendency to hurt. You can't honestly believe he loves you.

Her words struck me like a lightning bolt, leaving me reeling. I felt a surge of determination as I leapt to my feet, my voice rising with passion. Mema that's not fair you don't know him as I do, how can you say something so cruel, I hate you; I hate you, what happened to you could never happen to me, you said it yourself, I may be stupid but I could never be that stupid.

It was a powerful exchange, filled with raw emotions, but I truly believed in the strength of love and the promise it holds. Even amidst the whirlwind, I remained hopeful that understanding could pave our path forward. After all, love is a journey worth embarking on, no matter the challenges we face. When those words escaped my lips, I ducked instinctively, convinced she might be coming after me. When she didn't, a wave of guilt washed over me. Her gaze felt like a wounded animal hoping to escape its misery. Her eyes that once brought me peace during my childhood, now shimmered with deep sorrow, caused by me. Suddenly, Mema began to cry, and my heart ached for her. I wrapped my arms around her, desperate to console her, but it felt like nothing I did, made a difference. Seeing her shake uncontrollably filled me with fear for her well-being. I whispered apologies in a panic, but she couldn't hear me.

When she fell onto the bed, I felt a surge of urgency and dashed to Mrs. Bernadette's house. I arrived breathless, my mind racing as I struggled to get the words out. All that came out was an awkward scramble of, It's me, me, me. With her calm demeanor, Mrs. Bernadette urged me to slow down so I could explain. It didn't work, and I blurted out, Me. It's Mema. Her eyes widened with concern as she asked, What's wrong with your momma? Does she need help? I nodded vigorously, and together, we rushed out the door, though I found it hard to keep pace with her, even though she was no longer in her youth.

When we finally arrived at my house, I found Mema in the same spot, and my heart sank. Mrs. Bernadette rushed to her side, kneeling down to listen for a heartbeat, and at that moment, a wave of panic washed over me. I cried out in desperation, I killed her. I killed my mother. Tears streamed down my face as I called to Mema, I'm so sorry. I'm so, so sorry. It felt like the world's weight was on my shoulders, but deep inside, I clung to the flicker of hope that things could change. Gal, it's okay, your momma isn't gone. Why don't you take a moment for yourself? Maybe grab a warm glass of milk to help you calm down.

As I listened from the other room, Mrs. Bernadette spoke softly to Mema, asking what was wrong. I heard Mema express the deep pain she felt, saying she often wished for peace because the emptiness and struggles were too much to bear. The idea of losing control haunted her, she confided that some days she woke up not recalling what had happened the day before, terrified that she might have hurt her child without even knowing it.

Then, I heard her take a deep breath. Do you know what my child said to me? Mema's voice broke with sadness. Mrs. Bernadette responded with genuine concern, no, what did she say? And in that moment, I knew her words would carry more weight than any of us could have anticipated.

She said I was stupid for living the way we lived, and you know something, I think she's right; all these years, I've been telling myself I did it for her, but she wasn't there all the time, so now I wonder why I did it. For such a long time, I had believed that my sacrifices were commendable acts of Love for her. Yet, in the solitude of her absence, a wave of introspection washed over me, compelling me to question whether those decisions were indeed sacrifices or mere acts of misguided loyalty.

I burst into her room; the air thick with unspoken emotions. My heart raced as I faced her, fueled by a mixture of anxiety and urgency. I didn't mean it. You know that. I cried, my voice trembling as I fought to keep my composure. I understand your struggles, there was no other way for you. Mema, I love you so much, and I'm truly sorry for the pain I caused.

As I spoke, I could sense the tension slowly shifting. The hope for reconciliation ignited a profound belief that healing was possible and on the horizon. I envisioned the journey ahead, one filled with open conversations and mutual understanding, and for the first time in a long time, I felt genuinely optimistic about our future.

As I observed her, it became heartbreakingly clear that Mema bore a heavy burden in her spirit. She was trapped in a cycle of self-blame, convinced that she was the architect of the troubles that had befallen her. The mental pain that festered in her heart was profound, manifesting in the shadows beneath her eyes and the tightness of her smile. It pained me to witness her internal struggle like she was embroiled in a fierce battle against the very essence of life.

I can still vividly recall the cold, starry night we left that little house nestled in the woods, its weathered wooden beams creaking softly as we packed our belongings. Mema sat at the window, her silhouette framed against the dim light, with her gaze fixed intently on the darkened path outside. She looked as though she were waiting for someone special to materialize from the shadows, her eyes searching the night for an elusive connection that had long since faded. In the days leading up to that moment, I had sensed that same haunting expression creeping back into her demeanor, and it sent a chill racing down my spine. A short while before, she had reveled in her social life, inviting friends and filling our home with laughter and lively conversations. But now, she seemed tethered to that spot by the window, lost in a haze of memories and longing, as if clinging to a frayed thread of hope that had slipped through her fingers.

Mema's journey is a powerful testament to resilience and the capacity for change. Despite the shadows that loomed over her, I find myself holding onto the hope for brighter days ahead, a hope that one day, her laughter will once again fill our home with warmth and light.

EIGHT

One unforgettable afternoon, as I moseyed home from school, a peculiar mixture of excitement and dread danced in my chest. The moment I turned the key in the lock and stepped over the threshold, my heart sank a little. Mema was absent from her usual spot by the window, where she often gazed out at the world. My mind raced with possibilities, could it be that her persistent sadness had finally lifted? A flicker of hope ignited, and a radiant smile spread across my face as I contemplated the prospect of brighter days ahead.

Mema's voice, usually soft and tinged with melancholy, cut through the quiet as I entered. I found my family. Caught off guard by the passion in her tone, I momentarily wavered in my understanding. I stuttered, my confusion spilling out in a jumble of questions. For a fleeting moment, doubt seeped into my thoughts, and I hesitated, uncertain if Mema had genuinely lost her grip on reality, convinced she had been reunited with her family.

She asked me if I remembered the argument we had a few weeks ago, that was when I told her I was in love with

Robert. That realization made her see that she could never feel that way about anyone and that was the true reason for her going over the edge. She begged me to forgive her because she realized Robert was indeed good for me. That day was the last time she spoke to her mother. After she said those words, it seemed to awaken something within, out of the blue Mema yelled, I don't know what kind of game y'all playing, getting this woman to call me and pretend she's my mother, but y'all can't fool me.

Those words left me in a chaotic whirlwind of emotions. It struck me like lightning; she seemed to genuinely believe she had conversed with her mother, weaving a narrative that implicated me in some sinister plot. My heart raced as I craved to shout my innocence, to plead with her that I wasn't part of any deception. Yet, years of experience had taught me that during these turbulent moments, she often struggled to grasp what was logical. Dreading yet another episode of confusion, I quietly retreated, following my usual route into my own room, shutting the door behind me with a heavy sigh. She must have really talked to her mother, I thought, torn between my desire for details and my understanding that Mema would reveal them when she was ready.

Days melted into a week, and Mema remained cloistered within her room, cloaked in an enigmatic silence that deepened my concern. Finally, I resolved to cross a line I had vowed never to breach again: I knocked on her door without waiting for an invitation. The last time that happened she told me to come in, and I did, and the next thing I remembered was lying on the floor in front of her closed door. Hesitantly, I stood before her door, hand poised on the knob, every instinct urging caution.

As the knob began to turn, I held my breath and stepped aside, bracing myself for whatever awaited on the other side. When she finally swung the door open, a radiant smile shone on her face, starkly contrasting the shadows that had lingered for so long. I've been waiting for you. You won't believe it, I found my mother, and we've talked. She declared, excitedly dancing.

At that moment, an overwhelming surge of warmth washed over me, reminiscent of the comforting embrace of a summer's day. I rushed forward, wrapping my arms tightly around her, feeling the rare sensation of safety and familiarity engulf us, reminiscent of cozy evenings spent in stories in our little house nestled among the woods. How did you find her? I breathed, my voice a mix of urgency and wonder.

Mema launched into her story with palpable excitement, recounting the extraordinary events. It began at the Circle Food Store, a bustling hub filled with colorful produce and the sweet aroma of baked goods, where she had overheard two women animatedly discussing a friend who still clung to the hope of one day being reunited with her daughter. Intrigued by their conversation, Mema approached one of the women, sharing her longing to reconnect with her family. Although seemingly more interested in details than forging a genuine connection, the woman had offered snippets of insight about her friend's daughter. Despite Mema's initial frustration at the interaction, hope burgeoned within her as she accepted the woman's offer to share her name and phone number, longing for a lifeline to her past.

After several days of silence, the long-anticipated call finally came through, her heart raced as she answered the phone. The woman on the other end expressed uncertainty about whether Mema was indeed her daughter, but the eagerness in her voice to meet was unmistakable. Their conversation was filled with tentative joy as Mema shared vignettes of our lives together, promising to reach out when she felt ready to gather.

Mema wrestled with lingering uncertainty about their connection following that first tentative interaction. But just days later, another call brightened her day, the woman, overflowing with anxiety and eagerness, was desperate to connect. As Mema ruminated on their discussions, a whirlpool of hope began to unfurl within her heart. Certainty began to replace doubt; she felt this woman could indeed be her mother. Deep inside her, she sensed that this moment was the culmination of dreams she had cherished, and an exhilarating thrill surged through her veins at the prospect of a reunion that could transform her reality at long last.

Mema held on to the hope that reaching out to her estranged mother might somehow infuse her life with a dash of happiness, lifting the cloud of despair that often seemed to envelop her. However, the conversation took an unexpected turn, igniting a firestorm of frustration that boiled beneath the surface. I noticed the telltale signs of her mounting anger: the tightening of her jaw, the flaring of her nostrils, and her eyes, now sparkled with an intensity that hinted at the turmoil within. Just as I was contemplating how to comfort her, she erupted with a fierce declaration, as long as there's breath in my body, that woman is not welcome in my house or my life. Do you understand me?

Her passionate declaration hit me like a sudden chill; it was a stark contrast to the tentative curiosity about her mother that I had always sensed stuttering beneath the surface of her pain. Seeking to dig deeper into her feelings, I cautiously asked her to tell me what her mother meant to her. With a renewed fervor, she shot back, I could never forgive her because it's been far too long, and there's been too much pain. My heart is crushed, burdened with a weight of hate that I can hardly bear. Some days, I even see you as the enemy, I'm fighting a daily battle to love you, and I'll be honest: some days, I fail miserably. When it hit me that our situation was wrong, I kept replaying the question, why me? It always led back to my family; their choices trapped me there, and forgiving them feels like scaling a mountain with no summit.

As the weight of her words settled like a heavy fog, a powerful urge to counter her anguish surged within me. I tried to remind her that her mother was also a casualty of circumstances, likely unaware of the silent battles Mema had fought in the shadows of her life. In a bid to introduce the idea of reconciliation, I cautiously suggested, what if you gave her a chance? What if understanding could lead to healing?

Her response was swift and sharp, I don't owe anyone anything. She would have tried to find me if she cared about me. What kind of mother just disappears and doesn't look back?

Desperate to help Mema see the shades of gray in their complicated relationship, I urged her to consider that perhaps her mother had tried, battling her own demons along the way. In a moment of heated urgency, I exclaimed, Mema, for heaven's sake, she's still your mother. Why wouldn't you want to know her?

With unyielding conviction, she shot back, I don't have a mother. If you wish to speak to her, go ahead. Here's her address, but remember: she is not my mother. Tossing the crumpled pieces of paper onto the nightstand, she stormed out of the room, irritation and unresolved heartache trailing in her wake. A whirlwind of thoughts consumed me as I sat in the aftermath of her emotional exodus. After weighing my options, I decided to reach out, believing that the connections we built could lead us toward healing. The address led me to Tchoupitoulas Street, a thoroughfare hugged by the gentle murmur of the river nearby, each drop of water carrying whispers of stories untold.

A few days later, in a delightful twist of fate, my grandmother shared with me that her name was Lillian, striking coincidence, given that my name was Lillian as well. The tales she spun revealed that Mema also had siblings, two sisters and a brother. Listening to my grandmother recount stories of their childhood breathed life into faded thoughts in my mind. They shared warm memories, recounting how the youngest daughter, with her exuberant spirit, would light up their home. Baby Lillian was a whirlwind of joy, often draped in her eldest sister's clothes, transforming mundane days into enchanted adventures where makeup was her magic wand.

Returning home from these visits with Grandma Lil, I felt an eagerness bubbling within me as I shared our enchanting conversations with Mema. Gradually, as tales of their shared history unfolded, hopeful forgiveness seemed to set in, and Mema eventually agreed to meet her mother face-to-face.

Their reunions unfolded like a complex tapestry, a mixture of warmth and unease. More often than not, they found joy in each other's company, engaging in lighthearted banter and discovering common interests. Yet, lurking just beneath the surface were shadows of the past that erupted unexpectedly, sending Mema spiraling into emotional chaos. During these moments, she would unleash her frustrations with an intensity that left both women reeling, accusing her mother of abandonment, of being lost to substances, of never showing a shred of love or care. When the air thickened with unresolved feelings, Mema would leave abruptly, each exit dripping with unresolved tension and unspoken words.

At first, this emotional landscape proved to be a rocky terrain for Grandma Lil, who struggled to comprehend the maze of pain and betrayal that Mema was navigating. Yet, as the days morphed into weeks, Grandma Lil began to understand the complexities of Mema's experience, peeling back layers of hurt that had long been buried. Mema's siblings found themselves caught in the crossfire, trying to support their mother while grappling with their frustrations about her volatile emotions.

Amidst this familial storm, Tyrone, her nephew-in-law, emerged as a steady and reassuring presence. His calm demeanor gave Mema a safe space to voice her feelings without fear of judgment or escalation. Conversations with him flowed effortlessly, free from the burdens that weighed down her other relationships. With someone outside the immediate family who offered genuine concern, Mema felt a glimmer of hope that brought a remarkable shift in her life. Under Tyrone's influence, she was drawn into church activities, where community and connection breathed new life into her soul. For the first time, joy flickered within her, lighting our home with an ambiance of peace and tranquility, a rare and treasured blessing amidst the chaos we faced.

Mema's journey was undeniably arduous, filled with heart-wrenching challenges, yet she slowly began to find her way through resilience and the unwavering support of those around her.

It took Grandma Lil a long time to tell Mema the entire story. She said, the tale of your disappearance clings to my soul like a shadow, a haunting reminder of a dark chapter in our lives. It all began with the difficult realization that she would need to prepare Mema for the harsh truth of the situation. She felt compelled to share the story with Mema, fully aware of the pain it stirs within her.

I can vividly recall that fateful morning; the details are etched into my memory as if painted in bold strokes. The sun streamed through the kitchen window, casting a gentle light that danced across the table, where I had set about my morning routine of making breakfast. With a heart full of warmth and optimism, I cheerfully called out to everyone, ensuring they were awake and ready to start the day. As my family gathered around the table, laughter and chatter filled the air, but an unsettling realization quickly swept over me, you were missing. At first, a flicker of reassurance crossed my mind; I figured you were merely in the bathroom, taking a little extra time to wake up. However, as the minutes stretched on and the house remained eerily quiet, anxiety tightened its grip around my heart. When I sent someone to check on you only to learn you were not even in the house, a cold wave of panic rushed over me.

Frantically, I rushed to our bedroom, desperately shaking your father awake from his heavy sleep. The unmistakable odor of stale alcohol permeated the air, evidence of the night before lingering in the corners of our shared space. When I broke the news of your disappearance, it felt as if the ground beneath us had shifted; his eyes widened in shock as the stark reality registered. Without hesitation, he jumped out of bed, dressed in a blur of movement, and we both sprang into action, urgency propelling us forward. We began searching the house, peering into every nook and cranny, calling your name into the silent rooms. When we finally resorted to calling the police, we were met with a chilling indifference. Their arrival did little to ease our minds; they methodically examined our home, finding no signs of a break-in. The cold truth was painfully clear, during the 1940s, the police often turned a blind eye to the disappearance of a black child, and we were no exception. To our utter disbelief, they suggested you wandered off at night, encouraging us to rally our neighbors to continue searching the area.

Days bled into weeks, each stretching out like an agonizing eternity filled with desperate searching, hope dwindling with each passing moment. Night after sleepless night, we held onto the fragile thread of hope, but the weight of doubt began to suffocate us. The police returned to assist, but their efforts yielded nothing but disappointment. Despite the tireless searches, there was no sign of you. Each night, I knelt by my bed, fervently praying, pouring my heart into the universe, clinging to the remains of my faith. However, as the days dragged on, it felt like the world was slipping into an oblivion where you no longer existed. Our loved ones began to lose faith, and the officers finally suggested we come to terms with the grim belief that you could not be alive, urging us to move ahead with our lives, resigned to the conclusion that the river had claimed you. But deep in my heart, I knew that couldn't be true; I had instilled in you the importance of avoiding that river from when you learned to walk. I vowed never to cease my search for you, you became my everything, the light that illuminated my darkest days.

As time passed, turning days into weeks, a tangible shift darkened the atmosphere around your father. The unfathomable grief of losing you morphed into a consuming tempest of anger directed at everyone and everything around him. Friends and extended family, those who surrounded us with comfort, insisted that his behavior was a natural response to the tidal wave of grief he was wrestling with and that he simply needed time to recover. Yet, I watched helplessly as he became a shadow of himself, plagued by sleepless nights and nightmares that left him gasping for breath. One particularly harrowing evening, amid his restless slumber, I heard him call out, Mr.

Tommy, please give me back my child because I miss her so much.

His words struck me like lightning; confusion and an overwhelming dread coursed through my veins as I shouted, what did you say? What did you mean, Mr. Tommy? Who is Mr. Tommy? Where is she? What has happened to her? My mind raced, struggling to comprehend his fragmented words, but he insisted it was merely a bad dream, attempting to slip back into slumber. Despite his reassurances, I could feel the tension thrumming between us, a heavy silence masking the truth he was hiding, a truth that cast a long shadow over our lives.

Years later, when illness caught up to him, the weight of unspoken words finally spilled forth, unraveling the tightly wound threads of our shared history. Anger and heartbreak washed over me as I listened to the revelations unfold, each word striking deeper than the last. I was left reeling by the stunning admission from the man I had loved for so long. For countless years, he had wrestled with the demons of that day, trying to piece together the memory of your vanishing. Finally, I learned of his entanglement with Mr. Tommy, a dark figure cloaked in desperation and regret. Your father had found himself entangled in a web of debt owed to this man, a sum so large it loomed over him like a haunting spirit, a weight he knew he could never lift.

On that fateful day that would change everything, a stranger knocked on our door to collect that debt. I wasn't home, and I can only envision the terror that enveloped you both during that encounter. The man, without hesitation, took one look at you and brazenly declared that Mr. Tommy would accept you as payment for what was owed. Your father was stunned, grappling with disbelief. How could anyone propose such a horrific exchange? He pleaded with the intruder to leave, promising he would find a way to gather the money, and for a fleeting moment, it appeared that was the end of the nightmare.

However, the menace of Mr. Tommy's debt lingered, and before long, one of his thuggish associates cornered your father at work, browbeating him for payment once again. This time, they were not after money, they issued a chilling threat, claiming they would take you, instilling fear that they'd inflict harm on everyone he loved if he did not comply. Caught in a moment of desperation and fueled by reckless intoxication, your father made an unimaginable decision, he surrendered you, convinced by a misguided belief that Mr. Tommy had a child who would be a fitting companion for you.

Mema screamed, oh my god, are you serious? I can't believe this, playmate; my life has been hell. They used me as a concubine for his son. I can remember sitting in my little room crying my eyes out, wondering what in the hell was going on; I can't and will never forgive him.

She jumped to her feet as if she was leaving, but Grandma Lil stopped her and said, baby, I'm not expecting you to forgive your father; that's not why I'm telling you the story because what he did was despicable. While he was telling me the story, I wanted to reach my bare hand down his throat and rip his heart out. I asked him how he could do this to his flesh and blood, but he never answered; he just lay there with tears in his eyes.

While Grandma Lil told the story, I stared into Mema's eyes; they seemed to change color with every word from my grandmother's mouth. Mema yelled, that dirty no good son of a bitch; I wish he were still alive; I would kill him myself.

Grandma Lil lowered her head and turned away; she said, I did kill him; I killed him. After being in the hospital for about a month, he got better; I guess he told me the story because he thought he was dying. They released him from the hospital in my care; I'll say two months later, he died, and believe me, it wasn't pleasant. He suffered a lot, and the strange thing about that was he didn't complain, not once; it was as if he felt he deserved it.

I guess Mema had thought that her family didn't want her, her whole life. She walked over to Grandma Lil and placed her hand on her shoulder. It's okay, I'm sorry you had to remember all that insanity. All the time I was in that horrible situation, I prayed that you would come for me. You know, mother, I'm here. I survived, so things weren't so bad. Grandma Lil could tell Mema wasn't telling the truth, so she asked her to tell her about her life, she needed to know.

When Mema began sharing her story with me, I was faced with the daunting challenge of grasping the breadth of her experiences. The more time I spent living alongside her, the more I was drawn into her world, a world colored by the shadows of her battles with depression, disorienting blackouts that left her feeling lost in her own mind, and unpredictable behavior that confused those around her. Each moment spent with her served as a window into the profound depth of her suffering, illuminating the complexities of her pain. As she gradually unfurled the layers of her life, I began to see that each retelling was not just a recollection of events but a powerful testament to her remarkable resilience and unwavering spirit.

Mema described her childhood room in striking detail, remembering it as a dismally small space, no bigger than a closet. The cramped quarters served as a constant reminder of the emotional and physical confinement she felt during her formative years. She recounted how, every morning, a man would come to visit her, bringing his son along. Initially, her sleeping arrangement consisted of cold, hard floors that left her body aching and vulnerable, a condition that persisted for far too long. Eventually, the man provided her with a mattress, though it seemed a meager comfort in light of her profound isolation. For months, silence enveloped her, trapping her in a world devoid of conversation or companionship until the boy began to stay longer, reaching out to engage her in dialogue. In a moment that shocked Mema to her core, he revealed that after her birth, his father had chosen to allow a group of Black individuals to care for her until she would be deemed ready to return to the outside world. The boy explained that her early memories had slipped away, nearly forgotten, simply because she had been too young to remember the life she had known.

Mema's reflections were often haunted by the harsh realities of her conditions. The room could become unbearable, filled with an oppressive air that pressed down on her spirit, leading her to believe anything that might offer her a lifeline, a way to cope with the chaotic and often terrifying nature of her existence. When her gaze would meet that of Grandma Lil, whose eyes sparkled with earnestness and understanding, I could almost feel the weight of her memories casting a shadow over her heart. Yet, beneath that heavy veneer of sorrow, a remarkable strength shimmered, an indomitable hope that somehow continued to flicker within her. Mema's story is one of survival against unfathomable odds, a powerful journey I feel deeply honored to witness and grateful for her willingness to share with me.

Mema said, it was so hard for me, somewhere down the line I decided to stop fighting them. They began telling me these crazy stories from the very beginning, and sometimes I believed them. Everything shifted dramatically when I was told that I had been found in a critical condition, someone had left me for dead on a farm. The gravity of that revelation weighed heavily on my soul, propelling a cascade of questions into my mind. I remembered the exact moment I was dropped off, a memory tinged with a blend of confusion and solitude. I realized that I possessed an inherent courage that had long been dormant. This spark urged me to seek the truth and dig deeper into my past.

I consciously decided to embrace not just mere survival amid the swirling chaos of my situation but to actively thrive and uncover the remarkable truths that lay just beyond my reach. Outside the protective cocoon of my room, the atmosphere was vibrant with the sounds of lively chatter, laughter ringing like music, and the hurried shuffle of footsteps echoing through the corridors. Yet, despite the bustling life around me, it felt like an eternity had passed before I finally encountered anyone beyond the family. They delivered my food, occasionally, when the rest of the household had settled into their evening routines, I could break free from my seclusion and explore. Those precious moments of wandering through the house, tracing my fingers along the cool walls, and stepping into the inviting expanse of the yard became my cherished connections to a world that beckoned me.

Then, after what felt like an eternity of silence, Danny began to make regular visits, bringing with him the fresh breath of friendship. His father had imparted a wise lesson to him, reminding him that even creatures in the wild sought interaction and that it was equally essential for us as humans. At first, I found contentment in simply listening to him as he spoke with animated enthusiasm, feeling a sense of hesitance settle in my chest at the thought of interjecting my voice. However, as the days turned into weeks, our bond began to blossom, thriving on shared laughter and the exchange of stories. I entertained him with vivid stories that I had made up about farm life, painting pictures of sun-kissed mornings and the rustic charm of my upbringing while expressing an earnest curiosity about the wonderful people who had nurtured and shaped my existence. Each conversation was a delightful step into a world rich with possibilities, a tapestry woven with threads of genuine connection, lifting my spirits and reigniting the spark of hope for the future I dared to envision.

One day, I asked Danny if it would be possible for me to go back for a visit, and he jumped up and yelled, hell no, you're mine. You'll never go back, your ungrateful nigger.

You'll never leave me. We have given you a good home, and I've spent this entire time keeping you company; how dare you talk to me like that. He got up and ran out of the room because he was so disturbed by my question. I didn't see him for a long time, and no one came in to feed me or let me out at night. The next thing I remember, I was in bed, and a black woman was standing over me, I yelled Mother, Mother, you're here. The woman asked Mr. Tommy what was wrong with me and why I was skin and bones. I heard her say I needed to go to the hospital. She then asked me my name, but I couldn't remember. I looked around the room, and Mr. Tommy was standing in the corner and I was very confused. He asked the woman to leave the room because he needed to talk to her. He came back and gave me some medicine, but I never saw the woman again.

When I started feeling better, I was told I was old enough to work in the house, and the son no longer came to my room, which was a blessing in disguise. I can't believe I had to endure all that to get rid of him. While outside of the room, I noticed that other black people were working. One day, as I was eavesdropping, I overheard them talking about me, they wondered what I was doing working there and why I wasn't in school. I remember asking myself school, what was that? They also wondered where my parents were. I continued to work with no one talking directly to me, and as time went on, I began to understand what was going on in the house and realized something was wrong with how I was living. One night, the son came into my room; he said he needed me, which surprised me because I hadn't seen him in a long time. This time, he was drunk, and to this day, I can still smell that scent because it was the same smell that hovered over my father when he left me to deal with these monsters.

The son laid his smelly body on me the way he used to, but this time I fought back. I refused to submit to his demands because I knew I could no longer live that life. He came short of killing me that night, but I didn't mind because I was no longer afraid of my destiny. He beat me so badly that when his father saw me, he was taken aback, and I was not allowed to leave the room for weeks until all the marks were gone. When I got well, he told me I had to leave, so I left and found a little house in the woods where I lived for five years. I didn't tell a soul about my past because I didn't want to return to that room. Months after I moved out of there, Lillian was born. I didn't know what was happening to my body; it kept getting bigger and bigger; one night, I woke up in pain. It was getting worse by the minute, and I didn't know what to do. Suddenly, there was a presence, I could see a silhouette standing above me, and my body began to relax. When the baby came out, I cut the cord, and it felt like someone took her out of my arms, I thought I saw them hold her up toward the heavens, but when I woke up, the baby was lying right next to me.

I tried to remember what happened but was too groggy to think clearly. After a couple of days, I began recalling the events of that night, and the first thing I remembered was the release of pressure from my stomach and my legs spreading to allow the baby to emerge from deep within me. I heard a voice tell me to cut the cord. When I saw the baby, it frightened me because there was blood all over her, and she was screaming. Frantically, I wiped away the blood to see where it was coming from, but I didn't find anything.

After a while, she stopped crying and went to sleep. I realized I had a baby and was a mother, and my job was to protect her. I had to learn what she needed and how we would survive.

After three months, I finally had to go back to that house to work because I didn't know anything else, and I worked for them for about four more years. I lived with so much fear that they would find my baby and take her away, and that fear is still a part of me.

Grandma Lil grabbed Mema, held her tight, and told her she was sorry. Then she looked to the sky and said, Lord, why, my child? What did she do to deserve this? What did I do?

Grandma Lil died two years after she entered our lives, and her last words to Mema were, I have always loved you, daughter, please forgive me. Mema took the death very hard, but her new family couldn't help her much because they didn't know the whole story. The little help they tried to give, she refused. She had finally begun to love and understand her mother, and now she was gone.

HerStory

NINE

After meeting Mema's family and uncovering the mystery behind her disappearance, I hoped this newfound understanding would help her embrace a new chapter in her life. However, as it turned out, she was still weighed down by confusion and restlessness. I asked her what was troubling her thoughts out of genuine concern, and her response caught me off guard. She shared that she couldn't recall the faces of those family members, only a vague memory of a farm. My heart raced as I exclaimed, Mema, what farm? There wasn't a farm. You have to believe me; you made the farm up in order to survive. It pained me to see her struggle, so I proposed that we speak to other family members, and thankfully, she agreed.

Something extraordinary happened when we arrived at Grandma Lil's house, where my Aunt Caroline lived. Mema paused on the porch, taking in her surroundings. With a sense of uncertainty in her voice, she shared that she didn't feel connected to that place. There were no vivid memories of joy or laughter with her siblings, leading her to wonder if perhaps she had a different family out there, waiting for her to be found. Looking into her eyes, which flickered with a yellow-orange glow, I felt a mixture of concern and empathy. It was as if she were lost in a maze of memories that didn't lead her home. Slowly, she turned and walked out of the yard, and as she passed by me, her gaze felt distant, as if she were looking through a fog. Alarmed, I called out, she walked onward, seemingly oblivious to my words, amplifying my worry. Her expression perplexed me; her eyes shifted between a bright fire and a void. It was a sight unlike any I had ever witnessed.

She began to make her way home, and I desperately yelled out, urging her to share why she was leaving. To my dismay, she continued without uttering a word. Finally, she halted, exclaiming that she urgently needed to return to where everything began. It felt vital for her to reconnect with her earliest memories and to find herself as if it were a matter of profound importance. She gently told me I didn't have to accompany her, but it would mean the world to her if I did. I was determined to support her, so we headed home, where Mema quickly packed a bag before stepping out again. I tried to ask what her plans were, but she didn't respond, she simply walked towards the bus stop with unwavering purpose.

We hopped on the Galvez bus, which can be transferred to the Desire bus, and stepped off on Gentilly Road, embarking on a route filled with shared memories.

As we walked, something extraordinary began to take shape. I felt its warmth when I held Mema's hand, but it seemed more significant than I remembered. Glancing up, I was surprised to see her appear taller and more youthful than I ever recalled. I looked down at myself in a surreal twist and realized I had transformed into a four-year-old child. A stream of emotions coursed through me, yet the memories of my life remained intact, I remembered everything vividly. Mema looked radiant, her beauty shining through, but the weariness in her eyes lingered. I hadn't immensely appreciated how young she must have been when we first left.

As we continued walking, she seemed in a trance, unaware of the transformation around her. Eventually, we paused to catch our breath, allowing me to absorb the changes in our surroundings. The landscape had morphed dramatically since our last visit, where once there were only trees, water, and railroad tracks, now thrive lively houses, bustling stores, and delightful restaurants.

After a while, we stopped at a charming sandwich shop called We Never Close, where we treated ourselves to delicious hot sausage po-boys. The meal filled me with warmth, and after indulging, we walked for about an hour before taking a well-deserved break. Then, I must have drifted into a deep sleep, only to awaken with a start, my heart racing. Although I couldn't recall the details of my dream, one memory clung to me, the sensation of Mema cradling me in her arms, whispering, I love you. I'll always love you.

I looked into her eyes, feeling a rush of comfort and familiarity. Then, almost magically, everything shifted back to normal. I excitedly recounted our strange and wonderful experience, and Mema confirmed it: briefly, we had stepped back in time together. I hadn't fully grasped why our journey was necessary, but the clarity washed over me, I needed to be there for her during this significant time. In her soothing voice, she reassured me, encouraging me not to fear whatever lay ahead. The way she emphasized, no matter what, tugged at my heart, reminding me of a moment from our past when she guided me to follow a path down a mysterious road I had never encountered before.

Sitting in her comforting embrace, I pondered the adventures awaiting us, recalling the first time we shared such a tender moment. With curiosity shining in my eyes, I asked her about the dream that had lingered in my mind for so long. She smiled, and as she began to speak, I felt a sense of anticipation surge within me, ready to embrace whatever stories lay ahead.

Yes, I vividly remember your dream, and it resonated with me because I once felt a similar loneliness, an emotion I look back on with compassion for myself and you. When I was younger, my dreams often revolved around the farm where I grew up. Yours may have occurred in a different setting, but our feelings were unmistakably intertwined.

In my dreams, I would lie on lush Saint Augustine grass, gazing up at an expansive sky painted in the most stunning shades of blue, punctuated by fluffy white clouds billowing through the air. I would let my imagination run wild, watching the clouds morph into playful shapes, sometimes resembling horses, dogs, cows, or even the faces of loved ones. It felt like a little slice of eternity; I could lie there for hours. When the gentle breeze and the wonders of the sky eventually beckoned me to sit on my trusty tree swing, I would sway with joy and calm. But then the familiar feeling of dehydration would come, a little itch that nudged me to get up and head inside for a drink. Oddly enough, it always felt like something was trying to hold me back, creating a struggle within. The door would be locked, and I'd call out, feeling desperate. Hearing my mother's voice from the other side, saying I didn't belong, would tug at my heart. I would pound the door, pleading, please let me in, I belong here. Those dreams repeated themselves, night after night.

When I returned home that day and saw the emotion reflected in your eyes, unloved, unwanted, and scared, it struck a chord in me. I knew those feelings well, and I wanted you to know that you deserve love and security. I wish to shield you from ever experiencing that sense of isolation.

I often wondered why my mother never engaged with my dreams more and why her gaze was so sorrowful as she held me close. After she told her own story, I began to see things more clearly; her dreams seemed to echo a past she believed in, reinforcing the idea of a life rooted in that farm, which was, in her mind, a truth. After she shared her story, we cuddled close and drifted off to sleep, comforted by each other.

We set out bright and early the following day, walking down Chef Menteur Highway towards the railroad tracks. Together, we journeyed along the tracks, hoping to step back into the past and reclaim something lost.

As we approached a house, Mema's expression changed; her eyes glistened with tears, her lips quivered, and a deep crease appeared on her forehead. In a poignant moment, she stopped and fell to her knees, crying. Unsure of what to do, I knelt beside her, allowing a supportive presence. Finally, after a moment of emotion, I asked her what she wished to do. Her response was clear: we needed to go inside. This was something we had to confront.

The house stood smaller than I remembered, and inside, it felt even more cramped. Perhaps after so many years in her little room, Mema felt this was just right. The old furniture lingered unchanged, whispering stories as I approached the mattress by the window. Taking a deep breath, I was struck by the familiar scent that enveloped me. We speculated that someone might be living there, as the conditions suggested, so we decided to wait in silence; however, no one came. We embraced our surroundings and lived off the land as we had.

One morning, the sound of the front door creaking open jolted me awake. I saw Mema leap to her feet out of the corner of my eye. Who's there? she called out, her voice a mixture of courage and fear. To our shock, a white man stood in the doorway. As his eyes locked with Mema's, she fainted. I felt paralyzed by fear and uncertainty, struggling to react. What in the hell are you doing here? Who are you? he shouted.

With a trembling voice, I mustered the courage to respond: My name is Lillian, and that's Mema; she's, my mother. His gaze shifted as he asked about Mema's health, frantically wondering if she needed a doctor. His demeanor changed when he spotted the tears streaming down my face; he softened, apologized for his harshness, and asked for my help to move Mema to the sofa.

As he approached, an intriguing feeling washed over me, like we had shared a moment before. We gently lifted Mema and settled her onto the sofa. He went to the sink for a glass of water, he sprinkled some on her face, and slowly, her eyes fluttered open, meeting mine. It was as if she was silently asking, what just happened? But then, she turned to him, suddenly exclaiming, you no good bastard. before fainting again. I could see the confusion on his face; clearly, he was just as bewildered. He locked eyes with me, his voice filled with concern, what's wrong with her? Do you know me? Who are you? He splashed more water on her, but this time, she remained still. In a moment of desperation, he poured the entire glass on her. She gasped for air, her hands flailing as she locked her gaze onto mine, and for a long moment, we just stared at each other as I felt a mix of worry and intrigue.

I quickly grabbed a rag to dry Mema's face, and to my surprise, she suddenly focused on me, asking, Girl, what's wrong with you? The whole situation was so puzzling; I glanced at the man, hoping he could shed some light, but his confusion mirrored mine. They were both staring at each other, caught in a strange moment. Then, as he moved toward the door, she yelled, Who the hell are you? He paused, turned his back to us, and simply said, my name is John, before stepping outside. I asked Mema if she knew him, but she stared back at me, perceptibly silent. She got up and walked towards the door, telling me, stay in the house and don't answer the door for anybody, before leaving. As the door clicked shut, that exact strange moment washed over me again. I was four years old and retreated to my favorite spot, on the mattress in the corner under the window, trying to make sense of the baffling events that had unfolded.

Mema returned home late that night. When I asked where she had been, she looked at me, bewildered, replying, you know I went to work. Her response left me feeling lost, as her demeanor suggested she might not be fully present to help me understand. She entered the kitchen and started cooking, and while I wanted to dive into our peculiar situation, I realized it didn't feel like the right moment; after all, who would listen to the questions of a four-year-old? I sensed this strange chapter wouldn't last forever, so I resolved to wait for things to stabilize. We could delve into our questions together once we returned to the present.

Dinner passed, and soon it was time for bed. The following day brought relief; I was delighted to see signs of normalcy again. Mema was peacefully sleeping on the sofa, looking absolutely beautiful, so I let her rest more. When she finally stirred, I was curious about her whereabouts the previous day. She repeated that she had gone to work, but I pressed further, wondering if she was aware of the unusual shifts in our reality. She acknowledged that things felt different when she returned but couldn't quite articulate what had changed. While uncertain, she encouraged taking life one day at a time. There was so much more I wanted to ask her, especially about John and if he was my father, but something held me back. Deep inside, I felt a lingering connection to him that I couldn't explain, and I found myself contemplating Mema's quest for understanding, and what I was searching for, too.

As we settled in for another conversation, a knock at the door startled me. Mema intuitively suggested it was John and called for him to come in. Every time he was near, that mysterious sensation bubbled within me. He greeted Mema, but she didn't respond, her demeanor uncertain. He then turned to me, saying hello. Before I could react, Mema urged me to go outside, wanting to speak with him alone. I hesitated, wanting desperately to stay, but John kindly reassured me, saying I was a big girl now. Mema squinted her eyes in annoyance, sparking another wave of curiosity within me about the interactions unfolding around us. The energy in the room shifted, and I felt a hint of anxiety about what lay ahead.

Mema calmly spoke; She's no one's girl, she's a remarkable young woman, and it's essential to recognize. I felt defined by who I belonged to for much of my life, but she is her own person. John tried to clarify his intentions, but Mema seemed to expect more.

Your challenge is a lack of reflection; you do not consider the impact of the actions of your family. Because of you and your father, it has been difficult for me to live with my story, a story that many find hard to believe. Just seeing you brings back overwhelming feelings. I have worked hard on my journey, and I hope one day you can understand the depth of what I experienced.

He looked at her with a deep sadness before lowering his gaze, which clearly frustrated her. That's one thing I truly hate about you: your inability to stand up for what's right. I've always loved you, and would have followed you to the ends of the earth.

At that moment, I felt a strange disconnect as John moved toward her slowly. It was as if everything around me faded, but my ears remained tuned to the conversation. I could hear a man and a woman's voices, though I couldn't see their faces.

John, I love you with all my heart and want to build a life together. I can't go on like this any longer, your brother's aggression is escalating, and I'm genuinely scared for my life. If I don't take action now, I fear he will kill me. This situation has to end. You need to find the courage to speak with your father.

In that moment, the urgency of her plea filled the air, fueled by hope for change and the desire for a future built on love and safety.

I'm afraid I can't take that step because you were brought for him, and only he can make that change happen. That's just how the situation is.

Why not have a conversation with your father? He'll be understanding and supportive.

I noticed footsteps retreating and a dragging sound hinting at sadness. Hearing Mema's cries made me long to comfort her, but I felt lost. Then, I heard footsteps returning, this time, they sounded like two people. Suddenly, the door burst open, and I gasped as Mema let out a scream.

John, please, wait. Why are you doing this?

The other voice urged, Go ahead, son. Do what you want. She won't stop you. Soon, your brother will hand her over to you.

I could hear Mema's heart-wrenching pleas, and then, with a strength I hadn't heard before, she declared, I will never be yours.

I found myself on the sofa when I awoke, but she wasn't by my side. Glancing out the window, I spotted her standing gracefully beneath one of the majestic cypress trees. I stepped outside, joining her in silence. She turned to me, and in a soft, familiar voice that warmed my heart, she spoke, connecting us in a way that felt both meaningful and comforting.

Do you remember being there?

A wave of memory washed over me as I tried to grasp the elusive fragments of my past. I wish I could have wrapped you in the comfort you sought, but uncertainty clouded my mind. Seeking clarity, I turned to her, curiosity driving my inquiry about what had unfolded. She explained patiently, illuminating the truth: my absence from that time was not a choice but a fact, I had simply not been born yet. At that moment, I was a traveler exploring her past, a world that existed before my arrival. It initially felt chaotic, a puzzle missing vital pieces.

As she shared her story, she recalled a pivotal moment when someone entered her room, and that person was John himself. After witnessing his brother's cruel actions, John stepped in with a mix of concern and protectiveness in his eyes. That sick motherfucker, he exclaimed, his voice filled with emotion as he took in the sight of her injuries. This wasn't just a reaction; it was a powerful declaration of loyalty and care. In that moment, he became her champion, fiercely defending her and affirming the strength of their bond. It was a beautiful reminder of how deeply compassion can shine through even the darkest times, illuminating the path to healing and hope.

In a moment of unfiltered boldness, John had even confronted his brother, standing up for her in a way that filled her heart with gratitude. When the brother visits ceased, a heavy sense of longing settled over her, yet she felt warm as she silently thanked God for bringing John into her life. His kindness, like a light in the darkness, made all the difference, and she cherished the bond that had formed between them, one that transcended the chaos of her beginnings.

She thought he had stopped his brother from assaulting her and was so happy, but the happiness didn't last long because he returned. He came into her room and told her he hadn't been in to see her because he had gotten married. He realized that what he had done to me was wrong. His statement shocked me because he spoke in such a soft, caring, unnatural voice. He said he would ask his father to let me go; as he spoke, she sat listening, too afraid to move. He began walking toward her with his arms stretched out, hoping she would find it in her heart to forgive him someday. She sat there with her eyes downcast because he was the one she hated and feared the most. She had to be careful not to make him angry because she knew the animal he could be. The closer he got to her, the more she noticed his face changing, and believe her, it wasn't anything nice. He grabbed her and said this would be his last time. She began fighting, trying to get away, but she couldn't. He threw her on the bed, got on top of her, and told her that no other woman could ever take her place. He reminded her that she was born for him and no one else. He started babbling, saying things like his wife could never satisfy him the way she could. He tried to explain to his wife what he needed, but she couldn't understand. he knew she understood him; he wanted her and no one else but her. When he finished his business, he ran out of the room like the coward that he was.

When she next met John, she shared that his brother had visited her and recounted his actions. John confidently reassured her that she needn't worry about his brother any longer and that he wouldn't return. She felt a flicker of doubt since he'd made similar promises before, she never crossed paths with Danny again after that conversation. Honestly, that brought her a sense of relief and peace.

Six months later, she and John were talking and laughing when he grabbed her, gave her a long kiss, and said he loved her. She was happy because she had also fallen in love with him. He said he wanted to marry her, and they would live together with no one to answer to but themselves. They sat down talking when she asked him if he knew where she came from. She saw his facial expression change, but he didn't answer; he just looked at her through those caring eyes and held her tightly in his arms. He didn't know where she came from and thought she should focus on her future and leave the past behind.

One day, he came in and said his father forbade him from seeing her anymore. She told him they should run away.

Apparently, his father found out about the plan and got him drunk, then forced him to come into her room, beat her, and rape her. John couldn't face what he had done, so he left the house; she couldn't believe he would do something so horrific to her, so the way she dealt with it was to blame it on his brother. She was so angry that she blocked him out of her mind completely; it was as if he'd never existed.

I was deeply moved by the heartfelt stories Mema shared with me that afternoon. It marked the first time she ever mentioned his name. As she spoke, the air was thick with emotion, revealing a battle she had waged within herself for years. John had been more than just a fleeting figure in her past; he had opened her eyes to the concept of self-worth, articulating in gentle tones that she deserved more than the life she was living and that genuine love was not merely a fantasy.

Yet, the power of his affirmations twisted into something more painful. The very love that had once breathed life into her spirit also became a ghost that haunted her, leading her to unknowingly redirect her anger at him. In her turmoil, it was easy to blame his brother for her pain, who had always withheld the affection and respect that she so desperately needed. The weight of that unvoiced neglect was a heavy burden she carried.

As we stood there, hand in hand, our fingers entwined tightly, I noticed how her gaze drifted upwards to the sky, which was transitioning into a darker evening shade. The colors melted from soft blues to deeper indigos, sprinkled with the first twinkling stars. It's getting dark; let's go inside, she said softly, her voice barely more than a whisper. There was a sense of urgency in her tone, a desire to retreat from the emotional exposure of the moment. We walked into the little house, the familiar scents of old wood wafting through the air, offering solace and safety.

Inside, I felt the intensity of what she had just shared wash over me like a tide. It became clear that her journey was filled with sorrow and complexity, each layer revealing more about her struggles. I could sense the depth of pain she carried, overlaying her genuine resilience. And in that moment, I found myself filled with a profound empathy, hoping with all my heart that this journey she was embarking upon would lead her toward the liberation and healing she sought. Together, we stood on the precipice of change, our spirits intertwined, looking resolutely toward the comforting promise of brighter days ahead.

HerStory

TEN

The following day, I settled into the inviting embrace of the sofa. At the same time, Mema busily worked her magic in the kitchen, the rich aroma of spices wafting through the air. Suddenly, a sharp knock echoed through the house. This time, Mema didn't hesitate; she instinctively knew it was John. A flicker of anxiety crossed her face as she called for him to go away, but he brushed her words aside and pushed the door open, striding in with determination.

When John entered, he confronted Mema, his voice steady yet charged with emotion. The past was painful, he declared, but that doesn't mean you can keep me away from my niece. Mema's reaction was immediate and intense, her expression shifting like a tempest. A storm of feelings whirled across her features, fierce and protective as if her gaze could pierce through him like lasers. You've got it all wrong, asshole, she shot back, her voice rising passionately. She isn't your niece. Where on earth did you get that idea?

The tension in the room was palpable, hanging thick in the air like the scent of Mema's cooking. She was so angry she picked up a knife and ran toward him, yelling I'm going to kill you. Before I could react, she stabbed him in the shoulder. He pushed her away, then grabbed his wound and asked her if she was crazy. I swear it looked like Mema was foaming from the mouth, you damned right I'm crazy, and you know why; how could anyone keep their sanity being around you and your family? Do you remember the last night you saw me? Do you know what happened that night? He had a look of denial on his face as if he had no idea what she was talking about.

Dumb ass, you raped me, you know what I'm talking about, you raped me, and you have the nerve to stand there and act as if you don't remember. She's not your niece; she's your daughter.

His face underwent several contortions when I looked at him, and then he began denying the possibility. Mema kept repeating she's your daughter; she's your daughter. It must have finally sunk in because tears started running down his face; he said he didn't know and asked for forgiveness. He then dropped to his knees. Mema hovered over him with the knife in her hand, and I thought for sure he was a dead man kneeling. Calmly, she told him it wasn't that he didn't know but that he didn't care. John looked sadly over at me and mumbled he didn't know, but I stared at Mema and then back at him. He looked so pitiful that I wanted to say something soothing, but I couldn't undermine Mema's feelings. So, I told him no human being should have her memories, and even if he had known, it wouldn't have made a difference because what his family did to her told me that no one cared about what happened to her or to me. Mema told him that even though he might have made her happy for a while, he proved he was no better than the other family members. He said he had honestly forgotten what happened that night. He remembered that he had decided to stand up to his father and tell him he was in love and wanted to marry her. His father told him that was out of the question because he had his opportunity years ago, but he felt sorry for his girl and helped her escape. John explained that when he turned thirteen, he received the family gift, and at first, he was excited because his father had prepared him for this great event, but when he saw her, he realized she was a scared little girl, and she needed to be with her family. He said he would never forget Antoinette; she was about eight years old and had the prettiest brown eyes; when she smiled, they looked like two shiny pennies. His father tried to get him to do all types of evil things to her, but he didn't have the heart for that type of behavior. They became friends, and one day, when he visited her, he noticed that she had bruises all over her body. She said his father and little Danny entered her room and did this to her. Right after that incident, John brought Antoinette a bus ticket to Canada in hopes that she would find a family and have an ordinary life. Years later, he received a letter saying she was okay.

John said that when his father brought Mema to the house, he wanted to stop them, but he didn't know how. He watched his little brother do some cruel things and decided that the least he could do was to try and show some kindness so he would go in and talk to her, and after years of being with her, he fell in love. After the night his father got him drunk, his head was so messed up that he had to get away, so he left town. When he returned, he looked for her, but she was gone.

John wanted us to know what happened to his brother. One day, Danny came running home looking like he had been running from a pack of wolves; sweat was dripping from his entire body. His dad tried to get information out of him, but he couldn't understand a word he was saying, so he called Danny's wife, Debbie, to find out what was going on. She explained that things weren't good between them because Danny sometimes sat in his chair and cried for no apparent reason. When she tried to find out what was wrong, he would get angry with her and throw things around the house. His bizarre behavior occurred while they were having a dinner party. Their friends were traumatized by his actions because they had never seen this side of him, and this particular episode was so violent everyone thought that if he didn't get help, he would harm himself or his family. Debbie tried to get him to see a doctor, but he considered her request conspiracy.

One day, he told her he missed his favorite gift and explained what gift he was talking about; she stood there listening to him, not knowing what to say. Then, his following statement was more than she could handle; he told her he would give them the same gift when his boys turned thirteen. That's when she knew something had to change; she told him he would have to see someone, a doctor, or he could no longer be a part of her family. He started seeing a psychiatrist, and things seemed to be getting better. A new problem occurred when their neighbor's grandchild came down for the summer; he looked at her in a way that she had never seen a man look at a child. The last straw was when he started talking about owning her. One day, they argued, and he told her he would get the woman waiting for him; that was the last time she saw him.

After speaking with Debbie, Danny's father turned his attention to Danny, sitting in the corner with sweat glistening on his brow. Danny expressed his exhaustion from being labeled as crazy simply because he wanted to do for his children what his father had done for him. While his father tried to engage him in conversation, it was clear that Danny had lost his mind. This realization was painful for his father; he had always emphasized that others wouldn't understand their family's traditions passed down through generations. In his view, everyone adapted just fine, yet his son struggled to accept their customs. She was deemed less valuable once the male married, and John's attachment kept her safe from the family's harsh realities.

Months later, John received a call from his father that shattered him, his brother could no longer cope with reality, and the police had come to report Danny's tragic suicide. The way his father delivered the news was astounding; it felt as if he were recounting a minor injury rather than the loss of his son. John felt a wave of disbelief wash over him, realizing his father failed to see his actions' profound impact on Danny, ultimately contributing to his brother's distress. His father insisted that the family tradition had to carry on, placing the burden on John to ensure his children would receive the same gift at thirteen. At that moment, John firmly declared that the legacy had ended with Danny.

For so long, John had lived under an overwhelming cloud of doubt, thinking that Mema had left this world, heavily influenced by the turmoil of his father's life. But everything changed one memorable afternoon. While he attentively observed the chaos of his father's household, a wave of indescribable joy surged through him as he uncovered an astonishing truth: Mema was alive. Inspired, he followed her through the thick woods, ultimately discovering her nestled in a little house that seemed to leap from the pages of a storybook.

This newfound reality sparked a sense of optimism and renewal within John. What had felt like loss transformed into a source of hope, as he recognized that the family bonds, though complicated, could lead to unexpected joy and connection.

With a spark of curiosity in his chest, he took a cautious step closer to her world, feeling the pull of her life as she focused intently on her work. When he glanced inside, an unexpected scene unfolded: a warm, inviting home with love. The air was thick with a sense of belonging and comfort, enveloped in the gentle gleam of afternoon sunlight filtering through sheer curtains. And there, at the heart of it all, was a beautiful baby girl, her tiny hands reaching out and her laughter ringing like soft chimes, bubbling forth in pure joy. The sight wrapped around him like a cozy, familiar blanket, awakening a yearning deep within his hear, one he thought had faded into memory.

As days gracefully morphed into weeks, his visits to Mema's home became the highlight of his routine, each one steeped in an eager anticipation that brightened his mood.

He delighted in showering the baby with little tokens of affection, small bags of delectable snacks and sweet treats that transformed their shared moments into vibrant celebrations filled with laughter and warmth. Each visit was a tapestry woven with snippets of, playful exchanges, and the glittering magic of connection. However, one unforgettable day marked a pivotal moment in their relationship. As he stepped into the house and caught her gaze, time seemed to stand still, and he could swear he heard the faintest whisper of dada escape her lips. That single word hung like an invisible thread in the air, creating ripples of emotion that entwined them in a delicate bond. Overwhelmed with a mixture of joy and confusion, he instinctively chose to step back, reluctant to disrupt the tender happiness unfurling between them.

Often, he found himself lost in thought, reflecting on Mema's demanding job, a role that seemed to consume her life, and wonder, why did she stay. He recalled his father's insistence that she had simply never learned anything different, his words echoing in the corners of his mind. A painful memory resurfaced, pulling him back to a day that still left scars on his heart, the day the child had dared to step outside, only to face the cruelty of the kids. When they pushed her down, a fierce surge of protective instinct welled up within him, almost compelling him to break his vow of distance. The overwhelming urge to rush to her side and shield her from the hurt was intoxicating, a primal need that threatened to overwhelm him.

Yet, when he finally decided to seek out Mema again, he faced the bittersweet reality that they had moved. A wave of loss washed over him, filling him with a yearning that felt heavy in his chest. But he was not determined, and his heart brimmed with hope as he went to his father's house in search of answers. Upon arriving, he was struck by how drastically time had altered his father; worry etched deep lines across his once smooth forehead, each crease telling its own story. When he inquired about Mema, he found his father caught in a fog of confusion regarding her absence, a moment that deepened his sense of longing. Yet, a flicker of recognition ignited in his father's eyes when he mentioned the grandchild. John told him he should hope some redneck bastard didn't decide to keep their family tradition going with his grandchild. His father yelled, *that's my grandchild, and I have the right to see it.* John told him he must be out of his fucken mind because, for one thing, she was not an it, and what rights? What did he know about rights? He had a child living in his house under animalistic conditions; what about her rights as a human being? If her family came to this house and blew his head off, it would be justified; John told him to look in the mirror because he was the reason his son had killed himself.

When his father passed away, the moment was enveloped in a profound stillness that wrapped around the once-vibrant old house like a heavy shawl. The laughter that used to echo off the walls was replaced by an eerie hush, a quiet melancholy settling over each room. After Mema's departure, the home slowly transformed, its lively spirit dimming as shadows began to creep into the corners where sunbeams once danced freely.

One gray afternoon, John felt an almost magnetic pull to return to his childhood refuge, which held countless memories. As he pushed open the creaking door, a flood of emotions crashed over him, each wave heavy with nostalgia. The familiar scent of aged wood and faint traces of his father's pipe tobacco hung in the air, awakening deep-seated memories that had long lain dormant.

His gaze fell upon a heart-wrenching sight: his father's frail figure, now diminished by time and illness, lay resting on the well-worn rug by the fireplace. This rug, once a stage for playtime antics and family gatherings, now seemed to absorb the silence like a sponge. It was a space that had once overflowed with laughter, love, and warmth, now tinged with sorrow. With a heart swelling with respect, John gathered his father's remains. As he dug a small grave in the rich, moist earth, the ground exuded a fragrant scent of damp soil and fresh grass; he mumbled goodbye and closed the hole.

After he poured out his heart, she finally spoke. I once believed that leaving this vile place would lead me to a more fulfilling life, she began, her eyes glistening with emotion. But that journey has often felt daunting and isolating. Now, I've returned with a newfound purpose, to uncover the roots of my own existence. Can you help me discover any insights about where I truly belong?

John told her his father never mentioned anything about where she came from or who her family was; he just said that she was for his brother. He stared at her with loving, lustful eyes and said, you know I still love you and want to marry you. For less than a split second, when she heard those words, I thought I heard her exhale, but I think there was too much pain between them for that to mean anything.

I came here for one reason: searching for my past; I guess you still don't realize what I went through. To you and your family, it was just a game, but to me, it was my life, and until you live the life I had to live, you'll never understand me. There's so much hatred in my heart toward you, fool; I find it hard not to kill you right here and now. You say your father died the way he lived; I pray to God you die the same way, if not worse. I could tell Mema was getting angrier.

Man, I can't believe you're standing there asking me to marry you; you're one sick bastard. Haven't you done enough to me? This place must be hell; I must have done something mighty bad in my past life to know the likes of someone like you and your family.

He asked Mema if he could keep in touch with me, and she yelled: Hell no, you don't have a daughter; she's, my child; just because you lay on top of me doesn't make you a father; besides, you raped me, you sick motherfucker. She turned to me and said, tell him who your father is.

I felt sorry for him, but I knew she was right, so I told him I didn't have a father; I only had a mother; she's the one who fed me and taught me right from wrong. Mema looked at John and shook her head: You're not worth shit to either one of us. Come on, baby, let's go; it's beginning to smell bad here. We walked out of the door, leaving him in tears; as we walked down the same road we came up, we heard a scream. I love you both; please, come back. I don't want to live without you.

We then heard a gunshot; Mema turned and said, that's the last of those evil bastards. When we returned to our house,

I noticed she seemed even sadder than before; she would sit in a corner saying, who am I? I'm who, I am who? I tried talking to her, but it didn't seem to help; one day, when I got home, I noticed a letter on the table addressed to Mema. I took it to her; she looked at it and sat it on the table but said nothing. The letter sat there for a couple of days, and when I asked her why she hadn't opened it, she stared blankly ahead and said: I believe that exploring and understanding our roots, as well as our identities, is of profound significance, and I wish to elaborate on the reasons for this strong belief. At first glance, examining who we are or tracing the origins of our lineage may seem trivial or even secondary to our daily lives. However, a deeper investigation reveals that our innate need for connection, community, and a sense of belonging is woven into the very fabric of our humanity.

When you sit down and listen to someone passionately recount the stories of their heritage or the intricacies of their family history, it's as though you can almost feel the emotional resonance accompanying those narratives. There's an undeniable pride in their voice, a warmth that spreads like sunlight, illuminating the beauty of being part of a legacy that stretches across time and generations. This rich sense of continuity is essential and can be shockingly fragile. When people lose touch with their pasts, they can experience a disorienting sensation akin to drifting in an open sea, as if unanchored from the essence of who they are. This lack of clarity can leave individuals struggling to find meaning and purpose.

Moreover, when our understanding of history is obscured or absent, we often find ourselves overly reliant on the perceptions and judgments of others to construct our sense of normalcy. If those external perspectives are tinged with negativity or bias, they can corrode our self-esteem and warp our self-image, leaving us feeling inadequate or unsure. In contrast, when we receive encouragement and positive reinforcement, though often a rare occurrence in many environments, it can act as a transformative force, radically shifting our outlook on life and instilling a sense of hope and possibility.

It is fascinating to observe how, throughout history, humanity has often sought scapegoats to blame for its myriad difficulties. Yet, amid these challenges, there is always a pillar we can rely on, our past. No matter the complexities or trials it may hold, it remains an integral and unchangeable part of our individual and collective stories. By embracing and reflecting on our history, acknowledging both the triumphs and the struggles, we uncover a more profound sense of empowerment. This connection to our past unites us with others who share similar stories and propels us forward with a sense of purpose, confidence, and optimism as we navigate the future, I never had that connection.

ELEVEN

Yesterday marked a poignant moment for me as we gathered to celebrate Mema's life on the fifth anniversary of her joining the celestial family above. Just six months prior, she began to show signs of fragility, and during heartfelt conversations, she urged me to think carefully about my future, what I would do when she was no longer with me. I didn't fully comprehend her concerns then, but reflecting now, I see she was aware of her journey's impending conclusion.

The funeral was beautiful on a stunning spring day when the world bursts with color. The neighborhood was alive with vibrant flowers, and the sweet scent of spring filled the air. Spring was Mema's favorite season; she reveled in the beauty of nature awakening, feeling rejuvenated with each emerging blossom.

A few years ago, Mema had asked her nephew, Tyrone, to sing her beloved song, Amazing Grace, if the day ever came if she would depart before him. She believed Tyrone possessed one of the most magnificent voices she had ever heard, and hearing him sing was always a moving experience. The way he sang that day, there was something truly magical in the air. People often likened his voice to that of Paul Robeson, and in that moment, I understood precisely why. The room was filled with a serene stillness, only interrupted by the melodious chirping of birds outside, almost as if they were providing a heavenly chorus. Tears streamed down my face, my heart raced with every note, and I felt this overwhelming wave of emotion that took my breath away. It was as though the beauty surrounding us made it hard to inhale. Overcome, I suddenly jumped up, needing to escape, but someone gently grasped my arm. The next thing I remember is sitting back down with Mrs. Florence fanning me, giving me the comfort I desperately needed.

When Tyrone finished singing, I found the courage to share a few words. I wasn't sure what to say, but my heart was set on expressing something meaningful. As I approached the front of the church, an image of Mema's radiant smile and sparkling eyes flashed into my mind, bringing a warm smile to my face. I spoke from the heart, saying, Mema, I love you, and I know you did your very best for me. I paused, looking upwards, and added, wherever you are, may your heart and soul be filled with love and peace. I'll love you forever.

I felt a strong urge to say more, to share her incredible journey and the challenges she faced, but I sensed that the moment had spoken volumes. I knew deep down that Mema would want me to embrace life and move forward, trusting that we would reunite again someday, hopefully, not too soon. Although I felt this clarity during the service, afterward, I grappled with the realization of how much I would miss her. She had been my companion for so long. Mrs. Florence, frequently visited to keep my spirits up but eventually suggested I take some time alone to reflect on the next chapter of my life.

Two months after her passing, I found myself reflecting on the memories that haunted me. Her stories felt woven into my narrative, yet I understood I needed to clear my mind and embrace the path ahead. So, I began to take walks outside. Initially, it was a challenge, but I gradually started looking forward to my strolls, finding solace in the fresh air. One morning, I awoke feeling invigorated, realizing that my life was regaining balance. With this newfound perspective, I visited Mrs. Florence to assure her I was okay. She had been encouraging me to reach out to Robert, and with my spirit revived, today was perfect for reconnecting. Just as I was about to find his number, I heard a knock on the door, and to my surprise, it was him.

Walking into my home, Robert looked as handsome as I remembered years ago. It had been nearly five years since our paths had last crossed. We reminisced about our high school days, and he expressed how much he missed me. He also offered his heartfelt condolences regarding Mema. He had attended the funeral but felt uncertain about approaching me afterward, unsure of what to say. He admitted he believed Mema didn't like him, which, to him, was the reason our relationship faded.

Now, sitting together, I felt a wave of warmth. Moments like these remind me of how beautiful human connections can be, even though the trials of life. I look forward with hope, ready to forge new paths while carrying Mema's legacy, which is always in my heart.

The day before Mema and I embarked on our journey back to the little house in the woods, I had a significant conversation with Robert. He was preparing to leave for Southern University in Baton Rouge the following day and wanted me to join him on this new adventure. However, my heart was firmly set on staying with Mema, who needed my support. Robert had plans to live on campus and believed he could find nearby accommodations for me, but the thought of leaving Mema was not something I could bear. That encounter marked the last time I saw or heard from him, yet it was one of those bittersweet moments that linger in my memory.

During that conversation, filled with homesickness for our cherished memories, Robert declared, Lillian, I still love you. No one compares to you. His words held so much weight, and when he asked how I felt, I found myself lost in his captivating gaze for a moment before admitting that I wasn't entirely sure. That uncertainty weighed heavily on me, especially when he left for college, and the calls and letters I had anticipated never materialized. It was painful to realize that what I thought was a remarkable connection might have been more of a solo endeavor.

Robert felt that Mema and I were navigating through some difficult times and sensed that I couldn't juggle a relationship with him alongside my responsibilities. He often thought of me while balancing school, football practice, and a job, which understandably added to his sense of overwhelm. As time passed, he secured a job near the university in Baton Rouge, and although life moved quickly around us, he always intended to return to me. Now living back in the city and working at Dillard University, he surprised me with a heartfelt proposal, getting down on one knee and saying, I love you even more than ever. Will you marry me?

At that moment, memories of Mema's past flooded my mind, especially when I thought of John's proposal to her. I couldn't shake the feeling that if she had accepted his offer, she might still be with us, our family intact. Not wanting to follow in those footsteps of hesitation, I took a leap of faith and answered, yes. I love you and would be thrilled to be your wife. The joy on his face was infectious, he jumped with such exuberance that he nearly grazed the ceiling fan.

Oh, I promise to cherish you and shower you with love. Let's get married soon before you change your heart. he exclaimed, bolting out the door, shouting, she said yes. She loves me. I'm the happiest man alive.

After he left, I couldn't wait to share the news with Mrs. Florence, so I headed to her house. She was overjoyed for me, and amid our conversation about the past, she reminded me of that challenging time when I contemplated taking my own life. I had meant to ask her about that poignant memory, especially since no one seemed to remember her having a daughter. She expressed her concern and desire to guide me, ensuring I chose a path that led to my happiness.

We laughed, acknowledging that we would be celebrating my wedding one day. I happily informed her that the wedding was scheduled for the Sunday after next, and when I asked if she would attend, she enthusiastically replied that she wouldn't miss it for anything. While she recognized the tough years with Mema, she urged me to look forward and live for the future, as Mema had often gotten caught in past difficulties. Her encouragement was a reminder that this new chapter was about hope and possibilities. I'm excited as I navigate this journey and can't wait to embrace the future.

After we tied the knot in a heartfelt ceremony surrounded by our loved ones, we embarked on an adventure to find our dream home. We stumbled upon a charming abode in the picturesque Sherwood Forest neighborhood of New Orleans East, a community vibrant with lush greenery and tree lined neutral grounds. The moment we stepped through the door, it felt electric; the air was thick with possibility and excitement, marking the beginning of a thrilling new chapter in our lives. For the first time, an overwhelming sense of completeness washed over me, a feeling I longed for.

Our new house was a delightful two, story dwelling featuring four spacious bedrooms illuminated by natural light, two pristine bathrooms adorned with tasteful fixtures, and a cozy living room that exuded warmth. A cheerful dining room, with windows that offered a view of the picturesque garden, beckoned us to gather for meals steeped in laughter and love. The den, a serene escape filled with soft lighting and inviting armchairs, provided an ideal spot for quiet evenings of reflection or reading. The kitchen, perfectly sized for us, promised a space filled with the intoxicating aromas of home-cooked meals as we create memories with family and friends.

As I wandered through this beautiful home, I couldn't help but reflect on my humble beginnings. It felt like a world away from my past, and the thought of Mema brought a pang of nostalgia to my heart. I could vividly picture her strolling through our delightful gardens, marveling at the flourishing flowers, and resting beneath the magnificent magnolia tree that stood proudly in the front yard, providing a perfect shady oasis on summer's warm, sultry days. To add a personal touch to our porch, we lovingly retrieved a collection of cherished rocking chairs from the attic, one of which was particularly special, bearing the name Old Man Joel, 1892 on the back.

As life in our new home settled into a comforting routine, I began to spend a significant amount of time with Mrs. Florence. At first, our conversations were light and friendly, but as I got to know her better, a slight concern for her well-being began to gnaw at me. She seemed too fragile to navigate life on her own, wrapped in an aura of gentle kindness that made it hard to envision her without support. After confiding in Robert about my worries, I discovered he felt the same way. He recommended inviting her to move in with us, a fantastic proposal that warmed my heart.

With each passing day, while Robert hustled off to work, Mrs. Florence and I would settle into the comforting embrace of those old rocking chairs on the porch. The rhythmic creaking of the wood became a familiar soundtrack to our long, heartfelt conversations, where stories flowed like the sweet tea we sipped. I often wished Mema had shared some of Mrs. Florence's nurturing warmth and wisdom, yet I understood that each person carries a unique journey.

One sunny afternoon during our porch gathering, Mrs. Florence's eyes sparkled as she recounted a poignant memory from years ago involving Robert. She spoke vividly about when she witnessed him, just a boy, making a poor choice, stealing. Despite his youthful innocence, he had not noticed her presence. She shared how, instead of chastising him, she invited him into her home, and amid their conversation, she presented him with a gift, none other than the very object he had taken. The surge of embarrassment that washed over his young face was something she had never forgotten. With great compassion, she encouraged him to return the stolen item and apologize to the store owner, creating a pivotal moment that would alter the course of his life. That day marked the last time she saw him compromise his values; it sparked a transformation that redirected his path. In stark contrast, the boys he had been with drifted into a life of crime, and many months later, tragedy struck when they lost their lives during a robbery attempt. In many ways, Mrs. Florence's compassionate intervention had been a lifeline for Robert, and, ultimately, for me.

Every morning, I cherished our walks together; the golden morning light wrapped itself around us as we strolled leisurely down our quiet streets, exchanging stories and laughter. Robert and I would tie our shoelaces and hit the pavement, jogging three miles on Saturdays and five miles on Sundays. Each of these runs was painted with the colors of our dreams and aspirations. We spoke animatedly about where we envisioned ourselves living in the future and dreamt about our retirement. While I pictured us comfortably settled amid the familiar comforts of our cozy neighborhood, Robert often dreamt of adventures in sun-soaked California or the electric atmosphere of New York City. These dreams became one of our few playful disagreements; deep within, I knew I would follow him anywhere, yet the playful brainstorming about our future was always a delightful way to connect. Reflecting on those moments now, I never could have imagined professing that I had a perfect life, but standing at that crossroads truly felt that way.

Then, one fateful morning, Mrs. Florence knocked on my door, her cheerful spirit radiating. She was there to coax me out for our daily walk, but a wave of dread washed over me as I lay wrapped in my blankets. Nausea clung to me like a heavy blanket, and the thought of breakfast made my stomach churn. When Robert returned home, however, a flicker of hope ignited within me. I mustered the courage to share my symptoms, and he immediately sprang into action, booking a doctor's appointment for the very next day without hesitation.

The doctor's visit felt like a whirlwind. After a thorough examination, the atmosphere shifted dramatically as he delivered the stunning news, it seemed I might be pregnant. My heart raced at the thought, a whirlwind of emotions flooding my system as the doctor promised to run a few tests and call with the results in a few days.

Coming home, an exhilarating glow enveloped me as I shared the incredible news with Mrs. Florence, who was absolutely overjoyed for us. Her warm, genuine excitement felt like a ray of sunshine as she reveled in the possibility of a new life blooming in our home. I could hardly contain my nerves and excitement as I dialed Robert's number. When he answered, his initial silence sent me a rush of anxious concern. But then he quickly asked if I was okay. Before I could respond, he hung up and rushed home, the usual twenty-five-minute commute miraculously compressed into mere moments.

When he burst through the door, nearly startling me with his enthusiasm, he shouted, we're having a baby. My heart soared at his exuberance, though I reminded him that the doctor's news was important; we would need confirmation. But Robert, his eyes alight with joy, interrupted my thoughts, exclaiming, Hold on. I'll make that doctor tell me exactly when our baby is coming. What's his number? I need to know when I'm going to be a dad.

With a mix of disbelief and laughter, I watched as he dialed the doctor's office, vibrating with excitement. At that moment, Mrs. Florence gently took the phone from his hands, her demeanor calm and nurturing as she apologized for his exuberance. With sparkling eyes and a playful smile, Robert turned to me, excited as he said, shouldn't you be resting? Can you feel the baby kicking yet? I can just tell it's a boy. Can you picture me as a dad? In that precious moment, our home was filled with laughter and joy. I knew, without a doubt, that our journey ahead would be an extraordinary adventure rich in unforgettable memories.

It was a staggering revelation for me, an epiphany, to uncover the depths of his longing for a son or even just the sheer joy that a new baby would bring into our lives. The next day, he surprised me by taking a day off from work, his excitement intense as he immersed himself in household tasks. I could hardly believe his lengths; he must have inundated the doctor's office with at least twenty calls, each laced with palpable anticipation. Eventually, with an understanding but gentle tone, the doctor's secretary had to step in and ask him to refrain from calling for a while, recognizing that his enthusiasm was obsessive.

Throughout that entire day, he showered me affectionately, spending hours tenderly rubbing my stomach, his gentle and reassuring touch. His questions flew out like fireworks in the night sky, each one more thrilling than the last: Is he moving? Can you feel his heartbeat? How much do you think he weighs? His genuine enthusiasm was charming, wrapping around me like a warm blanket. I felt utterly drained but content when the sun sank low in the sky. I fell asleep with a smile etched on my face, my heart swelling with love for him and all the possibilities ahead.

As dawn broke the next day, he dutifully returned to work, but his spirit remained buoyed by the excitement of our impending journey into parenthood. Throughout the day, I could almost hear the excitement crackling in his voice every time he called, eager to listen to updates and share in the anticipation. Part of me reveled in this attention, highlighting our bond. However, another part felt slightly overwhelmed by the sheer volume of his enthusiasm. I adored him deeply, and I knew he cherished me, but sometimes his enthusiasm spun me in delightful, yet dizzying, circles. Mrs. Florence, a calming presence, did her best to help him find a bit of relaxation, though it seemed nothing could temper his fervent excitement. Every evening, he would rush home, often arriving in record time, which sent waves of anxiety coursing through me as I worried about his reckless driving.

As days went by, the doctor recognized the urgency of my tests and decided to personally intervene with the lab to expedite the results. It was clear that my husband's relentless calls were creating a sense of urgency for him and the entire medical team. When the doctor finally shared the results with me, I hesitated. In a moment of anxiety, I asked him to hold off on informing Robert immediately, fearing the overwhelming emotions that would wash over him. Yet, fate had other plans; Robert had received the call moments prior.

Panic surged within me as I immediately reached out to his workplace, only to be met with a concerning report from his boss that he had bolted out of the office as if summoned by an emergency. My heart began to race, a chaotic symphony of worry and anticipation. The minutes felt elongated with each tick of the clock, each second heavy with tension as I waited for him to return. After thirty long minutes with no sign of him, anxiety transformed into sheer dread. Just then, Mrs. Florence stepped into the room, her expression grave, her eyes glistening with tears that spoke of an unspoken tragedy.

My heart began to sink, and an icy wave of panic coursed through me. It's Robert, she finally said, her voice choked with emotion. He was in an accident just a couple of blocks from here. I was walking, enjoying the fresh air, witnessing it all unfold. I heard a car barreling down the road at an alarming speed, an awful, deafening roar that echoed through the street as I crossed. It all happened so quickly and was terrifying to witness. Apparently, he didn't see when the light changed, and suddenly, he ran straight into the intersection. The impact was catastrophic, colliding with another vehicle before crashing into a pole. At first, I didn't even recognize that it was his car, but my heart sank like a stone as I got closer. I rushed to the scene, desperate to see if he was all right, but the sight was devastating. He appeared badly hurt, and just as the paramedics were pulling him from the twisted wreckage, he looked directly at me, his face etched with pain and fear, and uttered words that would be burned into my memory: My wife is having our first baby; I don't want to die. His eyes were filled with terror and undeniable love, and he managed to apologize, asking me to tell you he was sorry. Soon after that, they covered him with a sheet.

My heart shattered like glass, the weight of despair crashing around me. No, Robert. Robert, I love you. Please don't leave me. I cried out, the anguish clawing at my throat, tears cascading down my cheeks. Every fiber of my being ached for the love we had shared, the laughter, the dreams, the future we had envisioned together, now hanging precariously in the balance.

.

HerStory

TWELVE

I woke up in the hospital with Mrs. Florence by my side, but I couldn't remember how I got there. Her facial expression conveyed that something horrific had happened. Hoping to trigger my memory of whatever was lurking in my mind, I squeezed my eyes shut. When I opened them again, I still couldn't understand how or why I wasn't at home. I turned to Mrs. Florence, expecting her to say something, but all I saw were eyes that reminded me of Mema's sad eyes. This frightened me even more. In my mind, I was yelling for her to speak, yet she remained silent, staring blankly at different spots in the room, tears streaming down her face.

When I called out for Robert, a memory surged forward, I remembered Mrs. Florence telling me that Robert had been in a car accident. My body felt weak as if made of rubber, and my head bobbled back and forth. Mrs. Florence reached over and held me in her arms, telling me to take it easy because she didn't want me to lose my baby. She once again explained what had happened to Robert. I couldn't believe my gentle, compassionate, loving husband was gone. I thought it had to be a nightmare, so I began pinching myself, hoping to wake up screaming, with my caring husband holding me in his strong arms and reassuring me that everything would be okay. But that didn't happen.

I could hear Mrs. Florence calling for help, but I had no idea what her problem was. Then, a nurse came running over; she grabbed my arms and tied them to the bed. I didn't understand what was wrong until I looked down at my arms. They were covered in bruises and blood. I realized this was no dream.

I was in an incredibly challenging situation, surrounded by pressure and uncertainty. They needed to ensure my safety and that of my baby before allowing me to go home. When I finally returned, I was touched by how Mrs. Florence had taken care of all the funeral arrangements. Honestly, the details of the service are a blur to me; the stress I was under made it hard to hold onto anything, even my own name, a common reaction during such intense trauma.

After the funeral, I wandered about in a haze, trying to navigate this new reality. Mrs. Florence was so supportive, but she recognized that the healing journey was one I had to take on my own. In those early weeks, I experienced haunting dreams of Robert, with tears in his eyes. Each time I reached out to him, my hand would pass through him, and he would vanish. I would wake up screaming, and Mrs. Florence would rush to my side, finding me trembling and drenched in sweat. She never needed me to explain; her understanding gaze said it all. She would comfort me back to sleep, and I would find her quietly keeping watch by my side in the morning.

This went on for what felt like an eternity. But one morning, I realized that Mrs. Florence wasn't there. That was actually a positive sign, I had slept through the night. It was a wake-up call for me to focus on reclaiming my life. My most challenging moments were during the evenings and weekends. Evenings were hard for obvious reasons, while weekends were filled with memories of discussions about our future that now felt distant. I often found myself alone, reflecting on all that had changed and what my next steps would be. But even in these moments, I clung to hope, knowing that I would find my way again with time and support. Amid this chaotic time, one of the few things that genuinely uplifted me was the simple joy of walking. It cleared my mind and lifted my spirits in remarkable ways. Mrs. Florence and I ventured out into the early light each morning, filling our lungs with invigorating fresh air. During our strolls, she shared heartwarming stories from my past, her voice radiating warmth and encouragement. It was so wonderful to hear her express deep pride in my strength. I listened closely, finding comfort in her words, which felt like a beautiful tapestry of hope wrapping around me. Those meaningful walks and conversations became a soothing balm for my soul, easing my worries.

However, one morning, I woke up feeling unable to get out of bed, sharp pain slicing through my back and legs, a reminder of my restless night. With a heavy heart, we agreed to take a break from our morning walks until after I delivered the baby. The absence of our daily ritual left me feeling profoundly isolated. I sat in contemplative silence for hours, reflecting on what an incredible father Robert would have been. I could imagine the joy of welcoming a child into our lives and creating a beautiful new chapter together. But those sweet daydreams soon shifted to an overwhelming tide of anger and frustration. I struggled with many unanswered questions: Why couldn't he have been more patient during this challenging time? How could he leave when I needed him most? And how would I navigate this journey without him beside me?

Yet, amidst these feelings, I realized I could face the future. I'm determined to move forward, hoping for what lies ahead.

Becoming a single parent was never something I imagined, and I often wished for Mema's presence and support during this challenging time. I could picture her joy at becoming a grandmother, and it made me reflect on how precious family is. It was hard to ignore the feeling of loss, especially with many of my loved ones no longer with me. Yet, I fought those thoughts, reminding myself I still had my baby and Mrs. Florence. She worked tirelessly to support me in staying strong, emphasizing that while I couldn't go for walks outside, moving around the house was still crucial for both of us. Motivated by her encouragement, I pushed myself to remain active, but balancing my health and preparing for my child often left me with little energy.

That particular day, the weight of the world felt particularly heavy. I was overwhelmed and caught in a wave of emotions I couldn't shake. For the first time since Robert's passing, the tears flowed freely. I had held in my feelings for so long out of fear that the floodgates would never close once open. Mrs. Florence noticed my struggle and gently suggested I visit the hospital to ensure everything was okay. She understood my feelings and reminded me that I needed to think about my baby, who needed my strength. I admitted I was trying, but the pain felt unbearable at times. I constantly missed Robert and Mema and worried about raising my child alone. Her reassurance that my feelings were completely normal was comforting, and encouraged me to face them, promising that I would emerge stronger.

Taking Mrs. Florence's wisdom to heart, I began to reflect on my emotions, allowing the stress to dissipate gradually. One evening, as I sat in the living room, lost in thought, a knock at the door jolted me from my reverie. When I opened it, a young woman stood there, searching for her sister. I explained that I didn't have a sister and was about to close the door when she said, I think you're my sister. My confusion stopped me, and I opened the door wider to hear her out.

I don't have any sisters; are you sure you have the right place? My mom had only me, I replied, genuinely puzzled. Who are you?

She introduced herself as Gail and revealed that John was her father. Stunned, I stood there speechless for a moment, absorbing the information. Are you okay? she asked, taking a step forward. I stepped back, processing this unexpected twist of fate, and eventually invited her inside.

As we sat on the sofa and talked, she shared that on the last night she saw her father, he mentioned me and explained that he had never spoken of me because he hadn't known he had another daughter. It was astonishing, I had a sister.

Excited by the news, I invited her to stay with us as she had just arrived in town.

After showing her to the guest room, I tried to rest, but my mind was racing about her unexpected arrival. Some of me wondered if she was who she claimed to be, after all, Mema had told her story to many people. The anxiety crept in as images flashed through my mind, causing me sleeplessness as I worried about what I had let into my life.

Despite my fears, deep down, I felt a glimmer of hope. The idea that I could share this experience with someone else, especially family, was a comforting thought. After all the heaviness I had been facing, I couldn't help but feel optimistic about this unexpected connection. Whatever the truth was, I knew I would navigate this journey with strength, fueled by my determination to create a loving environment for my child.

The following day, when I stirred from my slumber, an unsettling surprise greeted me: she was gone, leaving behind no trace, no whisper of her presence. It felt as if she had emerged from the shadows of my dreams and, just as mysteriously, slipped away into the atmosphere. A twinge of disbelief settled in my chest; had it all been a figment of my imagination? Yet, the vividness of the memory clung to me like morning fog, haunting and palpable. It sparked a curious thought: could I have siblings out there, flickering just beyond my reach? Eager to share this extraordinary experience, I hesitated about confiding in Mrs. Florence. The intrigue felt too strange, almost surreal, to articulate. Besides, she wouldn't return from her trip for a few more days, and a part of me hoped that clarity would grace my mind by then.

I drifted through a haze of reflection all day, pondering what this encounter might signify. Just as I was about to turn my attention to dinner, a sharp knock shattered the silence. A wave of mixed emotions flooded me, hope mingled with apprehension, as I feared it might be her again. Gathering my courage, I approached the door and swung it open. There she stood, and a phantom returned. I froze, astonished and captivated by her unexpected appearance. She looked different this time, her complexion was ghostly pale, a stark contrast to the night's warmth. Disbelief flared in her eyes at the sight of me also.

Can I come in? she asked, her voice tentative yet insistent. I longed to say yes, but the words caught in my throat like a stubborn knot, and silence draped between us like an unwelcome fog. Then she reached out, eyes searching mine, and asked if I remembered her. A million thoughts rushed through my mind, but my voice was lost; I could only gaze at her, grappling with the reality. Noticing my inability to respond, she stepped closer, concerned, etching her features. Are you okay? You look like you've seen a ghost. Her genuine worry jolted me from my stupor, and I managed to shake my head, mustering a response. Yeah, I'm okay ... this morning, when I woke up, and you were gone, it felt too surreal to be real. Please, come in. Where did you disappear to?

That morning had left me encumbered with uncertainty. I wandered through the park, the crunch of leaves beneath my feet echoing my scattered thoughts. Why had I been so driven to meet you in the first place? I yearned for you to reveal something about my family, particularly the dark tapestry woven by my father, grandfather, and uncle, all three of whom had succumbed to despair. A dark fear nestled in my heart: would I follow in their footsteps? The weight of depression sometimes felt insurmountable, leaving me adrift without direction. I remembered my father's last words before he passed away; he had spoken to my mother about visiting an old friend. Their marriage seemed more like a fragile facade, held together by strands of obligation rather than love. On the final night, I saw him, and he hesitantly mentioned that I had a sister named Lillian. After his death, my mother deteriorated, her spirit waning like a candle flickering in the wind. You don't owe me anything, but if you could share any fragment of insight, it would mean the world to me.

In a moment charged with unspoken emotions, she turned to me and asked if I might be her sister. My heart raced, and uncertainty flooded my thoughts as I replied, If John was your father, then perhaps you are my sister.

The following morning, as we settled down over breakfast, she leaned in, her eyes bright with hope and inquiry, eager to unravel the mysteries of our shared lineage. She told me I was her last hope in uncovering the truth about our family. I genuinely desired to aid her, yet an instinct told me to pause. I had just navigated a profound loss, and the narratives she sought were entwined with a sorrow I wasn't yet ready to confront again. I hoped she would grasp that now wasn't the opportune moment.

Despite my reservations, Gail opened up, sharing her story in fragments. Her mother's realization after her father's death, that love should never be a burden, resonated deeply with me. Gail had carried the weight of unreciprocated affection for far too long, feeling ensnared until it was nearly too late. She expressed that my knowledge could be the missing piece she desperately sought. I assured her I would share what I knew, but only after my baby was born, gently reminding her that the truths I carried weren't particularly uplifting.

This delicate connection felt fragile and hopeful, like a new leaf emerging from the winter frost. In a world marred by uncertainty, we could walk this uncertain path together, illuminating the darkness, one cautious step at a time.

During our conversation, I noticed a curious expression on her face as she seemed to be staring at my stomach. Then, genuinely concerned, she asked, Where's your husband? I felt a wave of emotion surge through me, and despite my efforts to stay composed, the tears began to well up in my eyes. I turned my head away to conceal them, but ultimately, I couldn't keep from crying. Just then, Mrs. Florence entered the room, took one look at Gail, and with a mix of confusion and protectiveness, asked, what are you doing here, and who are you? Lillian, are you alright?

I took a deep breath and explained that Gail was my father's daughter, my half-sister. Mrs. Florence then turned her attention to Gail, asking if she had proof of that relationship. Gail confidently presented her birth certificate, which I took to Mrs. Florence, but it was evident that she was still unsure. To provide additional verification,

I asked Gail if she had a photo ID, and she kindly handed me her driver's license. This seemed to settle the matter for the moment.

As I entered the kitchen to prepare dinner, I could still hear Mrs. Florence diligently questioning Gail about her family background. She asked for the names of Gail's grandfather and uncle and their addresses. Even though Gail answered correctly, Mrs. Florence wasn't quite finished; her inquiries continued about Gail's mother, how she had found me, and her purpose for being here.

Once dinner was ready, we all gathered around the table. Despite the warmth of the meal, Gail was eager for information. She asked me about my first meeting with our father and how often I had seen him. I gently explained that she would need patience as I couldn't share everything simultaneously. She responded earnestly, expressing her impatience, saying she didn't think she could wait.

I completely understand your eagerness, I replied, but you must bear with me. It's a difficult story, and I have to be mindful of my own emotional state, especially with my baby coming soon. I lost my mother a few years back and my husband just a few months ago. I want to be strong for the baby, and I hope you can appreciate that.

After finishing the meal, Gail and I decided to walk. We exchanged stories, shared a few laughs, and wiped away some tears, both in awe that we finally had each other as sisters. I asked Gail about her life before she found me, and she shared that she had remained in her childhood home after her mother passed away. She recalled how her father had mentioned that she had a sister. Initially, she felt hesitant about seeking me out, but as time passed, she realized I was her only family. That prompted her to move into her grandfather's house to sift through a mountain of paperwork.

While organizing, she stumbled upon a will revealing that her father had left the house to me, which puzzled her. It sparked the determination to find me. Without an address, she revisited the small house in the woods but found it empty and desolate. Years before, she had recognized that only one road was leading out of those woods, so she took it. Upon reaching town, she began asking around, but no one had any answers until a kind old lady, after a brief description, pointed her in my direction.

Gail then shared with me that after my uncle passed away, his wife Debbie, moved away, leaving that family behind. She felt a deep bitterness toward them, believing they were responsible for her husband's illness and eventual death, wanting to protect her children from experiencing anything similar. Curious, Gail inquired whether I knew her uncle, but before I could respond, she added with a hopeful grin, you don't have to answer that now. After the baby arrives, you'll fill me in on everything you know, right?

Her enthusiasm and eagerness were palpable, and it filled me with warmth to know that despite our complicated beginnings, we were embarking on a new path together as a family.

HerStory

THIRTEEN

Every morning, Gail and I eagerly set out on our familiar walk, and sometimes, Mrs. Florence would join us, bringing a lovely warmth to our little routine. It was heartwarming to see how quickly Gail grew fond of her, just like everyone else in our neighborhood. I'll never forget those strolls when Gail, with a mix of nostalgia and yearning in her eyes, would share how she wished her mother had been more like Mrs. Florence. It was a glimpse into her heart, revealing that she had faced her own struggles, reminding me of my experiences with Mema.

One afternoon, I found myself resting on my bed, suddenly feeling a sharp, unusual pain ripple through me. Initially, I brushed it off, thinking it might be a sign that the baby was ready to greet the world. I waited anxiously, but the anticipated contraction didn't arrive. Eventually, the pain pulled me into a restless doze, and when I awoke, I was hit by an intensity that took my breath away. I tried to cry out, but all that escaped me was a soft whisper. Fear washed over me as the pain escalated, making it difficult to call for help. Just as I thought to rise from the bed, it felt as if the baby was tossing and turning inside me.

Tears rolled down my cheeks as I sat at the edge of my bed, and just then, Mrs. Florence rushed in, her eyes filled with concern and urgency. Are you okay? she asked, hurrying into my room. With a pained expression, I told her, I think it's time. No sooner had I spoken those words than another sharp pain surged. Yes, it's time. I exclaimed, my voice trembling. Mrs. Florence quickly went to grab my bags from the closet, and in a moment of panic, I cried, Oh God, I think the baby's coming.

Suddenly, Gail burst into the room, her eyes wide with alarm and determination. Is it time? she shouted, urgency in her voice. My expression must have said it all. She scooped up her keys in an instant and dashed out the door. I could hear the engine roar to life, and for a brief second, dread filled my heart, was she really going to leave me? But as I stepped outside, relief washed over me; the car was running, and Gail was anxiously pacing in front of the Cadillac. Admittedly, her driving could be a wild ride, and in this heightened moment, it made me a bit wary of our safety. I silently prayed that we would make it to Charity Hospital in one piece. Each time I cried out, she pressed harder on the gas. By the time we arrived at the hospital, she was practically shouting, what should I do? What should I do?

Calm down. Mrs. Florence interjected, trying to bring some order to the chaos. You're driving us all crazy. At this rate, we might need to check in ourselves.

As we burst into the bustling lobby of Charity Hospital, a nurse at the front desk maintained an air of calm amidst the commotion. Mrs. Florence called out for help, and the

Nurse rushed over, her sense of urgency palpable. She seated me in a wheelchair, and I felt the cool metal against my skin as she launched into her questions, my name, age, husband's name, insurance details. Mrs. Florence, flustered, chimed in, Are you serious? Can't you deal with that later? She's about to have a baby.

The Nurse assured her, maintaining her professional demeanor, that it was hospital policy. I smiled weakly at Mrs. Florence and gently said, it's okay; I can answer the questions. After gathering my information, the Nurse wheeled me down a sterile corridor, my breaths quickening, my heart racing. When I caught sight of the hospital room, it felt like a wave of relief washed over me, and I collapsed onto the bed, thankful for something to hold me up.

As I lay there, trying to calm my nerves, another nurse entered to prepare me for what was to come. She explained the procedures, and even though it felt surreal amid the pain, her calm demeanor reassured me. I must have looked nervous because she assured me this was all standard practice. Once she finished explaining, I leaned back against the pillows and let my thoughts wander. I prayed silently for strength, hoping she wouldn't inherit my hair if I had a daughter. But remembering Robert's confident assertion that we were having a boy brought a smile to my face; I shifted my prayer to hoping he would have his father's hair instead. Just thinking about Robert warmed me; I knew he would be thrilled if he were here. I could vividly recall the happiness we shared and the deep love that bound us together, and now this baby was a beautiful symbol of that love.

But then, the pain returned with more urgency than before. I cried out for help, my voice echoing in the seemingly quiet room, only to be frustrated when no one came. I raised my voice, and finally, a nurse rushed back in. Oh please, it can't be that bad, she said, somewhat dismissively, as she checked to see if the baby's head was visible. When she saw nothing, she left, muttering as she exited, I've got to find me a new job; I can't take much more of these screaming women.

As I began to drift into a troubled sleep, my mind wandered to my own birth story. Mema had faced those waters alone, unaware of the changes happening to her body; all she felt was exhaustion and the weight she was bearing. How daunting it would have been to navigate this experience alone struck me. I hoped desperately that I hadn't caused Mema as much trouble as this boy was causing me.

Then, out of nowhere, the pain surged again, fierce and uncontrollable. Oh God, I think he's on his way. Somebody, please help me because this baby is coming. Nurse! I screamed, desperation filling my voice. The Nurse rushed back in, her composure wavering as she snapped at me to lower my voice, because I wasn't the only patient in the hospital. But when she peeked beneath my gown, her expression changed dramatically. Oh God, his head is nearly out.

As I entered the delivery room, a whirlwind of activity surrounded me, with doctors and nurses moving with purpose and determination. While their swift actions initially took me aback, I quickly recognized that I was in capable hands and felt a surge of trust in their expertise. The excitement of welcoming my baby filled the air, and I could feel tiny movements inside me, a beautiful reminder of the life soon to join us.

With a warm smile, a doctor approached and encouraged me to give a mighty push. As I did, I felt an incredible sensation of my baby emerging into the world. I curiously asked about my baby's hair color, noticing the puzzled look around me. While most mothers often inquire about their baby's gender or health, I was eager for this detail. Finally, someone joyfully announced, His hair is black. Overwhelmed with gratitude, I replied, Thank God, embracing the excellent news with a heart full of love and anticipation.

Before I knew it, I was gently waking up, and Gail and Mrs. Florence were beside me. Someone exclaimed, what a fine boy you have. Curiously, I mumbled, what color is his hair? I could hear Gail chuckle as she replied, That's an interesting question. Then Mrs. Florence chimed in, His hair is black. A wave of happiness washed over me, knowing my child would have a brighter path ahead, free from the challenges I faced. This moment was filled with hope and joy, and I felt so grateful for the love surrounding us.

They stayed with me until visiting hours ended, providing comfort during a challenging time. After they left, the doctor came in warmly and encouraged me to walk down the hall when I felt up to it. The following day, I woke up feeling surprisingly good, especially after everything I had just experienced. I decided it was the perfect time to take that first walk. As I strolled down the hall, a wave of excitement washed over me when I returned to my room to see the nurses bringing the babies around for their feedings. I sat on my bed, a flutter of joy in my heart, knowing it would soon be my baby's first feeding.

However, as I awaited my turn, the minutes stretched, and I began to feel worry creeping in. Had something gone wrong? I kept reassuring myself that all would be well and that they would bring my little one to me soon. But as time passed, I decided it was best to check in with the Nurse to find out why I hadn't received my baby yet. I pressed the call button and waited... but there was no response. At that moment, a wave of panic began to rise within me. I sprang from my bed and rushed toward the door, eager to find someone to help me, but the hallway was empty. In desperation, I called out, Nurse! Nurse! Where's my baby? What has happened?

Suddenly, a nurse came rushing toward me, her voice steadying as she said, hey now, take a deep breath. You need to calm down; let's not make this more stressful than it has to be. Just relax, and I'll get your baby right away.

By then, my anxiety had reached its peak. You've lost him. Where is he? I need my baby now. My heart raced as I demanded answers. The Nurse, trying to keep the situation under control, warned me that if I didn't lie down, she would have no choice but to give me something to help me relax. In a moment of sheer panic, I found myself darting down the hospital corridor, shouting that they had lost my son. It wasn't long before I noticed a group of nurses rushing over, concern painting their faces. One Nurse had what appeared to be the largest needle imaginable.

Oh no. You can't use that on me. I exclaimed, my anxiety bubbling over.

They managed to gently hold me down and give me an injection, and I have to admit, if it had only been two of them, I'm not sure they would have succeeded. The last coherent thought I remember was a heart-wrenching cry: Where's my baby? Someone took him.

The night's memories blurred into a peaceful sleep, and when I opened my eyes the following day, I saw my beautiful baby beside me. As I gazed at him, tears of joy streamed down my cheeks as I realized he looked just like his father. Holding him close, I felt an overwhelming surge of love. Just then, a nurse entered the room and noticed my tears. What's going on? she asked.

At that moment, I looked up and replied, Isn't he wonderful? She smiled and asked for his name, and I proudly replied, Robert, just like his father. Curious, she asked, where is he?

Without thinking, I responded, He died in a car accident. As the weight of those words sunk in, I felt an immense wave of grief wash over me. It was the first time I understood that Robert wasn't returning. I tried to pack away my tears, yet the mix of sorrow and the excitement of new beginnings was almost too much to bear. The Nurse touched my shoulder gently, I'm sorry to hear that. But I assure you, you and your baby will be alright. Last night, we didn't lose him; the Nurse who was supposed to bring him to you didn't find you in your room. She went on to deliver the other babies, intending to bring him back to you when she finished her rounds. We couldn't give him to you because you were upset, so we had to help you rest.

You're a powerful woman, you know, she added softly. It took three of us to calm you down, and at one point, I really thought we wouldn't win that little battle.

I told her that the doctor had encouraged me to walk more, as it would aid in my recovery. She agreed enthusiastically and suggested that I let a nurse know next time so they could accompany me on my walk. I apologized for my earlier actions, and she reassured me, saying, you wouldn't believe how I would react if I thought my child was missing.

Throughout the day, I sat with my baby, contemplating what our lives would hold. What adventures lay ahead for him? And how would I explain to him about his father? Gail and Mrs. Florence walked in as I was lost in my thoughts. Mrs. Florence greeted me with empathy. We heard you had quite the day yesterday. When we visited, they shared the story of everything that unfolded here. I felt compelled to share how your grandmother experienced a loss.

At that moment, I felt supported and surrounded by love, hopeful for our future.

Mrs. Florence gently cradled the baby and beamed; I'm your grandmother. Can you say 'grandmother'? I joked that if he answered her, I would muster the strength to drag myself out of this hospital and head straight to Hollywood alone. We both chuckled at the thought, but then I spotted Gail sitting quietly with her head lowered and tears streaming down her face. Concerned, I asked her what was troubling her.

With a radiant smile breaking through her tears, she exclaimed, I'm an aunt. I can't believe it. Just three months ago, I felt so alone, and now I have a beautiful sister and an adorable nephew. This is truly one of the happiest days of my life. Lillian, I love you. Mrs. Florence, I love you. And you, sweet little one, I love you most of all. I never imagined I would be an aunt. It's clear to me that there's a loving God who wants everyone to experience joy and happiness in their lives.

Her heartfelt words filled me with reflection, reminding me of Mema, who never knew the depth of happiness. I couldn't help but wonder what she would think of Gail and this precious new baby boy.

After three days, we were finally discharged from the hospital, thanks to my daily invigorating walks, which helped me heal faster than expected. I was overjoyed to be back home with my little one. I would scoop him up each morning and lovingly tell him how much he meant to me. No matter what challenges lay ahead, I promised to always show him my love, he would forever be my number one priority.

HerStory

FOURTEEN

After the first week of sleepless nights, I was genuinely amazed when the boy began to sleep through the night, as if he sensed I needed the rest. I, on the other hand, was struggling to find peace. Each time I closed my eyes, my thoughts raced, bombarded with vivid memories that I couldn't quiet. I would reflect on our little house in the woods, my mother's resilience, and my grandmother's heartbreaking past. I often found myself recalling a time in my childhood when I thought a happy life was out of reach. And most prominently, I missed my husband dearly, feeling a tug of love for him that was both comforting and bittersweet. Snatching even two hours of restful sleep felt like a rare gift. The combination of loss, caring for my baby, and overwhelming fatigue left me feeling drained. I expressed my heartfelt gratitude to Mrs. Florence and Gail, who were absolute angels during this time. They stepped in to care for the boy when I needed a moment to rest, and their unwavering support truly made a world of difference. I couldn't have navigated this journey without them.

After a few months, Gail and I resumed our lovely walks while Mrs. Florence stayed back to enjoy some quality time with the little one. I could tell Mrs. Florence was relishing her role as a grandmother, as she was completely attentive to every little sound the boy made. It's heartwarming to see such affection.

During one of our walks, I noticed that Gail seemed a bit restless, so I decided it was the perfect time for our long-awaited conversation. I was pleasantly surprised when she responded that she had been eager for this chat! I began by sharing the story of how my mother met her father, and her reaction was priceless, she had no idea they had known each other since she was just four years old.

Before diving deeper, I felt it was essential to give her a glimpse into my mother's past, as it was woven with challenges that shaped her. I gently explained that my mother had faced immense hardship, losing her sense of belonging when separated from her family. I noticed Gail's expression shift; she was genuinely intrigued but clearly felt the weight of what I was sharing.

With a deep breath, I prepared to reveal a difficult part of my mother's story. I knew it might be upsetting, but I wanted to be open and honest. I told Gail about how her grandfather had made a decision to purchase/take my mother for her uncle Danny when she was just a small child. As I spoke, I could see the surprise etched on her face, and she leaned in with curiosity, asking, what does that have to do with my father? Are you saying your mother lived her life as a slave?

I reassured her, urging her to be patient with me. I was committed to sharing my mother's story in a way that honored her experience and connected us all.

Mema arrived into a viper's nest. Her innocence, a fragile shield against the leering gaze of depravity. In that den of vipers, she was not a child, not a person, but a vessel, a plaything for your uncle's cruel whims. Each sunrise brought a fresh wave of violation, each sunset, a deeper scar on her soul. And your uncle, that vile serpent, reveled in her torment, his depravity a festering wound in the heart of humanity. His actions, a symphony of cruelty, orchestrated to strip her of dignity and leave her spirit shattered.

I revealed the inventory of my mother's trauma, each repulsive, horrifying, sickening, and outrageous act her uncle committed. Yet, John, your father, offered a sanctuary of sympathy. Theirs was a bond of laughter and shared secrets, a love that yearned for marriage, denied by a cruel patriarch. But darkness descended when your father, led by his own father into a drunken stupor, violated her in her very room. The hands that once offered comfort became instruments of a betrayal so profound it shattered the delicate tapestry of their affection.

Gail sprang to her feet, eyes wide with emotion, and exclaimed, That's not true. You're lying. My dad would never act like that; I know him better than anyone. I can't believe you'd say something like that. I just hate you.

With that, she dashed home, quickly packed up her things, and left without a word to anyone. When I returned, Mrs.

Florence had just returned from the store and noticed Gail's absence and asked what had happened. I hesitated, thinking about what I'd said, and guessed that Gail was struggling with some challenging family history. Mrs. Florence wanted to know the details, and I realized I needed to take a moment to reflect on my words, perhaps I hadn't handled the situation the best way.

I retreated to my room, taking a seat on my bed, and as I pondered what had transpired, I realized just how much I liked Gail and how she seemed to care for me. I questioned why I had told her that particular story. Deep down, I was overwhelmed by my own feelings about my family's experiences and may have inadvertently wanted to hurt her the way her family had hurt my mom in the past. I recognized that I could have approached her with more compassion, especially since he was her father, and she loved him dearly.

A gentle knock on the door interrupted my thoughts as I sat there contemplating how to move forward. It was Gail. I welcomed her in with an open heart. She sat beside me, vulnerability shining in her eyes, and apologized for her earlier outburst. We're sisters, she said softly. I love you. Moved by what she said to me, I returned an apology, acknowledging that I could've been more understanding of her feelings.

I took a deep breath and shared my perspective on John, explaining how his family had caused significant pain for my mother that she never entirely overcame. When I first met John in the woods, he didn't even realize I was his daughter; he mistakenly thought I was Danny's child. He never mentioned his family, but our last encounter was when he asked my mother to marry him. It was bittersweet; deep down, I sensed she might have had feelings for him, but the wounds from the past were too deep for her to overlook. Honestly, those wounds lingered with me, too.

The news of his passing didn't shock me. I could see in his eyes the same haunting sorrow my mother carried. It was clear that the weight of their shared history was too much for him, just as it was for her. However, we must let go of their past and not let it shape our future. What matters now is that we have each other and can create something new going forward.

With an understanding smile, Gail asked if it would be all right for her to stay with me. I smiled back, heart full of hope, and assured her, of course. You can stay as long as you want. Together, we can embrace the journey ahead with open hearts.

HerStory

FIFTEEN

Time truly has a way of slipping by, doesn't it? It's hard to believe that six months have passed. One sunny morning, I could have sworn I heard my little boy say, good morning, Mommy. Mrs. Florence and Gail found it amusing and teased me, mimicking him in a playful baby voice, bursting into laughter as they did. Yet, I remained confident in what I had heard. Determined to capture this remarkable moment, I invested in a tape recorder, my own evidence.

Discovering how children have this unique way of flipping the script was a revelation. Whenever we were alone, he spoke so clearly. But once I hit record, he would either go silent or babble like an adorable little baby. It was as if he sensed my intentions. Eventually, I realized he would share his voice with the world in his own time, and I decided to be patient.

About three months later, during breakfast, what a delightful morning. He surprised us by clearly asking, Can I have some more, please? Mrs. Florence and Gail exchanged astonished glances, their mouths ajar, unable to contain their disbelief. After all, my little one was only nine months old. I stayed calm and casually prepared another bowl of cereal, pretending not to notice the stunned expressions on their faces. All day, whenever our eyes met, I simply shook my head with a chuckle, what a joyous moment.

My main concern as a mother was ensuring my child felt abundant love. I wanted him to know he was cherished, and I hoped to receive that love back in return. Interestingly, with Mema, I felt she never expected that same connection, which had caused some distance between us at times. But everywhere me and my baby went, people couldn't help but light up in his presence. His joyful spirit drew smiles and laughter from everyone, especially the older folks in the neighborhood who loved to squeeze his cheeks, which he found hilarious. Their laughter was contagious, and we all found ourselves in stitches before long. It warmed my heart to see the love being shared all around.

Reflecting on my relationship with Mema, I understood her challenges. She loved me the best way she could; however, it felt like she had missed out on experiencing true, unfiltered love herself. Ironically, love is indeed one of the most beautiful experiences life has to offer. Yet, I recognized that it could be painful when misused, Mema's situation was a powerful example of that.

Despite the heartache of losing my husband, I found myself surrounded by hope. I was forging a bond with my sister, and Mrs. Florence was a steadfast support during this difficult time. Most importantly, I was blessed with a strong, healthy baby boy who filled my life with joy. One night, however, an uneasy feeling washed over me, and after a heartfelt prayer, I drifted off to sleep.

The following morning, I awoke with a shout for Robert, and Mrs. Florence rushed in, concerned. I confided in her that I felt an overwhelming longing for my husband. The emptiness of his absence was suffocating, and I ached for his love; I felt alone in a world where I couldn't quite find my footing. Please help me. I don't want to go on without him. My heart felt heavy with the weight of it all, I longed to be loved and craved his presence back. It felt incredibly unfair that it had been taken away just when I had found the love I had always yearned for. Life seemed to play the cruelest tricks, and I couldn't help but sense that Mema's struggle with love had mirrored my own experiences in some ways.

In those charged moments, anger bubbled within me. Mrs. Florence's response shocked me: I love you. What about the boy? He needs you. I shot back in a moment of raw emotion, you're not Mema. I need my mother. The voice that escaped me caught even myself off guard, echoing Mema's tone right before her emotional upheavals. Looking into Mrs. Florence's eyes, I could see the pain my words had caused. She gently reminded me to focus on what I could control and let go of things beyond my reach.

Yes, I understood what she meant; however, there were times when I couldn't shake the memories of Mema's turbulence. After having Robby, I often felt her lingering confusion and despair tightening its grip on me.

The hardest part was knowing the depth of my pain compared to what she endured daily. That awareness weighed heavy on my heart. Frequently, it crept up, attempting to take control of my emotions, and I had to fight to keep it at bay. I often wondered how Mema lived through such a life, as I was sure no one deserved to endure such suffering.

Life, with all its ups and downs, offers moments filled with love, laughter, and hope. I held onto those beautiful moments with Robby and the love surrounding us, pushing through the clouds of sorrow. Together, we would navigate this journey, creating bright memories that would shine on even the darkest days.

I've been feeling the weight of missing Robert, and it's been quite challenging. Although I've done my best to keep it under wraps, there are moments when the intensity of emotion becomes overwhelming. Mrs. Florence, often reassured me that she understood my struggles. While I miss my closeness with my husband, I've clarified that my main concerns extend beyond intimacy. The topic makes me uncomfortable, and just thinking about it can bring a wave of calmness, so I hesitated to discuss it openly. I sensed she recognized this because whenever I became frustrated, she casually introduced conversations about intimacy, aware it would lead me down a path of reflection.

Eventually, Mrs. Florence brought up Mema, believing I was in a place to process it. She shared that Mema had deep worries for my future, particularly concerned about me inheriting her disposition, fearing I might grow into a bitter woman. This moved me because it showed how much Mema truly cared. Mrs. Florence promised Mema to always stand by my side, which meant the world to me.

One day, my emotions hit a low point. I struggled to eat, found myself distancing from Robby, and lashed out at my loved ones, feeling overwhelmed by their presence. One of those mornings, I stumbled upon Mrs. Florence in the kitchen. As I approached her, a sudden urge to react with frustration whispered in my mind, but as she turned to me, her gaze held a familiarity, that she could sense my internal struggle. To my astonishment, tears began to stream down her face. This deeply affected me, as she had always been so resilient. Asking what was wrong led to a profound conversation.

I'm reflecting on a moment I shared with your mother during her final days, she shared, her voice filled with emotion. I fought passionately to illustrate that life holds value, but she had convinced herself that hers was over. She asked me for my thoughts on life, and I suggested that it's a blend of joy and sorrow, each emotion playing a vital role in overall balance. But then she halted me, wondering if a life filled solely with anguish and emptiness was still worth living. She was in so much pain, and I could feel her despair.

Mrs. Florence continued, I urged her to seek help, but I sensed it wasn't what she wanted to hear. She had already made a heartbreaking decision. I promised her to keep this to myself, yet seeing you like this brings forth fears that you might think along the same lines. This path isn't inevitable for you, there are alternatives. You've experienced love, and the warmth of it returned, which sets you apart from her.

I felt compelled to point out that Mema also had someone who loved her dearly, me.

Your journey is uniquely yours, and it's essential to recognize that, Mrs. Florence assured me. Comparing your life to hers isn't fair; you are worlds apart. Holding on to her sufferings could dim your own light. Instead, embrace your brighter moments and remember the good times in her life. Positive reflections can gradually dispel negative thoughts. You must take charge of your own narrative. If you don't, there's a risk her story could echo into your own, affecting how your child perceive you. Your mother wouldn't want that for you, and you don't want to follow that path either. Remember your words from her funeral, she is at peace now.

This conversation resonated with me deeply and filled me with hope. It was a heartfelt reminder that despite the pain of loss, I still had the power to create a vibrant life ahead. By embracing joy, loving moments, and the bonds that lift me up, I knew I could honor Mema's memory while forging my own path, rich with love and purpose.

I truly appreciated what Mrs. Florence was expressing, but I often slipped into old habits after spending so much time living with her. Misery had a way of entwining itself into our daily lives, and there were moments when I struggled to remember what it felt like to live without it hanging over me. I managed to keep afloat because it was Mema's sorrow we were navigating, not my own. However, now that she's no longer with us, I feel the weight of that desolation, and, to be honest, it often feels overwhelming.

Growing up as someone who felt different, coping with the loss of my parent, and facing the untimely departure of my husband created a narrative that resembled her life, a life filled with heartache. It's a challenge to not get lost in her despair, as it resonates so deeply with my own feelings of grief and loss. Mrs. Florence once shared some profound wisdom with me, she said, you must dig deep into your soul to discover the strength to challenge and change this cycle. If you don't, there's a risk you might find yourself walking the same path she did, and then it will be your little one's responsibility to break the chain. If he can't, his children will grow up with these shadows looming over them. This cycle will linger unless someone finds the courage to stop it. I know you can't bear the thought of Robby experiencing a childhood like yours.

With sincerity, I assured her that I would never allow that to happen. I love Robby dearly, and the thought of him enduring such pain motivates me daily. Mrs. Florence looked at me in her emotion-filled voice and said, please, don't use such drastic language. Doesn't that sound all too familiar to you?

Her words resonated deeply, and I realized that these burdens of the past had no place in my future. I wouldn't allow them to interfere with my beautiful bond with my son. The love a mother feels is unconditional and shifts your perspective, highlighting the importance of prioritizing someone else's well-being above your own. Just picturing what must have gone through Mema's mind when she returned home to find her baby all alone brought a wave of sadness over me; it's unfathomable to think about leaving my child unattended for hours.

At one point, I wondered if Mema lacked strength, but I'm beginning to appreciate that motherhood is a unique journey, different from being a wife, daughter, or friend. The more I reflected on her struggles, the more I understood the importance of finding a way to compartmentalize those memories, creating some distance between them and my family.

As I sat contemplating, trying to devise a plan to break this cycle, Gail walked in, sat beside me, and offered an apology. When I gazed into her eyes, I sensed mixed emotions swirling within her, prompting me to ask what was troubling her. She hesitated, sharing that she had something to tell me, something I needed to hear.

Then, in a surprising twist, she revealed that her valid reason for being here wasn't merely to reconnect with her sister. She had come with the intention of confronting me, blaming our family for the loss of her parents. Yet, she found herself sharing this because she had learned much about herself since we met and recognized the importance of letting go of her past. It became clear to her that she had to break free from the chains that bound her.

Initially, my impressions of her seemed wildly inaccurate, yet learning all this took me aback. When she first mentioned needing a place to stay, I instinctively opened my heart and home to her. Now, I sense that she is beginning to realize we genuinely care for her and are more than just acquaintances, we're becoming a family. This journey towards healing and understanding is a shared one, filling me with hope for all of us.

HerStory

SIXTEEN

Things were looking genuinely excellent for us. Mrs. Florence was in high spirits, buoyed by the companionship of Robby. Gail and I had formed a strong bond. We enjoyed spending time together, but City Park held a special place in my heart. It became our go-to spot for afternoon people-watching. I found it amusing when Gail introduced me to this activity, but soon I became fascinated. I wondered about the stories of those passing by, where they came from, where they were headed. In a way, it felt like I was part of a larger tapestry of life.

However, as life often teaches us, change is an inevitable part of our journey. When I thought everything was going smoothly, I noticed a creeping uneasiness settling into our little bubble of happiness. Gail started showing signs of restlessness, and despite my best efforts to comfort her, I sensed something was troubling her deeply. I had known her briefly, yet I could tell she was holding back and not candid. Inspired by Mrs. Florence's wise words about not bottling up feelings, I urged her to share what was on her mind, but it didn't make a difference.

Gail would sit on the porch for hours, lost in thought, seemingly unaware of the world around her. My concern for her grew because the sadness in her eyes was evident as if she had lost sight of hope. After weeks of her unusual behavior, she finally opened up to me. I had been waiting for this moment with excitement, hoping it would bring her some relief. When she revealed that she felt lonely, it struck a chord.

Even though we were family and had each other, something significant was clearly missing in her life. She reassured me that it wasn't about me; instead, she longed for the community and connections she missed. At first, I was confused by her mention of her people, but slowly, I began to understand. She was referring to her experiences and connections with white people. I was taken aback. Are you saying that because I'm black, we're different? I exclaimed. We're sisters Gail, part of the same family.

I wanted to comprehend her feelings; they simply didn't make sense to me. If we were just friends, I might understand the distance, but as sisters, how could we feel so apart? Gail gently asked me not to make it harder for her to express her thoughts. She spoke of a time when she might find the words to explain her feelings, but for now, she just felt a powerful longing to be around white people.

My heart sank when she told me it was time for her to leave. I desperately pleaded with her to stay, promising to help her work through whatever was troubling her if she just gave me the chance. Unfortunately, my words didn't change her mind. The very next day, she packed her bags and left. No amount of pleading could convince her to stay despite our best efforts.

For a long time, I struggled with her departure. I felt hurt and angry, trapped in a whirlwind of emotions. I even wished her ill, letting anger cloud my judgment. My frustration turned into rage that seeped into my interactions with Robby and Mrs. Florence. I felt like a storm, barely holding it together, ready to lash at anything around me. Despite Mrs. Florence's attempts to comfort me, assuring me that Gail's decision was not my fault, I was too caught up in my own turmoil to truly hear her.

Amidst this chaos, one day, I stood over my baby, overwhelmed and unsure of my feelings. I knew I needed to regain control, so I took a deep breath and stepped outside, shouting a mighty yell, Fight. You have to fight for your sanity; don't give in. In that moment of release, I felt a glimmer of clarity and hope wash over me. It reminded me that strength lies within us, even in the darkest times.

With renewed determination, I committed to supporting myself and honoring my sister's memory. Life is full of twists and turns, and while sadness is a part of it, so too is the resilience that allows us to rise again. We all have stories to share, and even though our paths may diverge, there will always be a connection, one that courageously strives toward understanding and compassion.

Robby was indeed growing up, and it filled my heart with pride. However, in the whirlwind of my thoughts and feelings, I hadn't fully grasped how deeply Gail's departure had impacted him. In moments when someone would mention her name, I would see Robby's little face light up with hope, darting his gaze toward the door as if he expected her to walk back in. But eventually, that glimmer faded, and he stopped searching for her. It was a poignant reminder of how children process loss, often quietly and in their own way.

At the same time, I began to notice that Mrs. Florence wasn't her vibrant self anymore. She seemed worn down and weary, and this concerned me greatly. The thought of losing her was unbearable, she was our anchor, our steady presence.

One day, as we sat together, she brought up a conversation from the past. Do you remember when I spoke with your mother before she passed? Mema believed that death was her only escape, she said softly. Her voice carried the weight of experience as she expressed that she, too, felt tired and sensed that her time might be approaching. Yet, she had made a promise to Mema, that she would always be there for me. She worried I wouldn't need her as much since I now had Robby. I stared into her eyes, I need you, Mrs. Florence. Robby needs you, too. I pleaded, hoping that my words would strengthen her spirit. Unfortunately, it didn't seem to alleviate her concerns, and I sensed that without Mema's promise weighing on her, she'd be ready to leave us.

The following two years rolled by without any word from Gail, a span filled with uncertainty and longing. Then, one day, a knock at the door changed everything. To my astonishment, it was her. My initial excitement echoed inside me but quickly faded into the shadows of confusion and hurt. Old feelings of rejection threatened to resurface, and I hesitantly asked her what had brought her back. However, remembering Mrs. Florence's wise words, I took a deep breath and laid aside my reservations, expressing my happiness to see her. Gail was gracious about my mixed feelings, offering to leave if I wanted. But I couldn't let that happen. Nonsense. Come in; you're still my sister. I exclaimed, a smile spreading across my face. We embraced, laughter spilling out and brushing away the clouds of uncertainty that had hung over us.

Curiosity bubbled within me, and I couldn't wait to hear about her adventures and why she had chosen this moment to return. Just as I was about to ask, little Robby burst into the room, his energy lighting up the space. Gail's face transformed in an instant as she beheld him. Who's that handsome young man? Wow, you've grown so much. Remember me? I'm your Aunt Gail, come give me a hug. Her warm welcome seemed to erase the distance from her absence, and I could see the beginnings of a beautiful connection being rekindled.

I suggested she nap before our heart-to-heart chat about the past few years. As she settled into her old room, Mrs. Florence and I exchanged glances, pondering the changes that had brought Gail back into our lives. Why had she stayed away for so long? What had changed?

The following morning was filled with anticipation as we shared breakfast together. I asked how her night had been and how well she had rested. Navigating our reconnected relationship felt delicate; she could hurt me again if I wasn't careful. But as we sat across, I realized she felt just as tentative. She broke the ice with heartfelt sincerity.

I missed you so much. Not a single day passed without thoughts of you, Robby, and Mrs. Florence. The way I left was not right, and I hope you can forgive me, I love you all so deeply. The look in your eyes the day I left haunted me, and I would never want to hurt you.

It was apparent just how much she had wrestled with her feelings. When I went home, I was confused, trying to understand why I left the people I cherished most. I had to embark on a journey of self-reflection. I initially questioned my biases, wondering if I was prejudiced. But I realized that it's vital to feel connected to something larger than ourselves, and in finding that connection, I discovered clarity.

I listened intently, unable to mirror her perspective, but I could empathize. I, too, had navigated a rocky path of anger and confusion after her departure. Mrs. Florence's kindness helped me reflect and realize that my anger stemmed from my love for her. Gazing into Gail's eyes, I decided to leave anger behind and allow our bond to grow deeper.

This beautiful reunion breathed new life into our family dynamics, igniting a fresh sense of purpose. Each day felt like an opportunity to cherish one another and embrace the joy of being together again.

SEVENTEEN

O ne bright morning, I awoke with a tightness in my stomach that made the idea of getting out of bed feel overwhelming. Robby was bursting with energy and enthusiasm, eager to visit Joe Brown Park. Despite his contagious excitement, I gently told him it would be best to postpone our adventure for another day, as I wasn't quite ready. He was on a joyous rampage, bouncing around the house with a liveliness I hadn't seen before. When Mrs. Florence came in and announced her plans for the park, Robby's excitement surged to new heights; I sighed in relief as I watched him dash towards her.

About forty-five minutes later, Robby burst through the door, jubilantly yelling. As if propelled by instinct, I leaped out of bed to meet him. Mommy, I don't love you. No, Mommy, I don't love you. he cried out, and I felt a surge of shock wash over me. Immediately, I knelt down and asked him why he didn't love me since my affection for him knows no bounds. His answer was a river of tears: Please, Mommy, don't love me anymore.

Wrapping my arms around him, I gently implored, what's wrong with me loving you, sweetheart? But he continued his plea, repeating, no, Mommy, don't love me, please don't. I realized I needed to understand what was distressing him, so I entrusted him to Gail for a moment and approached Mrs. Florence, hoping she had clarity about the situation.

When I found her in her room, she appeared absorbed, and I could feel my emotions bubbling inside as I sought answers. I've been waiting for you, she said, and I couldn't believe my ears. You've been waiting for me? Is that all you can say? What happened at the park? Why does my son feel this way? Please, help me understand.

She encouraged me to find calm in the chaos and took a deep breath before responding. Today at the park, Robby asked about his father. He was curious about who he was and where he could be. I hesitated about whether to discuss it with him before you had the chance to. As we walked, he said he felt his daddy didn't love us. I wanted to ease his thoughts, so I tried to explain that his daddy loved him and you very much, but he seemed to misinterpret what I said.

My response was too intense. You think? My son says he doesn't love me or want my love. What else could you have said?

I just wanted him to know his father cared deeply for him. But he was asking if he could see him, and I didn't know how to tell him his daddy had passed away. When he asked, if you love someone, don't you want to be with them? I just kept walking, unsure of how to respond. I fear he's confused about love and worried you might leave him, too. I'm truly sorry; that wasn't my intention.

Hearing her explanation filled me with profound remorse for how I reacted. Mrs. Florence has been a vital part of our lives, and I felt embarrassed for the misunderstandings that had caused me to raise my voice. Watching Robby's distress reminded me of my childhood pains, and the thought of that hurt was difficult to bear. I promised myself then and there that no one would cause him pain, no one at all. I've always known that Mrs. Florence profoundly cares for both of us, yet, in that moment, I let my fear overshadow my trust.

Despite her understanding demeanor, I still couldn't shake the image of concern etched on her face. She reassured me that, had she suspected anyone had hurt Robby, including me, her reaction would have been fueled by protective instincts. Yet a whisper of doubt lingered within me, after all these years, I should have more faith in people, especially in someone important to us. Perhaps I thought I had reconciled my past, but I still had work to do on trusting others and myself.

Reflecting on this experience, I realize communicating openly is vital, especially regarding our loved ones. The emotions we express and the misconceptions that unfold can profoundly shape how our children perceive love and trust. I remain optimistic that together, we can navigate these challenges, turning moments of confusion into opportunities for growth, understanding, and stronger bonds.

The incident I experienced left me feeling intensely weighed down. Even after two months, it felt as fresh and painful as if it had just happened. Finding clarity amidst those dark thoughts was challenging, almost terrifying. Mrs. Florence and Gail genuinely tried to support me during this difficult time, but it was as if I was speaking a different language, one they couldn't quite grasp. Truthfully, I was still trying to decode my own feelings.

Then, one beautiful day, I sat by the window, watching Robby play outside. His laughter and delight were like sunlight breaking through clouds, warming my heart. It was so fulfilling to witness his joy; as a child, I longed for those moments of carefree fun, and seeing him thrive was invigorating for me. As I savored the peace of the moment, an overwhelming wave of fear washed over me. Instinctively, I called out for him to come inside.

His curious gaze met mine as he asked why I wanted him. I urged him to come into the safety of the house. He began to walk towards me, but my anxiety drove me to rush out, scoop him into my arms, and dart back inside. My heart raced as I locked the door behind us, pulling him into my room. When he asked what was wrong, I whispered urgently, you need to be quiet, or they will hear you.

Who will hear me? he inquired, his little brow furrowing in confusion.

The white men, I told him, trying to mask my fear with reassurance. They're coming to take you away, but you don't have to worry. I will protect you.

I shouted at the door with fierce determination, demanding they leave us alone. Cuddled together in the corner under the window, we held onto each other, rocking gently while I sang "Amazing Grace", a song Mema often sang to soothe me during tough times. Just as I started to feel a moment of calm, a knock at the door startled us both. I raised my voice again, firmly insisting they couldn't have my baby and that I would fight to the end to keep him safe.

As the knocking intensified, Robby began to cry, and in a moment of instinct, I pressed my hand over his mouth, whispering for him to be quiet. I knew it was crucial to keep him safe, and even though he struggled, I held him close, whispering for him to calm down. Slowly, his rebellious movements ceased, and I cautiously removed my hand, hoping he had drifted into a peaceful sleep.

However, as I sat quietly, I felt an unsettling chill emanating from his tiny body. I gently laid him down to fetch a blanket, but in that instant, my heart sank, I realized he wasn't breathing. Panic enveloped me as I shook him, desperately calling his name, yet he remained unresponsive. My mind raced as I tried everything to wake him, but there was only silence.

Desperate, I shouted for help, hoping for a miracle as the door creaked open. My heart raced with fear, and for a moment, it felt like everything around me was closing in. When the door finally opened, I was surprised to see Robert standing before me. He said, you killed my son. Why? He was all you had left of me. Do you hate me that much? I shouted back, no, I love you. It was an accident. I love my baby, and I swear it was an accident. As I spoke, his image began to fade. I begged him not to leave me alone again, telling him that I loved him and that I needed to say so much more. As his voice faded away, I heard him say, you killed my only child. How could you do such a thing?

I started yelling for him to come back. While I sat there crying, another image appeared. It said, how could you kill your own child? He deserved better. What did he ever do to you but bring joy and happiness to your life? I couldn't figure out who this was, so I asked, who are you, and what do you want from me? I didn't kill him; it was an accident, and I was only trying to protect him from the men.

Then the voice said, I need you to listen carefully to what I'm about to say. I lived my life in misery, and it was all a waste of valuable time. I told myself I was living in seclusion for my child so she would never feel the pain I felt. I now realize you must live for yourself because if you do your best, you will have your best to give to your family. I used my past as an excuse for not living fully.

Just as I recognized Mema's voice, her image started to fade. I shouted, Mema, come back. Please don't leave me. The next thing I remember is Mrs. Florence and Gail standing over me and someone saying, Wake up. Wake up. You're having a bad dream. I jumped out of bed and yelled; I didn't mean it. It was an accident. I love my baby. I swear it was an accident. I heard one of them say, what are you talking about? What was an accident? We heard you screaming, so we came in to let you know your baby is okay. It was just a bad dream.

HerStory

I dashed into his room, and he looked as healthy and handsome as ever. I scooped him into my arms, overwhelmed with affection, and whispered how much I loved him. I promised myself right then that I would embark on a journey to become a better person. As those warm thoughts filled the air, Mrs. Florence stood beside me, comforting me, saying, I told you it was just a bad dream. He's perfectly fine. Would you like to talk about it? I nodded, feeling it would be hard to drift off to sleep again after such a vivid experience.

We moved to the living room, and I could still feel the remnants of my shaking body from the dream. So much was running through my mind, yet the words felt stuck. Thankfully, Mrs. Florence patiently gave me the space to gather my thoughts. Gradually, my feelings unfolded, and when I finally spoke, I could sense the weight lifting off my chest.

She listened intently and shared profound insights, saying, let me help you understand something important. This dream was trying to send you the same message I've been conveying for years: letting go of your past is crucial. You need to embrace the life you've been given and live it to its fullest. Remember, it's not about forgetting your mother; it's about not letting her fears shape your life. Every time a challenge arises; you fall into a cycle of feeling down. I completely understand your worries, but what I see in your eyes resembles the fear your mother once had. That's a dangerous path. You're allowing yesterday's shadows to cloud today's brightness, and carrying that pain into the present will only stifle your child's happiness.

What she said resonated deeply with me, but I still felt compelled to ask about those white figures who came to take my baby away. She thoughtfully explained that they might have been family members or my father trying to remind me not to dwell in the past. Even though no one had taken my child, I realized I was living under the shadow of that fear. If I continued down this path, it would be as if I was holding him back. I needed to cherish the memories of my loved ones, especially Mema, who cared for me deeply and wanted the best for my life. Thoughts of her love should lift me whenever I felt those dark clouds of depression looming.

I recognized that I didn't want to lose my family, so it was clear that I needed to change. I started viewing life more as if a heavy burden was lifted. For the first time in ages, I could savor life's moments. My family and I began engaging in fun activities together. One bright morning, I woke up with energy and prepared a picnic basket. By the time everyone else woke up, I was all set to go, and they were pleasantly surprised to see me up and about. I eagerly asked if they wanted to join me, and Robby's delight was infectious, he joyfully ran around singing, we're going on a picnic. We're going on a picnic. This moment sparked a realization: how much I had overlooked his happiness.

Mrs. Florence and Gail exchanged smiles, their eyes shining with warmth. I cheerfully told them I had packed enough delicious food for everyone, tantalizing pickles and crispy potato chips, scrumptious salami and liver cheese sandwiches, and hog head cheese with crackers just for Mrs. Florence, accompanied by refreshing cold drinks to wash it all down.

Our picnic was a delightful success. I couldn't remember the last time I fully appreciated the beauty of Joe Brown Park. The trees looked more vibrant, and the pond sparkled with pristine clarity. Even though I had visited this park countless times, that day felt unique and radiant, almost as if I saw everything anew. Everyone around me was also soaking in the moment's joy. I settled under a tree, taking it all in while reflecting on Robert. I felt his spirit watching over me with a warm smile, assuring me everything would be alright. I even pondered whether he and Mema were sharing a peaceful moment, and I was grateful for their visit in my dream. It left me with a comforting assurance that Mema had found peace.

From that day onward, I cherished a newfound sense of serenity and felt good inside and out. I made a powerful commitment to myself, vowing never to let anything pull me away from this peaceful and loving state of being. I was ready to embrace life as it blossomed around me, filled with love and happiness.

HerStory

EIGHTEEN

O ne sunny afternoon, I found myself cozied up by the window, relishing a moment of tranquility in my life. Just then, Gail walked into the room, tears streaming down her face. A rush of unease washed over me, I hesitated to ask about her troubles because, for once, things in my life seemed to be aligning beautifully, and I was reluctant to confront someone else's heartache. I decided to step outside, yet her soft cries lingered in the air, echoing like a haunting melody. Perhaps it was my own guilt that made her whimper feel endless. That evening, I found myself tossing and turning in bed, grappling with the weight of my inaction and reflecting on how I had overlooked her emotional needs.

The following morning, I overheard Gail confiding in Mrs. Florence. She expressed her disbelief about my lack of support when she needed someone to lean on. It was heartbreaking to hear that she felt I had treated her rudely. A wave of anxiety washed over me as the thought struck me that she could have been in such despair that it led her to contemplate something tragic. Of all the people in her life, she had believed she could count on me. Thankfully, Mrs.

Florence offered some comforting words, explaining that sometimes we all need a moment of solitude to gather our thoughts. Gail seemed to grasp the message, but deep down, I was acutely aware that my response could have been more compassionate.

Standing in the hallway, listening to their conversation, a feeling of sadness settled within me. I kept pondering why I had acted that way. Why do I find myself hurting the ones I care for the most? What kind of person am I? Retreating to my room, I wrestled with the confusion of my behavior. I sat on my bed, sensing the familiar pull of depression trying to invade my thoughts. But I resolved then and there, not this time. I realized this struggle didn't stem from my past; my discomfort was rooted in my treatment of Gail, and I acknowledged the validity of my feelings, I hadn't acted with the kindness she certainly deserved.

Determined to address the situation, I went to the kitchen, where they were still talking. I gently asked Mrs. Florence to give us a moment alone. I settled beside Gail, who remained still, lost in her thoughts, as she gazed out the window. I remained silent, giving her space to process her emotions or voice her frustration towards me. After a while, I took a deep breath and said, you have every right to be upset with me, and I sincerely want to apologize for hurting your feelings. I hoped to convey that while my intentions felt justified at that moment, I recognize now how misplaced they were.

Throughout my life, I often found that misfortunes stemmed from others' problems, leading me to focus inward and withdraw from emotional challenges. However, the past few months awakened me as I delved into self-discovery, seeking to understand who I was and why painful feelings often surfaced in my life. I realized I was living in extremes, either enveloped in love or consumed by sorrow, with no room for anything in between. In moments of joy, I rarely took credit for my happiness; conversely, when life turned sour, I internalized that pain deeply. This cycle, which had persisted for years, was beginning to shift. I felt a stronger sense of control over my emotions and a renewed belief that I held the key to my own happiness.

As I reflected on our earlier encounter, I recognized that when you came in crying, I instinctively braced myself for the weight of your sorrow. The last thing I wanted was for your sadness to become my own, especially since I had already endured so much. I refuse to let negative feelings consume any more of my precious time. While I am not asking for your forgiveness, you must understand my mindset. I genuinely care about you and want to work towards healing our connection. Let's take this moment together to move forward and support one another.

Throughout our conversation, Gail's gaze remained fixed out of the window, so I gently asked, Gail, did you hear me? When she turned to me, her eyes glistening with unshed tears, she spoke with a quiet intensity: Absolutely, I heard you. But it's important to understand that you are not the only one who faced difficulties growing up. Just because my father lived with us doesn't mean my childhood was free from challenges. I loved him deeply, and I knew in his own way he loved me, too. Yet, life at home was far from perfect. My father was a runner, someone who would suddenly run away from our family, leaving us all confused and hurt. It often felt like he couldn't bear to be with us for even a moment longer. Out of the blue, he would pack his things and vanish for weeks, leaving us with unanswered questions about where he had gone and when he might return.

Each time he left, I would lie awake at night, listening to my mother's heart-wrenching cries. This left me feeling bitter and angry at him for causing her so much pain. I remember an agitated moment when I overheard them arguing. He shouted, I don't love you, and if you hadn't gotten pregnant, we wouldn't even be together. It struck me deeply when he said, 'Besides, she's probably not even my child. I was about ten, and his words cut me like a knife. I ran into the room, overwhelmed with emotion, and yelled at him that I hated him and wished he would just leave.

Despite my feelings of hurt, I cherished him more than anything. I would pray fervently to bring him back each time he left. When he returned, the atmosphere would brighten momentarily, but I could always see in his eyes that his departure was just around the corner. Each homecoming seemed to allow us just enough time to rekindle our love and trust before he slipped away again, leaving us heartbroken.

One beautiful day, while he was gone, I was sitting under my favorite tree, soaking in the sunshine, when I heard footsteps approaching the house. My heart raced with hope, but it wasn't him when I looked. The wave of disappointment I felt still lingers in my memory. In the last year of his life, he started leaving every night, and my mother bore the brunt of that heartache. Despite her tireless efforts to keep him home, nothing seemed to work. I could sense her losing faith in our family staying together, and I thought I could fill that gap.

I tried everything I could think of: pretending to be sick to keep him close, engaging him in deep conversations to distract him from leaving, and even staying out later to trigger his worry for me. But I would return home every time to find he had vanished again. No matter what I did, it felt like an invisible force was pulling him away from us.

As I observed Gail's demeanor, I sensed something else weighed heavily on her mind, something more profound than she was sharing. She fell silent again, her gaze fixed on the window, her expression reminiscent of something that tugged at my memory, though I couldn't quite identify it. Suddenly, it hit me, and I yelled, no, Gail, please don't!

She remained unblinking, staring into the distance as if caught in a trance. I implored her to talk to me, but she seemed worlds away. Quickly, I moved closer, resting her head on my shoulder, but there was no response; it was as if she had retreated into her own space. Gradually, she stood up and quietly made her way to her room, leaving me with concern and a desire to better understand and support her.

Later that evening, I decided to check on Gail. As I gently opened her door, I noticed her tears were still flowing, and my heart went out to her. I walked over and sat beside her on the bed, eager to support her however I could. How can I help you? I asked, trying to create a safe space for her.

Without hesitation, she leaned in, resting her head on my shoulder, and expressed, I'm so ashamed. Her sudden outburst caught me off guard, and I instantly felt the weight of her emotions.

Curiosity and concern intertwined as I asked her what made her feel this way. She opened up about a painful realization, feeling like her father, who struggled to love his family. At that moment, I could sense the deep conflict she was experiencing within herself.

Gail then shared her story with me, explaining that after leaving there, she returned home and met a man named Donald. They ended up marrying because she was pregnant. Yesterday was my daughter's birthday, she said, tears streaming down her face. My heart ached for her as I processed this incredible revelation, she was married and had a child. It was hard for me to grasp the magnitude of what she had gone through. I wanted to delve deeper into her feelings and her life circumstances. Do you love him, or at least love your child? I blurted out, my concern for her growing more assertive.

Absolutely, I love them, she responded with conviction. But I left because I believed they were better off without me. She continued explaining how, upon returning to her mother's house feeling lonely, she started talking to Donald, who lived next door. Their friendship blossomed into something more as they enjoyed terrific moments together. It was clear she had developed strong feelings for him despite initially insisting she was not looking for anything serious.

As they began dating, they shared delightful evenings, savoring meals at Copeland's, enjoying movies, and listening to captivating music on Bourbon Street. With time, Gail found herself unexpectedly falling in love. She tried to suppress these feelings, yet love, with its relentless nature, took hold of her heart. One evening, she invited Donald over for dinner, and their chemistry was undeniable. That night, they shared an intimate connection that left a lasting impression on her heart, one she would cherish forever.

However, things progressed rapidly after that special night. Within a few months, they were married, and soon after, she discovered she was pregnant. Confusion washed over her. Despite her love for Donald, she wrestled with the feeling that she couldn't stay. I left him twice by the time I was five months along, she recounted, her voice trembling. I guess I felt like I needed some space. It was heart-wrenching to listen to her struggle, especially when she shared that when she returned to this place, her child was just three months old.

Gail expressed that she had convinced herself it was for the best that she wasn't part of their lives, but now, uncertainty clouded her thoughts. It was clear that she was grappling with monumental decisions and deep emotional pain. Listening to her story made me realize that supporting her through this journey was vital. With time and understanding, I hoped she would find clarity and strength to embrace whatever path lay ahead, remembering that love can heal and open new doors, even in the most challenging circumstances.

I made it a point to stay non-judgmental as I encouraged her to immediately reach out to her family to express her heartfelt apologies and desire to come home. She swiftly shared that she was eager to return, especially because she missed her daughter. When I inquired about her husband, she admitted feeling uncertain about him. She thought she still had feelings for him but didn't want to replicate her father's pattern of being in and out of their lives. While she dialed her family, I seized the moment to speak with Mrs. Florence and share what Gail had confided in me, although I sensed Mrs. Florence was already aware of much of it.

As soon as Gail finished her call, she beckoned me back into her room; no trace of tears left, and instead, a radiant smile lit up her face. She excitedly shared that her husband loved her and wanted her to come home, mentioning she probably wouldn't recognize her daughter, Nicole, who had grown so much. The joy emanating from her was palpable; she was glowing. Her cheeks had a lovely pink hue, and her voice was infused with excitement. Honestly, I thought she might faint from overwhelming happiness, I've never seen someone turn so red so quickly. When I asked about the sudden brightness on her face, she revealed it was pure joy at the thought of reuniting with her family. I was so relieved because I had briefly worried, we would have to take her to the hospital. We both chuckled as I approached her and shared a warm hug.

With a sparkle in her eye, Gail mentioned she had something else to share. She asked me if I remembered the reasons behind her previous departure. She explained that returning to her mother's home initially filled her with a sense of belonging, but eventually, that feeling faded, leaving her bewildered. For a while, I thought there was no place on this planet where I belonged, she confessed. Then, with a smile, she added, I met this incredible Black man. To make a long story short, I married him.

She glanced at me with a playful grin and teased, close your mouth before a fly goes down your throat. That's right, Donald is Black. We laughed, nearly rolling on the floor with amusement, as it dawned on me that she had initially left to be around what she called her folk. Just then, our laughter was interrupted by a knock at the front door. Gail jumped up, her excitement bubbling, and exclaimed, They're here. I'll get it.

When she opened the door, there stood Donald, holding Nicole in his arms. He looked over Gail's shoulder and cheerfully greeted Mrs. Florence, saying, Nice to see you again. Then he turned to me and said warmly, you must be Lillian. I've heard so much about you and have been looking forward to this moment.

Gail and I shared a knowing glance, mirrored by Mrs. Florence's radiant smile as she turned to Donald, asking, how have you been these past weeks? Robby then greeted, Hi, Uncle Donald and Nicole. Gail, bubbling with curiosity, asked, someone tell me what's happening.

Mrs. Florence gathered everyone, saying, Alright, everybody, let's sit so I can share the story. Gail, when you first came back, I noticed something was different about you. I patiently waited for you to open up, but since you didn't, I took matters into my own hands and went on a quest to find out what was happening. I promise you; it wasn't easy. I searched for months. When I was ready to give up, I ran into Donald and Nicole at the park, and the pieces started coming together. After a week of conversations, I learned he had searched for you for nearly six months.

When I asked him if his wife's name was Gail, he looked at me intensely and asked, What do you know about my wife, and where is she? I reassured him you were safe and told him where you were. Robby and I visited them often, and Donald expressed a wish to keep it from you until you were ready to make your own decision about returning home. I feared you had forgotten them for a time, but gradually, I saw signs that you were thinking about your husband. A couple of weeks ago, you called Robby' Donald,' and I knew it was just a matter of time until you realized you needed your family back. All the while, I was talking to Lillian about both of you. So, when I finally got through to her, I knew you would be my next success story. Lillian, I hope you can forgive me for keeping this from you, but there was a lesson in it that I believe is truly valuable.

This heartfelt sharing brought us all closer, filling the room with optimism and excitement about Gail and her family's futures.

NINETEEN

A few days after our gathering, everything felt genuinely excellent. There was such a warm and uplifting atmosphere, and my memories of my mother were filled with beautiful moments that brought me joy. Robby and Mrs. Florence, whom he lovingly called Grandma, continued their lovely daily walks together, often inviting Nicole for the adventure. When they returned, Robby always excitedly shared fascinating stories from their outings, many of which sparked our curiosity.

One day, he came bursting through the door with a wild story about an unusual incident at the park. Mrs. Florence had decided to take a little nap on a bench, and when Robby tried to wake her, he panicked because she didn't respond at first. It was frightening for him, and he ran to get help. When he returned with a police officer, they worked together to gently rouse her. Just as it seemed like all hope was lost, her eyes suddenly flew open. Trying to understand the situation, the officer asked if she needed to see a doctor. Mrs. Florence chuckled and reassured everyone that she could hear all the commotion and wanted to wake up but felt unable to do so. Out of sheer curiosity, Robby asked her why she couldn't wake up, and she responded by saying she had been talking to God. This made Robby pause with wonder. When I asked him if she had ever lied to him, he shook his head emphatically. I told him that if she said that's what she was doing, that was her truth. I never questioned her wisdom because she had always felt like a guardian angel to me, and I cherished her insights.

As Robby's first day of school approached, I navigated a swirl of emotions. Part of me was excited, thankful for the time I had spent with Mrs. Florence, even if it hadn't been as much as I had hoped. I wondered how she would handle the news of Robby starting school, especially since they were inseparable. I had an underlying confidence that she understood this was an essential step for him. Yet, the night before school, my mind raced with worry. I tossed and turned, wondering about Mrs. Florence's feelings, if Robby would miss us, or if he might cry and want to return home with me. It was clear that I had been worrying unnecessarily about so many things.

On the morning of his first day, I woke up to find them cozy and ready. Robby looked adorable in his grey khaki pants and white polo shirt, radiating excitement. They stood before me, calm and poised, while I felt like a bundle of nerves. They gently reminded me to hurry so he wouldn't be late for this special milestone. A flood of memories from my own childhood fears rushed into my mind, and I struggled to set those feelings aside. But when I looked into Robby's innocent eyes, I couldn't help but see hope and the possibility of disappointment. I reminded myself that he was unique, about to embark on his own journey. If I shared my anxieties, I knew he might sense them and feel hesitant. So, I took a deep breath, focusing on the exciting path ahead of him, ready to support him with open arms.

As we arrived at the school, we were greeted by the joyful sounds of children swinging, sliding, and dashing around, happily playing together. My little one's face lit up with a radiant smile, and before I knew it, he was off, diving right into the fun with the other kids. I was pleasantly surprised by how effortlessly he adapted as if he had been waiting for this moment all along. Just the night before, I had prepared a heartfelt speech to reassure him about being a big boy at school and to ease any fears he might have had. I couldn't help but feel relief that my words weren't needed and a twinge of disappointment that he seemed so secure without us.

Standing there, I forced back tears as a wave of realization hit me, as it does for many first-time mothers: my baby was growing up. I called out to him, wanting to steal a moment before I left, and he came running over. I wrapped him tightly, pouring out my love and assuring him I'd return before he knew it. Yet, I could tell my words barely registered. He immediately dashed back to join his new friends and continue the adventure.

On our way home, Mrs. Florence caught my eye, and it seemed she understood my heartache at leaving my child with unfamiliar faces. That was tough, wasn't it? But you handled it beautifully, she said, offering me her support. I thought about how I might have looked composed on the outside, yet inside, I was fighting the urge to scoop him up and take him back home with me.

Reflecting on my childhood, it felt like times had truly changed. I remembered kids clinging to their mothers on the first day of school, crying, but now, I watched as parents around me wore expressions of shock and bewilderment. It felt like we were all collectively navigating this transition, waiting for the first tear to fall, some did, and it was a bittersweet moment of solidarity.

I thought I had managed to push my worries aside in the mornings, but the walk home often overwhelmed me with a profound sense of loss. It was as if I had sent him away or someone had whisked him off. This experience opened my eyes to my grandmother's feelings many years ago. One morning, as we walked back, I confided in Mrs. Florence about my fears, that one day, I would arrive to pick him up, and he wouldn't be there. She offered comforting words, reassuring me that these feelings were completely normal and echoed the sentiments of many other parents, so I didn't need to connect my emotions to past family concerns.

Mrs. Florence explained how the start of school signals a new chapter in a child's life. As kids begin to show their independence, it's natural for parents to feel a shift in their relationship. Initially, children rely on us for everything, but as they grow and forge their own identities, it's common for parents to feel a sense of separation. However, she gently reminded me that these feelings will fade over time. While it may seem like I'm losing my baby, it's genuinely a beautiful new beginning for both him and me, filled with growth and discovery ahead.

HerStory

TWENTY

O nce I set aside my fears, I discovered immense joy in the conversations Mrs. Florence and I shared during our walks to and from school. It felt like we discussed everything under the sun. I considered taking the boy to school on weekends to continue our delightful chats. As we headed home one morning, a man stepped before me and cheerfully said hello. I responded quickly with a hi but kept walking. This brief encounter stirred up a long-buried memory of my first meeting with Robert. Every morning, at the same spot he would be waiting for me.

As we continued our walk, I could feel a mix of anxiety and curiosity bubbling within me. Something about that man felt unsettling, prompting me to wonder who he was and where he came from. But as time passed, my anxiety transformed into genuine intrigue, and I began anticipating our encounters. Eventually, he gathered the courage to introduce himself. He told me his name was Patrick, a resident of New Orleans East, and shared that the first time he saw me was while jogging to Joe Brown Park.

I introduced myself, Mrs. Florence, and then Robby. I invited Patrick to join us on our morning walks to school whenever he could. Mrs. Florence enjoyed our conversations immensely, but her mood shifted when he became a regular part of our group. Patrick and I talked non-stop throughout our walks, especially on the way home, while Mrs. Florence had to listen. It wasn't long before she began to walk ahead of us, keeping a good thirty feet in front, and as soon as we got home, she would head straight to her room. At that moment, I didn't pay much attention to her feelings; I was too engrossed in the budding relationship between Patrick and me.

Our conversations were filled with laughter and warmth, and I could feel myself falling in love all over again. I once thought I'd never love anyone the way I loved Robert, and while I insisted to everyone that Patrick was just a friend, deep down inside, I knew he meant so much more.

One day, after dropping Robby off at a classmate's birthday party, I returned home to find Mrs. Florence waiting for me at the door with an upset look. She seemed worried and asked me point-blank what was happening between Patrick and me. I brushed it off, insisting that we were just friends, afraid she might think I was trying to forget about Robert.

Her questions made me reflect on my true feelings. Initially, it was a muddle of emotions, but as I stepped back to gain perspective, everything clicked into place. During our walks to school, Patrick eagerly shared stories about his life. He'd grown up in Pontchartrain Park, had a fantastic school experience, was active on the debate team, and dreamed of becoming a politician. After high school, he attended Southern University of New Orleans, majored in Business Administration, and worked as a consultant. When I asked about his family, he mentioned he hadn't found time for a family or marriage, potentially sensing my reluctance to share my past.

One day, he invited me to dinner. Although I hesitated and initially declined, feeling it was all moving a bit too quickly, he reassured me that it wouldn't be a date, Mrs. Florence and Robby could join us. Excited by the idea, I went home and asked Mrs. Florence if she wanted to join us. To my surprise, she agreed. We all headed to Mandinas for dinner. I ordered a delicious fried seafood platter filled with catfish, shrimp, and oysters, so much food, but I couldn't resist trying it all. Patrick opted for crawfish étouffée, a dish I had never tried before, having only boiled crawfish in my culinary experience. Mrs. Florence and Robby chose smothered potatoes with rice and some chicken. That evening was filled with laughter and connection as we got to know one another in a fresh and enjoyable context.

After that delightful night, Patrick encouraged me to take our relationship more seriously. I explained that I wasn't quite ready for that as I had been alone for so long and wasn't prepared to give up my independence. I was surprised and touched by his reaction; he was incredibly understanding. Perhaps he decided that the best way to win my heart was to build relationships with Mrs. Florence and Robby. He began taking Robby to ball games and inviting Mrs. Florence to various events for seniors in our community, hoping their support would help me see the wonderful man he was and make it easier for me to embrace the possibility of a shared future.

One day, while having a heartfelt conversation with Mrs. Florence, I gathered my courage to share something growing in my heart, I was falling in love with Patrick. I recalled the deep sadness I felt when Mema passed away and the complicated emotions I experienced when Robert returned to town. Despite my attempts to resist my feelings for Robert, my heart had a mind. After Robert's tragic death, I thought I might never love again. Yet I felt those emotions stir within me again, and I was ready to embrace them. My son adored Patrick, and I believed I was also falling for him. Mrs. Florence listened and shared that she had also come to love Patrick, but she gently reminded me to distinguish love from lust.

Reflecting on her wise words, it was essential to seek another perspective, so I reached out to Gail. I poured my heart out, sharing what I was experiencing and Mrs. Florence's insights about Patrick. The idea of making a mistake that could affect my life for years weighed heavily on my mind. Although I recognized Patrick as a genuinely lovely person, I wanted to tread carefully. I didn't want to risk hurting him or having my heart broken again. When Gail asked what my heart felt, I confessed I wanted to shout how my heart and body longed for him. I could hear her laughter bubbling through the phone. Eager for her to meet him, I invited her and Nicole to join us for lunch, hoping it would allow them to connect.

That Saturday, we all gathered for lunch, and when I mentioned to Patrick that Gail and I were sisters, his surprise was precisely what we anticipated. People often reacted with sheer disbelief at this revelation. After getting over that initial shock, I could sense a slight discomfort from Patrick around Gail. The following day, Gail and Nicole came over, and I was curious to hear her thoughts on him. When she asked if I loved Patrick, I replied honestly, saying I believed I did. However, she shared Mrs. Florence's sentiment and pointed out that something about him seemed slightly off. Nevertheless, she encouraged me to follow my heart and do what was best.

As we continued to date, Patrick took me on delightful adventures, like the remarkable museum at City Park. We enjoyed a charming ferry ride across the river and leisurely shopping on Magazine Street. Gradually, he became an integral part of our family, and both Gail and Mrs. Florence felt comfortable with him. One magical evening over dinner, Patrick looked into my eyes and told me he loved me. After more than a year together, I realized I wanted to spend my life with him. Then came the moment I eagerly anticipated, he asked if I would marry him, expressing his readiness to commit. My heart soared with joy, and I wanted to say yes right away, but I paused to consider everyone involved in this life-changing decision.

I couldn't wait to share the exciting news with my family, so when I got home, I called Gail and invited her and Nicole over for dinner. When they arrived, I discreetly took Gail aside to tell her about Patrick's proposal, and I could see her excitement was practically bubbling over. However, I held off on sharing the news with the rest of the family until I spoke with Robby, knowing he would be thrilled for me. After dinner, I took Robby for a stroll. He kept glancing up at me as we walked with a massive smile. I asked him what had him so cheerful, but he just shrugged and looked away. Suddenly, it clicked, Patrick must have asked him for his blessing.

The joy around me was palpable as my family celebrated this new chapter in my life. I reassured them that Patrick was excellent for our family. Mrs. Florence, ever the voice of reason, reminded me, you've been on your own for over seven years, so be certain it's coming from your heart and not just the need for companionship. Patrick is the first man you've allowed into your life on such a level. Before you answer him, please ensure you're feeling love. If you believe it is, you have my full blessing. But if there's any uncertainty, it's important to address that first.

In that moment, I felt both grateful and reassured, ready to embrace whatever the future held. This journey was about love, growth, and the incredible possibilities ahead, and I was eager to see where it would lead us all.

I finally decided to say yes to Patrick, full of excitement and hope for our future together. However, the next day, I received a surprise call from him. He mentioned that he had to head out of town for business and wouldn't return for two weeks to hear my answer. I was a bit taken aback, this was entirely unexpected, as he'd never left town when I'd known him. My mind began to race with all sorts of possibilities. Was he having second thoughts about this big step? I turned to Mrs. Florence, who always had a knack for providing comfort and insight. She wisely suggested that Patrick might just need some time to reflect on the immense responsibility he was considering. After all, jumping into marriage is a significant decision.

Three weeks rolled by without a single word from him, and I started to feel a wave of worry wash over me. What if something unfortunate had happened? This anxious energy spiraled into a cloud of sadness. I found myself fixated on the phone, convinced that if I stared at it long enough, it would ring, and Patrick would be on the line, saying, I love you, I miss you, and I can't wait to come home. I waited by the phone all day, hoping for that magical moment despite everyone urging me to step outside and take a break. I just couldn't risk missing his call.

One afternoon, Robby approached me and said, Mommy, I love you, please love me back. His sweet words pierced through my fog of worry. I looked at him and replied, oh, sweetheart, I love you more than anything. Why would you ever think I didn't? He innocently explained that I was waiting for Patrick to call instead of enjoying time with him. His honesty struck a chord in me, and I knew I needed to change my focus. I suggested we go to Audubon Park together, and he took off to fetch Mrs. Florence. I overheard their delightful conversation where she encouraged him, believing in the power of our bond to lift me out of my slump. It made my heart swell with gratitude.

When Robby and Mrs. Florence reappeared, I felt a surge of warmth. Mrs. Florence, with her vibrant spirit, said, don't be upset with him. I encouraged him, knowing you both needed this. I assured them I had no hard feelings; I loved them dearly. Hand in hand with Robby, we set off for the park, and I felt a wave of relief wash over me.

Oh, what a joyful day we had. It had been a while since I'd spent uninterrupted time with Robby, and I was reminded of the sheer joy he brought into my life. Watching him gleefully dash from the swings to the slides filled my heart with happiness. I noticed him playing an imaginative game of hide and seek on his own, and I couldn't help but smile at his boundless energy.

When we returned home, I was astonished to find Patrick waiting for us. I thought to myself, really? After all this time, I finally decided to step out, and here he is. As I approached him, I resolved to stay composed and simply greet him. But as soon as I got close, a burst of emotions took over, and I slapped him across the face, crying out, get out of my face.

He quickly held my arms and apologized, explaining that he'd needed time to process everything and felt confused about our future.

Confused? What do you mean by needing time? I said, trying to keep my emotions in check. You should have thought things through before proposing. The least you could have done was to check in and let me know you were alright. I sat by that phone day and night, desperately hoping to hear from you. I was so worried about you. I couldn't bear the thought of losing another person I love.

At that moment, I realized the depth of my feelings, for Patrick and the trust and connection we were building. Regardless of the uncertainty, I approached the situation with openness and hope for our future together. After all, every incredible journey begins with a few bumps.

I wrapped my arms around him, feeling a surge of emotion as I exclaimed, please, don't ever leave me again. You are such an important part of my life. As he hugged me tightly, I felt his warmth and commitment radiating through the embrace. With a sparkle in his eyes, he declared, I need you too. Let's get married as soon as we can.

And so, our wedding went off without a hitch, and I was on cloud nine, basking in the joy of our union. However, as life often unfolds, I wasn't fully aware that this bliss would face challenges sooner than expected. The first hurdle emerged when he proposed that Mrs. Florence move into an elderly care home. I stood my ground, explaining that I had promised her a home as long as I was alive. After all, she'd been here even before we met. My dedication to her welfare began to clash with his desires, and the tension in our home escalated. I clarified that this home meant more to me than just a place, it was a sanctuary for Mrs. Florence, and I couldn't just cast that aside. Unfortunately, this revelation didn't sit well with him.

Patrick began to feel possessive, wanting my constant attention. It led to arguments whenever I sought a moment alone. As I reiterated that Mrs. Florence was here to stay, we also found ourselves embroiled in disputes about Gail and Donald.

Patrick and Donald engaged in heated disputes every time they visited, leaving me perplexed. The situation grew worse, and eventually, I stopped inviting them over. Initially, it felt like a relief, but soon, I realized how much I missed Gail. Determined not to let Patrick come between us, we started meeting for lunch, and our conversations often revolved around relationships with our husbands. It was comical to realize how trivial their arguments seemed to both of us.

I confided in Gail about my unease with Patrick, his insistence on putting Mrs. Florence away, his indifference towards Robby, and his overwhelming focus on me. To my surprise, Gail shared that Donald suspected Patrick of harboring prejudices against her and Nicole, which might explain their clashes.

Returning home after an enlightening lunch with Gail, I was confronted by an irate Patrick. He was upset that I had gone out without telling him, which spiraled into a tempest of complaints. Not wanting to engage, I retreated to the bedroom and slammed the door, thankful he didn't follow. That evening, as I shared the discussions I had with Gail to Mrs. Florence, I noticed a profound fatigue behind her eyes that I had overlooked for far too long.

Where's Robby? I asked, and she replied he'd spent the night at a friend's house. A wave of realization washed over me: I had been so consumed by my struggles that I overlooked how my actions affected the people I loved most. I was back in a whirlwind of unhappiness, losing sight of my marriage and my child in the chaos and confusion. My life felt like a train speeding off the rails with no brakes.

One day, as I sat in my room deep in thought, Mrs. Florence approached me and said something that struck a chord. Lillian, I'm really disappointed in you. You have so much potential, yet you keep falling apart when things get tough. My goal was to support you, but it's time for you to tackle these challenges head-on. I thought my presence would help, but I'm tired; I can't bear this weight for you anymore. Her words hung heavily, leaving me with clarity and renewed responsibility.

She made a poignant remark about Patrick's attitude, suggesting that he might harbor biases against different races. Feeling compelled to seek answers, I called Patrick to the room and asked him about his issues with Gail and Donald. As he spoke, I was taken aback to discover he believed interracial marriages were wrong. My heart raced, and I found it hard to comprehend. You're joking, right? Gail is my sister. I exclaimed. His shock response was equally stunning, asking if she had been adopted.

I took a deep breath to center myself. No, we share the same father, I replied calmly.

His voice rose, filled with incredulity. Your father was a white man. Why didn't you tell me this before we got married?

This was my moment to show him the love we had built. I asked, would it have changed how you felt about me? I'm still the same person you fell in love with. He hesitated but then diverted the conversation, claiming I spent more time with Mrs. Florence and Gail than with him.

With compassion, he urged us to consider moving to Baton Rouge for a fresh start, just the three of us. But the thought of leaving everything I knew felt impossible. I lovingly reassured him that I wanted him to be a part of this family, but asking me to abandon the ones I cared for was too much.

At that moment, I could see a path forward. We could bridge these gaps through deeper understanding and appreciation if he genuinely wanted us to be a family. I felt a flicker of hope, knowing that love could help us navigate this storm and find stronger shores.

Things have really taken a positive turn between us lately. One day, he opened the conversation and asked me about my past. Initially, I hesitated to share my story, worried about how he might react to what happened with my mother. But then it hit me that he absolutely deserved to know the whole truth, so I decided to share the entire story, no matter how painful.

When he expressed surprise that I could still talk to Gail after everything, I gently reminded him that she wasn't involved in what happened. His response was eye-opening; he said, I was a better person than he was for being able to do that. It made me think about our values and differences. That moment was crucial, based on the sincerity in his voice and the look on his face, I knew I had a choice to make. If he couldn't accept my past, it was probably best that we part ways, and I told him it was best for him to leave at that moment.

After that heartfelt conversation, I felt energized and ready to take action in my relationships. I called Gail and invited her and her family over for dinner. When everyone arrived, I took a moment to gather everyone's attention. I turned to my son and apologized for not being there for him as much as I should have. I told him how much I loved him and asked him to come over for a hug; that moment felt healing.

Then I turned to Mrs. Florence, who has been such a guiding light. I wanted her to know how grateful I was for her unwavering support through thick and thin. She showed me how to live a more authentic and stress-free life, and I expressed my deep love for her, which meant the world to me.

Next, I reached out to my sister Gail and shared my hope that she could find it in her heart to forgive me. I truly cherished our sisterly bond and wanted her to know how important she was to me. I addressed Donald and Patrick, clarifying that they could accept our family as it is or step away.

In a touching moment, Donald apologized for the struggles we faced and expressed his love for us all. He came over and embraced me, and we shared a moment of reconciliation. However, Patrick reacted differently. He stood up suddenly, his chair clattering to the floor as he went to the bedroom and packed his things, proclaiming that he could see he wasn't wanted.

As he walked out the door, I felt a wave of emotions; I wanted to call out for him to stay, but I realized that would mean compromising my newfound sense of self. I had to let him go. It was a bittersweet moment, I was sad because I loved him, but I was also relieved and empowered to finally take charge of my life.

The following nights felt long and lonely as I reflected on my love for him and my choices for our family. I recognized that my actions were for the greater good and focused on healing. Though I didn't regret what I said, I felt a pang of sadness over his departure. During that time, I leaned into my connections with Robby and Mrs. Florence and rediscovered joy in our walks and park outings.

A few weeks later, I was pleasantly surprised when Patrick resurfaced. He explained that he needed time to process everything I had shared. He reached out to me, love in his eyes, saying he wanted to come home. My heart soared at the thought of reconnecting with him, but I also gently reminded him that my life was now intertwined with Robby, Mrs. Florence, Gail, Nicole, and Donald. It was important to reiterate that his return would mean accepting us as a whole.

As he walked away, my heart swelled with longing, wanting nothing more than to go after him. Deep down, I believed that one day, he would understand the importance of our family bond.

.

TWENTY-ONE

With Patrick moving out, I found myself at a crossroads, contemplating my future and the exciting possibilities that lay ahead. While it's easy to cast a shadow on the emotions of loneliness that might creep in, I knew that wallowing wouldn't be the best use of my time. Instead, I decided to focus on keeping myself engaged and active. I remembered what Robby had once shared about Mrs. Florence and her presence in the park. I committed to learning more about her background and whether she had any relatives nearby. I couldn't recall her ever mentioning family, and it sparked my curiosity. Perhaps she had faced challenges similar to those of Mema, which might explain the connection we shared.

Though I recognized that a conversation with her would have been the most straightforward approach, I couldn't resist unraveling the mystery of her life through my own research. I began chatting with neighbors and was pleasantly surprised to learn that some had known Mrs. Florence for more than fifty years. They spoke of her as if she had always been a part of their lives, a constant and beloved presence. This discovery made me realize that uncovering her story wouldn't be easy, so I ventured back to the old neighborhood where our paths first crossed, hoping someone there could shed light on her past.

When I visited Mrs. Bernadette, I was greeted with warmth. She was delighted to see me, especially since I hadn't visited since Mema's funeral. We reminisced about my mother and her struggle, and she reflected on our first meeting, remembering how joyful I was to see her grandchildren. I also mentioned Robby, describing him as a cheerful little boy. Mrs. Bernadette acknowledged that my upbringing had its challenges but emphasized how proud she was to see the beautiful young woman I've become. However, in the midst of our heartwarming chat, I realized I hadn't gathered the information I had set out for. Just as I was about to leave, I paused and turned back, asking her how long she had known Mrs. Florence. I wasn't surprised when she encouraged me to speak directly with Mrs. Florence and hinted at her being tired, suggesting we continue our conversation another time.

As I walked away from Mrs. Bernadette's house, I felt a gentle wave of discouragement lift my spirits. On my way home, I fortuitously bumped into a woman named Tyra, who was around fifty years old. To my surprise, Tyra shared that she had known Mrs. Florence for her entire life. She recalled that Mrs. Florence had been a dear friend of her mother, who once described her as looking the same now as she did during her childhood. Tyra's mother had even mentioned that Mrs. Florence was friends with her grandmother. I found this intriguing yet difficult to believe. There was something enigmatic about Mrs. Florence that had me contemplating the truth behind these stories.

Could it be that I was going a little mad, considering that everyone I spoke to seemed to have known her all along?

Determined to get to the bottom of this, I decided to bring Tyra's story back to Mrs. Bernadette, thinking she might have some insight into why Tyra would share such an extraordinary claim. The following day, I returned to Mrs. Bernadette's house and recounted my conversation with Tyra. However, she reiterated that if I wanted answers, I should go directly to Mrs. Florence.

Navigating my approach to Mrs. Florence proved tricky. I had this nagging feeling that she was aware of my inquiries; after all, she always seemed to have her finger on the pulse of the neighborhood. As the weeks turned into months, I still hadn't found the courage to have that discussion. Then one bright morning, she confronted me about my curiosity. I don't understand why you haven't come to me, she said, her gaze piercing yet kind. I've always been open with you, and we've shared some significant moments together. What do you need to know?

Feeling a rush of emotions, I replied candidly, I wonder who you are. Robby told me about that incident in the park, which made me think about everything we've been through over the years. You knew about my struggles, the dark thoughts I had and my mother's passing. You were aware of Gail's marriage and her child. So, I'll ask again: who are you?

Mrs. Florence suggested that I shouldn't concern myself with her identity but instead focus on discovering who I truly was. I gazed at her, deeply contemplating her words.

In that moment, I realized I had yet to define that for myself. As she encouraged me to seek the answer within, she promised to share her story when I was ready to understand my own.

This exchange stirred something within me, an exhilarating sense of possibility and self-discovery. I felt more determined than ever to embark on this journey, both to unearth the layers of Mrs. Florence's life and to explore my own identity with newfound vigor.

I decided to set aside my curiosity about her past. At that moment, I never imagined that this choice would linger in my thoughts so frequently, at least once a day. I began to see that, while I had made great strides in my journey, I still had some self-discovery ahead of me. Letting Patrick go was the first step in reclaiming my life, and the more I reflected on it, the more I realized how monumental this achievement would be. With Patrick no longer in the picture, I finally had the chance to focus on myself, and deep down, I knew that one day I would be able to truly stand on my own.

As the summer came to a close, Robby was all set to embark on the adventure of third grade. It was heartwarming to see how much he was starting to resemble his father. There were moments when he would dash around a corner, catching me off guard. Half the time, I found comfort in seeing Robert's spirit live on through Robby, but the other half of me felt a bittersweet ache knowing that Robert would never get to know his son.

During this time, Robby unexpectedly developed a passion for sports. Whenever we visited the park, he eagerly joined in on games, with football quickly becoming his absolute favorite. It amazed me how those older kids welcomed him to play with them, allowing him to dart around, dodging and weaving through the crowd. There were moments when I felt a rush of protective instincts and wanted to jump in, but I knew he needed this freedom to play. Thank goodness he always came back unscathed. Everyone raved about how he might play for a professional team someday. A few weeks before school started, I asked him if he was excited to return, and he answered with an enthusiastic Yes. because he missed his friends. I couldn't help but feel a wave of joy wash over me, knowing he looked forward to school and the friendships there. Reflecting on my own experience, where the first day always brought worries of staring and laughter directed at me, I realized how grateful I was that I chose to have children despite my past fears.

On that special first day of school, I woke up to find both Robby and Mrs. Florence ready and eager. We walked him to school together, and later, we joyfully reunited at the end of the day. Sometimes, Gail and Nicole joined us, with Mrs. Florence and Nicole chatting away, while Gail and I caught up, leaving Robby to play with his friends without a care in the world. He seemed perfectly content with us walking him to school, fully aware that we cherished our little routine. One day, during our stroll, Gail confided in me about her struggles with Donald. He wanted to move closer to his family, over a hundred miles away in Baton Rouge. It had been tough, weeks of discussions, but she realized it was ultimately for the best. As much as I wanted to convince her to stay, knowing I needed her in my life, I understood that she had to make the right choice for her family. I let go of my impulse to wallow in why me thoughts, reminding myself that it wasn't about me, which helped me redirect my focus on what truly mattered. As planned, Gail and her family made their move at the end of the month.

When Patrick left, I dedicated myself to spending more quality time with my family, which included Gail. With her departure, I found myself grappling with how to fill my newfound spare time. I had looked forward to shared experiences together, but it seemed that just when I found my footing, life tossed something unexpected my way. I often wondered why I faced such challenges, sometimes even raising my voice in frustration, God, why me? It was then that I recalled Mema's comforting words: Those are my words, and they will do you no good. Taking a deep breath, I closed my eyes. When I opened them, the tension about Gail's leaving dissipated, and I felt a release.

Every now and then, I would receive a call from Patrick, and I could sense his excitement about Gail's move. Though he tried to mask his joy with a semblance of sympathy for my situation, his happiness was hard to conceal. It occurred to me to invite him back, but I recognized that my motivations stemmed from loneliness rather than genuine desire for reconciliation. I knew that wasn't the right reason to want him back. Instead, I decided to channel all my energy into Robby. My first step? Signing him up for little league. I wasn't entirely sure if baseball would be his thing, but as soon as I mentioned it, he leaped to his feet, exclaiming, Baseball. I love baseball. Thank you, Mom, I love you. It was a heartwarming moment. I suggested we head to the park for practice since the season was still a couple of months away, and I made it clear that if he wanted to play ball, he needed to keep up the good work in school.

It felt good to embrace this new chapter with Robby, and I couldn't wait to see where this journey would take us both.

Every evening, after a long day, Robby would head straight into his room to tackle his homework, and then we would make our way to the park for some quality time together. It was always a joy to watch the vibrant scene unfold around us, with children playing baseball and laughing. One day, when Robby approached a group of kids to see if he could join their game, they told him he could play, if he could find someone else to join him. That's when I noticed Anthony, a little boy sitting alone on a bench, who seemed a bit lonely. I encouraged Robby to invite him to play. Anthony was much smaller than Robby, almost too small to be on the field, but the kids welcomed him with open arms. That moment sparked a beautiful friendship, and as I watched them play, my heart swelled with joy at their undeniable excitement.

After their first practice, Robby excitedly told Mrs. Florence that he would be playing baseball on a real team. With a knowing smile, she said, I know you're going to be a little Jackie Robinson. It struck me how she seemed to have an instinct for what was to come, which gave me pause. Usually, I wouldn't think much of someone making such predictions, but Mrs. Florence had an extraordinary insight that intrigued me. Curiously, I asked her what the future held for me, and she simply advised me to be patient; I would understand in time. I chuckled softly at her wisdom as I headed into the kitchen to prepare dinner.

After dinner, Robby was eager to hit the hay; he could hardly wait for another exciting day. The next morning, after dropping him off at school, I decided to surprise him. I picked up a baseball, a bat, and two gloves, hoping to join him in his practices. When he got home and saw the new gear, his reaction lit up the room: Oh man, are those for me? Thank you, can we practice after my homework? His enthusiasm was contagious, and he dashed off to complete his assignments, barely able to contain his excitement.

As I waited for him, I noticed Mrs. Florence gazing out of the window, looking sorrowful. When she told me she felt like there was nothing she could do, I felt a pang of concern but didn't think much of it at the time. Later, however, she called me into her room and shared that she had to leave. I was bewildered and asked her to explain why. I didn't want to accept her departure and ended up raising my voice, pleading with her to talk to me. But despite my efforts, she simply walked away, leaving me feeling helpless and foolish.

The following morning, as she packed her belongings, uncertainty washed over me. I never imagined she wouldn't be part of our lives. The thought was deeply unsettling; I always believed she would be by my side, an unwavering support. Yet amidst this turmoil, I knew I had to focus on Robby and help him cope with her leaving.

Once we found some time to talk, we both opened up about our feelings. Robby shared that, deep down, he felt she wouldn't abandon us if she believed we couldn't handle things on our own. His words brought a wave of comfort and assurance, and I was reminded of the strength we had as a family. In the days that followed, I dedicated myself to practicing baseball with him. Initially, our practices were daily events filled with laughter and learning, but once the baseball season kicked off, we shifted to three times a week. I became known as the enthusiastic parent everyone loved, and our home turned into the favorite hangout spot for all the kids after the games.

As the baseball season wrapped up, I excitedly signed Robby up for football, a sport that I have always cherished. To my surprise, he was just as enthusiastic about it. However, just two weeks before the season was set to begin, his coach, a dedicated captain in the U.S. Air Force, received orders for reassignment overseas. The search for a replacement was on, but no one was available, which left the possibility of withdrawal from the league looming overhead. I couldn't let that happen, so I decided it was time to step up and fill the gap. When I asked Robby what he thought of me coaching the team, his face lit up as he exclaimed, That's a great idea.

I soon found myself embracing the role of coach with passion and dedication. My coaching philosophy was simple: every child should have the opportunity to participate, and regardless of the outcome of a match, we would celebrate together. Whether we won or lost, I believed the most important part was ensuring everyone had fun, and that approach forged a bond among the team that was truly special. Together, we created a supportive, joyful environment that made me proud to be a part of their journey.

Mrs. Florence had been gone for over a year, and periodically I would get a letter from her but was not able to write back because there was never a return address. Patrick began spending time with us, and we became best friends because I was able to be more honest with him and him with me. Through our conversations we learned a lot about each other, but I still didn't know why he disliked Gail but knew it couldn't be just because of her race. I felt that if we could get to the crux of this problem, we could make a new beginning. Then one day he was talking about his past and I noticed that his eyes were tearing, he said, at the age of sixteen, my world was turned upside down by an unexpected and devastating betrayal. A simple interaction spiraled into a nightmarish ordeal, as racial bias maliciously depicted me as a criminal, a young black teenager falsely accused by a white girl who claimed I had wronged her. Despite the unwavering support of my loving family, who stood by me through the darkest days, the legal system let us down in unimaginable ways.

My life took a shocking turn as I spent two harrowing years in juvenile hall, confined by the walls of a system that seemed indifferent to truth. Those painful years were rife with anger and deep frustration, fueled not just against those who had betrayed me but aimed squarely at the larger societal injustices that allowed such a falsehood to thrive unchecked. The sense of betrayal cut deeply, revealing the cracks in a system that was supposed to protect the innocent.

After I left here, with the guidance of dedicated counseling, I embarked on an incredible journey of growth, transforming my anger into a powerful force for compassion. I gained valuable insights into the complexities of my situation, which empowered me to forgive, not just myself for building walls around my emotions, but also those who were part of my struggles. My heart is now brimming with a sincere desire to heal and reconnect with my family.

We recognized the importance of revitalizing our marriage, and despite the challenges we faced, I could truly feel the spark returning between us. He once again became the wonderful man I fell in love with. It had been two long years since I last saw Gail and her family, so when Patrick suggested a visit, I was overjoyed. We spent two amazing weeks together, filled with laughter and joy, and I found myself wishing for even more time. This experience has filled me with optimism for the future, and I can't wait to create more beautiful memories together.

Upon our return, we were greeted by the delightful presence of Mrs. Florence. The moment Robby spotted her, he burst with excitement, shouting, Grandma's back. Grandma's back. He dashed over, leaping into her arms with uncontained glee, showering her with the biggest, sloppiest kisses you could imagine. The love I felt in that moment brought tears of joy to my eyes. I realized how much I had missed her and how immensely happy I was to have her back in our lives.

We gathered around to catch up, and she immediately asked me if I knew who I was. With a big grin, I confidently replied, yes, I do. Mrs. Florence had made a conscious decision to step away because she believed I needed to take charge of my life. She felt that as long as she was around, I might not recognize my own strength. It was bittersweet for her to leave, but she was filled with hope, knowing that I was ready to embrace a more fulfilling life.

That evening turned into a beautiful reunion as she and I stayed up talking late into the night, reliving the magic of our past conversations. She was eager to hear everything that had happened while she was away. Even as I shared our stories, I sensed she might already know them all. Then, echoing back to a question from our past, I asked her, who are you? She gazed into my eyes and replied, Trust your inner feelings; you already know. That made me reflect deeply, and it dawned on me that her identity was less important than the profound impact she had on my life. She was truly an extraordinary woman, and I felt a warm glow of gratitude for her presence.

As a few days passed, I began to notice something enchanting about her. It was as if an inspiring aura surrounded her. I was curious about where she had been and what experiences had shaped her, but I sensed that she would share when she was ready. After all, what mattered most to me was knowing how long she would be with us.

When I finally mustered the courage to ask about her stay, a peaceful silence enveloped the room. Her eyes seemed to delve deep into my heart, searching for unspoken words. Then she expressed what I had hoped she would say: I'm home to stay. At that moment, a surge of happiness filled me, those words were truly music to my ears. I wrapped my arms around her in a heartfelt hug, and when I looked into her eyes again, I found her beaming with joy too.

As we exchanged smiles, an intriguing thought crossed my mind, one I could tell she sensed. She responded with a knowing smile and said, No, I'm the direct result of it. Her words intrigued me, and I asked, The direct result of what? She replied, The direct result of your mother's childhood. I was taken aback and in amazement, I asked how she could know I was going to ask that question. She simply smiled and said it was just a hunch.

This beautifully layered moment reminded me of the intricate connections we share and how our histories shape us. The journey ahead seemed brighter than ever, filled with new beginnings and cherished relationships.

HerStory

TWENTY-TWO

With Patrick back in the picture, he and Robby quickly formed a wonderful bond, often spending delightful afternoons at the park. Sometimes, the adventures included Anthony and his little brother, Ronald, turning their outings into mini-escapades that echoed with laughter and joy. Their friendship blossomed almost overnight, which stirred up a twinge of jealousy in me, as if my precious moments with Robby were slipping away. It seemed that Robby had found his confidant in Patrick, and I was left feeling a little sidelined.

One day, as I strolled through the kitchen, I overheard something that left me shocked and confused: Robby calling Patrick Daddy. I immediately rushed into the living room, my heart racing. What did you just call him? I exclaimed, standing right in front of Robby, who looked taken aback, surprised by my outburst. His big, innocent eyes blinked at me in bewilderment as he asked, Called who, Mommy?

Pointing emphatically at Patrick, I couldn't contain my surge of emotion. That's who. Don't play with me boy, did you really call him Daddy? When Robby nodded, my heart sank, and I felt a wave of anger wash over me. He is not your father. Your father passed away in that tragic car accident. Please remember that, and don't ever call him daddy again, do you understand? Seeing him break down into tears was gut-wrenching. No, Mommy, I don't understand, he sobbed, his confusion cutting deeper than I anticipated.

Seeing my son in distress struck me hard. I took a deep breath, placed my hands gently on his shoulders, and looked him square in the eyes. In that moment, I saw a reflection of fear, fear that reminded me of my own childhood when Mema would erupt in anger. When I released my grip, he dashed to Patrick and jumped into his arms like he was escaping from a storm. I dropped to my knees, tears flowing freely, and glanced up at Patrick, searching for comfort but only finding his own deep sorrow in his eyes. Robby wouldn't even look in my direction, and it hit me then, something within me had unleashed a monster from my past. Consumed by regret, I crawled back to my room and wept until sleep took over me. Patrick didn't join me that night, and honestly, I couldn't blame him; I wouldn't have wanted to be around me either.

Throughout our marriage, I had always hoped for a strong father-son bond to grow between Patrick and Robby. Yet there I was, feeling lost and disheartened.

The next morning, I made my way to the kitchen, where Mrs. Florence was savoring her coffee. As I walked by, I sensed a hint of disappointment in her presence, but more importantly, I noticed her understanding. She didn't push me to talk about the tension of the previous day, which encouraged me to retreat to my own space. I desperately wanted to confide in her, but I remembered her words about being less dependent on her. I knew I needed to face my emotions alone, so I took the next couple of days to reflect on what had transpired.

This wasn't the first time Robby called Patrick daddy, yet this instance hit me like a ton of bricks. I pondered whether my frustration stemmed purely from feeling like Patrick had taken my son away from me, but that seemed too simplistic. There was something deeper, and grappling with that understanding left me feeling very low. Each attempt to dissect my feelings took me back to Robert and the pure love we shared, and how I had envisioned a future together. But I realized now that those dreams needed to shift; I had to start dreaming a new dream with Patrick.

I spent three days in solitude, wrestling with my emotions until I could finally articulate the source of my anger. Once clarity washed over me, I gathered the courage to initiate a family meeting. In the living room, I could feel the anticipation in the air as they looked to me to speak. I approached Mrs. Florence, silently asking if she understood what was coming; her unwavering support enveloped me.

Then, I turned to Robby, ready to open my heart. Son, I'm so sorry for what I said. I love you dearly, and I can't express how much I regret upsetting you. And Patrick, I hope you can find it in your heart to forgive me as well. Lately, I've felt distanced from both of you, and it sparks memories of my own childhood when I often felt excluded.

When I heard Robby call you daddy, it shook me to my core because it felt like I was losing the last connection I had to Robert. In my heart, I've always viewed Robby as Robert's son. But I genuinely celebrate the bond you two are forming, and I sincerely hope we can move forward together as a family. Can you both find it in your hearts to forgive me?

There was a silence filled with emotion; Patrick seemed genuinely puzzled about why I was feeling upset.

While I was sitting in my room, reflecting on my feelings, I realized that I hadn't fully accepted Patrick as my husband. It wasn't that I didn't love him; rather, somewhere along the way, I convinced myself that no other man could fill the void Robert left behind. I had kept Robert close in my heart to help cope with the pain, but now I understood, I truly loved Patrick.

As I turned to leave, our eyes connected, and I felt the familiar warmth of Mrs. Florence's presence envelop me once more. Her gaze resonated with the feeling that something monumental was about to unfold. I could almost hear her thoughts, even without her having to say a word. It was as if she understood the depths of my heart and the journey I was on. With a gentle smile, I sensed her saying, you handled that beautifully, and I'm so proud of you.

Feeling grateful, I turned to exit the room. Just then, Mrs. Florence called out, you know, you only needed to say it once; I heard you loud and clear the first time. I almost replied but realized that our connection ran deeper than words. Instead, I smiled at her and made my way to my room. Moments later, Patrick entered and settled beside me on the bed.

I get where you're coming from, he began, his voice steady and sincere, but I need you to know that I'm not trying to replace Robert. I always knew that you would carry him in your heart. I just wish you wouldn't compare us; that feels impossible for me, and honestly, it hurts. I love you deeply and want to spend my life with you, but I need to feel like I'm your priority, too.

He stepped closer and kissed me, and in that moment, all the love I had kept locked away surged forward. I realized he was my one true partner, and my heart was full. That night, Patrick and I connected on a profound level, and in the weeks that followed, he was the only one on my mind.

I tried to reach out to Mrs. Florence again, but she didn't respond. Doubt crept in as I questioned if our earlier exchange was just a figment of my imagination. After a while, I discovered that I was pregnant. A wave of anxiety washed over me as I thought of telling Patrick, fearful memories of losing Robert flooded my mind. I knew I would need to share the news soon, but I wanted to wait for the right moment. As my belly grew and morning sickness hit, I sometimes felt so unwell that I wished I could cry out for help. Eventually, I decided it was best to visit the doctor, and once he confirmed I was indeed expecting, I knew it was time to take action.

I called for another family meeting. As I approached Mrs. Florence, I looked into her eyes and sensed, for the first time, that she was unaware of what I was about to reveal. When I shared my pregnancy announcement, her surprise was utterly genuine, and I could see a glow of grandmotherly joy lighting up her face. In a burst of excitement, Patrick jumped to his feet, rushed to me, and placed his hand on my stomach, exclaiming, It's a boy.

In that moment, panic surged through me. No. I can't go through that again. I can't bear to lose you, Patrick. Please, don't leave me. I shouted, recalling how Robert had always known we were having a boy and how that knowledge had led to such heartache. I hurried over to Mrs. Florence, resting my head on her shoulder, and whispered, I'm not sure I have the strength to face this again. Please, tell me it will be okay.

With all the love and wisdom, I felt her reassurance surrounding me, and in that moment, I realized I wasn't alone on this journey. There was hope and possibility, and together, we would find a way forward.

TWENTY-THREE

Every morning when Patrick headed off to work, a wave of anxiety washed over me, making me feel as if it might be the last time I'd see him. It was a heavy thought, and one day, I decided to share my feelings with him. To my surprise and relief, he began calling me several times a day, just to reassure me that he was safe and that he loved me.

One sunny afternoon, Mrs. Florence and I found ourselves by the window, admiring the spirited football game unfolding outside. Robby was having a blast playing with his friends Anthony, Ronald, and their new buddy Paul. Watching them, I couldn't help but smile; they were all incredibly talented and fiercely competitive. After each game, they would get into playful debates about imaginary rules. Their animated discussions sometimes reached a volume that made us worry they might come to blows, but they were simply energetic kids letting off steam.

At that moment, I suddenly began to question my earlier belief that my connection with Mrs. Florence was merely a figment of my imagination, just a fanciful notion. I chose to challenge that idea yet again. In a moment of earnest intent, I mentally called out her name as loudly as I could. To my delight, she sprang to her feet, and I felt a comforting calm wash over my mind. Are you crazy? Do you think I'm deaf? she exclaimed, and I couldn't help but feel a rush of relief. I apologized for startling her and explained my uncertainty about our connection and why I hadn't heard back from her before. She explained that when Patrick and I sealed our bond, she had to withdraw to allow the process to unfold.

She expressed confusion about my fears of losing Patrick, pointing out that Robert and Patrick were two distinct individuals. Then she shared some profound insights. Let me explain something to you, she said warmly, everyone is on this planet for a reason, each with a unique purpose. Her words resonated deeply with me, prompting thoughts of Mema and her struggles. I wondered what her purpose was and why she had to face so much pain.

Mrs. Florence continued with kindness; Mema didn't have to suffer; she had choices. Even though some of her decisions may not have been right for her, she often didn't fully embrace her ability to choose. Many of her choices were conscious, but the most damaging ones were made on autopilot. Her upbringing clouded her perspective, making her feel trapped in a cycle of sadness. She often wanted to change her reality, yet she didn't know how. I tried to remind her that she could take charge of her life and do things differently, but she seemed unable or unwilling to see the possibilities. To her, the sadness felt normal. Even in moments of joy, she didn't grasp that life could offer so much more. When your mother returned to the house to reconnect with John, the chance for a relationship didn't present itself immediately, but had she been patient, she might have found happiness. Life often presents us with choices at critical junctures.

I couldn't help but wonder if this philosophy applied to Patrick and me as well.

Every significant decision indeed arises from a fork in the road. In your situation with Patrick, things reached a breaking point, prompting you to explore a different path. Yet somewhere along the way, you realized that life with him still held value, and you believed that with some commitment, improvements could be made. When you recognized your desire to be together again, you began to envision a new future. It's important to note that you can't change your trajectory until that fork reappears; reconciliation doesn't mean that things immediately revert to how they once were. Instead, it opens the door to a fresh path. Had you continued on your previous course, your life would undoubtedly look different today. Now that you and Patrick are moving forward together, remember that you hold the reins to your destiny.

Curious about her abilities, I asked Mrs. Florence if she could read anyone's thoughts. She replied with a warm smile, no, not everyone. My thoughts drifted to Robert and I asked, did you know he was going to die?

With a somber expression, she replied, I can't predict these things. If I can't foresee it, I can't intervene. Life can bring unpredictable heartbreak. I have faced many tragedies, and that moment was one of the hardest in my life.

Even amid uncertainty, her confidence and wisdom shine through, reminding me that while we can't always control our circumstances, we can always choose how we respond to them. The journey of life may be unpredictable, but it is filled with opportunities for growth, hope, and connection. I'm grateful for the lessons and love that surround me as I navigate this path.

With a heavy heart, she headed to her room, but it wasn't long before her wonderful son Robby bounded in with excitement. Mommy, I can't wait for my little brother to arrive. he exclaimed; his enthusiasm infectious. When he's here, I'll teach him all the fun things I know. We'll play baseball and football together, and I'll even help him learn how to read.

I smiled, letting him know it would be a little while before his brother was big enough to join in on those games. Robby chuckled back at me, eyes sparkling with a mix of innocence and wisdom. I know, Mommy. I mean when he's older. He placed his hand on my belly, eager to feel the baby stir. Each time there was a lively kick, his surprise and delight shone brightly in those big, beautiful brown eyes.

As I approached the end of my eighth month of pregnancy, I noticed my little one becoming quite the energetic acrobat. There were days when it felt like he was performing somersaults, making it a challenge just to get around. If I wanted to take a break and rest, it turned into a little adventure of carefully sneaking up on a chair to slide down into it, a feat only I seemed to appreciate.

However, Robby began to grow a bit frustrated with the situation, noticing how my discomfort seemed to overshadow my joy. The happy moments of him feeling my stomach transformed into a distant memory as the pain sometimes would make me cry out. Whenever that happened, his instinct kicked in, and he'd rush over to wrap his little arms around my shoulders to comfort me, being mindful to keep his distance from my belly, sensing the turmoil within.

I missed the comfort of my connection with Mrs. Florence during this time, it was like a missing piece of a puzzle. If we were in tune, she could probably feel my discomfort, and I wouldn't wish that on anyone. Yet, I missed the tranquility our bond brought me. Communicating with her became a bit of a challenge, often leading to misunderstandings. Our mental connection had allowed us to express our true thoughts and feelings without the mix-ups that can happen in spoken words. It made me appreciate, even more, the depth of our relationship and the ease it brought to our conversations. Despite the challenges, I remained optimistic about the joy the new addition would bring to our family and looked forward to those shared moments of laughter and love.

About two weeks before my due date, there was a bit of an unexpected twist in our journey. My doctor decided it was time for some tests, and I found myself at Charity Hospital for a sonogram to check the position of the baby. To my amazement, I learned I was having twins. One little one was cleverly tucked away at the top of my belly, which explained the discomfort I had been feeling when trying to find a comfortable position. With this exciting revelation, the doctors made the decision to induce labor, which meant I didn't have a moment to share the wonderful news with all my loved ones.

As they prepared to wheel me into the delivery room, I quickly asked a nurse to call my husband. I requested that she let him know about the doctors' decision and advised her to tell him to drive safely, oh, and please, don't mention anything about the twins just yet. However, in the bustle of the moment, things got a bit chaotic for the nurse. She was able to contact Mrs. Florence instead, asking her to spread the word to the family, so Patrick didn't receive my message after all.

By the time Patrick made it to the hospital, I had already welcomed our two beautiful baby boys into the world. We had toyed with names during my pregnancy, if we had a girl, she would be named Audrey, and if it was a boy, Roland was the chosen name. Funny enough, the only name that rhymed with Roland was Noland, and it turned out to be the perfect fit for our second son. When the nurse informed me that Patrick had arrived, he went straight to the nursery to catch a glimpse of our little ones.

A nurse told me that as the nurse brought one of our boys to the window, she couldn't help but smile at the image of Patrick standing there with a proud grin lighting up his face. But then, another nurse approached bearing our second baby. She said she would never forget the look on his face as confusion started to wash over him. In an instant, he felt a wave of wooziness and, bless his heart, he collapsed right there. It dawned on him that he was now the proud father of not one, but two precious baby boys.

I'm not sure how pleased the twins were at that moment, but I knew Patrick would soon redeem himself as a fantastic dad.

When Patrick got to my room, he looked at me and shouted, Baby, baby. We had twins. Did you know? I couldn't help but reply with a laugh, no, honey, we have three boys. His eyes widened with complete disbelief for a split second, but he quickly responded, you know what I mean. With only one name in mind, he was eager to discuss what we should name the twins. I reminded him of our decision to name one son Roland. Then a thought struck me, there was a book I'd read by Noland Hall about overcoming challenges and attaining success, which had truly inspired me. The name felt like a wonderful choice for our son. When I shared my thoughts with Patrick, he loved it instantly: Roland and Noland, the perfect names for our little angels.

As I continued to bask in the joy of our new family, I asked about Robby and Mrs. Florence. He reassured me that he wanted to make sure everything was alright before picking them up, but he took a moment to give me a sweet kiss on the forehead before he left. Our adventure was just beginning, and I couldn't wait to share it all with our growing family.

After he left the room, a friendly nurse came in and offered me something soothing that made me feel a bit drowsy. As I began to drift off, I distinctly felt the warmth of Mrs. Florence's presence enveloping me. The final thought I had before falling deeply asleep was of the pure joy she radiated upon realizing that I had twins.

Then, I gradually drifted into a slumber filled with warmth, only to be stirred by the gentle sounds of the most cherished people in my life surrounding me. Groggy and still in that blissful haze, I wondered if I was dreaming. Just then, I heard a reassuring voice say, no, you're not dreaming. A smile crept across my face at the thought of Mrs. Florence nearby, and I tried so hard to open my eyes, yet they felt too heavy.

Relax, Mrs. Florence's comforting voice urged me gently. Don't strain yourself; we'll be right here when you wake up. As she began to hum my favorite song, I felt myself surrendering to the drowsiness, slipping back into a peaceful slumber.

At some point, the sweet sounds of chatter stirred me again, and this time, I managed to open my eyes. The sight before me filled my heart with joy: Robby, Patrick, Mrs. Florence, Gail, Nicole, and Donald were all there, beaming with happiness. Donald looked at me, shaking his head with a smirk, we surely have our hands full, don't we.

Gail added that they immediately dropped everything to rush home once they heard I had the baby. As my vision adjusted, I noticed Nicole standing behind Donald. Curious about the young lady beside him, I asked, who is that standing behind you? She stepped forward with a big smile and said, It's me, Nicole, Aunt Lil. My heart swelled in disbelief. I exclaimed, oh my goodness, is that really you? How much you've grown. Where did the time go?

As I took in the scene, I realized Robby was no longer present. I turned to Patrick, instinctively asking about him.

Patrick looked around and opened the door, calling out, why are you crying? Come in here; your mother wants to see you. But to my surprise, he hesitated.

Wishing to have a moment alone with Robby, I kindly asked everyone to step out for a bit. When he finally entered the room, his tears flowed even harder, pulling at my heartstrings. I knew Robby well enough to understand he didn't cry without a reason; something in him was deeply upset. I gently called him over, only for him to stop mid-stride, saying, no, mommy, I don't want to.

My heart ached as I inquired why. He simply replied, you're my mommy, and I don't want those babies. Once they come home, you won't have time for me anymore. Can we just leave them here, mommy? Please?

Come here, my sweet boy. You know I will always have time for you. You're my firstborn, which makes you incredibly special to me. I was hoping you would help me take care of the twins.

Though I hoped my words would ease his worries, I could see that something deeper was troubling him. As he walked closer, he remarked, Mommy, you have beautiful hair. He then reached out to touch my hair, running his fingers through the strands. I wish I had hair like yours.

His innocent words touched me deeply, especially since I remembered anxiously asking about his own hair color when he was born, relieved he didn't resemble mine. As I relished this sweet moment, a wave of panic washed over me. I hadn't yet seen my babies.

With urgency, I called out, Nurse. Nurse. Where are my babies? I want to see them now. I attempted to sit up, but weakness held me down. I called out once more, please. I need to see my babies. Just then, Patrick rushed back into the room, his voice filled with concern, he looked at Robby What's wrong? Are you okay? What did you do to her?

In a burst of emotion, I shouted, don't yell at my baby. Please, never yell at him again. It was all a blur from that moment, the last thing I heard being the nurse kindly asking everyone to leave the room for a moment.

The next day, I floated in and out of consciousness, my blood pressure and heart rate fluctuating dangerously. The medical team monitored me closely as they sought to understand why my vital signs were so erratic before I could be discharged. Upon awakening, I found a nurse smiling gently beside me.

Hi there, do you remember me? she asked, her face oddly familiar. I couldn't pinpoint where I'd met her before, but she began to piece it together for me. I remember you from your first child. I often wondered how you and the little boy turned out. I was the nurse who sat by your side ten years ago when you were worried about yourself and your child after losing your husband.

It felt heartwarming to reconnect in such a meaningful way. It was a bittersweet reminder of the journey I had traveled, but also a beacon of hope that filled me with gratitude and excitement for what was to come.

Absolutely, I remember you. You reassured me that everything would turn out just fine, and you were right, it truly has. When she asked me about my problem, I struggled to recall the reason I ended up in the hospital. Don't you remember having your babies? She gently prompted, I glanced down at my stomach, and in that moment, I was bewildered; it seemed like my baby was still with me. I hesitantly asked, are you sure I already had my baby? Her warm smile radiated comfort as she assured me, you've had twins, two wonderful boys. They will be with you soon, I promise.

As I processed this, memories began to resurface. I felt an overwhelming desire to know where my son was. The nurse kindly explained that he was probably home, tucked in bed since it was the dead of night. I was momentarily anxious that I had scared him, but she reassured me that he was only a little upset when he left. She planned to reach out to Patrick in the morning, so they could be here bright and early to greet me when I woke up. I asked to see my babies, but she advised me to rest and gather my strength for the new day. Just before leaving, she playfully remarked, we really need to stop running into each other like this, which made me smile as I drifted off to sleep.

When I finally opened my eyes again, Robby was standing beside me. He looked sincere and remorseful, saying he was sorry and promising that he would never upset me like that again. Please, don't be angry, he pleaded. I smiled back, reassuring him, I could never be mad at him. I started to explain why, but the look on his face showed he was curious. I told him, it's because I love you, and it wasn't your fault.

Just then, the nurse brought in the twins. I felt a rush of hesitation as I prepared to look at them, but I noticed Robby staring at me with concern. I slowly looked down at my baby boys and felt a pang of fear; they had white hair. In that instant, my heart sank, knowing the challenges that may lie ahead for them. Yet, as Robby gently placed one of them in my arms, something magical happened. The moment our eyes met; all my worries melted away. He placed the other baby in my other arm, grinning as he said, See, Mommy, they have beautiful hair just like you. I couldn't help but respond, you're right, they do indeed have beautiful hair.

I curiously asked, why were you crying the last time we spoke? He replied, I was scared you would love them more because they looked like you. I told him with all sincerity, I have enough love to share with all of you equally. As he enveloped me in a big hug, I felt his sigh of relief, and I knew in that moment that he understood my love was boundless. I asked where his father was, and he said everyone was waiting downstairs, respecting my wish to see him alone first. Smiling, I encouraged him to go fetch everyone now that I had reassured myself about him.

As he left the room, I reflected on the delightful quirks of life. I hadn't realized how much he cared about my hair, and the knowing that he loves it brought a newfound sense of joy. From this day forward, I'm determined to instill in my sons the importance of loving themselves entirely. I'll teach them that some will appreciate them for who they are, while others may not; they should choose their friends wisely. I've learned this from my own insecurities, I almost missed out on meeting Robert because of them.

I heard the excited footsteps of family approaching down the hallway. When they entered, I gleefully proclaimed, Aren't they beautiful? This is Roland, and this is Noland. I asked Robby if he'd like to hold one of his new brothers. I carefully placed Roland in his arms, and with pure enthusiasm, he introduced himself, hi, I'm your big brother, Robby, and I promise to always protect you and your brother.

Gail and her family stayed with us for two wonderful weeks. Before they left, Robby proudly called for a family meeting. Now that I'm a big brother, I'd like everyone to start calling me by my real name: Robert. Robby is a baby name, and I'm no longer a baby, just look at me. He pointed proudly toward the sleeping twins. In that instant, I couldn't contain my pride; I could see my little boy blossoming into a responsible big brother. From that moment on, everyone affectionately used the name Robert, and it filled my heart with happiness to see him stepping into this new role with such confidence.

HerStory

TWENTY-FOUR

The arrival of the twins certainly turned our lives upside down. Their unexpected entrance brought a delightful whirlwind of energy into our home. However, along with those bouncing baby boys came new challenges we hadn't anticipated. Life became a beautiful chaos, leaving all of us a little overwhelmed but endlessly entertained. At first, I didn't quite notice the subtle shift in Robert. But when he brought home a report card that showed some unexpected grades, I felt a wave of concern wash over me. This was so unlike him; he had always excelled in school.

I tried reaching out to him, hoping to understand what was troubling him, but it felt like he was building walls between us. I couldn't believe that the twins could be the source of his struggle; after all, he adored them and took it upon himself to walk them in their stroller every weekend, beaming with pride and glowing under the attention he received from passersby, especially girls his age. It was evident he cherished every moment with them.

One day, bathed in the unusual calmness of our home, I realized how truly peaceful it could be without the sounds of baby babbles and giggles for just a moment. It felt refreshing. In that serene silence, Mrs. Florence called out to me, nudging me to have an earnest conversation with Robert because she sensed he was in need of that connection. She insisted that today was the day to break through. Communication is key, she reminded me, and I nodded, grateful for her wise perspective.

I shared my frustration that Robert hadn't been opening up to me. Sitting nearby was Patrick, so I turned to him for insight. I asked if he had noticed anything different in Robert. When he hesitated to answer, my determination to uncover the truth intensified. Just as I felt my expression shift toward exasperation, Mrs. Florence broke the tension with humor, saying, Lillian, make sure you're mentally connecting with him. Ask again, but this time, really open up your heart. We both laughed, and soon enough, Patrick was caught in our moment of lightness, glancing curiously between us. I quickly composed myself and asked him to keep an eye on the twins while I took Robert for a chat.

When Robert walked through the door, I was ready. I handed the twins over to Patrick and Mrs. Florence and invited Robert for a stroll to Joe Brown Park to have a heart-to-heart. To my relief, he agreed. As we walked, I anxiously opened the door to our conversation by asking if he was feeling angry with me. His response was a negative shake of his head. I hesitated before asking if he felt upset with Patrick. Suddenly, tears welled in his eyes, and in that moment, my heart sank, I knew we had stumbled onto something significant.

It dawned on me that he was grappling with feelings tied to Patrick that had likely been amplified by the presence of the twins. As we sat in the park, Robert finally let out what had been weighing on him: They are his children, and I'm just a stepchild. His words hit hard, and as he spoke through his tears, I could see the depth of his hurt. He had been feeling neglected, desperate for connection.

When we returned home, I was torn between the urge to shield my children from hurt and my responsibility to address it. I called Patrick into our room and laid bare everything that Robert had shared. I expressed how vital it was that we pay attention not only to the twins but to all our boys. I told him, I love every one of my children equally, and I want them to know it. I don't know what's happening between you and Robert, but it needs to change. I refuse to see any of my children suffer, and I would rather navigate this journey alone than let that happen. As I looked into Patrick's eyes, I urged him to remember who Robert was to him.

Mrs. Florence, still within earshot, asked if I was okay after the confrontation. I nodded but wondered if I had been too hard on Patrick. She reassured me that no, it was important he understood how essential it was for him to connect with all his sons, including Robert.

Later, Patrick took the time to visit Robert in his room. After a meaningful conversation, they unearthed something significant: Robert missed that routine of walking to school together, a cherished ritual that had disappeared since the twins arrived. Patrick vowed to walk with him until he felt comfortable venturing out on his own.

The next morning, Robert came down for breakfast radiating happiness, I knew he and Patrick had taken a big step toward healing their relationship. Patrick made an intentional effort to spend extra time with Robert, whether on walks, outings, or cozy afternoons on the couch watching sports. What stood out was that Robert simply craved those moments of one-on-one connection with his dad.

I'm filled with admiration for Patrick's commitment, recognizing how crucial it is for our family to maintain strong bonds. Together, we're learning and growing, navigating the delicate balance of raising three energetic boys while ensuring each feels cherished and supported. It's a journey full of highs and lows, but I am confident that with open communication and love, we will thrive as a family, ready to embrace all the joyful noise that comes our way.

I can hardly believe how much the twins have transformed in just eighteen months. Their hair has blossomed into a stunning sandy brown, softly glimmering in the sunlight and reminding me of the golden hues of summer days. Though I can't pinpoint the exact moment this change took place, it came with a profound lesson on self-acceptance and inner beauty. My son, often shares his wisdom: true beauty radiates from within and is more about how we perceive ourselves rather than how others see us. Hearing this heartfelt insight from my little one resonated deeply within me, like a soothing melody that lingers in the heart.

When Robert turned thirteen, it was a moment bursting with excitement and promise. He and his tight-knit group of friends, Anthony, Ronald, and Paul, decided to join their school's football team, their faces lighting up with eagerness and determination. Although they were the youngest players on the roster, their passion and energy made them shine like stars on the field. At first, I felt a knot of anxiety in my stomach; the potential for injuries weighed heavy on my mind, especially considering how much taller and more muscular some of the opposing players were. Yet, Patrick's calming words wrapped around me like a warm embrace, reassuring me that Robert understood the game well and would take care of himself. Deep down, I held an unwavering belief in the boys' potential, sensing they were destined to make an impact, even if others expected them to spend most of the game on the sidelines.

When game day finally dawned, anticipation coursed through me like an electric current. As the sun shone down, bathing the field in a golden hue, I watched with delight as Robert and Paul sprinted into the huddle, their faces brimming with enthusiasm and determination. Then, in a heartbeat, it happened, Robert scored his very first touchdown. The sheer joy spilling from his face was simply priceless, a moment that encapsulated the thrill of victory. He celebrated with an infectious little dance, his moves echoing his father's lively spirit from years past. He pointed enthusiastically and glided left, then right, desperately searching the stands for me. When our eyes finally met, he dropped to his knees in pure jubilation, pointing skyward, this was a moment to be etched in time, one filled with love and triumph.

As I watched him bask in his success, tears of overwhelming joy welled up in my eyes. It struck me as a beautiful reminder that his father was with him in spirit, bursting with pride, cheering him on alongside sporting legends like Ernest Davis, the first African American Heisman Trophy winner, who paved the way for so many. My heart swelled with indescribable happiness, knowing that Robert wasn't merely playing football, he was crafting lifelong memories, fully embracing each exhilarating moment, and celebrating the enduring love of family. I thought, what an incredible journey were embarking on together, each step filled with joy and discovery.

I recall, how the twins love to go to the park. The first time I took them along, it was a sunny day at the park, everything was going smoothly until both kids decided they absolutely had to use the same swing. With a few swings available, it was amusing to see their determination. They were extra animated that day, and before I knew it, their playful fun turned into a little tussle. A crowd quickly gathered, and it felt like a spontaneous show. Most people found it adorable, until I heard a sudden, alarming scream. In just that moment, Roland had picked up a rock and hit Noland in the face. I had only turned away for a heartbeat, but instantly rushed back to check on them. The onlookers were taken aback; one woman even admitted she thought it was just harmless play. Thankfully, Noland was okay.

I was so angry, and irritated because when I was alone with them, I had no peace. I wanted to scream to the top of my lungs, that it was just the terrible twos. When I looked down at Noland's face there was blood running out of his mouth, I wiped the blood to see how bad it was and when I looked over at Roland, I swear that child was smiling. I slapped him so hard it scared me, and everyone in the park began staring at me like I was the problem, so I grabbed their hands and started walking home. Both of them were screaming, and I wanted so bad to leave them right there, but I saw a police car driving by. That day the walk home seemed extremely long, and people were staring at us from all directions. I wanted to get home as quickly as possible because my head was pounding, and I felt as if I was about to fly into a rage.

I was feeling overwhelmed by the noise, so I gently picked up Noland, hoping to soothe him. To my delight, he quieted down. I then reached for Roland, who was getting a bit too wild, and before I knew it, I was walking down the street, cradling both boys. Suddenly, they started fighting with each other, and I felt the urge to put them down for a moment. While I tried to draw strength from thoughts of Mrs. Florence, who usually brings me so much peace, I found myself without her reassuring guidance this time. It was a bit of a challenge, having to pause a few times to separate the two rascals, but I kept my spirits up.

When I finally got home, I was greeted by the sight of Robert peacefully asleep on the sofa. Mrs. Florence had mentioned that she picked him up from school because he wasn't feeling well, but thankfully, he didn't have a fever. A bit of soup and some rest, were just what he needed.

Despite my best efforts to calm things down, the twins were still at it, creating chaos all around. I tried to gather my thoughts, but the noise echoed in my mind, making my head throb. All I wanted was a moment of peace. Robert was tossing and turning in his sleep while Mrs. Florence sat beside him, soothing him with her gentle humming. Feeling overwhelmed, I leaped to my feet and exclaimed, Alright, enough is enough. My sudden outburst startled Robert, he opened his eyes, and he looked up at me with wide eyes, as if I had completely lost my mind. Meanwhile, the twins continued their rambunctious antics, engrossed in a brawl that looked straight out of a wrestling match.

I walked over and grabbed Roland by the back of his shirt with one hand and Noland with the other, lifting them slightly off the ground. As I held them there, a wild thought crossed my mind: what if I slammed these two bad asses together? I couldn't help but chuckle at that thought. However, Mrs. Florence caught on to my thoughts and gently warned, Lillian, don't. In that moment, a wave of calm washed over me, the tranquility I had longed for earlier. I confessed to her that I was at my wit's end; the boys' antics were truly driving me up the wall.

With a knowing smile, she advised me to look at them, my precious little ones. She reminded me that, deep down, I had an abundance of love for them and that I would never want to harm them. As I glanced down, I saw their sweet faces, and it melted my heart. I gently set them down, but a rush of shame flooded over me. I couldn't comprehend how I had even entertained the idea of hurting my own children. Reflecting on when Robert was a baby, I cherished every moment spent with him, as he was such a joy. Mrs. Florence reassured me that I couldn't compare the twins to Robert; they each had their unique personalities and quirks, even differing from one another.

As I was chatting with Mrs. Florence, Patrick walked in, and I felt a rush of emotion. Without thinking, I jumped up, dashed over to him, and slapped him across his face, exclaiming, you're driving me crazy. Those little rascals of yours are terrible.

In the background, I could hear the twins crying, and occasionally, their banter turned into little scuffles. Patrick took one look at Noland, who was pouting, and asked what had happened. I explained that his brother had hit him with a rock at the park. I took a deep breath, looked into Patrick's eyes, and sensed a hint of disappointment there. I wanted to convey my feelings, but it was a bit jumbled in my mind, so I decided to give myself some space and retreated to my room.

I flopped onto my bed, letting my thoughts swirl around me. As I started drifting off, I reflected on the whirlwind of the day and wondered why I had reacted that way. After a refreshing day and a half of sleep, I woke up to discover that Patrick had been a fantastic caregiver, tending to Robert and the twins. I noticed Robert was peacefully snoozing on the sofa, likely still feeling under the weather, and I couldn't resist checking in on him.

Hey, how's Robert doing? I asked, genuinely concerned.

He's feeling a bit better today, but I think he still needs a break from school, Patrick replied with a reassuring smile.

Standing in the doorway, I swayed slightly, it was both amusing and alarming at the same time. Patrick quickly came over to steady me and guided me to sit beside Robert on the sofa. I turned to Patrick, a little guilty, and asked, Did I really slap you earlier? He nodded with an understanding look, telling me it was probably just my mind playing tricks on me from being under the weather.

I'm so sorry. I said sincerely, knowing there's no excuse for losing my temper. He responded with a warm smile, assuring me he understood, but gently reminded me to keep it together next time.

During my recovery, I felt a unique connection with Mrs. Florence; her calm presence truly seemed to guide my healing. After a few days of cozy rest, I was back on my feet. Everything seemed to find its rhythm again: Robert was ready to head back to school, Patrick was getting back to work, and Roland and Noland were still the lively troublemakers they had always been.

That year was a real learning curve for me, who knew kids could be so spirited? But just as quickly as it had begun, the fighting dwindled when they turned three. Sure, they still bickered occasionally, but at least it was less combative.

Fast forward a bit, and the twins were gearing up for kindergarten. I was thrilled to see Gail and her family move back into the neighborhood. Robert had just started his first year of high school, shining on the football field and catching the attention of university coaches who were already scouting him. I couldn't be prouder of him. His grades were stellar, he was well-liked by his classmates, and the future looked positively bright for him. It felt wonderful to see everyone thriving, and despite the ups and downs, life was shaping up splendidly.

The first day of school was quite an adventure for the twins, who are definitely not the early bird types. I had quite the challenge getting them out of their cozy beds, and even when they were up, they were a bit reluctant to embrace the day. By the time we finally made it out the door, we were running a little behind schedule. Mrs. Florence kindly joined us on the walk to school, and the twins had a lot to say along the way, mostly expressing their desire to stay home.

When we arrived at their classroom, I could see that they were hesitant about staying. I gently explained that I would be stepping out but promised to return to pick them up after school. That's when their teacher invited them to the playground, and the moment they spotted the other kids and toys, it was like a switch flipped, they dashed off to join the fun.

As I stood there watching them, my mind drifted back to Robert's first day of school. I remember feeling a wave of sadness wash over me as I walked away from him, not wanting to leave his side. But this time, I felt a comforting anticipation for some peaceful alone time at home, something I hadn't experienced since the twins were born. Just as they really got lost in their play, it was time for me to go. Walking home, I couldn't help but think about the mix of guilt and relief I felt, what a unique feeling it was to carve out a moment for myself after so long. I glanced at Mrs. Florence, and I could see she, too, was deep in thought. When our eyes met, we shared a knowing smile, which felt incredibly supportive.

Mrs. Florence brought up Robert's first day, and I remembered how difficult it was for both of us. She had reassured me back then that with time, it would become easier, and it truly has. But I never expected it to feel this smooth. I found myself wondering if I loved the twins any less than I love Robert, and she immediately reassured me that my love for each of them is different but equally profound. She reminded me that when Robert was five, I was still healing from the grief of losing my mother and his father. Now, I'm in such a different place, which makes all the difference.

As we continued our stroll and chat, something made me pause right in the middle of the street. Mrs. Florence, a few steps ahead, didn't notice at first. When she turned back and saw me standing where Robert had had his accident fifteen years ago, I sensed she understood that my emotions at that moment were something I had to process alone. Eventually, I joined her again, and with genuine concern, she asked if I was okay. I nodded and assured her that I was.

As soon as we reached our front door, the phone started ringing. It was the school, apparently, there were some issues with the twins, and they needed me to come back. When I arrived, I found Roland and Noland in the principal's office, tears streaming down their little faces. The moment they spotted me, they rushed over, wrapped their arms around my legs, and pleaded to come home. It took a little while for them to settle down, but once they calmed, I explained that they would have to stay until the end of the day when I would be back to pick them up. Unlike my earlier feelings of optimism, this time leaving them was bittersweet, knowing they were feeling so upset. But I reminded myself that every new beginning can come with its own set of challenges, and we can all navigate this together.

HerStory

TWENTY-FIVE

I've recently noticed some changes in the twins, and it's been quite a journey. A couple of months ago, they were full of energy, running around the house with the wild enthusiasm of WWF wrestlers. Their meals were lively affairs filled with chatter and laughter. But lately, something shifted. Instead of their usual playful banter, I found them sitting silently in front of the TV, seemingly lost in their own world. I completely understood that adjusting to school was a big change for them, yet it felt like a different version of my boys had emerged.

Initially, I thought this might be just another phase, similar to the changes they experienced around two years old. However, after a couple of weeks of observation, I decided it was best to reach out to their teacher for insights. One morning on the way to school, I was pleasantly surprised to see Roland and Noland holding hands tightly. They've always enjoyed being around each other, but this was a new level of togetherness, as if they were keeping each other from drifting apart.

As I approached the school, I went to the principal's office for my appointment with their teacher. I almost gasped when the secretary informed me, they were in different classes. My heart raced. No one had told me about this separation. I couldn't believe my boys were apart all day long. Determined, I asked to speak with the principal, expressing my strong desire for them to be in the same class. He explained that he thought it would be beneficial for them to develop their individual identities. With a mix of disbelief and concern, I asked him what he meant; after all, they were just five years old.

It was daunting to see the impact of this situation on my children. I knew my boys well and felt that the separation was causing more harm than good. After an intense discussion with the principal, he finally agreed to place Roland back in the same class as Noland. When I left the office, I reminded both of them to always share their feelings with me about school or anything else. Their smiles at that moment warmed my heart, and from then on, their attitude toward school transformed completely.

It's astonishing how they've grown, especially when I compare them to Robert at this age. Now, halfway through the school year, the twins have proudly declared they no longer need us to walk them to school. They confidently announce they're not babies anymore, a statement that is both delightful and bittersweet. Of course, they can still be a little reluctant to get out of their cozy beds in the morning, but once fueled by breakfast, they dash out the door, ready to conquer the day.

One particular morning, after they headed off, a wave of anxiety swept over me. It felt like something ominous was going to happen, and I couldn't shake that dreadful feeling. I realized I would need to check on them, trusting my instincts. As I prepared to leave, I noticed Mrs. Florence's calming presence, which helped ease my racing heart.

Lillian, she reassured me, don't worry. They're fine. Remember those difficult moments when Robert was young? You had those strange feelings and worries too, right? It's important to reflect on those experiences, acknowledge them, and then let them go. Don't allow fears to overshadow your life, it's time to move forward.

Reflecting on her words throughout the day, it dawned on me that these anxieties were mine to conquer, not connected to the twins. With newfound clarity, I was ready to embrace my boys with all the affection I had been holding back. When they returned home that afternoon, I couldn't help myself, I showered them with hugs and kisses. They looked at me, a bit puzzled by my affectionate display, and I simply told them I had missed them. Their delightful smiles and warm embrace melted away any lingering fears I had, and from that day forward, I felt a renewed sense of peace.

It's amazing how much our little ones can teach us about love, resilience, and navigating the challenges of life together. I'm filled with optimism as I watch them grow, knowing that we're all on this journey side by side.

One lovely morning, after the twins waved goodbye and set off for school, Mrs. Florence and I were enjoying a warm cup of coffee in the kitchen. Suddenly, Gail popped by, and asked if we could chat privately. With a friendly nod, Mrs. Florence gracefully excused herself and headed to her room. As she passed by, I couldn't help but smile at the thought, if only she knew about the special unspoken bond, she wouldn't have felt the need to ask. Mrs. Florence playfully said, No, Lillian, it's a private conversation between you two. I chuckled at the idea of our chats being private since our connection was so strong. I assured her I'd catch up with her later, and just like that, we slipped into what I now affectionately call the infamous click, an unmistakable signal that Gail and I were completely alone.

Gail, quickly inquired about our community coffee. Of course, we had some. As I poured her a steaming cup, I could see her eyes light up, and she shared how much she missed both our delicious coffee and our cheerful chats while she was away. It warmed my heart to see her smile. But as she prepared to leave, I noticed a hint of sadness in her expression. She truly didn't want to part with her beloved New Orleans, yet she felt the pull to be with her husband and daughter. It was a bittersweet choice, but it was the right one for her, even if she didn't fully realize it yet. When she arrived at Donald's mother's home, Vivian, she discovered just how warmly welcoming family could be. Vivian went above and beyond, introducing Gail to her circle of friends, some of whom became fast friends for Gail as well. Nicole, Gail's daughter, found her tribe too, especially with Paulette, as they became inseparable, sharing adventures and laughter together.

Donald reminisced about a delightful double date to a neighborhood Christmas party with two brothers, Lionel and Gerrod. They had all grown up so much, and it filled him with joy to see those familiar faces again. Meanwhile, he reconnected with his high school pals, LB and Kevin, and their weekends soon turned into lovely fishing escapades. Gail, a massive fan of fried fish, confessed that the cleaning part was quite the chore. But that task turned into a beautiful bonding moment between her and Mrs. Vivian, those fish-cleaning sessions became a cherished connection.

Every Saturday, Gail and Vivian made a ritual of shopping together. Initially, it was enjoyable and full of laughter, but over time, Gail experienced a bit of frustration. It wasn't true dislike, more of a love/hate relationship. If she really hated it, she could have easily said no, yet there was something delightful about their adventures, even if they ended up in playful banter. Gail would tease Vivian about how shopping trips seemed endless, as Vivian was always eager to browse and try on everything, even though there was no intention to buy.

Whenever Gail voiced her hunger or fatigue, sharing how her knees ached, Vivian, with her characteristic spunk, would simply laugh it off, insisting they weren't done yet. She had a playful way of calling Gail born lazy and raised tired, a quirky saying that always managed to crack Gail up. Vivian even cheekily suggested Gail see a doctor about her knees, as it was amusing to her that someone so young could complain so much. With all the ups and downs, Mrs. Vivian was undoubtedly a colorful character, enriching Gail's life in ways she never expected.

Every Saturday, Vivian and Gail embraced the joy of shopping together. Occasionally, Donald and Nicole would tag along, and they often found themselves puzzled by the duo's strong friendship, especially considering the playful arguments that frequently accompanied their outings. Donald struggled to understand how two people could love each other so much yet engage in such lively debates. Yet, Vivian and Gail shared knowing smiles, recognizing that this spirited dynamic was a vital aspect of their bond. Beneath it all, Gail cherished Vivian's vibrant and energetic spirit, which added so much color to her life.

Vivian had a true love for television, often seen lounging in front of her screen whenever she was at home. One of the most memorable incidents took place on a sweltering summer night when Vivian and Gail were nestled comfortably on the couch, a fan's cool breeze drifting around them. Out of the blue, the fan suddenly stopped working. concerned, Vivian jumped up to figure out the issue and discovered that the fan's plug was frayed.

Gail, full of optimism, assured Vivian that she'd handle the repair. She omitted the part about never having fixed a plug before, having only witnessed it done a couple of times. Confident that she could manage, Gail cut off the damaged plug, stripped the wires, and wrapped them around the screws. Feeling a touch of uncertainty, she turned to Vivian and asked her to plug it in, knowing her friend was fearless.

As Vivian walked over, she couldn't help but reflect on how today's youth often seemed timid in comparison to her own spirited past. With nostalgia, she spun exaggerated tales of her childhood, like braving the snow while walking uphill to school and doing homework in the glow of flickering candlelight, struggling to make out every other word. Vivian was not only beautiful but also possessed a wonderfully quirky sense of humor.

Whenever Gail voiced her concerns about the fan repair, Vivian would always respond with one of her outlandish stories. But when Gail finally plugged in the fan, an unexpected spark flew out, plunging the whole house into complete darkness. It was so dark that Gail couldn't even see her own hand in front of her face. Panic washed over her as she heard Vivian yell, I'm blind. I can't see. and the sound of Vivian bumping into the walls and furniture filled the air.

In a moment of sheer confusion, Gail shouted, where are you? But all she heard were Vivian's frantic cries. Just then, the absurdity of their situation hit her, and she burst into laughter, realizing that they must have blown a fuse. Upon hearing Gail's laughter, Vivian exclaimed, are you laughing at me? Did you plan this? Now I can't see.

Gail couldn't stop giggling, understanding that Vivian didn't quite see the humor yet. So, she called out, You're not blind. We blew a fuse. The whole house is dark. Once Vivian understood what had actually happened, she too, began to laugh. They ended up on the floor, sharing a fit of giggles like carefree children, just as Donald and Nicole entered the room.

What's going on in here? Donald asked, amusement written all over his face. Gail, still chuckling, struggled to find the right words, but Vivian managed to explain, we blew a fuse. Donald looked bewildered and questioned, what's so funny about blowing a fuse? As Gail attempted to reply, she stammered, We, we blew a fuse, and your mother thought she was blind, and with that, they both laughed even harder.

Donald shook his head with an amused grin, saying, you two deserve each other because you're just a little crazy. They playfully pointed at one another, both insisting, you're crazy, before dissolving into laughter once again.

Once the laughter settled, Gail remarked that it had been ages since she had laughed that hard, her spirits noticeably lifted from the experience. Once she left, I found myself eager to share this delightful story with Mrs. Florence. But just as I was ready, the phone rang, it was Gail again. She wanted to chat, so I enthusiastically suggested we meet at the park the next day. When I arrived, I spotted her sitting under a tree, looking a bit troubled. What's wrong? I asked, ready to support her in whatever way I could. She said,

I deeply miss Vivian. It's hard to believe that she's been gone for six months now. Sometimes, I still catch myself expecting her to walk through the door, ready to share one of her hilarious jokes and brighten the day. The whole experience happened in the blink of an eye, and I wish more than anything that I had had the chance to say goodbye. I don't remember missing my parents this much. One day, Vivian wasn't feeling quite right, and before we knew it, Donald took her to the hospital, only for us to receive the heartbreaking news that she had passed away that same day. When Donald called to share the news, I was in disbelief. My mind raced, convinced it was some kind of cruel joke, hoping it was just Vivian's playful spirit at work. But when Donald came home, wrapped me in a comforting hug, and whispered that she was gone, my world felt like it had collapsed. In that moment, reality hit me hard, I realized that I would never again hear her infectious laughter or experience the warmth of her embrace. Even attending her funeral felt unbearable; I couldn't look at her still form because I wanted to forever cherish the vibrant and joyful person she was in life.

After she passed, things felt different with her friends. It was as if they suddenly noticed the differences between us. I tried to go out shopping, hoping it would lift my spirits, but I was only reminded of the deep conversations and playful debates I had with Vivian. We could talk about anything and everything.

While Donald and Nicole had their bond, I felt adrift. Even though they tried to include me more, it didn't fill the void left by Vivian's absence. Their connection seemed so special, and while I loved Nicole dearly, we weren't as close as I wished we could be. Sometimes I found myself wishing we shared a deeper bond, but I understood that it was what it was. I grew restless, longing to return to my own space, yet Nicole and Donald weren't ready for that step. Even so, the thought of returning alone crossed my mind several times. I didn't want to disrupt their family dynamics again, and weeks turned into days of feeling ignored and unseen. That is until one day, I decided it was time to take charge of my life. I started visiting a peaceful park near the state capitol, just a place where I could sit, breathe, and gather my thoughts. It ended up being a great way to clear my head and improve my mood.

While I was sitting on a bench, a girl approached me and introduced herself as Louise. She asked if I was new to the neighborhood and expressed genuine curiosity about me. At first, I found it a little unusual that someone I had just met would want to know so much, but as we got to know each other better, I realized that her inquisitive nature was simply part of her charm. On our initial meeting, she shared that she was a student at Louisiana State University. She had longed to return to school for years but felt it was too late until a close friend encouraged her to take the leap.

Louise and I quickly forged a delightful friendship. We often enjoyed outings to the movies or I would help her with her studies. When I was with her, I felt truly alive, our conversations flowed effortlessly. One day, when she invited me to go shopping, a wave of emotion hit me, and suddenly I found myself crying uncontrollably. In that moment, thoughts of Vivian surged back into my heart with such intensity. I shared stories of Vivian with Louise, she walked over to me, wrapped her arms around me, and held me tight. From her comforting embrace, I sensed that she too had experienced a significant loss. I noticed the sorrow in her eyes, and before long, tears began to stream down her face. I gently asked her who she had lost.

Louise revealed that her dear friend, who had encouraged her to go back to school, had tragically passed away from cancer during their first semester at LSU. Her friend had known she was nearing the end but chose not to tell Louise until her final weeks. She wanted Louise to focus on her education, understanding that life is unpredictable and that it's crucial not to put off what truly matters. The connection between Louise and me grew stronger over time, and I felt an unexpected bond with her, deeper in some ways than with my own family. I had tried explaining to you my desire to feel a sense of belonging, but the words often eluded me. I believe there's something uniquely special about the connections among Black individuals that transcend other backgrounds and shared histories. Initially, I thought my friendship with Louise stemmed from that bond, as if I had discovered the key to understanding my connections, but soon I realized that our friendship was built on much more than that.

One sunny afternoon, Louise and I were sitting on our favorite park bench, chatting away as we often did. Suddenly, we noticed a group of young men playing basketball nearby. Louise turned to me with a frown and expressed her belief that young people like them were associated only with negative things, violence, drugs, and promiscuity. She lamented how the headlines in the Times-Picayune were always filled with stories of crime and despair, and remarked that every time she saw a black woman, there seemed to be a swarm of children following her around. She even speculated about how these women ended up pregnant when they hardly ever seemed to be with any men. I was taken aback and speechless as she looked at me, wondering what was wrong. I struggled to respond.

Her comments felt deeply personal, even though she didn't know my family and had no idea I was married to a black man and had a beautiful daughter. It brought me some solace to think that if she really knew my family, perhaps her views wouldn't be so harsh. After that conversation, I decided to take a break from the park for a while; I needed time to sort out my feelings and how to approach the situation.

After a couple of weeks, I felt ready to return. I reminded myself that Louise's views should not stand in the way of our friendship. When she inquired about my absence, I casually explained that I had been visiting relatives in New Orleans. Yet, each time we were together, I worried about her eventually discovering my family. Can you believe it, Lillian? There was a time when I became uncertain about my own thoughts and feelings, but I did realize one important thing: whenever I wasn't with Louise, I genuinely missed her. She had become such an integral part of my life.

One day, while we were enjoying some window-shopping downtown, I spotted Donald approaching us from a distance. Suddenly, my heart raced and I felt a wave of anxiety wash over me. In a moment of panic, I ducked into the nearest store. Louise noticed my sudden change and could sense something was off; I was visibly shaking. She enveloped me in a warm embrace, asking if I was alright. In a moment of insecurity, I lied and blamed it on feeling under the weather. Without hesitation, she took me to her house, and as we settled in, she asked again what was going on. Yet I remained silent, unable to admit that my husband was approaching or that I felt ashamed of him, or that my daughter's identity was a source of fear instead of pride. Would she see them the way she'd spoken about others?

I feared that if Louise knew Donald was my husband, our friendship might come to an abrupt end. I truly valued our bond and needed her support in my life. Lillian, you have to understand, I was never ashamed of you, and I don't think I was ashamed then either, but in that moment, facing the reality of Donald approaching, I felt like everything I held dear was slipping away.

After leaving Louise's home, I returned to find Donald waiting for me on the porch. He asked where I had been, but I couldn't bear to meet his gaze. I found myself staring at the ground, feeling an intensity in his eyes that pierced right through to my heart. I told him I had been at Louise's, but deep inside, I sensed he knew there was more to the story than I was sharing.

This journey of navigating friendship, love, and identity is certainly complex, but I hold hope that sharing these difficult moments will pave the way for deeper understanding and connection.

After that pivotal day, everything took a wonderful turn around the house. Donald began to spend more quality time with me, and I found myself forming a delightful bond with Nicole. To my surprise, we genuinely enjoyed each other's company and could talk about anything and everything. One afternoon, Donald and I settled on the porch, basking in the warmth of comfortable silence, just appreciating each other's presence. After a while, he broke the quiet with a thoughtful question: You know, my mother passed away almost a year ago, and you haven't mentioned her since. Can you share why that is?

This question struck a chord, and as I reflected, tears began to flow. I opened up about how profoundly I missed her. It had become impossible to go shopping without thinking of her or to sit on the porch without hearing her laughter echo in my mind. Even while watching television, I felt her spirit beside me, sharing the moment. Donald, too, admitted he often found himself in tears when he thought of her; he hadn't realized how much I was grieving. He pulled me close and reassured me that everyone who knew her shared the love and sense of loss.

That heartfelt conversation was a turning point for me. I learned the importance of accepting painful parts of life, and after our talk, I felt a weight lift off my shoulders. Allowing myself to express my feelings about Vivian made room in my heart to embrace the love I have for my family. I realized I had leaned on Louise as a distraction, as spending time with her kept my grief at bay.

One sunny day, I decided to take Nicole to the park. While we settled on a bench, enjoying our shared laughter and love, Louise unexpectedly approached and sat next to me. I asked Nicole to go play, and she stood up, gave me a sweet kiss, and skipped off. As I looked into Louise's eyes, I noticed her surprise at our interaction. I explained that Nicole was my daughter and that I am married to a wonderful Black man, a love that fills my heart.

Realizing she was unaware of my marriage, Louise seemed taken aback. I candidly shared that after her comments about the young men playing basketball, I felt unsettled about revealing my family situation. She tried to reverse the blame, suggesting my expressions led her to believe I felt differently about those men. I smiled genuinely and clarified that any expression she saw was rooted in my anger and sorrow from losing a friend without saying goodbye.

I told her about the day I had gone to her house feeling unwell, that I had I saw husband walking toward us and I was ashamed of him at that moment. we talk about it for a little while, and it led to a moment of understanding, and we suggested starting anew. I proudly introduced Nicole to her, and in a pleasant surprise, I discovered that both she and Donald had attended Broadmoor High School.

Lillian, not a single day passes where I don't reflect on that experience. It's a mystery to me why it unfolded the way it did, and the thought of my actions can be disheartening.

Gail, listen, when someone navigates a tremendous loss and keeps it bottled up, it can lead to unexpected behavior. It's crucial for individuals to find perspective, and I believe you've managed to do just that.

I shared this story with you because I needed someone who would truly listen and allow me to express what had been weighing on my heart. I recognize you mentioned that my actions were influenced by my loss, and while I appreciate your understanding, it's still challenging to reconcile my feelings. I experienced shame regarding my baby, not because of her being part of me, but because of society's perceptions. Her skin tone differs from mine, but honestly, the differences are hardly noticeable. Yet, I internalized that disparity and felt embarrassed. How can I wish for others to see her as the incredible individual she is if I allowed stereotypes to cloud my vision?

It's a journey, and as I embrace my truth, I am optimistic for the future and the connections I continue to nurture.

After Gail finished the story, she cried and cried as if she needed to release the pain and though I tried to comfort her, nothing seemed to help.

I told her seeing her color was not the problem it was her definition of what she saw that was causing the problem. I wasn't saying that it's a conscious thought, but it was part of her upbringing, and she should talk to Donald about this. She said she couldn't find it in her heart to tell him that she was ashamed of him and was afraid of how he would react. I went through the same sort of thing when I lost Robert and missed him so bad I wanted to die, and even being pregnant with his child I didn't feel like I could break through my woes. It was easy for me to think there was no happiness out there for me, but Mrs. Florence tried to help and told me I couldn't die because I needed to think of my baby. I told her I didn't care about her or the baby I only wanted to die and be with Robert. I felt ashamed for years behind that but it happened, and I couldn't take it back but at least I knew why it happened.

One day, during a lively chat with Donald, he brought up Gail's friend Louise. Curiosity sparked, I wanted to see what insight he had. He opened up about how he sensed Louise was struggling with some shame and wondered if she had avoided him at the mall. Initially, he felt hurt, but after reflecting on her challenges, he compassionately chose to put aside his feelings to support her. It was heartwarming to see him extend that kindness! In time, it became clear that his support made a difference, and Gail started to brighten up. It's moments like these that remind us of the power of empathy and friendship.

HerStory

TWENTY-SIX

When Robert turned fifteen and embarked on the thrilling journey of tenth grade, I noticed a fascinating transformation in him. While it initially left me a bit puzzled, it also filled me with curiosity to discover what was brewing in his mind. Suddenly, he began to spend more time in his room, diving into music or getting lost in captivating TV shows. It was as if the world outside his door had faded away, and nobody in the family, not even the twins, could coax him out of his cozy sanctuary. Of course, this sparked a swirl of concern in me, especially as this retreat seemed to deepen. Wanting to reconnect, I encouraged Patrick to have a heart-to-heart with him. Robert, however, insisted that he was perfectly fine and just preferred some alone time. Patrick, with his easy-going nature, reassured me that this was all part of the normal teenage experience, a classic sign of puberty, and we should respect Robert's evolving need for space.

As Robert began coming home later from school without explanation, I sensed it was time for a genuine conversation. One beautiful afternoon, I seized the opportunity to invite him for a leisurely walk in the park, a cherished spot where we had enjoyed countless meaningful conversations over the years. My hope was that our familiar surroundings would inspire him to open up. As we nestled onto an inviting park bench, I wrapped my arms around him and gently asked about what was happening in his life. Instead of the lively conversation I yearned for, he simply gazed ahead in silence. In that moment, I realized how much he had grown; I would need to approach him with the understanding and respect he deserved.

I lovingly reassured Robert that I was always nearby, eager to listen whenever he felt ready to share his thoughts. With all my heart, I reminded him he could always count on me. Yet, when we returned home, he quietly retreated back to his room, leaving me with a twinge of helplessness. It was disheartening to witness him in struggle, and I felt like no number of words or efforts could bridge the distance. To lift his spirits, I decided to whip up his favorite dish: pork and beans. The moment I began sautéing fresh onions until they were caramelized and fragrant, before adding a delightful blend of smoked sausage, hot sausage, and beef franks, I felt hopeful. The delightful aroma wafted through our home, creating a warm and inviting atmosphere that I hoped would evoke happy memories from our family dinners.

As the delicious scent spread through the house, family members began to trickle into the kitchen, intrigued by the enticing smells. When Robert finally wandered in, he broke out his signature little dance and gave me a hug that melted my heart, but when he said he wasn't hungry, a wave of urgency washed over me. Deep down, I sensed that something more was going on with him, and I felt a determination to get to the heart of it. After dinner, as I gazed out the window, I pondered how I could create an environment where he felt comfortable enough to share his feelings once again.

In the midst of my reflections, a comforting presence arrived, Mrs. Florence, after all these years, she still had an uncanny ability to sense when I needed a boost. With a gentle sigh, I shared my worries about Robert and quietly asked for some space to collect my thoughts. Her heartfelt response, remember, if you need me, I'm only a thought away, resonated within me like a soothing balm, reminding me of the strong connections in my life, before I heard the tender click of her departure.

I felt hopeful knowing that with patience, understanding, and love, we would find a way through this maze together, ready to embrace whatever lay ahead.

In the following days, I found myself brainstorming different ways to encourage Robert to express himself. Yet, despite my best efforts, nothing seemed to work. As I became increasingly immersed in solving his problems, other relationships and responsibilities began to fade in my periphery. I was determined to show both myself and Mrs. Florence that I could tackle any challenge, but in reality, all I was doing was absorbing Robert's troubles as if they were my own. This didn't benefit either of us.

I sensed that Mrs. Florence could feel my internal struggle, especially since I had inadvertently distanced her. To break through, she cleverly sent the twins to ask if I would take them to the park. At first, I hesitated; I wanted to stay buried in my thoughts. But the twins, with their delightful persistence, made it impossible to say no. Maybe a little fresh air and fun would do us all some good. As I passed by Mrs. Florence, I asked if she'd like to join us. After a moment of hesitation, she saw my hopeful expression and agreed. I knew she had orchestrated this outing, much like she had done for Robert in the past when I faced my own challenges. In that moment, I felt a sense of optimism. Sometimes, we just need a little nudge from those who care about us to get back on the path to connection and joy. Together, we could all find our way back to each other and create that beautiful space for open conversations and understanding.

When we arrived at the park, it was heartwarming to see the boys jumping right into a game of football with their friends. Meanwhile, Mrs. Florence and I found a spot on a bench. I sensed she wanted to dive into a conversation, but I felt it was time for me to tackle things on my own. She shared her concerns about how I seemed a bit lost, trying to fix what wasn't broken, and overlooking other important parts of my life.

Mrs. Florence gently reminded me of how important it is to lean on others during tough times. She encouraged me to let her in instead of shutting her out, reminding me that we all need a little support every now and then. As I pondered her insightful words, I realized that my struggle was only leading me further into unhappiness. So, I made the decision to open up to her, and I could practically see her face light up with joy.

When I admitted my confusion about what my son was going through, Mrs. Florence encouraged me to think back to my own childhood. While my struggles revolved around making friends, he had so many around him. But then, a memory struck me: it was around his age that I met his father. Mrs. Florence's encouragement for Patrick to connect with Robert sparked my curiosity, did she sense an underlying issue I wasn't seeing?

She assured me that sometimes, events fall into place for a reason, and while she couldn't interfere, it was important for me to trust the process. Admittedly, that thought gave me a sense of unease, especially since it reminded me of things she'd shared about his father. But then she quickly reassured me that everything would be alright.

Don't forget, she said with a warm smile, you have two other boys who will be fifteen someday too. I chuckled and replied, if they face issues like this, I'm not sure I'll make it through. With a little laughter, it felt like we were already on a path to brighter days ahead.

That night, as we settled into bed, I felt a strong desire to encourage Patrick to reach out to Robert. He had some reservations, pointing out that their earlier conversations hadn't led to much progress. Patrick thought that Robert would initiate contact when he felt ready. However, I firmly believed that this was an ideal moment for them to reconnect. I sensed that Robert was just as eager for this dialogue, yet Patrick's hesitation was evident.

After he turned away, my heart ached with concern. I gently reminded him how much it hurts to see our children struggling. His silence was difficult to bear, and as I lay awake, contemplating our situation, I was surprised to hear Mrs. Florence call my name.

Lillian, he needs to tackle this issue collectively with Robert. This is crucial for both of them, she said, her words striking a chord within me. I felt reassured that, with more encouragement, Patrick would recognize the significance of addressing this matter now rather than later.

I decided to take control of the situation. The next morning, I headed to Robert's room and told him that his father wanted to chat. He went to our bedroom. After about forty-five minutes, Robert emerged looking relaxed, something I hadn't seen in a while. I was eager to speak with Patrick and find out what they had talked about.

When I walked into the room, Patrick was smiling, but there were tears in his eyes. I asked him how it went, and he said, it was fine. We talked about girls, you know, he's growing up.

He excitedly shared that he has a girlfriend named Natalie. They chose to keep it a secret since her parents aren't on board with her dating yet. I could tell that his struggles were really weighing on him, especially since he felt unable to open up to you. As Patrick began to dive deeper into his story, he encouraged me to sit down, saying, Grandma, I think this is a moment where it's best if you take a seat before I keep going. I felt his eagerness and concern in every word.

I remember thinking to myself, what did he call me, then it hit me like a coconut thrown from the Zulu float, was he trying to tell me I'm going to be a grandmother? I yelled I don't believe you, where's Robert, he grabbed my arm and said, wait a minute he's scared already, he doesn't need you yelling at him. The next thing I remember was yelling, pregnant, he's just a baby, pregnant, how did this happen, I mean why, where did we go wrong? I'm going to kill him, where is he?

Patrick kindly suggested that I take a moment to breathe and collect my thoughts. Robert shared his experience with me, recounting how when he and Natalie first fell in love, they felt an undeniable connection and were excited about a future together. Their relationship blossomed, and after they shared an intimate moment, they both sensed something truly special between them. They made a thoughtful decision to wait until they were a bit older before considering marriage. However, they soon learned that every choice can lead to unexpected consequences, they discovered they were going to be parents. Patrick expressed some regret, feeling partially responsible because he hadn't discussed the topic of sex with Robert more openly. I felt a surge of passion as I responded, partly? Oh, come on. Let's be honest, it's entirely your responsibility. I've been encouraging you to have that conversation for months. If you had been more open with him, I truly believe we could've navigated this situation much differently.

Lillian, I completely understand where you're coming from, Patrick replied with sincerity. I'm already aware of my shortcomings as a father. My past experiences impacted me in ways I never fully grasped until now. Seeing how down Robert has been hit me hard, it took me back to a time I promised myself I would never revisit. I didn't have the strength to reach out to him, and because of that, I feel like I've failed him. I explained what happened to me at his age, and he walked over and embraced me with a hug and said, dad, this isn't your fault. I'm stepping up and taking full responsibility for my actions. That moment felt transformative; it was such a relief to have an open and honest conversation with him, as I no longer felt like I was carrying secrets.

I was curious about Robert's plans moving forward, and asked Patrick, what Robert intended to do about this unexpected situation. He explained that once Natalie's parents found out they would likely need to figure out a place for her to stay.

Robert came in the room; he was ready to discuss things with me. Just be patient and hear me out before responding, he encouraged gently. I couldn't help but feel a bit disappointed at his hesitation to speak with me directly, as we had always enjoyed open dialogue.

Robert sincerely apologized, Mom, I'm really sorry I didn't talk to you sooner about this. I was just too embarrassed. But if Natalie's parents decide to kick her out, I want to marry her. I realize I don't have a job right now, and I honestly have no clue how I'm going to support them, but I know I have to take responsibility since I played a part in this.

I listened intently as I asked about his future, his education, to be specific. He told me that if they had a place to live, he planned to finish high school, but college would depend on how things unfolded. Though there was determination in his voice, I could see he was grappling with the weight of his new reality. Suddenly, he paused, his expression shifted to uncertainty, and he softly admitted, "I'm going to be a dad, and I'm scared." He laid his head on my shoulder, tears streaming down his face. In that moment, I felt the gravity of our situation, I was watching my child prepare to welcome another child into the world.

I gently suggested to Robert that Natalie's parents needed to be informed, and I asked for their contact information. After reaching out to them and inviting them over, I made it clear to Robert that he needed to take the lead in sharing this news. It was a big moment for him, but I felt optimistic that this would be the beginning of a new chapter for all of us, filled with challenges but also immense love and growth.

Getting them to visit was a bit of a challenge since they weren't familiar with us. I really wanted to emphasize how important this meeting was, and even offered to go to them if they preferred. When they finally arrived, I was thrilled to see they brought Natalie along! It all made sense why my son admired her so much, she was absolutely lovely.

Natalie's parents, Maxine and McKinley, who everyone affectionately calls Bube, arrived with such warmth. As soon as they came in, Natalie joyfully rushed over to Robert and wrapped her arms around him. It was a bit of a surprise, especially since her father looked ready to step in. Understanding his hesitation, Robert gently pushed her away. I could see he was nervous, and I wished I could assure them about everything. Still, it was Robert's turn to stand tall and handle this like a responsible young man.

As everyone settled in, Robert took a deep breath and said, Mr. and Mrs. Wiggins, Natalie is carrying my baby. What a moment that was. I guess I should have asked him how he was planning on breaking the news to them. If I would've known what he had in mind I would've told him it wasn't a good idea to blurt out to the parents that he had made love to their daughter and now she's going to have a baby. Bube jumped up and grabbed him around his neck and yelled, you snot nose little bastard, I'm going to kill you, I'm going to kill you dead. Natalie began screaming, Patrick, Maxine and I were trying to get him off of Robert. After we pulled them apart, Bube walked over to Natalie and told her she wasn't welcome in his house ever again. Maxine yelled No, please not my child, someone tell me it's not true, Bube looked at his wife and said, I'm leaving and if you want to come, you can.

They left Natalie with us, and I made the decision to move her into Robert's room for the time being. Robert, being the wonderful brother that he is, settled in with the twins. I knew I had to come up with a simple yet reassuring way to explain this change to them, considering they were just five years old. I could imagine their little minds racing with questions about why their big brother was suddenly sharing the room with them.

The next morning, Robert headed off to school, while Natalie stayed behind feeling a bit under the weather and without any fresh clothes. Mrs. Florence mentioned that as she walked past Robert's room, she heard Natalie weeping, prompting her to check on her. She described how scared Natalie appeared, unsure of what to expect.

When I entered the room where Natalie was sitting quietly on the bed, I introduced myself warmly. Since we hadn't had the chance to properly meet before, I told her she could call me Mom. I could see a spark of relief in her eyes as she managed a little smile. I wanted her to know that she was welcome to stay with us for as long as she needed. However, to my dismay, she began to cry again. I assured her not to worry, reminding her that her parents would likely come around eventually. After all, this situation was hard for everyone. I wrapped my arms around her, feeling her small frame tremble with emotion, and whispered reassuring words that everything would be alright.

Then, just as I was comforting her, there was a gentle knock at the front door. It was Maxine, her face brightening as she carried a bag filled with Natalie's clothes. I invited her in, but she had to decline as Bube was waiting for her in the car. She promised to return once he went to work. When Maxine eventually came back later that day, I could see the glimmer of hope in Natalie's eyes, although I sensed that her heart still longed for the comfort of her family.

That afternoon, I felt a pang of disappointment thinking about how Robert had left Natalie alone on her first day with us. When he returned from school, I called him to my room and asked him to bring Natalie along. I took a deep breath and said, look, even though you've expressed responsibility for both Natalie and your baby, it seems like your life hasn't quite adjusted to this new reality. I want you to understand that things have changed significantly, and they will continue to change. This morning, you went about your routine like things was the same. You need to realize that you're no longer just one person but part of a bigger family now.

What happened today isn't acceptable. You knew Natalie was in an unfamiliar place and needed support. I truly hope she can find it in her heart to forgive you. Now, let's talk about moving forward. What are your plans? Are you thinking about getting married?

Through this conversation, I aimed to guide him gently yet firmly, instilling the importance of responsibility and care for those around him. Together, I believe we can create a loving environment for everyone involved.

They exchanged glances for a moment, and then Robert turned to me with a serious request to step out, wanting to have a private conversation about their future. I moved to the living room, where Mrs. Florence was patiently waiting for me, eager to discuss the unfolding situation. Honestly, I never expected to find myself in this scenario with Robert, a young man who has always been so responsible. Mrs. Florence reassured me that Robert was still the same person we all knew; he just hadn't fully grasped the impact of his actions yet. While welcoming a child into the world is one of life's greatest gifts, she acknowledged that this moment felt more like a mistake than a blessing for them, considering how young they both are. They truly didn't understand what laid ahead, and she urged me to be cautious not to let this mistake define their lives forever.

I expressed to her that having a baby does indeed lead to a lifelong commitment. While it's true I could argue that they are still children themselves and that Robert isn't quite a man yet, nor is Natalie a woman, my heart reminded me that none of that matters once pregnancy occurs. In just nine months, they will find themselves navigating parenthood, whether they feel prepared or not. It's crucial for Robert to step into this role now, and although this situation arose from a mistake, it's one that carries lasting implications.

After some reflection in my room, Robert called for me to return. Him and Natalie was determined to get married out of love and a shared desire for their baby. Looking into their eyes, I saw the fear and uncertainty of youth. I shared my thoughts with them.

You're still the same young people you were before this happened. If you genuinely want to get married, I support that decision. However, I must emphasize that it's not appropriate for you to sleep together under my roof. You need to recognize that this marriage is largely influenced by the baby, and while I can understand the desire to embrace parenthood, cohabiting may lead to more complications.

Here's the plan: Natalie, you will stay in your own room while Robert keeps sleeping in his brother's room. You can continue with football since it seems to be a promising path for your college aspirations, but all other activities should be put on hold for now. Natalie, there is a school designed for young pregnant women to help you stay on track academically, and I'm here to support you in enrolling.

Once the baby arrives, you'll have the chance to rejoin your regular school, and I will gladly help with childcare.

I want you both to understand that this is genuinely a second chance, a rare opportunity that not everyone receives, and I encourage you to make the most of it. If, in the future, you decide you want to take the next step in your marriage, we can have another discussion. Just keep in mind that making that choice means you're ready to embrace your roles as adults, husband and wife, mother and father, and as a family.

The following day, I took Natalie to register for school, a step I felt hopeful about. When I got back home, I reached out to Maxine to share the details of my conversation with the kids. She agreed with my approach, but mentioned that her husband was quite upset, encouraging me to allow him some time to come around.

When the twins came home, I felt it was important to explain the changes that were happening. I was initially hesitant, concerned about how they would process this information. But when I told them that Natalie would be living with us, Roland chimed in without hesitation: Mommy, we know Natalie and Robert are getting married, and she's having a baby. My surprise was palpable, and then Noland added, yeah, Mommy, Robert already told us. With that, they both casually walked off.

From the other room, I could hear Mrs. Florence laughing. She remarked on how Robert had beaten me to it, clearly amused by their early knowledge, and she chuckled again, sharing in the lightness of the moment. It was a relief to see the humorous side of such a serious situation, igniting a little optimism that we could navigate this journey together.

As time passed, Robert and Natalie developed a wonderful friendship, working through their studies together with great enthusiasm. Robert even brought Natalie to his football practices, and it became clear that wherever you saw one, the other was never far behind. By the time the school year came to a close, both had blossomed into solid A students, largely thanks to their dedicated study sessions together. Initially, I had some concerns about the possibility of them engaging in a romantic relationship again, but I soon realized their commitment to their education was genuine and strong.

Fast forward to when Natalie was eight months pregnant, and it was heartening to see how excited they both were about becoming parents. They had truly grown throughout this journey, embracing the challenges with optimism. On July 29th, the moment we had all been waiting for arrived: Natalie went into labor. She mentioned that she hadn't slept well that week, which worried me a bit. Later that morning, while I was busy organizing the twins' room, Robert burst in, bubbling with energy, Mother, it's time. It's really time. Come on, we have to go. His excitement was contagious, and even as he dashed in circles, I couldn't help but smile.

Curiosity took over when I didn't see Natalie in the kitchen, and I rushed to ask, where was she. Robert, still in a whirlwind of excitement, replied, she's in the bedroom, that's where I left her. I hurried to the bedroom, and there she was, calmly sitting on the bed, enjoying breakfast as if it were just another day. It struck me as odd, but I quickly assured her I was there for her. She mentioned feeling a few sharp pains, so I suggested timing them and calling me when they were about ten minutes apart.

Meanwhile, Robert was a bundle of nerves. Patrick was trying his best to soothe him, but it was quite a sight to see; he oscillated between laughter and tears. I encouraged him to pull himself together because Natalie needed him to be strong and composed at that moment. If she sensed his panic, it could add more stress to the situation and impact the baby. After urging him to see if Natalie needed anything, he paused, wide-eyed, proclaiming, Mother, what am I going to do? I'm going to be a father. I'm just too young. How will I provide? Who will take care of him? It almost made me laugh, but I held back, reminding him that we were all here to support him.

Watching him struggle with those fears tugged at my heart, but I knew I had to stay focused. Patrick suggested I keep an eye on Natalie while he calmed Robert down. I dashed back to her room, only to be met with the alarming sight of her lying on the floor. I called out frantically, Patrick, get in here. Something's not right with Natalie. Amid the chaos, I could hear Robert in the background, clearly in distress. I rushed to Natalie, who explained the intense pain that had overcome her while she was finishing her breakfast. Just then, she cried out, Ooh, Ooh, here it comes again.

Each scream Natalie let out was echoed by Robert's frantic yells, which only added to the tension. I quickly sent him to Gail's house to fetch Mrs. Florence for assistance. While I gathered Natalie's suitcase, Patrick took the wheel and drove us to Charity Hospital. Upon arrival, I felt a surge of worry as I noticed the intensity of Natalie's pain. The doctor immediately asked about any complications during her pregnancy, and thankfully, Natalie assured him that she had attended all her appointments and everything had seemed normal up until that morning.

In the meantime, I called Maxine to update her and told her to come to the hospital right away since Natalie was having challenges with the delivery. Maxine and Bube arrived together; she came straight into the room where Natalie and I were, while Bube remained with Patrick in the waiting area. Robert, Gail, Donald, Nicole, and Mrs. Florence arrived about thirty minutes later, and it was clear Natalie was becoming weaker. The doctor started voicing concerns for both her and the baby, indicating they might need to act quickly if things didn't improve.

Natalie, feeling vulnerable, cried out for Robert because she desperately wanted him by her side. I hesitated to bring him back since he had seemed so unprepared earlier, but her insistence left me no choice. I walked out to find Robert and urged him to step up because his wife truly needed him right now. To my relief, he stood tall and declared, Mother, you're right. I want to be there for my wife; she needs my strength. In that moment, I realized my boy had stepped into a role of maturity, ready to embrace fatherhood.

When I returned to Natalie, I found Robert by her side, holding her hand, speaking words of reassurance, and reminding her that everything would be okay. Though

Natalie would cry out from time to time, Robert stayed strong, gently rubbing her stomach and encouraging the baby. Then, with urgency in her voice, she exclaimed, go get the doctor. The baby's coming.

When the doctor arrived, he smiled and nodded, knowing it was the perfect moment. He turned to Robert and asked if he wanted to be present for the incredible moment of their baby's birth. Just thirty minutes later, they welcomed their beautiful eleven-pound baby girl into the world. The doctor shared that the reason mom faced some challenges was simply because their little one was snug and cozy, making it a bit tight in there.

When they brought Natalie back to the room, Robert couldn't contain his excitement. Mom, did you see how big our daughter is? She's simply amazing. Watching her come into the world was unforgettable, and even the doctor was impressed. He mentioned he'd never delivered a baby this big before. And when the nurse announced her weight, eleven pounds even. Everyone erupted into applause. Have you had a chance to hold her yet?

I told him my granddaughter was beautiful; she looked just like her mother. Natalie asked for her father, she wanted to know if he saw the baby, I didn't want to upset her, but I could see she already knew the answer so I told her no, when he found out she was ok he left. Natalie turned her head and began crying, Robert sat on the bed and put his hand on her shoulder and told her he was sorry he caused her so much trouble. If it wasn't for him, they wouldn't be here and her life would be problem free and asked her to please forgive him.

She said, Robert, I love you and what we did was wrong only because of our age, not our feelings. I don't regret the love I feel for you, and perhaps someday we'll have more children. Robert jumped to his feet and yelled, oh no, this is it for me, I'll never go through this again, I love you, but I could never put you through that again, never.

After saying that he got up and left the room, he was obviously traumatized. I went after him and explained that pain was part of child bearing, and it was well worth it, then I took him to see his daughter so he could see what I meant. As we stood at the window watching his little girl, tears came to his eyes, and I could see he understood what I was saying, he said isn't she wonderful?

Natalie named their daughter Asia, after her father's mother. Natalie and Asia came home after four days. For the first two weeks, she was good, waking up about four times a night and always going back to sleep but after that she started crying most of the night. Natalie could no longer handle her alone, so Robert started staying up with her. One morning when I got up, I saw Robert sleeping with Natalie and was horrified because I thought we had an agreement. He assured me that the only reason he was there was because he couldn't get Asia to go back to sleep, and when she was in his bed, she disturbed the twins. He only meant to laid there until she went back to sleep but was so tired he fell asleep also.

As the school year kicked off, it was such a delight to see Asia finally sleeping more soundly. Her newfound rest seemed to uplift our entire household. Robert and Natalie joyfully returned to their school. After their busy days, they would eagerly take Asia on long, leisurely walks that often stretched for hours, perhaps they sensed I could use a little break from the whirlwind of our daily lives.

Every morning, I would rise early, filling the kitchen with the mouthwatering aroma of bacon, eggs and toast as I prepared a hearty breakfast. After making sure the baby was fed and comfy, it was time to wake the twins. Getting them up felt like a heroic endeavor; despite being first graders now, they still resisted the morning light like sleepy little bears emerging from hibernation.

Amidst all this, I noticed Mrs. Florence spending quite a bit of time with Gail. It was hard not to sense that something significant was developing between them, and I felt genuinely intrigued to unravel that mystery in due time. Exciting developments seemed to be in the air.

TWENTY-SEVEN

Robert and Natalie achieved remarkable success by graduating with honors and earning academic scholarships. As they embarked on their college journey together, I stayed behind with Asia, filled with pride for their accomplishments. Before their departure, I engaged in a heartfelt conversation about their outlook on marriage now that they had reached adulthood. They recognized that while their love had evolved, it was no longer the kind typically associated with a husband and wife. Their prime focus was ensuring a bright future for Asia, which they believed was best achieved by pursuing their education. Once they completed college, they planned to reassess their circumstances, with the possibility of one or both returning for their daughter. They were incredibly grateful and determined to make the most of their opportunities. The future was uncertain, but they committed to living purposefully and making every moment count. However, Natalie was honest about her two regrets: a longing for her father's love and respect.

In the meantime, Mrs. Florence was spending more time at Gail's house, but she remained a strong source of support for me. I felt a steadfast connection with her throughout the challenging moments involving Natalie and Robert as if she were sending me reassuring thoughts to stay centered. Curious about her frequent visits to Gail, I asked her about it one day. She shared that Gail was facing her challenges and believed that distancing herself from her family was the best solution. Although Gail struggled with feelings of disconnection, we understood that it was her journey to navigate, and all we could do was be there for her, supporting her decisions, regardless of our personal feelings.

Watching Gail's situation unfurls left me with a sense of helplessness. I sincerely wanted to assist her and guide her toward making positive changes. Nicole, was grappling with the emotions surrounding her mother's sadness. She confided that sometimes it felt as though Gail looked at her with disappointment as if wishing her away. My heart ached to hear those words; they stirred up painful memories. I comforted Nicole by assuring her that her mother's feelings didn't reflect a lack of love. I encouraged her to express her feelings to Gail, and she agreed that now was the perfect time. The emotional toll on Nicole was evident, and it was a heavy burden for her to bear.

After their conversation, it was encouraging to see Nicole appear more at peace with their relationship, and I hoped they had made a breakthrough. However, my optimism was short-lived. Gail asserted her need to leave in search of clarity, which left me in disbelief. How could she go knowing how much it hurt Nicole? It felt as if Gail was disregarding her daughter's feelings entirely. Within a week, she had left, leaving Nicole devastated. I wanted to comfort her but struggled to articulate the emotions involved, no words were to justify Gail's repeated behavior. Seeking guidance from Mrs. Florence, I found a way forward; she suggested I share some personal experiences that might bring insight.

I took the opportunity to explain my relationship with Gail, the connection she once had with her father, and my experiences with my mother. After our conversation, Nicole seemed to grasp our shared struggles better, even though I knew it didn't remove the pain of Gail's departure. It was a difficult chapter, but through understanding and love, I hoped we could all navigate these turbulent waters together.

It had been weeks since anyone had heard from Gail; understandably, concern was mounting among us. Donald reached out to his relatives in Baton Rouge to check if anyone had seen her, but sadly, no one had seen her. As the days passed, my initial worries morphed into frustration; I felt she must realize how much we cared, yet she seemed distant. Thus, when I finally received a call from her, I asked if she had reached out to her family. When she confessed, she hadn't, I encouraged her to hang up and call them before we chatted further.

When she didn't return my call, I decided to swing by and see Donald. As I expected, he hadn't heard from her either. I shared my brief exchange with her and suggested he should hear from her, too, it was important.

Two weeks passed before I finally heard from her again. She explained that she hadn't contacted Donald because she felt unprepared to talk to them. I gently told her that regardless of her struggles, she shouldn't distance herself from family and certainly not put that burden on her daughter. I wondered if she truly understood how much they were suffering in her absence. Losing my patience, I urged her, what's going on? At the very least, let them know you're okay. The importance of Gail's family in her life was undeniable, and it was crucial for her to reconnect with them.

While she responded that she couldn't reach out, I took a deep breath to steady myself. What do you mean you can't? Just imagine how your daughter feels without you. I implored, evoking the image of Nicole's face, worried and longing for her mom. Gail replied that Nicole belonged to someone else, not her. That struck a chord as she snapped back fiercely, No. Look, Lillian, I must go; we'll talk later.

The next time we connected, I could hear the tears in her voice. She was lost, unsure of where she was or how she had ended up there. All she could remember was waking up on a bench in a park surrounded by trees. My heart ached for her as I tried to pinpoint her location. She described being near a children's playground, so I brought Mrs. Florence into the conversation for a calming presence. After a short while, I heard Mrs. Florence ask if a newspaper was nearby. With some effort, Gail found one and discovered it was from Walterboro, South Carolina. Just then, the call disconnected, leaving us in suspense.

This situation escalated my worry levels. We faced a tough decision about informing Donald, but I ultimately believed it would only add to his struggles. He had enough on his plate with everything he was already confronting, and revealing this would make things worse for him and Nicole. I decided to wait by the phone, hoping she would reach out again.

Finally, she called with a request to see me. I quickly took down the address, ready to support her. Leaving Mrs. Florence to care for Asia and the twins, I assured Patrick I would return in a couple of weeks. Though he was hesitant, he recognized how essential this was for me. Before I set out, I informed Donald about Gail's recent calls. I reiterated my commitment to being there for her, hoping this would clarify the situation deep down.

By supporting Gail, we could take small steps toward healing and reunification. No matter how difficult, every moment spent with family can help reignite connections that may feel fractured. I remained hopeful that together, we could find a path forward.

I arrived at Charleston International Airport at eight o'clock that evening, and there was Gail, waiting for me with a warm smile. I had braced myself to see someone deeply shaken, but to my delight, she stood tall and confident. I felt a wave of relief wash over me, mixed with curiosity from the unusual phone calls I had received from her.

As we made our way to her apartment, I was pleasantly surprised to find it nestled right in the vibrant heart of the Black community. That night, Gail began to open up about her journey since leaving New Orleans. Initially, she wasn't sure where she was headed but found solace at her friend

Louise's house in Baton Rouge, where they spent a couple of days talking and reconnecting.

Gail expressed the importance of a conversation with Louise that day in the park. She bravely addressed a comment she felt was racist, challenging Louise on her views regarding Nicole and Donald. With passion and conviction, Gail emphasized that everyone deserves the right to love and build their families with whomever they choose. She passionately expressed that everyone deserves the right to love, marry, and raise children with whomever they choose. Then, she playfully challenged the girl by asking if she would consider marrying a Black man. The girl's response was immediate and intense. Marry? Are you serious? Not. However, with a softer tone, she quickly admitted she hadn't had the opportunity to get to know a Black man on a deeper level. Gail couldn't help but smile, recognizing that this moment had unveiled the girl's genuine feelings.

During the remainder of her visit, they intentionally avoided conversations about race, focusing instead on current events, the weather, and light-hearted discussions. Gail was wise enough to understand that she wasn't there to change Louise; her goal was to confirm her suspicions.

After departing from Baton Rouge, something inspired her to head north, leading her to Walterboro, South Carolina. Before moving to her new apartment, she had lived on the other side of town, where most white people resided, thinking this was the key to finding the connection she so deeply craved.

I reminded her that she had been on this quest for connection since we met years ago. This search led her to leave my home when her baby was still very young, and here we are again, identifying the same challenge. She seemed to be disrupting so many lives in her pursuit, and all I wanted was for her to pause, reflect, and consider a more fulfilling path.

Sighing, she confessed, Lillian, I wish I understood what drives me like this. There's an emptiness in my life, and just when I think things are improving, this overwhelming feeling hits me, it's almost unbearable. I wish I could put my finger on it.

HerStory

TWENTY-EIGHT

When I woke up the following morning, I couldn't believe that Gail was gone or that she would leave me here all by myself. I thought that she went to the store, but after a while I realized that I was alone and there was no indication of where she was or if she was coming back. During our conversation last night, I threw some serious questions at her which seemed to make her uncomfortable. I called Mrs. Florence and asked if she heard from Gail. She couldn't believe that Gail would leave me alone like that and suggested that I stay for a while to see if she would return. I hung up the phone and turned to look around the apartment, and to my surprise I was reminded of our little house in the woods not because of the way it looked, but because of the way it felt, the solitude and despair in the air.

While I waited, I told myself that when she returned, I would stay in control and remain emotionless, but when I saw her face two days later, I couldn't help myself, I yelled, Where in the hell have you been, you invited me here just to leave me in a strange place alone, are you crazy.

She stood there looking at me with teary eyes and told me she was sorry and didn't know what was happening to her. The only thing she remembered was waking up and being enticed to leave, and she knew it was wrong but couldn't stop herself. Her confusion seemed to calm me, so I asked her to tell me what was going on in her life, she told me before she moved on her own, she lived with a man. Being with him made her happy at first, but after a while the emptiness returned and she realized she was only using him. She and Donald hadn't been sexually involved for some time because she wasn't attracted to him, and it got to the point where she didn't want him to touch her. She began to think he was the problem and worked up the nerve to talk to him about how she felt. When she finished, she could see the hurt in his eyes. She tried to tell him that it was something inside of her that was wrong, but she could see that didn't ease his pain. I told Gail of course he was in pain, why wouldn't he be, he loved her with all of his heart. She tried to tell me she didn't say it to hurt him like that but I assured her that it did.

I didn't want to hear any more of her bullshit because I was convinced that she had lost her mind again, cheating on her husband, this was unacceptable behavior. I just wanted to leave, but instead I asked her if she had contacted her family yet, when she told me she still wasn't ready to talk to them, I felt the blood rushing to my head and yelled, you're not ready? What are you waiting for? Why are you doing this to them? The very least you can do is call Nicole. I tried to explain to her what I thought was going on with you and she understood, but after you called me and didn't call her it hurt even more. I saw it in her eyes, so call them, please Gail, call them. I can understand you falling out of love with Donald, but for heaven's sake, Nicole is your daughter, forever, do you love her, do you?

Gail had the nerve to try to get an attitude, of course, I love her, what kind of question is that, why would you say something like that to me? I told her it was the question her daughter asked me all the time and if she loved her, then why was she putting her through so much agony. She doesn't understand why her mother refuses to talk to her. Gail was staring at me with teary eyes and said, yes, I do love my baby. I had finally gotten through to her, then I reiterated for her to do the right thing and call. She went to the phone, sat down on the sofa and said, Nicole, this is your mother, and I love you. I'm sorry I haven't called before this, but I've been trying to work out some of my problems.

I stepped outside to give her privacy, and met one of her neighbors, Mrs. Phyllis; she saw me sitting alone, came sat beside me and began a conversation. I could tell that she was a very nice person, she reminded me of Mrs. Florence. It was almost as if I knew her from somewhere else. She told me she had lived in Walterboro all her life and had two daughters who lived close by. I told her I was visiting my sister, after I said those words, I saw that familiar look of skepticism on her face then she smiled. I said, yes, she really is my sister. Are you surprised? She stared at me for a second or two and said no, not really because you two look alike. We both laughed as we sat there talking and joking about things. I was glad she was Gail's neighbor and thought maybe they could become friends, and perhaps she could help her figure out what her problems were.

When I left, Gail seemed to have stabilized herself, and since she had called home to talk to Nicole, I didn't feel that there was anything left for me to do. Two days after I returned home, I found a letter in my purse, it said, I find myself very lonely these days, I know I have Nicole and Donald but still I'm lonely, it feels like something very important is missing from my life. Is it Lillian, whom I long to be close to or is it Mrs. Florence I'm missing? I don't feel that myself and I are one, and I've tried so hard to explain this to everyone, but they don't seem to understand. I love Donald so much, but love isn't enough, our relationship makes me feel as if I'm sometimes being smothered by him. My life feels so one dimensional when I'm with my family, and I need more. This city fits my ambiguous mood, and I feel drawn to it in a weird way. There's something about it that makes me want to experience life in a new way, and find my true destiny. There is only one thing that stops me, fear, I'm afraid of finding out that there's nothing out there for me, or finding out that I don't belong anywhere, and that's what scares me the most.

That's where it ended, the letter sounded like a page out of her diary. I wanted to show Mrs. Florence this letter, but she was asleep, I tried to wait until she woke up, but she was taking too long. In my mind I yelled Mrs. Florence, can you hear me, and I heard her mumble something then I yelled again, Mrs. Florence can you hear me? She said yes, I hear you, what do you want that couldn't wait until I got up? Before I could answer her, the twins walked in so I told her when she got up call me, the line would be open.

Roland and Noland were having one of their infamous arguments, I asked them what the problem was and

Roland said, yesterday in class they were studying history, and the book said black people's freedom came in 1865, but the teacher said our freedom didn't really start until the 1960's, and we're barely free today. Noland agreed with the book, but Roland felt that he needed to open his eyes. They wanted to know my opinion on the subject, I told them that they were both right, on December 18, 1865, Slavery was abolished in America, and the 13th Amendment was formally adopted into the U.S. Constitution, but in reality, real changes were slow to come and didn't make great impacts for the majority of people until the 1960s, and still today, we're fighting for our fair share of everything from housing to employment and on and on. Roland said, mother when I grow up, I want to make changes in people's lives. He looked so serious as I looked into his eyes. They both walked out of the room saying see I told you so, mother agrees with me then I heard the other one said no, she agreed with me. I just smiled as they walked away.

I heard Mrs. Florence say Lillian I'm awake, what was so important that you couldn't wait? I told her I found a letter in my purse that Gail must have put there for me to read and wanted her to read it, and tell me what she thought. She said she would be out soon, so I waited about fifteen minutes, and when she hadn't come out, I yelled Mrs. Florence, are you coming. I didn't get an answer so I yelled again, Mrs. Florence are you ok, still no answer so I became frightened and ran to her room but she wasn't there, so I yelled again Mrs. Florence, where are you. She came out of the bathroom and said girl, what's wrong with you, can't a woman do her business? I told her she frightened me, and why didn't she answer me?

I've shared that our mental connections were disrupted during those private moments. If only you had called me, I would have gladly listened. Please keep this in mind, it can save you from unnecessary heartache. Now, let's talk about that letter.

After handing it to her, she read it and reassured me that it wasn't as confusing as I initially thought. Reread it; you'll uncover the wisdom she's trying to share with you. Call me when you begin to see it, she encouraged.

The first time I revisited the letter; I struggled to grasp Mrs. Florence's message. But then, it struck me with such clarity. It dawned on me that Gail had never formed strong connections with anyone. I wondered why she placed so much importance on bonding; it didn't seem that essential to me then. Now, with fresh insight, I see the value in it. It reminds me of Mema, who, although she had a bond as a baby, lost it when taken from her family, leaving her feeling adrift. In contrast, I formed deep bonds with my mother, Mrs. Florence, Robert, Patrick, and, of course, my children. Life can sometimes be perplexing, and having someone to communicate with is key.

The letter revealed that Gail had never allowed herself to bond with the people in her life. Despite her challenges, I thought she had found a connection with Donald, perhaps with Nicole, and even with Vivian. Yet, I still don't fully grasp the depth of this bond concept. Maybe that's not the only lesson hidden within the letter; I felt Mrs. Florence's presence guiding me.

Lillian, you're making progress. Keep pondering this, she advised.

When Gail finds herself in difficult situations, she often feels isolated and tends to run away, much like her father did with her mother. That realization made me pause; she shares qualities with him. During our conversations about her father, she intensely disliked his sudden departures, especially when she needed him the most. I asked Mrs. Florence, Is that the key?

Yes, you're spot on in many ways, but there's one final piece, the most crucial. People who haven't established proper bonds often feel an overwhelming urge to fill this fundamental human need. Without it, loneliness seeps in, despite the number of people surrounding them. You know the saying about being alone in a crowd? Gail lives that experience daily. She constantly seeks relief, yet she's unsure how to find it.

She said she needs you because she trusts you to stand by her during tough times. So, Lillian always endeavors to be there for her; she truly isn't a bad person. Remember the fork in the road I mentioned? Gail has lost sight of it, which contributes to her unpredictability. Reflect on this, and perhaps, just perhaps, you hold the key to helping her.

Our journey together has the potential for growth and deeper understanding. With empathy and patience, we can make a difference.

HerStory

TWENTY-NINE

When I received Robert's touching letter about their upcoming return for Thanksgiving, I was absolutely thrilled. It truly warmed my heart, especially thinking about little Asia, who had missed them way more than we could have ever imagined. Their move for school unexpectedly shifted her mood, which caught all of us off guard. The transition has been quite challenging, and we certainly weren't ready for the depth of her feelings. I vividly remember the morning after they left when Asia came into my room with tears in her eyes, exclaiming, Grandma, where are my mommy and daddy? It broke my heart to see her hurting. Although I tried my best to console her, it was clear how deeply their absence affected her. We hadn't fully understood just how impactful her first experience of separation would be.

Before they left, we had talked about college life, but the concept was hard for Asia to grasp. This was the longest she had been away from them. Seeking some support, I reached out to Mrs. Florence, whose nurturing spirit always brings comfort. I hoped Asia would feel a sense of security in her care. To my surprise, when I placed Asia in

Mrs. Florence's arms, she wrapped her tiny arms around her neck and said, Grandmama, I want my mommy and daddy. With such compassion, Mrs. Florence held her close, gently rocking her while saying, I know you miss your mommy and daddy.

Reflecting on this from my own room, I thought about how this was the first time Asia called me Grandma. While I had expected that moment to fill me with happiness, my main focus was on being there for Asia during this tough emotional time. It's certainly bittersweet, but together we'll get through it.

I woke up feeling energized, ready to embrace the day ahead. The house was peacefully quiet, creating a calming atmosphere. As I peeked into Mrs. Florence's room, I saw Asia peacefully snuggled up to her, both lost in sweet dreams. I smiled, knowing the twins were still sound asleep, only to be stirred by the delicious aroma of frying bacon, a breakfast treat they absolutely adored. As I busied myself in the kitchen, the anticipation of cooking filled the air. Just then, I heard the familiar sound of the twins waking up. They appeared in the doorway, rubbing their eyes and sporting sleepy smiles. I reassured them that breakfast would be ready shortly, and they eagerly dashed off to the bathroom. I chuckled, knowing the usual playful bickering about who would bathe first was on the horizon.

It was a light-hearted routine that sparked their lively banter. Their arguments over trivial things were almost endearing at just eight years old. I even tried creating a list once to settle the disputes, but that only worked briefly before they found something else to debate. It became clear that their disagreements were part of their unique bond, and I found joy in watching them learn to navigate their differences, all while growing closer in the process. By the time they were finished bathing, breakfast was calling. They arrived at the table with those infectious, sunny smiles, no signs of bumps or bruises from their little skirmishes.

Mrs. Florence and Asia were still in dreamland, giving me a moment to gather my thoughts. As I settled into the morning routine, I took a moment to connect with Mrs. Florence's thoughts and sensed a flicker of fear. It puzzled me, and just then, I heard a thought whispering, Mommy and Daddy don't love me anymore. A wave of sadness washed over me, it felt like I was tapping into Asia's emotions instead. This fleeting insight transported me back to my own childhood. I remember sitting down with my mother, who told me to walk down that road if she didn't return from work. I could feel the fear rising within me as I replayed that memory, and my heart ached at the thought of my granddaughter experiencing something similar. I found myself wishing I could shield her from that pain. I was jolted back to the present by Noland's lively shout, you're burning the bacon. The urgency in his voice snapped me back to the task at hand, and I quickly finished preparing breakfast.

After we gathered around the table, the twins ignited another debate about the words lay and lie. Their zest for discussion was truly impressive. Watching them, I couldn't help but think they might make great leaders someday, passionately voicing their opinions on various topics. As breakfast concluded, the debate only grew more animated.

They spotted their reflections in the mirror, and one exclaimed, don't we look just alike? The other quickly disagreed, stating, No way. My head is different, and I'm definitely more handsome. Their friendly banter brought laughter to the room.

In that heartfelt moment, Mrs. Florence walked in, cradling a sleepy Asia in her arms. She gently handed Asia over to me, and I wrapped my granddaughter in a warm embrace, pouring all my love and the love of her parents into that hug. As a few tears slipped down Asia's cheeks, I was struck by a deep desire to connect with her, yet I found myself unsure of her thoughts. Just then, Patrick strolled in, ready to start his day with breakfast. I easily passed Asia to Mrs Florence while preparing a plate for him.

I felt an exciting urge to share my thoughts with Mrs. Florence, yet a familiar sadness pinned me down, tied to Asia's feelings. Once I finished Patrick's breakfast, I sensed Asia's need for comfort. I sought a quieter space in the living room, hoping to create a serene atmosphere for her. Settling by the window, I honed in on her soft cries for mommy. I longed to soothe her spirit, whispering gentle reassurances that her parents would be back soon, but her distress lingered.

Before long, Mrs. Florence returned, cradling Asia once more, and lovingly placed her back into my arms. When our eyes met, an intense wave of emotions flowed between us, fostering a beautiful understanding. Mrs. Florence gently urged me to reflect on my own childhood feelings, reminding me that doing so would help Asia feel truly understood. It resonated with me; while our journeys may differ, our shared experiences of pain connect us all in profound ways. That's when I heard the infamous click,

I realized this was the first time in a long time that I was able to think back to my childhood and actually remember the loneliness. Through the years, I had convinced myself that the pain I suffered as a child hadn't been so bad, but as I sat hugging my grandchild, I became angry with my mother. She was never there for me when I was hurting, and I knew if she had, it would have made a big difference in my life. As I sat there holding Asia, I had a clear picture in my mind of a little girl about four years old sitting in a corner crying, I wanted to reach out and hug her. For a moment, she stopped crying, it was as if she felt my presence. She stood up and reached her hand out to me and as I reached out for her it was as if I was looking through a flickering light. I wanted so bad to hold the little girl in my arms, I just didn't know how, and then she said, please hold me, please, you understand what I'm feeling, please hold me.

The confusion I was feeling had become unbearable, I couldn't figure out how to get to her, and as the picture in my mind began to fade, the little girl started yelling, please, don't leave me alone, I need you, don't leave me here, take me with you. The voice stopped, and the little girl went away, I tried hard to get her back, but I didn't know where she came from or why she came to me in the first place. All day I tried to figure out a way to help Asia because she was still very unhappy.

The next evening, I went to Mrs. Florence room, since I couldn't enter her mind, I had to speak outwardly. I told her I couldn't help Asia, she said only three words to me, the little girl, so I went back to my room to mull over what she said, and still couldn't figure it out. I got up, went sat by the window and after being there for a few minutes, I heard Asia crying. I knew I had to do something so, I went to Asia and brought her back to the window seat. I sat there rocking, talking and singing to her, hoping it would calm her. Then I gave her some warm milk hoping that would help, but nothing I did made a difference. I called out to Mrs. Florence, What can I do, I can't stand to see her this way, it hurts me to see her suffering like this, please help me.

I began rocking back and forth harder and harder than all of a sudden, I felt the little girl enter my mind once again. She said, hold me, someone please hold me. I could clearly see her even though she had her back to me. The little voice kept crying out. She turned and reached out, please don't leave me here alone, take me back with you I belong with you. Don't leave me here. The little girl was looking at me, then the picture started fading. Don't leave me again, don't hurt me. I yelled, come closer, I don't know how to hold you, I'm sorry you're hurting, I'm sorry your mother hurt you, I'm sorry my mother hurt me. Mema, I'll never forgive you, it's your fault that I hurt so much as a child, why did you do that to me?

The little girl said I'm sorry I upset you, it's not your fault you can't hold me, just as it wasn't Mema's fault, she couldn't hold you when you were a child.

After she said those words, I could feel my adult body coming toward her. She looked at me and raised her arms

323

up. I walked over to her and held her. She said if our mother had known the pain, she would've been there for us. While standing there holding her, I could feel the spirit entering my body. She said, at last we are one.

I must have fallen asleep because the next thing I remember I was waking up, Asia was still sleeping, she hadn't slept this good since Robert and Natalie left for school. I couldn't wait to tell Mrs. Florence what had happened and when I focused, I felt her presence and knew the line was open. I asked her if she knew what happened to me because I wasn't sure, she told me to explain, that maybe she could help. I told her the whole story and that I didn't understand why it happened at this time because I wasn't having problems, Asia was. I didn't see how that was going to help my grandchild, sure it made me feel better to have another chapter closed, but what did this have to do with her? She asked me where was Asia, and I told her she was asleep. She then said, that little girl wasn't you, it was Asia she was angry with her parents for leaving her. Last night you and she bonded, she needed to bond to someone here. It was hard for you because of your experiences. You hadn't really bonded with her until now.

I told her I was able to read Asia's mind and she told me that wasn't true, I wasn't reading Asia's mind it was her mind I was reading because she had the connection. She said she knew the pain was too great for Asia to handle so she put in a line to give her some relief. Whenever I tried to reach her, our connection connected me to Asia. She said Asia would be all right, just keep reminding her that her parents love her.

HerStory

THIRTY

T he excitement was palpable in our home the day before Thanksgiving, with Asia bursting with energy and anticipation. She dashed around, cheerfully singing, my mommy and daddy are coming. They promised they'd be back for me. I gently reminded her that they would only briefly visit before returning to school. This time, she grasped what I meant. Later that evening, a taxi pulled up in front of our house, and to my surprise, four people emerged. I guess I had missed the memo about additional guests joining the family. When Asia spotted the taxi, her joy was contagious as she exclaimed, They're here. They're here. Instead of the warm embrace I expected, they were enveloping their friends. Realizing I needed a plan, I asked Asia to fetch Mrs. Florence.

Once she left the room, I contacted Mrs. Florence silently, hoping she could keep Asia engaged while I figured out the situation. The newcomers introduced themselves as a young man named Melvin and a lovely young woman named Tyneka. Eager to be a good host, I offered them some refreshments, then discreetly pulled Natalie aside to learn more about these unexpected visitors. However, she seemed preoccupied with finding where Asia was, pressing me with her concern. After some silence, she finally agreed to discuss things later, but I could sense she felt just as unsettled as I did. The tension and uncertainty in the air were palpable. When I inquired whether Melvin and Tyneka knew about Asia, Natalie hesitated before admitting they didn't. I couldn't help but express my worry, exclaiming, No? What will happen if she calls you Mommy? It's crucial to acknowledge her. Natalie responded, we haven't denied her; it hasn't come up. She then inquired about Asia's whereabouts, hoping to see her little girl soon. I reassured her, saying that Asia was happily with Mrs. Florence. She exited the room and tried to allay my fears, saying, don't worry, they're not staying long; they just have a four-hour layover.

I heard Robert joyfully chatting with Roland and Noland from the kitchen. Wow. Look at how much you two have grown. One exclaimed, Check it out; I'm taller than him. This playful rivalry sparked a lively argument, and Robert couldn't help but laugh, realizing that, in many ways, those boys hadn't changed at all. After enjoying those light-hearted moments, he returned to the living room, eager to share everything about the twins with his friends. Meanwhile, Natalie went to fetch Asia but returned empty-handed, sharing that Asia had worn herself out. So, Natalie and I cozied up in the living room, where we spent a couple of hours sharing stories and laughter. I felt relieved when Tyneka mentioned they had to head to the airport. I asked Patrick if he could take them, and soon, all four rose to leave. As I glanced out the window, my heart swelled as I saw them sharing a kiss, a sweet moment that brought a smile to my face. They came back inside, and as I turned to them, I asked if we could chat quickly. However, their minds were wrapped around thoughts of their baby. They attempted to rouse her from her slumber but to no avail, so they gently tucked her into bed before returning to me. While I waited in the living room, anticipation built within me. When they finally returned, I asked, can someone shed some light on what's happening? Are you two still married? What are your plans after college? I'm eager to know. They looked at each other, and then Robert spoke candidly.

Well, we don't have all the answers, Mother. We married for that beautiful child there when we were deeply in love. But now, we share more of a friendship. We still do everything together, but it often feels more like brother and sister. Curious, I probed further, So, how did you explain things to Tyneka and Melvin? That you're like siblings? He quickly responded, not quite. We told them we're friends. I cherish Natalie as a friend; it's a strong connection, and we both hope our love can transform into something that inspires us to spend our lives together. But right now, that's just not where we are. After he expressed those heartfelt thoughts, I could see a wave of sadness wash over both him and Natalie, as if they were finally confronting feelings they had kept bottled up. They spent a while silently gazing into each other's eyes, and I sensed they were searching for something profound. Then, a gentle acknowledgment of their love for one another flickered between them. Robert then turned to me with a request, Mother, can we have a moment alone? I think Natalie and I need to have an important talk. Tears glimmered in his eyes, and I stood up to give them space. Just before I turned to leave, I caught sight of him wrapping his arms around her, whispering, I love you. He then asked her how she felt about him, sounding just like his father did when he posed that same question to me over two decades ago. Though I didn't hear her reply when I glanced back, they were kissing, and my heart felt happy for them.

I woke up bright and early on Thanksgiving morning, excited for a special dinner. The family was coming together, and I couldn't wait to see everyone. The only one missing was Gail; we hadn't heard from her lately, which concerned me. Since I was preparing a whopping twenty-five-pound turkey, I had to start cooking immediately to ensure everything would be ready on time. This year, I'm thrilled to try out some delicious stuffed peppers and mirliton; thanks to Mrs. Florence and Nicole for growing those fresh ingredients. I recently got a fantastic recipe from Mrs. Bernadette, and I'm eager to see how it turns out. Of course, no Thanksgiving dinner is complete without my famous gumbo, which I always customize with extra shrimp for Noland and extra crab for Nicole. Once the gumbo is bubbling, I'll whip up some baked macaroni and cheese, followed by hot potato salad, because I've learned that the kids just won't eat it cold. After all the savory dishes, I'll reveal the desserts I prepared yesterday, which include bread pudding, sweet potato pie, and a luscious coconut cake. It will be a wonderful celebration filled with warmth, laughter, and delicious food.

When I peeped into the living room, Robert and Natalie were sleeping on the sofa, arm in arm. I wanted so bad to ask them if they were sexually involved with other people, but I realized they weren't kids anymore. As I walked into the kitchen, Mrs. Florence entered my thoughts:

No, they are not. Before going to college, they had to confront their feelings but didn't know how to stop fighting them after leaving. It will take some time for them to realize that what they seek in a relationship is right before them. The good thing is that they are still friends. Their friendship will hold them together until they are ready to start their family.

I felt a wave of warmth wash over me when Mrs. Florence popped into my thoughts, brightening my day. I questioned whether my efforts were truly beneficial, and she reassured me that I made a positive difference. The sun had just begun to peek through the curtains when Asia burst into the kitchen, her little voice ringing excitedly, Where's my mommy and daddy? I gently told her to lower her voice, explaining that they peacefully slept on the sofa. She marched over and snuggled on Robert's chest with a delightful determination. As he opened his eyes and saw her there, he responded softly before wrapping her in his arms. The comfort of each other's presence had lulled them back to sleep in no time.

Watching them, I couldn't help but think they were the sweetest little family, and it filled my heart with hope that one day they would genuinely be a united family. Around eight o'clock, Natalie sauntered into the kitchen with an appreciative smile, eager to thank me for everything I had done for her and Asia. Her optimism was infectious as she believed their family was on the right path to happiness. She recounted how she and Robert had felt uncertain about their relationship in their first college days and decided to take some time apart. As it turned out, being away from each other only deepened their feelings of loneliness. One day, Robert reached out, saying he missed his best friend, and that was all it took, they had been inseparable friends ever since. Reflecting on a moment from the night before, Natalie shared how lying in Robert's arms had made her realize those were the arms she wanted to be in forever.

With a flicker of worry, Natalie asked if her mother or father had come to visit Asia. I hesitated, but I knew I needed to be honest with her, it hurt to admit that they hadn't paid a visit since she left for college. While at school, her mother sent a few letters, but they never mentioned Asia, leaving Natalie uneasy. A shadow crossed her face as she turned away, tears brimming in her eyes. It was clear that, despite everything, she still loved her parents, and the distance was painful. She looked at me with hope and despair, Mother, was what we did so terrible? Can't they see we were just kids? Don't they realize people make mistakes? I don't know where I would be without your kindness. When I think of how they reacted, I feel this surge of anger, yet that doesn't diminish my love for them. I know two wrongs don't make a right, but their behavior feels unfair. I encouraged her to consider her parents' perspective when they learned about her pregnancy. She was still so young, barely fifteen, and feelings of betrayal had changed everything. I reminded her that she was no longer just their little girl and that letting go had likely been an overwhelming experience for them. Sometimes, people say hurtful things out of anger, and as that anger subsides, finding the right words to express remorse can be daunting. It's common for people to avoid reconciling because addressing emotions feels so intimidating. I urged her to reach out and express her feelings, as I sensed that too much precious time had already slipped away. With a

331

newfound determination, Natalie nodded, realizing I was right. She decided she was ready to talk to her parents right away. With a loving heart, she dressed Asia, and they set off together. I couldn't shake the worry from my mind, but then I heard a reassuring voice say, you don't need to stress; they'll be just fine. Feeling hopeful, I looked forward to what was to come next.

Later that morning, my phone rang as I was joyfully whipping up breakfast. It was Natalie, and she had a question: would it be all right for her parents to join us for Thanksgiving dinner? Without a second thought, I said yes. They're always welcome in my home, they're also Asia's wonderful grandparents. After hanging up, I felt a little spark of anticipation and wanted to share this great news with Mrs. Florence, but I couldn't help but think she might already be in the loop. As I busied myself in the kitchen, the delicious aroma of bacon sizzling in the pan filled the air. Just then, the twins popped out of their room like clockwork. I told them excitedly that we had guests coming and encouraged them to wear their best clothes for the occasion. From the bathroom, I could hear their playful banter about the meaning of Thanksgiving, it was so sweet to listen to. Just as I finished cooking, Natalie and her parents arrived, bringing a wave of warmth with them. When Robert spotted Bube, he greeted him, exclaiming, Bube, you made us feel so guilty that you'd give up your only daughter and beautiful granddaughter. I love them, and if that's a problem for you, that's something you'll have to work through. After college, we're planning to live together as a family. He strolled over to Natalie, gently took Asia in his arms, and confidently continued, how can you say what we did was wrong when it brought you your only grandchild? Look at her, she's a blessing. You might as well embrace this picture because it's here to stay.

Bube kindly walked over to Robert, and Robert returned Asia to Natalie with a warm smile. Just as Bube extended his hand toward Robert in a gesture of goodwill, Robert, caught off guard, reacted by throwing a punch that sent Bube to the ground. Natalie quickly set Asia down and rushed to her father, exclaiming, what were you thinking? On the ground, Bube reassured her, no, sweetheart, I deserved that. He turned to Robert and said sincerely, I just wanted to shake your hand to apologize and seek your forgiveness. Wow, you really pack a punch.

Robert's expression of realization showed that he felt remorseful. I'm truly sorry, he admitted, looking down. I must have lost my mind. He deeply cared for Natalie, and seeing Bube's actions hurt her and also affected him. It was a moment that hinted at the possibility of understanding and healing between them.

Bube stood up, determined to approach Robert, extending his hand again with a warm smile. As he got closer, Robert hesitated but reached out, only to be met with an unexpectedly powerful punch that sent him soaring across the floor.

With sincere concern, Bube said, what you did to my daughter four years ago hurt her deeply. As a father, her pain is my pain. Now it feels like we've settled the score. How about a handshake to move forward?

Robert slowly lifted his head with a chuckle and replied, just a favor, let's not have a repeat of that; I thought I was done for.

A moment of tension melted into laughter, filling the space with a newfound sense of understanding and camaraderie.

The twins burst into the living room, their cheerful good morning. brightening the atmosphere. They turned to Maxine and Bube, warm smiles on their faces, and called out, Hi, Mrs. Maxine. Hi, Mr. Bube. Evidently, they shared a sweet bond with them, prompting me to ask how they knew the Wiggins family. Just as the question left my lips, a delightful memory hit me: Mrs. Florence. I could almost hear her infectious laughter in the air. Natalie chimed in, promising to explain everything after breakfast, and I couldn't wait to hear more.

After our delicious meal, Robert, Patrick, and Bube headed outside for a chat. Roland and Noland retreated to their room, playfully squabbling about something trivial, while Asia and Maxine settled comfortably in the living room. As Natalie opened up, she shared how she felt determined that morning as she prepared to confront her parents. Yet, the closer she got home, a wave of fear crept in, almost making her reconsider. Still, she knew she had to muster the courage to face them.

When she arrived, Asia was peacefully asleep. She knocked gently, and her father answered the door. The moment Asia woke and saw him, her eyes lit up, and she exclaimed, Grandpa. Her baby leaped into his arms in an adorable flurry, catching her off guard. Shortly after, they shared some heartwarming moments while talking. He shared that before they learned about her pregnancy, he and Natalie's mother were contemplating a divorce, as things hadn't been going well between them. However, they had stuck together for Natalie's sake, and it was really Mrs. Florence's encouragement that had helped them reconnect.

Through open dialogue, compromise, and a genuine effort to restore their bond, they found it within themselves to forgive and love Asia fully, exactly how she deserved to be loved. He mentioned how often Mrs. Florence would bring Asia and the twins over for delightful visits, nurturing their relationship.

A moment later, Robert, Bube, and Patrick re-entered the kitchen, laughter bubbling. Curious, I inquired what had them in stitches, and Patrick shared the comical story of Robert's startled reaction when he accidentally socked Bube. Apparently, his fist had moved on its own, and Bube's astonished face as he found himself on the floor was pure comedy gold. Their laughter was infectious.

Then Nicole and Donald popped by, always a welcome addition to our celebrations, especially since they began spending their holidays with us. I fondly recalled that first Christmas when I stopped by to wish them well, only to find Donald struggling in the kitchen. He's an excellent cook, but he'd been under the weather that season. I jumped in to help him finish the meal, and from that day on, I made it a point to invite them over for every holiday celebration.

As they settled in, I felt a gentle tug at my heart, wishing to ask Donald about Gail. Yet, I hesitated, if he hadn't heard from her, I certainly didn't want to discuss a complex topic. Instead, I focused on the joyous atmosphere enveloping us, filled with laughter, love, and cherished memories in the making.

Nicole was delighted to see Natalie and Robert. Before they went to school, she and Natalie had become good friends, and for the rest of the day, they sat around talking and laughing together. Asia stayed by her daddy's side most of the day; occasionally, I noticed Nicole trying to get her attention, but Asia ignored her, which seemed to hurt Nicole a little. When their parents were at school, Asia and Nicole had become close. With Natalie gone, it felt like Nicole had taken on a motherly role for Asia. They would go shopping, visit the park, or play educational games together, but now Asia acted like Nicole didn't exist. Later in the day, I walked past Nicole and said, your baby is with her daddy now. She turned toward me and smiled, and that one statement seemed to put her at ease.

After everyone left, Mrs. Florence and I talked about Robert and Natalie's relationship. She mentioned they had bonded the night they fell asleep on the sofa. While she said they had bonded, I interpreted it differently and considered it more intimately. I could have sworn they told me they hadn't engaged in anything physical, but Mrs. Florence assured me they were speaking the truth; their mental bond formed as they lay arm in arm. Their minds had connected deeply, this kind of making love, though not always physical, is sometimes just as important. When Asia laid by their side, they united as a family.

HerStory

That Thanksgiving remains special to me because everyone was so happy. I had prayed that Natalie's parents would re-enter her life, and what better day for it to happen than on Thanksgiving? That year, I had a lot to be thankful for.

THIRTY-ONE

When Robert and Natalie graduated, they joyfully renewed their marriage vows and chose to settle in Pontchartrain Park, just a quick ten-minute drive from us. Asia was absolutely over the moon about having her parents nearby and finally having her own space to call home, complete with her own room and belongings. It was a beautiful new chapter for them. Robert landed a great job at the University of New Orleans, while Natalie could work part-time at Hibernia Bank, which meant so much to her as she valued the time spent with Asia. Every time I was with my son, my heart swelled with pride, knowing that his father was looking down with a beaming smile, whispering, Job well done.

As Robert graduated, Roland and Noland were fourteen and navigating their ninth-grade year. These two were engaged in spirited debates, they often found themselves on opposing sides of issues, which made for lively discussions at home. Their topics frequently centered around historical events, turning our dinner table into a mini classroom. I particularly cherished our conversations about the Reconstruction era. Noland felt it could have succeeded if everyone had adhered to the rules. At the same time, Roland passionately argued that there was never a genuine intention to follow them, making success impossible.

Throughout the years, these young men broadened my understanding of America and Black history. Roland viewed American history through the lens of his-story, emphasizing the dominant narrative often sidelining others. We encountered various perspectives, including some who controversially suggested that enslaved individuals were happy with their lot, believing they didn't have to worry about basic needs. However, we engaged in heartfelt discussions about the actual cost of such a life, where everything came at the expense of their very existence. It was clear to me that if anyone viewed such a reality as a reason for happiness, we had some profound misunderstandings to address.

These conversations not only fostered understanding but also deepened our connections as a family.

Noland has always had an inquisitive spirit and is genuinely curious about the challenges of our world. I distinctly recall a moment from his sixth-grade year, while we were driving, he spotted an elementary school across town that bore an impressive resemblance to a high school or a college campus. It struck him as unfair, and I found myself grappling with the uncomfortable reality of explaining why the stark difference existed between his school and that one, which was meant for white students. It felt as if he instinctively understood the answer. I will never forget the confusion in his eyes as he expressed his feelings about it not being fair. I silently agreed, thinking, you're right, my son; this isn't fair. How could I adequately convey to a child that such blatant inequalities were overlooked in our society?

Fast forward to their ninth-grade graduation, a truly unforgettable day where Roland and Noland delivered powerful speeches. At that moment, I had a profound realization: they would undoubtedly be drawn to public service. They devoted themselves to their debate team throughout high school, and their passion didn't end there. They also shared their voices at local schools, senior citizen centers, and libraries. Over time, Noland gravitated towards speaking engagements at educational institutions, while Roland dedicated himself to community organizations focused on helping at-risk Black youth. Their hard work paid off, and they earned scholarships to further their education upon graduation.

One morning, Roland approached us with a sense of urgency in his eyes. He wanted to discuss his future. While we understood his aspirations, we hadn't anticipated that he wanted to dive into community work before even starting college. He said, Mom, Dad, I know you envision me heading off to college, but not everyone is ready for that commitment. There is so much going on in our community, particularly among young Black men who are missing out on critical education and mentorship. This often leads to underemployment and disillusionment with the American Dream. Unfortunately, some feel they have to resort to desperate measures. I believe I can create real change. I have many ideas and genuinely feel this is my calling, so I hope you'll support me in this journey.

His enthusiasm and sincerity were impossible to ignore, filling me with pride and hope for the difference he could make in the world.

I felt a burst of energy inside me, wanting to shout, go to college. Your journey will still be waiting for you when you get back. But as much as I tried to encourage him, I knew giving him the space to make his own choices was important. I reassured him that our support would be unwavering regardless of his path. I then asked if he had any idea what his brother was planning. Noland was set to start college and hoped Roland could join him. But he fully understood why Roland needed to stay.

As fall approached, Noland began his college adventure, while Roland stayed home for the first month, finding it hard to get into a routine. I could see he missed Noland more than he anticipated. However, he pivoted towards his dreams once he adjusted to the quietness. It wasn't easy initially; he believed fiercely that everyone deserved an opportunity and a new outlook, someone to remind them of their invaluable worth and that any dream could become a reality with determination. I reminded him that it can be hard to see their true potential when people have faced challenges for so long. They've often believed the negativity surrounding them and felt they were doing their best. I suggested he focus on the small victories rather than the overwhelming larger picture. The little steps would add up, and people often don't realize their capability; it just requires persistence and faith.

One day at work, Nicole asked if they could talk after his shift. Feeling uneasy about discussing her situation at the center, they agreed to meet at the house. Roland had sensed that Nicole was struggling and was eager to lend a hand. She was tackling several challenges: not having graduated high school yet, difficulty in her relationships, a lack of friends outside her family, and an overall sense of gloom. Roland was ready to inspire her, believing they could work together to overcome these obstacles.

My heart swelled with joy when she came over for dinner that evening. It had been a while since we last shared a meal, and I couldn't wait to catch up. After dinner, though, I noticed a hint of worry on her face, as if something was weighing on her mind. It soon became evident that they needed a little privacy to discuss things. Respecting their need for space, I leisurely returned to my rocking chair on the front porch. Nestled under the shade of my beloved magnolia tree, which I affectionately call my memory seat, I settled in, knowing it would offer a comforting refuge for my thoughts to wander.

As the crisp evening air wrapped around me, my mind drifted back to Gail and a peculiar letter I had received from her following my first visit. Intrigued and determined to connect, I decided it was time for another visit. Upon arrival at her home, I was delighted to see how Gail and Mrs. Phyllis blossomed into wonderful friends. Their bond warmed my heart as Gail shared tales of spending hours chatting, with Mrs. Phyllis lending a compassionate ear and offering insightful guidance to help Gail navigate her challenges. Her wise counsel reminded Gail that life inherently ebbs and flows, that running away is never the answer, and that each day should be embraced as a precious gift.

It's remarkable how our past contributes to our identities, yet it should never be a chain that binds us. Instead, it can be a springboard, propelling us toward brighter horizons. We can genuinely flourish by reflecting on our experiences, analyzing them, and gently letting them go. If we allow our past to overshadow our potential, we risk being ensnared by its shadows, ultimately missing out on the beautiful possibilities.

Mrs. Florence's wise words resurfaced in my thoughts, and I wanted to speak with Mrs. Phyllis. Just as Gail and I were conversing, Mrs. Phyllis approached. I wanted to ask if she had ever known Mrs. Florence, and I gazed into her eyes, searching for a spark of recognition. My mind busily contemplated, do you know Mrs. Florence? She smiled back, a soft expression that made me curious and hopeful.

The chats with Mrs. Phyllis uplifted Gail, encouraging her to return home with me. Nicole and Donald were overjoyed to see her. As we settled in, Gail wanted Nicole to stay the night as she and Donald sought quality bonding time. I couldn't help but dream that this reunion might be permanent. Yet, like a delicate clock ticking away, I sensed Gail's restlessness returning, her longing to flee creeping back in. Despite the challenges, I remain optimistic about our journey ahead and the countless beautiful moments still waiting to unfold.

As I sat beneath the comforting shade of the tree, reflecting on Gail, I was momentarily interrupted by Nicole crying. Concerned, I decided to head into the kitchen to see what was happening. Roland reassured me, saying, Mother, we're just conversing; she'll be alright. Feeling that their talk was necessary, I retreated to the living room.

I heard Roland gently say, Nicole, it's important to recognize that you're an adult now. You are responsible for your life, and it's time to take charge of it.

Nicole responded with vulnerability, I get what you're saying, but sometimes I feel incredibly alone and abandoned. I just don't know where to turn.

Roland's sincerity shone through as he replied, I want you to know I'm here for you. Whenever loneliness creeps in, reach out to me. You're family, and I care about you deeply. I will always have time for you. How about we schedule a time to talk more at the center? With relief, Nicole said, no, I feel more comfortable talking here if that's okay with you.

Of course, he answered warmly. Let's dive in. What's on your mind right now? The room fell into a thoughtful silence for a few minutes. I considered getting up to check on them, but just as I felt the urge to break the quiet, Nicole finally spoke again.

Roland, when I look at our family, I see how well everyone's doing. Robert and Natalie are thriving; you and Noland seem grounded in your paths. Then there's me, I'm twenty-three and feel lost. I struggle to maintain any relationships because I'm terrified of ending up like my mother, always running away. I have such anger towards her for never being there for me. Sometimes, if she had chosen to stay home, our lives, especially my father's, would have been much happier. Just look at what her choices have done to him.

I remember when he was the pillar of our family: a loving husband, a dedicated father, a tall, strong, handsome man. Each time she left, she took a piece of him. Now, seeing him brings me sorrow. I cannot find it to forgive her for the hurt she caused him. His health has declined, and he seems incapable of love or joy anymore, all because of what she did.

Hearing her express such raw emotions was heartbreaking, but I also felt a spark of hope that they could navigate these challenges together with love and support.

As I sat there, genuinely listening to her, I couldn't help but think about my mother. The sadness in her voice resonated deeply, reminding me so much of what Mema had once felt.

Nicole, the first and most important step for you is to let go of your resentment towards your mother. Nobody is perfect. Holding onto that anger will only hold you back from truly loving yourself. I want you to ponder this, and then we can continue our conversation tomorrow. I'd like to talk to my mother about this if that's alright with you. She might offer insights to help us better understand your mother's situation.

Nicole agreed, expressing her trust in me for this discussion. Roland then gently asked if she would like to stay the night, but she declined, mentioning her promise to her dad to come home and prepare dinner. She committed to making smothered potatoes, knowing how much he cherished that meal and how it always lifted his spirits. As they walked past me, I wanted to run to her, embrace her, and tell her how much I cared. Yet, I knew this was not my burden but her mother's.

When Roland returned, we dove into a heartfelt conversation. He shared that he had no idea Nicole was grappling with such profound issues. He remarked on how her face reflected every emotion as she spoke, unveiling some of her darkest struggles. What astonished him most was that Nicole had always been part of our lives, yet her struggles had remained hidden. This realization prompted him to reflect on others he interacted with, how could they be in such difficult places without anyone noticing? He mused that perhaps their families had given up on them, but Nicole had taught him that this isn't always the case; sometimes, families simply don't see the pain that's there.

Roland felt inspired to advocate for open communication within families, realizing that helping just one person tackles only half the problem. He expressed a newfound curiosity about his aunt and her journey. He shared, When I decided to pursue this kind of work, I never imagined I would find myself trying to assist someone so close, a family member, no less.

I reminded him that everyone faces challenges throughout their lives. I revealed that he might be surprised to learn I had experienced a period in my teen years where I considered taking my own life. My struggles were far more complex than he could have envisioned. I explained to him that Gail's and my problems were traced back to our paternal grandfather. The way he raised our father contributed to the challenges we all carry today. Digging into family history can often uncover deeply unsettling truths.

Even though Gail wasn't there to support Nicole, she had Donald, who needed her. Unfortunately, when he fell ill, she sacrificed her life to care for him. Mrs. Florence and I did our best to provide support, but the reality was that she longed for her mother's presence. Over the years, Nicole had become skillful at concealing her true feelings, which made it hard for anyone to recognize the depth of her struggles. But now, she stands on the brink of releasing her pain.

I've spent years attempting to convey to Nicole that Gail's behavior was not a reflection of her worth, but she couldn't truly absorb that message. Hearing it from you will resonate with her in a way that brings her comfort and healing. Together, we can help her discover the love and strength she deserves.

Every time Nicole seemed to make some progress in understanding her mom, it felt like just as suddenly, Gail would leave again. I had hoped Nicole was coping better than she was, but it became clear that she was struggling. When she decided to drop out of school, it really highlighted that something was off. I reached out to her, trying to lend my support, but our conversations didn't quite hit the mark. That's when I thought it might be beneficial for her to connect with Natalie for help getting a job at the bank. It looked like a promising first step and helped her, but deep down, I knew it wasn't a long-term solution.

I've held back from sharing my experiences because they carry a lot of hurt. Yet, providing a clear picture of what he might encounter while working with individuals facing personal challenges is essential. I told him about my life and the trials Mema and I faced together. When I finished sharing, I could see how much it affected him. he said, you know, mother, the reality is that this situation could still be happening today. People often think, if it's not happening to me, then it's not real. This mindset needs to change, and I want to take action right here in my community.

During our conversation, I explained how societal norms impacted my journey, especially when I felt different. When I mentioned my differences, he gave me a curious look and asked, Mother, what makes you different? I smiled, reassuring him that what's important is how we move forward, not necessarily the specifics of my past. When he asked about Gail's role in our story, I shared everything I knew about her and how our paths crossed. I really wish I understood her struggles better. She seems caught in a cycle of running from problems that are still hard for her to identify.

The following morning, I was thrilled to see him still peacefully asleep in the same spot I left him. When he finally woke up, he intriguingly asked how I transformed into the firm and positive person he admired now. I took a moment to explain that my childhood was tangled with confusion. Our minds can only handle so much before seeking an escape, sometimes leading to puzzling choices.

An overwhelmed mind can plant thoughts that life might not be worth living. It was wise Mrs. Florence who taught me that experiencing confusion is part of being human; we all feel it at some point, just as we experience happiness. Emotions serve as signals that something needs our attention, and as I learned to navigate these feelings, my life began to take shape.

While I can't say everything is perfect now, I know our emotions make us who we are. How we respond to them defines our true essence. Gail hasn't entirely acknowledged her past, so she seems to block it out. My priority was that you and your brothers wouldn't have to escape from anything in your past. Many wonderful people resonate with these experiences, and it's crucial to remember that everyone carries their own emotions. I encourage you to take the time to listen to those who wish to share because you never truly know what someone has gone through until you learn their story. That understanding is the first step toward making a real difference in their lives.

Mom, I truly appreciate your perspective, and it's essential to recognize that the story of African Americans is deeply intertwined with a much broader history. Many of us often think of this history as something that happened hundreds of years ago, but in the grand timeline of humanity, that is just a blink of an eye. When we explore our past, we confront the painful reality that some of our ancestors were enslaved, which can be a difficult truth to face.

It's hard to consider the atrocities they endured, being treated inhumanely, suffering from violence, and facing unimaginable hardships. Focusing solely on that darkness might stir feelings of anger and resentment, but it's crucial to remember that this does not define us or our future.

The way history is often presented in schools can feel distant, as though it describes a separate, impersonal event. However, I believe it's vital to personalize these stories. They are about our family and our heritage, and we have every reason to take pride in our lineage. Yes, the past holds painful memories that should never be forgotten, but it also reflects the incredible strength, resilience, and hope of those who came before us.

Our ancestors prayed for freedom, not just for themselves, but for us. They endured so that we could have a brighter future. Now, here we stand as a testament to their strength. I genuinely believe that the way we rise from such adversity is a powerful reflection of who we are. We are a strong people, resilient in the face of unspeakable challenges, and that strength is something to celebrate and cherish. Let's continue to honor their legacy by living proudly and joyfully in the freedom they fought for.

As he spoke, I noticed tears welling in his eyes, and it was clear that he was deeply connected to his words. It was getting late, and he needed to prepare for his visit to the center. Before I left, I turned to him and asked what was fueling his passion. He replied, it's because some of my people are still acting as if we're in bondage, believing there's no hope for us. This mindset is still a struggle we face across the country, and sadly, it often diminishes the respect we truly deserve.

Given his passion, I felt compelled to share my belief that he has the power to bring about change. I encouraged him to pause before speaking, reminding him that if he wouldn't want his mother to read it in the newspaper, perhaps it's best left unsaid. I recalled a saying that really resonates: Use your ears twice as much as you use your mouth; that's why God gave you two ears and one mouth. Curiously, he asked if I had visited the Lower Nine Ward recently and suggested I check it out myself.

The following day, I took his advice and saw the situation firsthand. I was taken aback; I hadn't fully grasped how difficult things had become for our community. When I returned, I asked Mrs. Florence if she'd been there lately and shared my conversation with Roland. I could sense her wisdom and was eager to hear her thoughts. She expressed her belief that Roland has the potential to uplift others, and she was confident that he would eventually recognize his essential role.

In the ensuing months, Roland would discover that this journey wouldn't be without its challenges. He sometimes felt overwhelmed and contemplated giving up; he'd wrestle with self-doubt and question why he was pushing himself. But I knew he'd be okay. There will be tough times ahead, but he has what it takes to realize his goals and make a real difference. His journey may be challenging, but it is also filled with immense possibility and hope.

After our conversation, she went to Gail's house to be with Donald, who hadn't been doing well lately. I felt very disappointed in Gail because she still hadn't gotten her life together, and I could see how it affected her family.

Initially, she would be gone for about a month, but I hadn't seen her in years. Once, she called me from New York and asked me to visit her. When I arrived, she was living with a man. She introduced me as a friend, and it felt as though she was ashamed to acknowledge that we were sisters. I could tell he didn't want me there, and I didn't particularly want to be there, but she begged me to stay, so I did. One night I was awakened by loud voices; I heard him say get that nigger out of my house; I don't care if she's your friend. I could hear her speak softly; lower your voice, she'll hear you. I couldn't believe my ears, so I got up and packed my bags, I would have left, but it was two o'clock in the morning, so I went back to sleep. When I got up, Gail was in the kitchen, and her friend was gone. I was very angry with her and told her never to call me or ask me to come to her under these circumstances again.

I thought she needed help and wouldn't take that from anyone. Walking toward the door, I yelled, tell that bastard if he wanted me out of his house, he should've been man enough to tell me to my face instead of waiting until two o'clock to shout it to the world. She tried to justify his statement by saying he was drunk and didn't mean it. That really irritated me. I responded, Drunk? Are you serious? You left a loving husband and a beautiful daughter for a drunk? You must be out of your mind.

I was angry for weeks after I returned home. Mrs. Florence tried to connect with me, but I was too upset and didn't want her to hear all the harsh language I was thinking. A month later, Gail returned, and I was still upset with her. I tried to confront her whenever she was around, but I bit my tongue for the family's sake. She was home for a year, and I thought she had finally conquered her demons. But one day, when I went to talk to her, she was gone.

Whenever she came home, Donald seemed so much more alive, stronger, and happier; seeing a smile on his face was pleasant. I once asked him why he put up with her coming in and out of his life.

I have thought about this countless times. Since the first time she left, she sometimes sleeps with different men. I let her go because I can sense her struggles; her demons take over at times, and there's nothing she can do but leave. I stay with her for the sake of our daughter. She needs her mother, and I don't want to be responsible for Nicole losing her mother forever.

THIRTY-TWO

One afternoon Donald and I was sitting on his porch when Nicole came home, she asked if Roland was home yet, and I told her he should be there in about an hour. She sat with us not saying a word, when I looked into her eyes there was nothing there, and actually she had the family stare. I was angry with Gail because I knew Nicole's problems were partially her fault. After sitting for about forty minutes, I told her Roland should be home by the time we got there, and as we walked, she stared straight ahead not saying anything. When we got there, he hadn't gotten home yet so she went directly to his room to wait. I wanted to talk to Mrs. Florence, but she wasn't at home so I tried concentrating on her, but she was out of reach. I must have been thinking hard because I didn't hear Roland come up behind me, the next thing I knew he was standing over me. I told him that Nicole was waiting for him in his room. After a while I could hear them talking in the kitchen. Nicole said, where did I go wrong? My life feels like it's going nowhere, and I don't know what's going to happen to me? The reason I'm talking to you is a couple of weeks ago I was so depressed, I actually thought about killing myself, because I feel so alone sometimes. The only thing that stopped me was I knew my father needed me. I'm all he has and he's all I have.

When I heard her say those words, it brought me back to the day I sat on the porch thinking similar thoughts. That was such a hard time for me, and I never dreamed I would have a normal life.

I could hear the urgency in Roland's voice, he said, that's not true, I'm here for you. I've always been here for you. Look around you have a whole family to lean on.

After Nicole left, I told Roland that I overheard them talking and suggested that he ask Nicole if she wanted to do some part-time work with him, perhaps being around people her own age would help her self-esteem.

When he asked her to join his team, her heart filled with joy. It was the perfect opportunity for her. Soon after she started, she made the exciting decision to return to school and earn her diploma. Before long, she was thriving in her new role and began helping teenagers who faced similar challenges, making a meaningful impact in their lives.

Among those she worked with was Lamont, a remarkable young man who'd faced his share of struggles during his teenage years. Dropping out of high school at just fifteen, he didn't let that define him. At twenty-one, he decided to turn his life around and return to school, juggling night classes while working during the day. His determination paid off when he earned his GED and then went on to enroll at Southern University of New Orleans. He started working at the center, and it was clear that he had an eye for Nicole, wanting to get to know her better.

Unfortunately, Nicole was so focused on her own journey of self-discovery and progress that the sparks of interest from Lamont went unnoticed. He certainly wasn't shy about expressing his interest, frequently asking Roland to help him set up a date with her. Finally, Roland invited Lamont to dinner, knowing that Saturday dinners with Nicole and Donald were a tradition.

To me, Lamont radiated kindness and sincerity, but it was evident that Nicole wasn't fully aware of his feelings for her. It was heartwarming to see the lengths he went to try to catch her attention that day.

Then one day, Lamont dropped by our house looking for Nicole. I advised him that she was likely home, though I knew she wasn't. I realized that the way to reach her heart was through her father. Instantly, Lamont and Donald connected, beginning a wonderful friendship. Every day, they'd head out for walks, and I often overheard their fun debates about various sports events. I chuckled hearing Lamont declare that the Saints making it to the Super Bowl would mean hell would freeze over, to which Donald jokingly told him to keep his jackets ready, because he believed the Saints were destined for greatness every year.

As time went on, Nicole began to join their walks, and that's when it hit me: Lamont had truly captured her heart. By the end of that year, they were married and settled in with Donald. Lamont was a great encouragement for Nicole to pursue college, and not long after, she discovered she was pregnant. It was such an exciting time, and I could see that her life was finally on an upward trajectory. Both Donald and Lamont were over the moon with joy at the news. They say a pregnant woman carries a beautiful light, and Nicole was absolutely radiant as she continued her studies and eagerly anticipated her baby's arrival.

On July third, she welcomed a precious baby girl, weighing eight pounds and two ounces, and they chose the lovely name Shareese.

Fast forward to when Shareese was about three months old, Gail unexpectedly returned home after being away for four years. It was shocking for her to discover that her daughter was married and had become a mother. This time around, Donald's attention was devoted entirely to his granddaughter, making it clear where his priorities lay. On the other hand, Nicole found it difficult to reconnect with Gail. During Gail's visit, Nicole, Donald, Lamont, and little Shareese were inseparable, creating a close-knit bond that left Gail feeling rather overlooked.

After a couple of days of feeling left out, Gail approached me, expressing her frustration. I contemplated advising her to give them space, but then I recalled Mrs. Florence's wise words about the fork in the road and the importance of choices in life. I also understood that we couldn't predict how long Gail would be around.

Life was busy and filled with changes, and it was clear that nurturing these new relationships and dreams was the way forward for everyone involved. It was such an uplifting time, witnessing growth, love, and the beautiful bonds forming among them all.

I shared with Mrs. Florence how Gail was feeling and told her I wanted to help but I knew it was something she had to deal with. Mrs. Florence told me I did the right thing. She said, when Gail finally felt ready to stand on her own, she moved back to her mother's home, where she has been thriving for the past year.

I found myself quite perplexed by the news I was receiving. It struck me that Gail had been around for a whole year locally and hadn't reached out to visit. I began to wonder why Mrs. Florence hadn't shared this information with me, or why she hadn't kept Nicole or Donald in the loop. She had previously mentioned that there are certain situations beyond her control, and this seemed to be one of them.

When I inquired about Gail's whereabouts, I learned she had returned home, fueled by the feeling that no one wanted her to stay. Mrs. Florence encouraged me to visit Gail, pointing out that she had finally started to reconcile with her struggles. Donald and Nicole may act as if they don't need her, but at their core, they deeply wish for her return; they just harbor a fear that she might leave them again. When I asked for her new address, Mrs. Florence graciously handed me a piece of paper with the details and reassured me that Gail would be overjoyed to see me.

I was excited to tell Patrick about my plans to see Gail. His reaction was one of joy, and it felt nice that he understood how much I needed to do this. With a heart full of hope, I made my way to the address Mrs. Florence had provided.

As it turned out, when I arrived, there was no sign of her. Naturally, my mind began to wander, wondering if she was off in her own world again. Just when I was about to turn around and leave, I spotted Gail pulling up behind me. She stepped out of her car and approached mine, explaining that she felt a tugging in her heart to drive by the house, she had actually moved out two months ago.

I followed her to her new place, and as we parked in front of the house, a wave of nostalgia hit me, this was the same house where my mother and I had lived during my early childhood. I got out and stood there, overwhelmed with memories, as I watched Gail approach with tears in her eyes. Without saying a word, she wrapped her arms around me in a warm embrace that spoke volumes. I asked her why she was crying, and with a hint of determination in her voice, she simply said, let's go in.

As I opened the door, emotions flooded in, and tears streamed down my face; the house looked exactly as it did in my memories. Inside was a child peacefully sleeping on a mattress in the corner under the window, and it struck me profoundly, I had been that child once.

We settled onto the sofa, gazing at each other, and I took a moment to express my sorrow for how I had treated her in the past. I asked if she could find it in her heart to forgive me. To my surprise, she shook her head and replied with a smile, given everything I put our family through, I'm amazed you didn't slap me, kick me, and call me a dumb bitch. We shared a good laugh, and I took her hands, expressing how much I loved her and that I would never react that way. She was the sister I had always longed for during those early days in this very house.

Gail considered this house to be a truly special sanctuary in her life. Without it, she felt she'd still be wandering aimlessly, caught somewhere between simply existing and feeling lost. After spending three transformative years in New York, she made the heartfelt decision to return to her parents' home, wanting to ensure she was fully ready before embracing her true home once again. Initially, everything was going well, she was making strides forward. Yet, after a month are so, she started to sense herself slipping back into uncertainty.

Determined to regain that sense of direction, she planned a trip back to New York, packing all her belongings as she got into her car. However, fate had a different plan. The car seemed to steer her toward this wonderful house, where she ultimately chose to stay. This house became a profound teacher for her, revealing deep insights about herself and her family. Gail began to understand an important lesson: the past doesn't have to define our future. During her last visit, she expressed her desire to discuss all the valuable things she had learned along the way.

I noticed a little boy peacefully sleeping in the corner. Curious and full of warmth, I asked her who he was. With a proud smile, she told me his name was Marcus, and he was just four years old.

Let me take a moment to share my journey over the past five years. Walterboro turned out to be quite a blessing for me. I developed a wonderful friendship with Mrs. Phyllis, who bolstered my strength and encouraged me to return home. When I came back, I felt a genuine connection with Donald, but somehow, it wasn't enough to keep me there, and I returned to New York. However, after your visit, I decided it was time to mend my relationship with my family again. You may remember that I spent nearly a year here, and during that period, Donald and I grew even closer. Just a month before I left, I discovered I was pregnant. Curiously, I inquired if the baby was Donald's, but she seemed to tune me out, continuing with her story.

I didn't want to repeat the same mistakes I made with Nicole, so I headed back to New York. At first, it was a challenging process; Alvin was right there with me, working day and night. When I gave birth to the son, we named Marcus, things began to brighten up. I finally felt the beautiful warmth of love from him. That bond opened the door for me to accept love from others, which was truly liberating. Now, as I mentioned, I've been at this house for a while. Initially, I found myself just sitting around, trying to figure out my purpose here, but then the magic began to happen.

One day, while cozily settled on the sofa, I saw a little girl crying softly. She repeatedly said, I'll never be like my daddy, and then added, I love my daddy. It struck me right in the heart, I realized that little girl was me. Throughout my life, I'd either loved my father or struggled against the desire to be like him. That week, the little girl's voice lingered in my mind. Suddenly, a teenager's voice emerged, saying, I love my father, and I want to be just like him. The echoes of these two voices resonated inside me consistently. I began to explore when and why I transitioned from not wanting to be like him to genuinely wanting to emulate him. It suddenly clicked that this change happened when he passed away. I told you, all those memories flooded back when we discovered him, right over there in a pool of blood.

We both found ourselves drawn to that spot, soaking in the moment, and then she continued to share her story.

Seeing his body lying there struck a chord deep within me. It was a blend of hurt and guilt for the resentment I had harbored against him. In that moment, I made a heartfelt decision: I would always choose to embrace love for him and the way he lived his life. Even though I wrestled with those negative feelings, I realized, from the depths of my soul, that I didn't want to mirror his choices. Yet, here I was, standing in a way that reminded me of him. Can you relate to this?

I looked at her and said, believe me, I completely understand. I had gone through a similar experience with my mother. There were moments when I longed for her so deeply that I found myself acting just like her, although I had vowed not to. It took me quite some time to grasp the complexity of what I was experiencing, but once I did, the burdens I carried began to lighten. She shared that ever since she moved into that little house, strange occurrences had been happening. She wondered if she was losing her grip on reality because she found herself not just seeing her past but also reliving it.

I nodded, fully comprehending her feelings. I told her about the times my mother and I had visited that very house, years after leaving it, and how we too encountered some unusual happenings. My mother returned there in search of her history and, in doing so, uncovered painful truths she never fully understood. One of the most extraordinary moments was revisiting the night I was conceived, strangely, it felt like I was present in some way.

With a sense of encouragement, I asked her the question that had lingered in my mind for years: was she open to reconnecting with her family? Although she felt uncertain, one thing was clear: she didn't want to disrupt their lives only to retreat again. Her love for them was profound; she believed it was kinder to remain absent than to risk causing them pain. She had convinced me that she had truly transformed, over the past four years, she had dedicated herself to caring for her son without faltering, embracing responsibility that she never thought she could handle.

I encouraged her to consider coming back with me to give her family another chance. I'm confident they would be excited to meet Marcus, and I could see how thrilled he would be to bond with them. She shared her desire for us to stay a couple of days, hoping we might witness some extraordinary moment that could change everything. How exciting would that be?

THIRTY-THREE

The next day was filled with warmth as we gathered to share stories about our lives, and I was genuinely eager to learn more about Marcus. Gail shared that his birth was a smooth process, just like Nicole's, and he came into the world weighing a healthy seven and a half pounds. She then asked me to take a close look at his face, hoping I would see the resemblance she believed was there. She wanted reassurance that her perception wasn't just a figment of her imagination.

As I approached and focused on Marcus, I felt a sense of wonder. After looking back and forth between him and Gail, I exclaimed, wow, this little one looks like Donald. Gail smiled and proclaimed that he had looked this way from the beginning. She confessed, however, that she sometimes wondered if her emotions were coloring her vision, especially given her past. While she was completely confident in Donald being Marcus's father, she was concerned that people might assume she was spinning a tale based on her previous experiences. I couldn't help but think that many would be completely skeptical if they knew about her history. My curiosity piqued; I asked her if she had any reservations about Marcus's paternity.

No, she replied with conviction. I knew I was pregnant when I left, and while I was with different men, it never happened when I was with family. My choices led me astray, but that's a part of my story that I own.

We continued our heartfelt conversation throughout the day. When morning came, I woke up in the corner of the room, under the window. Instantly, I felt a sense of longing; I leapt up and looked around for Gail but found myself alone. The feeling took me back to my childhood, reminiscent of when I was four years old. I stood frozen in place, trying to shake off the unease that was creeping in, sensing something significant was about to unfold. Drawn towards the window, I felt an irresistible urge to step outside. Then, memories rushed in of my previous encounter with the two children I had met before.

Venturing outdoors, the scene played out just as it had on that day. When the little girl appeared before me, I locked eyes with her and shouted, it was Gail. In that moment, I snapped awake, my eyes flying open to see Gail sitting calmly on the sofa, her gaze glued to me. It was clear she understood the weight of what had just happened. Excitedly, I said, it was you who pushed me down that day. She grinned and clarified, yes, I was the little girl, but it was my cousin who actually did the pushing.

Moments like these remind us of the connections we share and how our past experiences shape our present. I felt grateful for the candid moments we shared, filled with insight and understanding.

I hadn't thought about that incident in years, but it came to mind recently. The last time my mother and I visited, John mentioned that he witnessed everything but misled us by blaming it on Danny's kids. Looking back, he wasn't ready to share the truth about having a daughter, which means I had a sister. It's intriguing how memories resurface; in fact, Gail reminisced about that night, too. When our father came home, he had a serious talk with her, some of which was verbal and some not so much. I asked if she recalled what Danny's son called me, and while she remembered, she was too young to grasp its meaning then. After her father's conversation that night, she didn't want to use that word again.

And speaking of that visit to New York, I wanted to share that I felt quite hurt when she introduced me as just a friend. Communicating how we think is essential, and I believe those conversations can strengthen our bonds. When Alvin called me a nigger and she didn't defend me, it made me feel that she felt the same way about me and her family. She attempted to explain her comment, saying he didn't intend any harm since he was also black. In fact, the term is often embraced within the Black community. Then she added, I'm surprised it offended you. I felt a rush of emotion and responded passionately.

Why in the hell are you surprised? Are you trying to say all black people should respond the same? You are saying if your skin is dark and you are of African descent, the word nigger should not offend you. Just because you hear people use the word does not mean that it's acceptable to all African Americans. Let me teach you something that I hope you'll never forget, nigger is your people's word, it's the label your people used, to rape and control us. And some people might have adopted it as some sort of term of endearment, but that's crap. I don't like to be referred to as one, and I don't want to hear it. Let me ask you something, do you consider your daughter a nigger? Is that why you run away from her?

I could see the shock on her face as she told me to calm down because I knew she didn't mean it that way, and for heaven's sake, I was her sister, and she loved me. I asked her to answer my question did she consider her daughter a nigger, and she said no, but... I told her to stop right there because I didn't want to have to flog her ass. She needed to know that my pride was thicker than my blood, and I would willingly give blood before I even thought of giving up a fraction of my pride. Most people learned pride, but I had to fight to get mine. I was so upset I had to step outside to cool off; after a while, I went back in.

Look Gail, I don't like the word, I taught my children the same, and I'm sorry I lost it, but something about that word gets to me. It probably comes from the day I ran into you and your cousin, my mother got furious because I was outside, but when she found out what I was called, the anger left her body. She told me because you looked at me as a nigger, you didn't feel guilty about throwing me to the ground because a nigger wasn't part of the human race. I don't expect you to understand what I'm saying, but for the good of your family, you need to try.

She told me she understood what I was saying, and no she didn't look at her children as niggers, what she meant was she'd heard black people call each other that all the time, and no one took it personal. I told her, all I have to say about that is they should have.

We kept the conversation flowing, and soon, Gail asked if I was ready to head home. After she packed her things, we left together, filled with a shared sense of camaraderie. As we drove away, thoughts of Mema filled my mind, and a warm smile spread across my face. I could almost hear her voice saying, I'm proud of you for standing up for your beliefs, and that thought fueled my spirit even more.

Once we returned, Gail came over to my house, and we brainstormed an exciting idea: I would invite everyone so they could meet Marcus all at once. I let them know Gail would join us but kept Marcus a delightful secret for now. By the time our guests arrived, Marcus had peacefully drifted off to sleep, blissfully unaware of the gathering. We playfully anticipated that he might wake up in this unfamiliar setting and let out a little cry, little did we know how right we were.

When the familiar sound of a baby crying filled the room, Nicole asked who was making the noise. With a chuckle, I called out, oh, he's looking for his mommy. Everyone's eyes turned intently toward the doorway, eager to see who was entering. As Marcus appeared, rubbing his sleepy eyes, there was a moment of collective surprise. Everyone exchanged glances between him, Donald, and me, their minds racing with questions. I proudly introduced him as Gail's child, turning to Nicole and saying, that's your little brother. Then, to Donald, I added with a smile, I think you know he's your son.

The room was charged with emotion as Donald looked deeply at Marcus and then back at Gail. He expressed his love for her, reminding her of the bond they shared while also acknowledging the challenges lying ahead. Gail's eyes glistened with tears as she apologized for any pain she may have caused, her hope for forgiveness evident in her gaze, especially directed towards Nicole. However, Nicole turned her head, and the atmosphere grew heavier. As Gail's tears fell, Donald rose with determination, approaching her and saying gently, Gail, would you step into the living room? I'd like to talk to you privately.

It was a moment filled with potential for healing and understanding, and I couldn't help but feel hopeful for what lay ahead.

When Marcus spotted Gail leaving, he couldn't hold back his tears. I reassured Gail to go on ahead; I would take care of him. As I picked him up, his tears kept flowing, I suppose I had forgotten just how emotional these moments can be. He looked at Nicole, almost as if he recognized her as part of his family. When she met his gaze, tears started streaming down her cheeks too. With open arms, she reached for him, and he instinctively leaned into her embrace. As soon as she held him tight, the crying ceased, and he nestled his head on her shoulder. It was such a beautiful moment. She turned to Shareese and said, this is your niece, and Marcus responded with a sweet little smile, as if he truly understood.

I overheard Donald mention that everyone was in the kitchen. I knew he meant Robert, Natalie, and Asia; they always kept us waiting. Sure enough, Natalie walked in, playfully complaining as usual, I'm sorry, Mother, but Asia made us late again. I couldn't help but chuckle, knowing it was true, every time I accompanied Asia, we showed up at their house at least an hour ahead. I had never encountered someone who changed outfits as frequently as she did. The moment Shareese spotted Roland, she dashed over with excitement, leaping into his arms and exclaiming, Uncle Roland, I've missed you. Her big kiss on his cheek brought an instant smile to his face. He laughed and playfully teased her, I missed you too, but didn't I just see you yesterday? Their joyful banter always lightens up the atmosphere.

Initially, they overlooked Marcus, but when they finally focused on him, they stared just like everyone else had. I introduced Marcus, ready to explain that he was Gail and Donald's son, but before I could finish, Robert jumped in with a grin, so, its Donald's son, right? But who's the mother? I playfully admonished him, saying, Come on now, he's Gail's son too. His laughter echoed in the room.

I decided to whip up something tasty for everyone, and as they enjoyed their meal, I invited Nicole and Lamont to step into my room for a moment of chat. Nicole gently set Marcus down to eat, and she and Lamont followed me, curious. I wanted to share my understanding of her feelings towards her mother. I explained that the Gail we know today is a different person compared to who she once was, she is stable and working hard to be who she needs to be. Nicole expressed her concerns, saying that she knows people who struggle but still treat their children with love and care. She wasn't quite ready to forgive Gail. I gently reminded her how much Gail really needs her, sharing a personal insight: You know how my mother dealt with her struggles? She took a tragic path. She didn't have someone like Alvin who offered her support through her anger. Nicole paused, curious, and asked, who's Alvin?

Your mother received exceptional care in New York, where she was guided to confront her challenges and learn how to navigate them. I truly believe she is ready to lead a normal, happy, and productive life, so please consider giving her another chance, what happened wasn't her fault. Do you love your mother? Or has she done so wrong that you would prefer to see her gone rather than be a part of her life? The only reason she left was to prevent burdening the family with her struggles. I visited her during that difficult time, and I can assure you, we should be grateful she was in that situation rather than even worse circumstances here. My frustration led me to stop visiting because it was too painful to witness her in such distress.

When I looked deeply into Nicole's eyes, I felt a connection; it was as if I was reaching her on a profound level. Then, we suddenly heard Marcus crying. She rushed into the kitchen, scooped him up, and comforted him with, don't worry, your big sister is here. I love you. When Gail returned to the kitchen and saw Nicole embracing Marcus, she paused for a moment, just staring at the two of them. It was a pivotal moment. Nicole gently set Marcus down, then wrapped her arms around Gail in a big hug. Marcus looked up at them, beaming with a smile. In that heartfelt moment, Gail apologized for the pain she had caused

Nicole. For the first time in her life, Nicole truly felt her mother's love. She told Gail that she loved her and expressed her hope that she would stay this time because they needed her. In an emotional embrace, tears streamed down both their faces, solidifying their bond. From that day forward, their relationship flourished into something beautiful, like a mother and daughter.

As I think about my journey through life, I'm filled with gratitude. I told Mrs. Florence; I genuinely love you; you mean everything to me. She responded, no, Lillian, it's you who has saved yourself. Your perseverance and hard work have brought you to where you are now. I've just been a friend beside you to offer guidance when you needed it. This is your journey.

I smiled, knowing those words were true. It's the journey we should cherish, not merely the destination. While I'm delighted to be here, I also recognize that every experience has shaped me. My feelings for you are beyond what words can express.

She returned my smile with warmth. Then, I turned to Patrick and thought to him, Patrick, I love you. You have always been a steadfast presence in our family and in my life. My feelings for you remain as strong today as they were from the start. Despite your quiet nature, your love for this family resonates profoundly.

Patrick met my gaze with a smile, and I felt an unexpected mental connection. I thought, Patrick, can you hear me?

I hear you loud and clear, baby, he replied. My heart soared at his words, and as we got up to go to the bedroom, I turned back to Mrs. Florence.

I know he can hear you, she said, smiling.

Before you leave, I've got a question for you, Lillian. Do you remember the dream you had as a little girl?

Oh, come on, Mrs. Florence. I've had so many dreams, which one are you talking about?

As I walked away, a vivid image popped into my mind: a wise old woman flying beside me, telling me I could soar and that we would meet again. I turned to Mrs. Florence and saw she was grinning.

Yes, that was me. I've been with you from the start. My work here is almost complete, but soon, another little one will have that same dream. Ta-ta for now...
Then I heard that familiar click.